Something
to Think
About

Something to Think About

Jack (Suitcase) Simpson

To order additional copies of this book, contact:
Xlibris Corporation
1-888-795-4274
www.Xlibris.com
Orders@Xlibris.com
66031

THE SOCRATES 'n SUITS TRILOGY

XLIBRIS has also published three books by Mr. Simpson.

Socrates is the widely acclaimed "Man of Athen, Man of Greece, and Man of the World."

It is said Socrates brought the critical study of fundamental beliefs, and the grounds for them, from Heaven down Earth.

Simpson thought it would be foolish not to get to know Socrates!

BOOK I is the story of aerial combat and test flying the world's first supersonic fighter.

BOOK II tells the story of Jack and the experimental testing of a "twice the speed of sound" fighter.

BOOK III discusses the synergy between a philosopher, fighter pilot, the lessons of history free enterprise!

BOOK I

LIBRARY of CONGRESS NUMBER: 2001117998

    ISBN#   HARDCOVER   1-4010-2265-7

             SOFTCOVER   1-4010-2366-5

BOOK II

LIBRARY of CONGRESS NUMBER: 2001118000

    ISBN#   HARDCOVER   1-4010-2372-X

             SOFTCOVER   1-4010-2373-8

BOOK III

LIBRARY of CONGRESS NUMBER: 2007901633

    ISBN#   HARDCOVER   978-1-4257-1967-8

             SOFTCOVER   978-1-4275-1966-1

CONTENTS

A FICTIONAL NOVEL;
WRITTEN IN A VICARIOUS MANNER

A few years ago I wrote a letter to a very sharp lawyer friend of mine to thank him for taking the time to tell me how much he enjoyed my BOOKS I and II, entitled *Socrates 'N Suits*. He, and others, also said that they like the way I write, particularly about my combat missions and a number of close calls during experimental test flights including ejection from a crippled experimental fighter and a crash landing of the first MACH 2 (TWICE THE SPEED OF SOUND) YF-104A. In recapitulating the salient facts of my intense flights they said, "You put me right in the cockpit; there I was, holding the stick with frightened intensity—etc. etc."

However, more than one or two, wondered why I spent so much time and research into philosophy. Easily answered! Philosophy, which was the nexus of all three of my books, (the recently published **BOOK III** of the **trilogy)** gave me the opportunity to learn to become a better man in my pursuit of wisdom. In this, I was offered a constant search for a general understanding of values and reality. In **Book III,** *The Synergy* Between a *Philosopher, Fighter Pilot, the Lessons of History, and Free Enterprise,* I constantly hammered home the thought that sales personnel must always sell "in the language of, and needs of, the customer." Well, my needs were, simply, as I said, to try to be a better man. And, *GREAT TREASURY OF WESTERN THOUGHT,* a 1700 page volume, edited by Mortimer J. Adler and Charles Van Doren, offered me "A Compendium of Important Statements on Man and His Institutions by the Great Thinkers of Western History." Just think! As I wrote, and studied, I slowly began to grasp, through over 100 renowned, experienced philosophers, MAN, LOVE, EMOTION, MIND, KNOWLEDGE, ETHICS, ECONOMICS, POLITICS, LAW & JUSTICE, WAR & PEACE, HISTORY, PHILOSOPHY, and the distinguishing features of RELIGION. Every time I had something to think about, sometimes for weeks before I penned, I always had a formidable experienced philosopher to fly my wing and give me guidance. Also the *GTOWT* gave me a parachute; it allowed me to open MY MIND!

SOMETHING TO THINK ABOUT is strictly fiction. The story, written by a sports' editor, centers on a consensus ALL AMERICAN high school half back, offered innumerable scholarships to some of the nations best schools, announces at his high school graduation dance that he is going to become a Monk. The love of his life, a brilliant and beautiful cheerleader is shocked, as is everyone else. She goes on to savor a vexing life in his perplexing career.

All of the names of the personnel portrayed in this fictional novel are real with the exception of our cheerleader friend. The half back, *his* brother, the CEO of the paper, the Sports' Editor, the Philosophy Professor, and others are actually friends of mine from high school. Of course all of the roles they play are narratives not based on fact. There are, however, two exemplifications that are narratives based on fact, but hidden with fictional narrative!

When you read the book you may say, "Hell, this could never happen." Not so!

It can!

And it did!

I thought about this printed literary composition for a long time. But as I grew more mature, read more, cogitated more, studied more about the man and the human condition, and in *The Grandeur and Misery of Man,* I remembered what I learned from Tolstoy, oddly enough from *War and Peace,* II Epilogue, VIII.

Man *is* the creation of an all powerful, all-good, and all-seeing God. What is sin, the conception of which arises from consciousness of man's freedom? That is a question for **theology.**

Man's actions proceed from his innate character and the motives acting upon. What is conscience and the perception from right and wrong in actions that follow from consciousness of freedom? That is a question for **ethics.**

Man in connection with the general life of humanity appears subject to laws which determine that life. But the same man apart from that connection appears to be free. How should the past life of nations and humanity be regarded—as the result of the free, or as the constrained, activity of man? That question *is* for **history.**

Jack Simpson, November, '06

ALL THE WORLD IS A STAGE,

AND ALL THE MEN AND WOMEN,

MERELY PLAYERS;

THEY HAVE THEIR EXISTS

AND THEIR ENTRANCES,

AND ONE MAN IN HIS TIME

PLAYS MANY PARTS!

SHAKESPEARE

AS YOU LIKE IT

FICTION

A LITERARY WORK, SUCH AS
THIS NOVEL WHOSE CONTENT IS PRODUCED BY
IMAGINATION
AND IS NOT NECESSARILY
BASED ON FACT!!

TIME

AN INTERVAL SEPARATING
TWO POINTS!
A PERIOD DESIGNATED
FOR A GIVEN ACTIVITY!
AND
CONSTRUCTED TO OPERATE
AT A PARTICULAR MOMENT!

SOMETHING TO THINK ABOUT

**TELLS A STORY ABOUT THE
LIVES OF FOLKS
NOT NECESSARILY IN A SEQUENTIAL MANNER!**

**FOLKS DUE ENTER
AND EGRESS
WITHOUT FALLING ALL OVER EACH OTHER!
I SIMPLY CHOSE WHEN—AND HOW!**

Jack Simpson
July 2007

DEDICATION

THE PASSING OF TIME TENDS TO
NUMB SIGNIFICANT EVENTS IN OUR LIVES,
UNTIL A NEW DAY REKINDLES BRILLIANCE;
IN THIS CIRCUMSTANCE
A BEAUTIFUL LADY!
THE LADY'S NAME IS DAGMAR
SHE HAPPENS TO BE
MY WIFE!!

THE CLASS OF 1944
CRAFTON HIGH SCHOOL
CRAFTON, PA.
YOU, LADIES AND GENTLEMEN, ARE
BEAUTIFUL TOO!
ALTHOUGH I LEFT EARLY
YOU WELCOMED ME BACK!
THE WHOLE CLASS TREATED DAGMAR WITH
UTMOST RESPECT AND CONVIVIALITY.

I AM FOREVER GRATEFUL! !

YES, MR. MONTEZ *IS*—
SOMEONE TO THINK ABOUT!
AND SO IS—
MS. BARBARA CLOSE

I met Hank Montez, the artist for the cover of *SOMETHING TO THINK ABOUT,* over 20 years ago at an aerospace company in Southern California. I was under contract from a vendor and needed someone to design a logo. Hank was head of an arts department assisting sales, customer relations, personnel etc. With a studio in his home, he jumped right on it and designed an outstanding identifying symbol.

Hank said, "In painting the illustration for the cover of the book, *SOMETHING TO THINK ABOUT*" the direction I received from Mr. Simpson was something of a mixed metaphor combining the Garden of Eden with the subjects, namely the Monk and the Cheerleader. Since there are so many different types of Monks and many interpretations of the Garden of Eden, I decided to research both subjects on the internet. Most of the depictions of Eden were very elaborate and complicated so I simply started with a stylized apple tree and added the serpent and additional foliage to provide the background for the Monk and the Cheerleader standing on a pebble pathway with their arms around each other as described by Mr. Simpson.

On the original sketch, I had the Cheerleader dressed in cheerleader attire which seemed logical. Mr. Simpson decided that she should be wearing a full-length gown and that is the story, or evolution, of the painting."

I might add, Hank also painted the cover of **BOOK I,** the first of a trilogy I wrote about philosophy, war, flight testing and business. The cover details Socrates, my mentor, and I in the cockpits of our Saber jets preparing to take off on my 50th mission.

Barbara Close, an exceptional freelance calligrapher brought style and character to the covers of the **BOOKS I, II, & III,** of the trilogy **SOCRATES N' SUITS**, the fictional accounting of actual events in the author's air combat, test flying, and business life. Her delicate printing also brought additional beauty to the cover of the author's fourth book, **SOMETHING TO THINK ABOUT**.

Ms. Close's studio is located in Santa Ana, California, where she is currently teaching a series of calligraphy classes as a certificate program which she designed herself.

Her work can be seen in Glen Epstein's calendars, the Artful Letter Calligrapher's Engagement Calendars and SfC's Artful Book of Days Calendar. She has exhibited her work in several juried shows throughout the United States. Barbara also participates in several calligraphy conferences and has taught at many of the International Lettering Conferences.

FORWARD

MAN IS AN IMAGING BEING

—Gaston Bachelard

I have been imagining situations (things) all of my life. When I was very young I imagined I was a "spurter" or "splasher" on a fire truck responsible for putting out big fires. When my Dad bought me a 2 foot square airfield made of tin with a painted runway and a transport, I imagined I was the captain and took off and landed that airliner hundreds of times. I used to fly forks or spoons around the dinner table (after dinner, of course). When WW II broke out, I cut out German and British fighters—the Focke-Wulf "FW 190," Messerchmitt "Bf 109," Supermarine "Spitfire," the Hawker "Hurricane," and the Boulton Paul "Defiant" fighting for life and limb over London in the Battle of Britian. I guess I had 30 to 40 aircraft pasted on the wall of my bedroom in this hellishly fought, protracted struggle, for air superiority. My imagination had planes going every which way—on fire, tails shot off, pieces flying out of the cockpit, wings folding back, in tailspins with twisting trails of fire and smoke. That dramatic battle was followed by an abrupt, explosive ending as the victim lost his gallant battle against gravity. I was kicking the hell out of those German pilots.

And then one day, my effervescent flights of fancy came to the realization of something desired. From March of 1944, when I became an Aviation Cadet in the US Army Air Corps, until September of 1952 when I won my wings in the US Air Force, I never gave up that mental image of flying my own fighter. I was delayed *eight* years because, in June of 1944, the government threw me, plus tens of thousands more, out of the Cadet program and into the infantry. Ever try six weeks of grueling, insistently demanding, eighteen-hour days of physical exercises plus running and marching mile after mile in 100-degree heat and 97% humidity! With sadistic, savage, merciless, and cruel chicken crap sergeants screaming at you *all* the time! We were destined to be cannon fodder for the invasion of Japan. The death tolls of Marines on Iwo-Jima plus the Marines and Army on Okinawa were repulsive and frightful. In the invasion of Japan, "Operation Coronet", the name of one plan, our government expected a million casualties.

Don't anyone ever tell me we shouldn't have dropped the atomic bomb!

After my discharge, a college degree was next in line. I graduated from St. Louis University with a Bachelor of Science in Aeronautics in 1951. I earned my wings as a USAF fighter pilot in 1952.

Yes, this book, **SOMETHING TO THINK ABOUT**, is fiction with one exception (you will learn of the anomaly). Therefore, by definition, an imagination is necessary. It is about an honorably discharged fighter pilot, Chuck Grube, in his new vocation as a sport's writer for the *PITTSBURGH (PA) POST TELEGRAPH*.

Charlie Grube is a successful pundit because it isn't good enough for him to *imagine* what is happening on the field of play. In his way of reporting, he must *vicariously* be there—in his helmet or cap, in his skates, on his starting block, crouched on the edge of the pool, in the air on his gravity-defying jump shots. He must be with him or her on the tennis court, on the golf course, on his or her skis, or his or her bowling alley.

I would say imagination could be classified as "knowledge of", while vicarious would be "knowledge about". For instance, today I only have knowledge "of" Paris, France, because I have never been there or studied the famous city in any way.

On the other hand, if I vicariously visited Paris, I would feel as if I was taking part in the experience or feelings of another, therefore giving me knowledge "about" Paris.

So, let's move on. Mr. Grube may, in his mind, heart, and actions be thinking "vicariously." Or, maybe thinks he could write a better column from his knowledge "about" the surprising circumstances surrounding the two main characters in this treatise. I am leaving it up to him.

I chose Charles Grube, I call him "Jolly Cholly", as the fictionalized sports' editor in this literary work, because he has been a friend since 5th grade. He was an "A" student, class leader, football star, successful business man, loving husband and father, a devout Christian, and what you would classify as a "class act".

Jack Simpson
Summer, 2006

INTRODUCTION
TO
SOMETHING TO THINK ABOUT

ON THE USES OF PHILOSOPHY

You are about to read a story about an All-American high school half back who turns all ears away from widely recognized grandiosity and brings public notice to his graduation dinner, "I am going to become a Monk"

This young man shows intelligence of a high order; a brilliant study. I have learned he has found pleasure in **philosophy.** He seems to have learned that most of us have found some golden days in the June of life when philosophy was in fact what Plato calls it, "that dear delight"; when the love of a modestly elusive Truth seemed more glorious than the lust for the ways of flesh and the worthlessness of the world

Our candidate for a monastery believes much of his life is meaningless, a self-canceling vacillation and futility. He believes we strive with the chaos about us and within. However, he believes that all the while there is something vital and significant in him and through **philosophy,** and deep religious study, he can decipher his own soul. He wants to seize the value and perspective of passing things knowing when the little things are little and the big things big, before it is too late.

As SPORTS' EDITOR for *THE PITTSBURGH (PA) POST TELEGRAPH,* I knew about our local hero's ability to outmaneuver a defensive opponent with the aid of some extra resource—the exact combination of brainpower and leg authority. I wanted to casually look into his brainpower.

I found out he loved to read and was, at the time, reading *THE STORY OF PHILOSOPHY* by Will Durant. It was published by SIMON AND SHUSTER, New York, in 1929. Here is what I learned he learned:

"To be a philosopher," said Thoreau, (Henry David, 1817-62, American author and naturalist) "is not to have subtle thoughts, nor even to found a school, but to love wisdom as to live, according to its dictates, a life of simplicity, independence, magnanimity, and trust." We may be sure that if we can but find wisdom, all things else will be added into us. "Seek ye first the good things of the mind," Bacon admonishes us, "and the rest will either be supplied or its loss will not be felt." Truth will not make us rich but it will make us free.

It appears to me that our friend will move from one game plan to another. This time, however, preparation will be for *his* heart and soul only; not for the minds and hearts of ten others.

Charles Grube
Pittsburgh, PA
May, 1954

SPORTS EDITOR TO
MONK'S PRAYER HISTORIAN

By: Charles Grube
Sports' Editor

I have been pondering all afternoon; just about chewed my pencil in half. What will I write about this 6-3, 211 pound phenomenal **All-USA first-team offense** running back with his remarkable statistics? I have to write something; look at the company he's in! A 6-4 quarterback from Arkansas completed 190 of 270 passes for, in his division, a single-season record of 3,817 yards, with 47 touchdowns with only six interceptions. A running back from Ohio rushed for 2,134 yards and 27 touchdowns, with a 9.6-yard per carry. Another running back from Lake Butler, Florida, at 5-11 at 185 pounds, rushed for over 1800 yards and scored 27 touchdowns. Another Floridian, at 6-8, 295 pounds is a two time first-team all-state lineman who did not allow a sack during his final two seasons. You know what! If that guy ever hit me I would starve to death bouncing. Another lineman, at 6-5, 325 lbs., from Alabama graded 96% without allowing a sack. He bench-presses 375 pounds and squats 575. And would you believe these young men are just leaving high school!

So, what can I compose, that hasn't already been inscribed, about this consensus All-American senior halfback so remarkable as to evoke disbelief. As Editor, Sports', for the *PITTSBURGH POST TELEGRAPH* I started calling him the "Drummer Boy" during Central Catholic's last game of the season three years ago. He was a sophomore substitute; the beginning of his glory days in high school.

I found it to be an easy nickname, and it stuck! His powerful legs, as he plowed into the line off tackle or guard, reminding me of the two heads of a bass drum being pounded and giving a booming sound of a low indefinite pitch of grunts as bodies, torsos, upper arms, and mighty shoulders collided to open enough of a cavity to let the deceptively attractive, artfully attained runner, maneuver through the line for the attained goal of a first down. And when he returned a punt, or a kickoff, the legs, quick stepping, slowing, followed by instantaneous acceleration, yet the legs were smooth in his steps, like the arms and wrists of a drummer with a snare—deceptively attractive limbs attaining ground by artful and skillful maneuvers. I can only think of his running as associated with a Gene Krupa masterful solo.

Yes, they were the days of grandeur for John Joseph Flynn and, also, for his "take your breath away" blonde cheerleader girl friend; a proverbial king and queen of their senior class. They were both articulate, easy going, and without the slightest thought or action of being overconfident or flamboyant. AND, they both had SAT scores of the highest magnitude. "Barney", as was his nickname, named after his father John Bernard, was given the choice of any college: Notre Dame, *any* Ivy League college, USC, Florida, Stanford, Villanova, Ohio State, Penn State—any college of his choice. And Elizabeth, or "Sparky", would be joining him. They made an absolutely beautiful couple.

I am in this conundrum—this problem having, to me, only a conjectural answer. Why? What changed his mind? Certainly he must of known his answer tonight, the night of the graduation dinner dance. "Sparky" was radiant, standing beside him anxiously waiting for him to announce his choice. She was prepared to go to the same college of his choice.

When "Barney" made his declaration, late in the evening after a "good time was had by all," just the astonished, bewildered look on Sparky's face offered irrefutable evidence that she did *not* know. I quickly scanned the room looking at his Mother and Dad, his football buddies, his coaches, the cheerleaders, the Chief of Police and his wife, the Mayor and *his* wife, all VIP guests of the principal, Brother Raymond of the Brothers of Mary. No one was moving! All were aghast at what was said. The countenance, the indication of emotion, the expressions that offered what? Approval or sanction! Did their demeanor show moral support or a penetrating query asking the question, "Is this guy out of his mind?"

"Barney" knew what to expect; his audience would tender a cross-section of dichotomy of thought. The Brothers of Mary would be happy thinking their good habits and solid Faith had an effect on him. His parents were put in a position of being in the midst of something of not knowing what to think—or say. And "Sparky" was in pure shock; her eyes were already watering—the beginnings of a heartfelt and intense cry.

John Flynn continued; he was ramrod straight as he moved his eyes and head slowly around the room. Confidence was his demeanor! Facing reality was one of his mental strengths!

"Ladies, gentlemen, Mayor Webster, Chief Ryan, coach McNeal, Brother Raymond, Mom, Dad, my teammates that made me what I am, and "Sparky", my cherished treasure—I have eyes too! No one person can fool me into believing he, or she, knew of my decision. I didn't really know myself until I stepped to the rostrum." I am speaking now to quell all potential rumors and half-truths.

He was looking directly at Liz. She was trying to behold his gaze while wiping her eyes with a fragile white square of cloth with a crocheted perimeter. "Sparky," he said, "remember it was during Christmas break when you and your family took your trip to Washington and I took off to ski at Deer Valley near Salt Lake. I knew where I was going; I knew what I was looking for; and I was scared to death about finding the answer to a very somber and pressing question."

He continued while looking over the suddenly surprised faces. Was the Lord Jesus inviting me to a Cistercian monastic life? I felt strongly about hanging on to my Catholic faith, my trust and confidence in myself—particularly in believing, one way or the other, I would have the moral and intellectual power to accept the answer. I ended up in the Wasatch Canyon with a pounding heart looking for the **Abbey of Our lady Of the Holy Trinity** I had so outlined on my HERTZ Salt Lake City/Ogden map. It is located in a town named Huntsville. I was shaking as I phoned The Guestmaster and asked for a meeting.

I met a very personable man pleasing in both personality and appearance. He said, 'Welcome, my name is Father Eugene; how may I assist you?' I explained why I was there. I told the gentleman my background, school, football, and Liz. 'But, over the past year or so,' I told him, 'I seem to be much happier when I pray by myself in the dark shadows of the interior of my church. And during Lent my going to daily Mass or giving up of something what seemed important like a good cold beer, wasn't a real sacrifice because I was happy doing it for God. I have been reading about monastic life, your Retreat House, a Monks Day and Prayers of the Monastery, and frankly I would love to give it a try after graduation with, let's say, a month at the Retreat House.'

Well, everyone," John Flynn said as he let his eyes traverse the dance hall, "it has been just about five months since I spoke to Father Eugene and I have decided to give up any thoughts of football."

A resonant gasp rippled through the guests like the flowing of small waves in a smooth pond invaded by a thrown rock. He held steadfast, adhering firmly and devotedly as to what he desired to say. His acknowledged quality of being factual permitted him to continue. "I have been accepted at the retreat house at Holy Trinity starting 7 July. Will the future offer me the life of a Trappist Monk? My actions are, I think, the only way to find out. To all of you, I wish the best of everything including good health and great wealth in whatever you're choosing.

And now, pardon me if I may borrow a line from a TV news program Liz and I saw not too long ago, 'Good night, and good luck!'"

He turned, and with a wave and a blown kiss to Liz, he left the stage.

It was "Barney's" short speech that made it easy for me to write my column the following day:

"As Editor, Sports', for the *PITTSBURGH POST TELEGRAPH* I had the pleasure of attending the senior class's graduation where John Flynn, everyone's All-American, was to make his announcement, after thoughtful attention, as to what college he would matriculate. As I write, and cogitate, I would offer to say his mind had a millstone around it; the decision "Barney" made must have been packed with an emotional burden.

Imagine! What was going through his mind? John Flynn, in a very short and incisive speech, informed the community that God would be his quarterback calling to assist in such efforts as the Liturgy of the Hours all within the hours of A Monk's Day.

Last evening, spent in study, after picking up what I thought would help my inquiry, I learned the abbey church is always open to retreatants for prayer and meditation, including the times of the monk's prayer. So God, as Flynn's quarterback, will be calling plays such as *Lauds*, or early morning prayer, *Sext*, afternoon prayer, and *None*, evening prayer. I have not determined the difference between gaining ground by running or passing but *Tierce*, *Vigils*, and *Compline*, as part of a Monk's day, appear to be important plays. *Tierce* has something to do with third so maybe God is calling plays on "second down and three" or maybe even "fourth and three." I did learn that *Compline* comes from the Latin completorium; evidently He's talking about completing passes. *Lauds* means praise and we all know "Barney" has had plenty of that.

Whatever the case may be, let us all say a quiet prayer that the process of passing from one stage to another that is, carrying the ball to carrying his faith, is, for him, just another dynamic process—of doing 'whatcha gottah do'"

Barney and Liz wanted to be alone. They had their arms around each other at the waist with Liz's head tilted to rest on Barney's shoulder. She had stopped crying. Every fifteen steps or so she would stop, turn to her left and kiss Barney on his cheek and lips while holding him closely. She repeated this process until they reached his car; a six-year old Ford coupe purchased with money saved by working on the ore trestle at Superior Steel. He worked on weekends, school breaks, and holidays with the exception of his football playing dates during the season.

They drove to a small but elegant club in downtown Pittsburgh. The *Club Exquisite* was designed, and designated, for couples over sixteen (but under drinking age) where they could dance, snack on finger food, and order non-alcoholic beverages until they could legitimately drink. At that time in their life they could go upstairs to the *Café la Liberte* to eat, drink, and dance the night away.

John Flynn and Liz danced and snuggled over a couple of "cokes", decided it was time to leave and headed for home. Several years later, after a couple of hours commiserating over a few drinks and dinner, they would leave *Café la Liberte* together in Liz's new *MUSTANG* convertible just minutes away from an incident that would diametrically change their thoughts on life and its pursuit of happiness.

Talk to you later!

THE RETREAT HOUSE
For Laymen!!

By: Charles Grube
Sports' Editor

The *PITTSBURGH POST TELEGRAPH* is a family owned and operated newspaper; for 93 years. The President, CEO, and Chairman of the Board today is David R. Latshaw. His older brother Paul, before David, was Editor-in-Chief for 36 years and "Father Time" Lawrence Latshaw *was* the big boss for 50 years. David's son Todd, a former twin engine Navy pilot, has started to work for the paper as a mechanic in the pressroom. David says, "That's where I started right out of the Navy a number of years ago and I continue to learn. Todd will have to go to school plus work his way to a top position; with no guarantees.

David and I were in high school at the same time—he as a senior and I, a freshman. That's why I didn't feel it too far reaching to approach him with an idea that would possibly affect my title as Sports' Editor. I called and made an appointment.

Myrna, Dave's personal secretary for the past six years, said, "Mr. Latshaw said he would be glad to speak with you. In fact he made it a point to tell me, to tell you, an appointment to see him was not necessary. His door would always be open for you. And would you like a cup of coffee?"

"Yes, Myrna. Please; black; thank you. And how's that husband of yours? Tell him I said 'hello'"

"I'll do that Mr. Grube. And thanks for asking."

Dave was already on his feet ready to shake my hand. He had a grip like a vise—a clamping device holding your hand and arm in position until he was ready to yield; same as my Dad taught me. Always stand up to shake a man's hand; give the hand a firm grip; look 'em in the eye!

"Good to see you Charlie," Dave said. "I hope your lovely friend Gloria is still as effervescent as always. Why don't you marry that girl? No! No! Don't answer that! You ex fighter pilots don't like to be put on the spot."

"Sir, Charlie said, "In all do respect, there is no such thing as an 'ex' fighter pilot."

"OK! OK! You win. Just don't forget to put me on the invitation list while I'm still alive and doing well. And speaking of doing well, you're doing a hell of a job on that kid Flynn. Congratulations!"

Myrna entered with two cups of coffee. Dave always had a drop or two of cream. As I was watching, Myrna measured it like a nurse with an eyedropper. "You know Charlie, gotta' watch my cholesterol. Anyhow, what can I do for you," Dave asked as he went to his desk and sat down. I sat in the leather chair slightly off to his left.

"Thank you for the note on Jack Flynn. In fact that's why I'm here," I said. "You are aware, I'm sure, that Mr. Flynn has decided to follow his faith and become a Trappist monk. Since everyone in the community was astounded with his announcement, I thought I would like to write a column or two about what a tough decision it was for him and what he might expect, first in the Retreat House and later in the Abbey. I mean, David, it's not going to be an easy time for Jack."

"Don't you think he knows it's going to be tough! I'm sure he has given it much thought. Just the notion of leaving that gorgeous cheerleader would give me a migraine."

"I already have the other half! (A migraine affects only one side of the head—author). Yes, Dave, I think he is aware but there are a hell of a lot of our readers who haven't the slightest idea and I thought it a good thought to let the readers know. It would only take a couple of columns. You know! While he's hot material it would be good reading. I could write in under **Sports,** or under the **Pennsylvania** section, or **Daily Read** or, you could even give me a leave of absence and I'll write it all up and you can insert when and in what part of the paper you desire."

Dave didn't say a word. He *was* sitting with his arms to his side, hands in front of his chin with fingers spread, touching at the tips; a virtual crane of bone and flesh. He slowly turned his chair about 130 degrees until he was looking out of his massive picture window harboring a dramatic view of "The Golden Triangle" where the Monongahela and Allegheny converge to form the Ohio River. The Ohio then flows northwest only to turn southwest to enter the Mississippi at Cairo, IL.

Dave always took his time about deciding things; today was no exception. As I was finishing my cup of coffee he turned to me and said, "You're right, Charlie, Flynn and his decision is on the minds of many people. Go ahead! Write the column; as many as you feel necessary and do it under your Sports' Editor column. We can't presage what might happen. No one knows whether or not this young superstar can handle it. Have no worry! They will follow what you write wondering, like we did as kids, at the Saturday matinee, as to what happened to our hero in the next movie cereal. Will he be Jack Flynn Armstrong the All-American Boy who will save the good guys from the bad? See the thrilling action at the movies next Saturday!"

"Gee, David! I haven't thought about those Saturday afternoons at the Chartier's Theatre for decades. Remember! It used to be a dime! At today's prices, you're lucky if you can make *one* end meet!

Anyhow, this whole subject could be interesting. *My* column, though, will have the best interests of John Flynn and his family at heart. Thanks! Give my love to your family. And by the way, I may have to visit one of these Abbeys to build an undistorted structure around my columns."

"I haven't complained about one of your expense accounts yet."

With that said, we stood, shook hands and I started to leave but stopped and said, "My first column will be about the **Retreat House** at the **Abbey** of the Holy Trinity. The retreat house is open to adult men, Catholic or not. Sounds interesting!"

"Charlie, if you decide to stay and pray, it's "OK" by me. But don't try to slip your offering into your expenses," Dave said with a smile.

I was pleased with our meeting; so much so I gave Myrna a quick kiss on her cheek as I said, "Thanks for being such a nice lady; and thanks for the coffee."

"Gosh, Mr. Grube," she exclaimed, "what did I do to deserve that?"

"Haven't you heard, Myrna. Nice guys, and gals, finish first!"

The elevator made a couple of stops on the way down. Funny thing about elevators—they seem to be able to change ordinary fun loving people into zombies. They look and behave like automatons—like robots. They walk into an elevator, don't smile, a quick 180-degree sweep with their eyes, a once in a lifetime nod, a stiff hutt, hupp, twrip, foah about face, a quick look up to see the floor, or figures, or somethin', then look down at their feet and stand there! Door opens, a side step or two, door slides shut, a look up, and then down to their feet until the downward migration ends. Door opens, a juggle of briefcases, clothing, books, umbrellas and rain gear, a rush, a dash, and everyone is gone. Usually, not a word has been spoken!

Sometimes when I get on an elevator with a friend I would say, "Gee Patrick, did you see the headlines today?"

He would answer, "No David, I didn't. What's the scoop?"

I would say, "A father of sixteen was shot. He was mistaken for a rabbit!"

Nothing! No smile! People would look at me as if I were nuts—but no reaction whatsoever. A sad way to go through life!

When I arrived at my desk, I sat down, and stared into a Grand Canyon of lights, offices, clothing racks, desks, machines, tons of paperwork, young ladies, office boys, and men and women. They were moving about seemingly in complete disarray and disorder, but what was actually a well-tuned machine hitting on all cylinders. When you consider the diverse and varied articles, essays, and commentary such as Astrology, Comics and Crossword, Global Reporting, Nation, TV, Opinion, and Sports, plus about thirty other subjects, a daily paper like the *PITTSBURGH POST TELEGRAPH* faces a gigantic task. It must take, without blunder and omission, this rapid inward circulation of alphabet and numeric and with the materializing of computers, word processors, and printing press offer the man on the street the activity of the world, the country, the state, the city, the hometown and, sadly, its Obituaries.

David Latshaw and his team run a hell of ah' railroad.

"Well," I said to myself. "I had better stoke up my own steam and get your railroad running. It isn't going to be easy writing a sport's column about a charismatic young football player metamorphosing into a monk. Gee, if a quiz show host asked me a word with an opposite meaning of 'charismatic' I could answer 'monk' and be right. Certainly I have respect for anyone's religious belief but, by nature, a monastery has to be about exciting as watching a manual cotton picker. Even picking strawberries would be a little more exciting 'cause you could put a few in your mouth now and then. But Dave runs a tight organization and he and his experienced staff seems to come up with the proper solutions to problems. Since you are part of it just make up your mind you will find a way to contribute."

I got up from my chair, headed toward the coffeepot and on the way something struck me. You mentioned 'solutions'! That's it! Remember Father Anton Niepp the Jesuit priest that was your philosophy professor during night school classes?

"Yes, I remember him," I said to myself. "He was from Lancaster, Pa. Same as my Mom—Lancaster county Dutch.'Pop's on the table and Mom's all et!'" In our *way* of speaking that meant Pop is eating and Mom has already finished dinner.

Father Niepp stopped by to see me in the not too distant past. He was on his way to Harrisburg to be the principal at a Catholic boy's school.

The good padre and I hit it off pretty good since he was a U.S. Air Force Chaplain for a few years and I had just finished my tour of duty as an air force fighter pilot. I remember he told me during our short encounter that it would not be easy entering the world of business and free enterprise. "But," he said, "Make sure you continue your studies of philosophy and history. Think through your readings, my friend—and learn. Learn what the lessons of history have to offer. The air force gathered all the knowledge and lessons of history in teaching cadets to fly—and learned. You *started* or began your pilot training in the same aircraft that cadets in WW II used to *finish* their flying for advanced fighter training. The lessons of history taught the training command that more mature men could handle a more developed curriculum. A sport's writer must also consider what I call four other *extensions*. They are **time, legacy, culture,** and **planning.**

Time could not be presaged in taking the fighter you flew from the drawing board to operational suitability. The aircraft builder's **culture,** the total product of human creativity and intellect took decades. It is the same for the Latshaws' *PITTSBURGH POST TELEGRAPH.* The **legacy** of the paper has been passed from one generation to another. And **planning;** that's a killer in most companies. My good friend, always have a plan particularly when you reach for pen and paper or keyboard in initiating your columns about our Mr. Flynn.

Sometime in the immediate future, I want you to look up a physicist by the name of Murray Gell-Mann. It won't be tough—he won the Nobel Prize for physics. See what he has to say about 'filling yourself full of the problem.' If you have a problem about meeting your standards for your column and are seeking a solution fill yourself full of it. You will solve your problem but not without paying the price of time. You will learn then, the solution presents, for free, a plan far beyond what is normal or customary. The thoughts of Gell-Mann may not seem important in calendar years, but the historical significance to you and the paper will be priceless.

Don't worry, Charlie. You will succeed in your particular niche of business. But let's go back to our philosophy class. Your gains through experience will give you knowledge and from that flows what?"

"Wisdom! Insight! And I hope the ability to gain sensible decisions."

"OK! Good! And if you make a decision what are you *not* going to be afraid of!"

"Making a mistake."

"Valid answer! And what will making a mistake offer?"

"The opportunity to learn."

"Excellent! Why weren't you this sharp in class?"

"I think I was in love with a redhead! A valid answer!"

"You always were a wise guy. But don't change! Remember to put down in writing what you learn. Make yourself a book of aphorisms—you know—your motto and proverbs from what your have learned from writing your columns. Every time I travel through Pittsburgh I'll give you a call for lunch or dinner—on you! We'll talk! And discuss! And brainstorm! I will not rescue you from failure; a good way to learn. Know yourself, be honest with yourself, be honest with others. And I'll help you with your golf swing. I understand you have more ways to slice than a delicatessen counterman."

"You can't get to me Father Anton. You're about as funny as a cry for help. Buy even if you make fun of my golf swing, I'll welcome you back with open arms and a bill for lunch."

"I won't mind. *JACK IN THE BOX* sounds good to me. Speaking of open arms, give me a hug and let's shake hands. I'm outta' here."

"We shook hands, and slapped shoulders as we gave each other a hug. Father Anton turned around and said, before he left, "You have done well, Charlie. Seems maybe you have lost some of your cocky fighter pilot attitude!"

"Wrong! Father Anton. Cockiness comes with the territory. Once a fighter pilot, always a fighter pilot! And, thanks for your few but profound words."

MURRAY GELL-MANN

Soon after my meeting with Father Anton, I stepped into a minefield for the pursuit of consecutive progressive achievement. In other words I got serious about my column. I hadn't planned to do anything that particular evening after Father Anton left. Since the public library was close to where I planned to grab a bite of dinner, decided to take a new approach to my Gell-Mann dilemma. I asked the librarian if she had anything about solving problems. "Like solutions in math or physics," she asked? I said, "More like business; you used the words 'solutions.' Have anything on that"? She looked through a long list but soon stopped and fingered one. The lovely librarian said, "I have a book here entitled *THE SEARCH FOR SOLUTIONS.* What do you think?"

I said, "I think I would like to marry you. Where may I find it?" We laughed. I looked for the book by reading a lot of numbers and decimals, and then—there it was, *THE SEARCH FOR SOLUTIONS,* by Horace Freeland Judson, HOLT, RINEHART, and WINSTON, New York, 1980.

I grabbed a chair and started to peruse; I found the chapter on Gell-Mann.

In *the book THE SEARCH FOR SOLUTIONS,* a conversation with Murray Gell-Mann makes a great case about thoughts entering the conscious at unexpected moments. Gell-Mann, a theoretical physicist at the California Institute of Technology, won a share of the Nobel Prize in Physics for *his* work on subatomic particles. In his early search, he first conceived the entities that may, after all, be the stuff that all other stuff is made of. He named them quarks.

When someone asked Gell-Mann where ideas come from, he replied (rather lengthily), "We had a seminar here, about ten years ago, including several painters, a poet, a couple of **writers,** (bold print by author) and the physicists. Everybody agrees on how it works. All of these people, whether they're doing artistic work or scientific work, are trying to solve a problem.

Any art that's worth the name has some kind of discipline associated with it. Some kind of rule—but it's not the rule of a Sonnet or a symphony, or a classical painting, but even the most liberated contemporary art, if it's any kind of art at all, it has some kind of rule. And the object is to get across what you're trying to get across, while sticking to the rules.

In our business, it is hard to find out what nature is up to, and there are all sorts of constraints—you have to agree with everything you already know, and you have to have a nice self-consistent structure, and so on. And so, when you have to account for something new or in the artist's case, when you want to express yourself within the rules—you run into problems. And the problems at first seem difficult, and perhaps insoluble. And you work very hard trying to understand, trying to fill yourself full of the problem, just to know what barriers you're trying to crack.

And after that, further voluntary effort, further conscious effort, *is* not so productive. And at that point, what the shrinks call the preconscious, I guess, seems to be more important. Processes that are outside awareness go on, which thrust up bubbles of ideas from time to time.

And that can happen when you're driving, or shaving, or walking—anything.

One of my ideas came in a slip of the tongue. I was getting up at a seminar—one person had just put forward a theory, and I was explaining why his theory was wrong, why it didn't work—and while I was explaining it, I happened to blurt out the correct way to do it. Just a slip of the tongue! And I recognized immediately that the slip would solve the problem."

"What was *that?*"

"Oh, it *was* the idea of 'strangeness," Gell-Mann said. "I was intending to say 'isotopic spin-three halves' and, instead, I said 'isotopic spin-one,' which for the particular kind of particle, was *unthinkable*. Unthinkable, but correct! Everybody had taken it for granted that the value was a half integer. And it wasn't. As soon as I mentioned an integral number, which nobody had thought of, I realized that the integral number was the answer."

Which led him to the name 'quarks.'

Gell-Mann's statement, 'you work very had trying to understand, trying to fill yourself full of the problem . . . ' to me smacks of sheer genius. Six words summing up what every man must undergo and endure in preparation for possible recognition and solution to the advancement of the state of any art, be it science, music, literature, or a business; (like running a newspaper) insert by Grube. And what a challenge in the competitive atmosphere of business today! To be able to expose ones self to complete saturation of a problem—trying to understand—trying to bear the weight—hoping the process bears fruit. It is a blessing, because every thought you may fail at first, the persistence will pay off. And the rewards will be the Gell-Mann of the business, literature, art, and professional community.

"Well, Mr. Horace from the chorus," I said to myself. "You and I are going to get along just fine. You have granted me a map, outlining the road to my pot of gold. Isn't that something to think about! As a matter of fact you have just given me the particular title that will be associated with my column according to Flynn, and other sports' stories—SOMETHING TO THINK ABOUT!"

Over dinner at the coffee shop in the Hilton, I took my first stab at what order I would put the **SOMETHING TO THINK ABOUT** columns. They would be in some type of order paralleling Jack's metamorphosis from Mr. Jack to **Monk** Jack. They would be completely separate from my regular column and would ensure that nothing more than Jack Flynn's relationship with his church and beliefs would be discussed. I may write a column about how his decision affected his lovely girlfriend Elizabeth "Sparky"

McGovern. I think her broken heart came from the fact the announcement was an astonished shock. We know nothing of her plans for the future and whether or not it includes college. We do know Liz, as she is known by her friends, models for the POWERS AGENCY, but she has been doing that since 6th grade. I'll say one thing. God himself must have touched her face; she is absolutely stunning. My guess is a local college and continued work for POWERS. But we'll see!

My first column will undoubtedly be an overview of what to expect. I know from research the first step for Jack should about the history of **Monks** and their evolution to present day. We should also address the Retreat House. The hurried pace of life today prompts many men to seek a place of peace and quiet in which to reflect on their relationship with God, to pray and to be renewed spiritually. We do not know how long he intends to stay at the RETREAT HOUSE; we know only that it is a stepping-stone. I have a fighter pilot friend that works at an aerospace company in the Salt Lake City area. He told me at a reunion two years ago that he attends a retreat for men once a year. I'll give him a call and find out if the retreat is in the Ogden area. Wouldn't it be a kick if it was located in Huntsville where Jack will be headed.

I will also will be informing readers of just what composes a retreat is and what we could possibly learn. Religion will play no part of any column; the RETREAT HOUSE is open to adult men, whether Catholic or not. There is no set fee; a free will offering according to one's means is requested.

A column will highlight my visit to Huntsville and a personal interview with the Father in charge. I understand the monks do change responsibilities. No matter! I would ask my friend Roland DeBeer, Col., USAF, (Ret), to request a meeting with me.

At the proper time I could report the conversation I have with Jack upon his return home. Since one has to be 21 years or older to enter the Abbey, we will all learn together. I am pretty sure he has to go to an approved prep school to mentally prepare for his new vocation. The column will take us into time not recorded so we will see what knowledge we gained; maybe we will gain some insight into Jack's thinking. In the meantime, I have to talk to Jack and get back to my sport's column. I have several ideas about what, and whom, I will write about in additional **SOMETHING TO THINK ABOUT** columns.

Talk to you later!

LEGACY & CULTURE

A lesson to be learned from the legacy of baseball, the business community and the Latshaw family.

A Two Part Series

By: Charles Grube
Sports' Editor

Why?? You, our resolute and steadfast readers ask! Why this two part series written by the *PITTSBURGH POST TELEGRAPH's* **Sport's Editor?**

Because after studying what is happening to baseball and football through free agency, corporate management in a frenzy of conglomerate growth, the Latshaw family is a shining star. I wanted you, our customers, to know how much the Latshaw's have supported you through their years of developing legacy and culture as the nexus for the *PITTSBURGH POST TELEGRAPH*. Although information is extremely sensitive and kept "under wraps," The *LATSHAW FOUNDATION* has given millions to the DUQUESNE, CARNEGIE TECH, and PITT schools of business, journalism, and literature. They radiate the principles of free enterprise through their constant concern for customers and employees. The Latshaw endeavor grows from within.

Bear with me!!

It's been said that the toughest feat in sports is to hit a baseball on the major league level. Yet for 56 consecutive games in 1941, Joe DiMaggio of the New York Yankees did just that, resulting in a baseball record that many believe will never be broken.

Joseph Paul DiMaggio joined the New York Yankees in 1936 and played his entire career with the Yankees; he retired in 1952. He was known as a "Thing of Beauty" for his versatility, fielding talent and hitting ability. He was elected to the Baseball Hall of Fame in 1955.

Theodore Samuel—Ted—Williams joined the Boston Red Sox in 1939 and played continuously (with exception of military service) for the team until his retirement in 1960. Williams was one of the greatest natural hitters the game has ever known; he attributed his prowess to *his* detailed knowledge of the strike zone. In 1941 Ted Williams won the American League Batting Championship with a .406 average; a record most experts believe will never be broken. He *was* elected to the Baseball Hall of Fame in 1966.

The older of the two baseball leagues, the National League, was organized in 1876. In 1900 the Western League regrouped as the American League and three years later gained recognition as the second major league. Although earlier rules existed, the American and National Leagues adopted joint playing rules in 1904.

The Committee of Baseball Executives appointed, in 1921, Judge Kenesaw M. Landis to the new post of Baseball Commissioner. Landis replaced the three-man National Commission, which had ruled professional baseball since 1903. Landis governed for 24 years.

Why a brief synthesis on DiMaggio, Williams and baseball history? Because it *is* my firm belief that legacy and culture are interlinked with stability, time, and therefore, concomitant performance; accompanied by a cornerstone of customs, ideas and attitudes shared by a group and transmitted from generation to generation.

Think about what has been said; joint playing rules since 1904, Judge Landis governing for 24 years; Joe DiMaggio and Ted Williams were given the platform of stability that enabled them to perform over a period of time that gave birth to their legacy. Joe DiMaggio didn't play by one set of rules and Ted Williams another. Joe DiMaggio didn't play for the Yankees one year, the White Sox the next, the Cincinnati Reds the next, and so on. The same with Ted Williams!

In the present day atmosphere of free agency and business short-term planning, constant instability of cohesive strategy and unrelenting emphasis on the bottom line, I see a pervasive lack of awareness by corporate executives of understanding the appreciating legacy and culture. Culture, not economics, is the cornerstone of corporate stability and growth. There is no culture or legacy with the Yankees anymore. Dollars have taken over their winning ways. No one grows within the team anymore; their contracts are purchased for the higher price!

This is not the case with the Latshaw family!

John Stuart Mill said in 1851, "The grand achievement of the present age is the diffusion of superficial knowledge." In my opinion, the grand achievement of the present day is the diffusion of superficial management.

"Culture" in a society as a whole, is "a general state of intellectual, material and moral development."

And what is a society? It is a group of people united for the promotion of a common aim. In the process of thinking through my reasoning on management's lack of understanding culture, I vicariously joined this "group of people" and brought together our collective material, intellectual and moral development into a corporation. We are supposedly united for a common aim. Is management leading us? Is management seeking the chance to look at all aspects of this collective material, intellectual and moral development before making decisions? I don't think so unless you study the Latshaw's way of building a business.

In "culture" we speak of the material, intellectual and moral development as a way of life; but that doesn't satisfy me. I also want time, maturity and legacy (continued superior performance) considered. Let us reflect for a minute on Bennett's observation on the acquiring of culture. To develop *anything* takes time, and if one's energy and aim *is* directed toward gaining knowledge and beauty, there is an accompanying gain of development and maturity. With maturity there is an understanding of one's self. Also, there is value to be gained by sharing the experience of attained knowledge and beauty with family, friends and business colleagues.

Whitehead said, in *AIMS of EDUCATION*, "Culture is activity of thought and receptiveness of beauty and humane feeling. Scraps of information have nothing to do with it. A merely well informed man *is* the most useless bore on God's earth. What should be our aim would be producing men who possess both culture and expert knowledge in some special direction. Their expert knowledge will give them the ground to start from, and their culture will lead them as deep as philosophy and as high as art."

The Latshaw's possess both culture and expert knowledge in some special direction—upward!

In a corporate environment expert knowledge shared and exchanged over a period of time creates an atmosphere for giving birth to legacy. I think that it would be fair to say that Henry Higginson developed a specific culture in the Boston Symphony Orchestra. History reveals the legacy of the orchestra has been handed down through a period of time by famous conductors, Symphony Hall, The Berkshire Festival, and the Boston Pops Orchestra.

Tom Watson, Sr., developed an acute no-nonsense business atmosphere and culture at IBM and handed it down to Tom Watson,

C. R. Smith created a culture of reliable and charismatic business travel at American Airlines and passed it on to Robert Crandall.

The Latshaws developed an acute no-nonsense business atmosphere and culture and one Latshaw handed it down to another.

"OK," you say, "I can't find argument with you about your definitions but how do legacy and culture relate?"

That's a fair question but the answer will not be an easy one. You have to think in terms of both words. The secret is: the *recognition* and *appreciation* of expert knowledge (CULTURE) and the *determination* to continue or hand down (LEGACY) generally accepted works of value and intellectual excellence. It's "recognition-appreciation—determination." It's the Boston Philharmonic—IBM-American *Airlines—PITTSBURGH POST TELEGRAPH!* It's your company!!! To uphold your company's position, strength, and customer satisfaction in the marketplace, you must have all three. You can't have one or two without the other. At the same time, as a company continually strives for knowledge and value, it must develop the ability, character, leadership and personal esteem of employees. Management sometimes forgets that employees ARE the company. If the company *is* to continue to have pre-eminent significance its employees, and I mean all employees, must be part of the continual effort for knowledge and value.

TO BE CONTINUED:

Talk to you later!

LEGACY AND CULTURE

PRIME DRIVERS IN PITTSBURGH POST TELEGRAPH MANAGEMENT

Part II of the series

By: Charles Grube
Sports' Editor

First, I want to thank all the fans and customers who have written to Mr. Latshaw and me regarding Part I of the series about Legacy and Culture. I did not ask permission from Mr. Latshaw; I just wrote the article because I thought it the right thing to do. Individuals, not organizations, create excellence. With their unique skills they lead others and prepare corporate strategy for the future and pass on a vibrant culture.

Families possess culture. In a family, parents develop children by caring for, and educating them. Parents set standards for propriety of speech, appearance, behavior, and educational excellence. As the children grow older they recognize and appreciate the family legacy and pass on to their children what they have come to learn and esteem.

Today, however, due to the effect of WWII and the Korean War, families were split up due to the serving our country. Or, the parents were given the opportunity for both father and mother to work, or a single parent had to labor, thereby creating the need for easy access to "fast food". Hence, parents do not have the real opportunity to sit down at dinner to discuss propriety of speech, appearance, behavior and educational excellence.

A corporation is a big family. Management should take time to develop its employees and train them to complement the strategies and goals of the company in its competitive growth. Goals and standards for excellence are set. Every member of the organization, from the CEO like Mr. Latshaw, to the lowliest clerk and janitor share responsibility; and through proper communication, accepts accountability for the organization's products and services.

Time begins to highlight and distinguish unique patterns with which companies manage and control. Time distinguishes their company from competition. To perpetuate the culture, each *Pittsburgh Press Telegraph* manager and employee passes valued features of quality along to succeeding generations. The manager and employee possess both culture and expert knowledge in some special direction. This is the basic story of the Latshaws and their paper!

The *PITTSBURGH POST TELEGRAPH'S* "culture" has, in the past, won high marks over many other newspaper chains for three reasons: employees share an unrelenting commitment to superior CUSTOMER SERVICE, management strives to hire and KEEP good people, and employees themselves enforce a high standard of PERFORMANCE. The *PPT's* "culture" has been PASSED ALONG so consistently to so many succeeding generations that no one who works for the family can escape it. If a new employee doesn't suit the paper's culture, fellow employees, not a manager, remind them to perform or resign. The *PPT's* standards and expectations bring non-performers to the company's notice quickly, and management doesn't waste time getting rid of employees *who* won't, or can't, adapt.

I would imagine most companies honestly strive for good customer service and they try to hire and keep good people. But that's not good enough. Management must realize the only reason they are even needed or the reason for the corporate entity itself is to perform in the needs of the customer. The communication of determination to excel must permeate the entire organization, and it is this philosophy, when passed to succeeding generations that nurtures culture and legacy. How? They Listen! Listen! Listen! To the customer's needs!

The Latshaw family *is* extremely economically successful. Their corporate stability and growth nurtures their success.

Customer satisfaction is the ultimate objective of every business. In truth, satisfaction is the only product or service. A home tool and appliance maker once thought it was in the business of selling one-and-a-half inch drill bits when it realized that its customers didn't really want one-and-a-half inch drill bits. All they wanted were one-and-a-half inch holes.

CHANGES IN MANAGEMENT

There is a proliferation of management changes today. It seems to be the thing to do; Japanese management style has become, in some disciplines, avant-garde. Also, there are a horrific number of management reorganizations and personnel shifts due to the junk bond/buy-out, amalgamation frenzy. One of the fastest and most sure ways to destroy culture and dim prospects for continued legacy *is* by revolutionary (rather than evolutionary) reorganization.

By working for this paper I have been in the discipline of learning, first hand, business management for a number of years. As most of the readers of my columns know, I have been going to night school and teaching business classes (one night a week) at Duquesne for seven (or eight) of those years. I have had the opportunity to study, first hand, innumerable companies. Overnight replacement of a high percentage of management personnel, overnight structural reorganization and the hiring of managers from competing firms with a history of changing jobs for a few dollars more creates mass confusion, cultural shock, and bureaucracy.

When was the last time there was a management change at the *PPT*? There hasn't been any change. Why change personnel if first, there *is* a better understanding of responsibilities and accountabilities. I know of no example when the Latshaw's raised heck because someone made a mistake. Why? Because they believe a mistake of *commission* is OK! A mistake of *omission* is trouble!

In all appearance and substance the new CEO wants to make a name for himself as fast as possible. He is under pressure to perform. This "fast recognition" parallels short-term planning and goals. This compression of time negates the ability to recognize and appreciate the intellectual excellence of the company.

"What is that," you ask?

Its employees! Its customers!

Hickman and Silva address these issues in a volume I am using to lecture. It is *CREATING EXCELLENCE*. For example, they directed their attention to Bausch and Lomb. Bausch & Lomb's instruments' group had at one time consisted of some thirty different product lines that competed against such successful giants as Hewlett-Packard. This loosely bound group of businesses had languished for almost a decade before Jim Edwards, an IBM whiz kid, rode to the rescue. The first phase of Edward's rehabilitation program was a wrenching *overnight* reorganization, creating four new divisions—three oriented to manufacturing and one dedicated to sales and service support for *all* product lines. In addition to the new divisions, Edwards brought aboard the matrix form of organization he had learned at IBM. The reorganization seemed brilliant because it united all the fragmented product lines under the direction of one business unit, thus taking advantage of economies of scale and share resources.

But, the loose-knit family at Bausch & Lomb didn't fall into step like the disciplined professionals at IBM, and Edwards found himself valiantly struggling to bind the family together with brochures and videotapes selling the new organization and mode of operation. Despite all his efforts, confusion blossomed, and the group grew demoralized. Before long the company announced a quarterly earnings drop of 32 percent, soon followed by Edwards' resignation. One former executive summed up the experience by saying, "Edwards didn't take the TIME to take the measure of the company, the employees, and the customers before he started." Apparently Edwards forgot for the moment that culture does not grow out of overnight reorganizations, policy directives, or matrix-style management.

I can't possibly imagine the Latshaw's allowing that to happen.

I am sure of one thing. IBM didn't install a matrix form of management style in a "wrenching overnight reorganization." It evolved through evolutionary common sense, keeping in mind people, product, and performance. And just because matrix "was in" at IBM doesn't necessarily mean it would work at Bausch & Lomb, or the PITTSBURGH POST TELEGRAPH for that matter.

A deep study of Legacy and Culture would offer many answers.

Jim Edwards should have taken into consideration the culture of the company. How did the company establish its name and perpetuate it for so long? You find that answer in people; not organization. People will tell you what's wrong, not an organization chart that you assign personnel to. And by people, I mean employees, subcontractors, vendors, and customers.

Jim Edwards should have directed the analysis of Bausch & Lomb in the language of, and needs of, the customer before making changes. Customers in concert with management will communicate to an organization what is needed to compete and grow; those needs are fulfilled by employees! One does not draw an organization chart and detail it with positions and names. It is the *function of—the detailed responsibilities* and accountabilities of—employees that dictate organization—not the other way around. If Bausch & Lomb's different product lines served different customers, why did they have to be shoved into one style of management? It is impossible for the customers and sales and service personnel to speak the same language. It is impossible to develop the rapport needed for what? The recognition and appreciation or expert knowledge!

Jim Edwards didn't take the time to ferret out, recognize, and appreciate knowledge and excellence in people. The Latshaws do!!

AN ADDENDUM

What I discuss now is an augmentation of my short essay, particularly about free agency in baseball and loyalty.

Before free agency who followed DiMaggio? Mantle did! Who followed Williams? Yastrzemski did! They continued, first hand, the legacy and culture of the Yankees and Red Sox.

To me culture is based on historical performance and communication—"transmitted from generation to generation—." The foundations of mathematics were so well laid by the Greeks that our children learn their geometry from a book written for the schools of Alexandria two thousand years ago. Modern astronomy is the natural continuation and development of the work of Hipparchus and of Ptolemy; modern physics that of Democritus and of Archimedes; it was long before modern biological science outgrew the knowledge bequeathed to us by Aristotle, by Theophrastus, and by Galen.

If the foundations of these great sciences contributed so immensely to the mental growth and culture of man, why would present day management allow the deterioration of employee mental growth and culture?

Because they don't understand! They think small! They move in revolutionary terms! For culture certainly means something quite different from learning or technical skill. It implies the possession of an ideal, and the habit of critically estimating the value of things by comparison with a theoretic standard. It takes time to evaluate and compare and it's impossible to find the right standard *if* one is in too much of a hurry.

Perfect culture should apply a complete theory of life, based upon a clear knowledge alike of its possibilities and of its limitations.

I did send Part II to Mr. Latshaw's office for approval. I did not want my sports' column to sound "too preachy". He sent me a hand written note and thanked me for mentioning the Latshaw family's pattern of management and added, "Who can go wrong in learning about the nexus of corporate strength and growth through Legacy and Culture."

Talk to you later!

JACK FLYNN'S IRISH EYES
ARE SMILIN'
SO IS HIS HEART!!

By: Charles Grube
Sports' Editor

I invited Jack to join me for lunch at the Chartiers Country Club, the area's center for all social activities for members and their guests. The Latshaws' have a corporate membership through the paper and as an executive, my lady companion, and I, are granted all privileges. My current girlfriend, Gloria, in one heck of a bridge player and enjoys the social atmosphere and the women she plays with—or against—or whatever!! I tried it but failed! I kept trumping my partner's ace or performing other acts of pure lunacy!

I *was* sitting at my table when Jack walked in at 1:00PM, our designated time. He was wearing a dark blue blazer with a lighter blue pair of slacks, and a white silk sport shirt open at the collar. A fire engine red colored handkerchief was tucked neatly in the blazer's pocket.

When he sat down I said, "Bless me Father for I have sinned. Since I sin in color, it *is* a lot easier for me to confess to someone in the same dress code. Confessing to someone in the colors of our flag makes it a little arduous to clean one's soul."

Jack didn't miss a beat. He cocked his right arm at the elbow, gave me the sign of the cross and said, "Go in peace and hand me a piece—of bread!"

I love a quick wit!

The waiter came to the table; Jack ordered tomato-basil soup plus a spring salad made up of apple, nuts and chunky blue cheese. It was tossed with a vinaigrette dressing. I had my favorite; a strip of top sirloin, medium rare, with melted chunks of blue cheese and a serving of hot broccoli. We both asked for ice tea; lemon but no sugar.

Over lunch Jack and I chatted about a number of incidental subjects; Jack's life since "the announcement", Liz McGovern, his plans for travel to Utah, and his mental attitude toward the huge step he decided to embrace.

Don't let anyone fool you. Jack Flynn is an intelligent, bright, discerning individual. He gave me straightforward answers. As to the announcement, he said I just stepped up and announced reality. I made up my mind after my ski trip to Utah. Maybe it was unfair to Liz; I really don't have an answer. I just did what I thought was right at the time. Yes, we were ready to attend college together but I am convinced I have to follow my heart and it is now pointing to the **Abbey of the Holy Trinity.** Hell, Mr. Grube, I have absolutely no answers until I step forward and try. You fighter pilots have a saying, "No guts, no glory." Why should not the same maxim apply to me or, for that matter, anyone who wants to step forward and try.

Pass me the crackers, please. Thank you."

I was pleased to see him so relaxed and enjoying his meal. We both said "Yes" to refills of iced tea.

"As far as Liz in concerned," he continued, "we had dinner the night before last. Let's face the tangible here. We are both broken hearted although mine is being mended, slowly, with a ray of light. We both wonder like all get-out about our future happiness. Liz told me her heart will be cured in time and in the interlude she is thinking about taking the modeling position offered to her by the Ford Agency. Liz is satisfied with Powers as they always schedule her at a convenient time. But then Liz says if she goes to school she may not be able to travel as Ford requested, so the final tally has not come up with an answer as yet. She *is* also perusing the summer courses of study offered by the local colleges, particularly at night. She would like to study radio broadcasting and TV. She is *so* "drop dead" beautiful but as she told me the other night 'That's today; I have to think about tomorrow.'"

"Smart lady," I said. "I'll tell you a story about another "drop dead" alluring lady. She was an applicant for employment as a stewardess for *AMERICAN AIRLINES*. She was from a small town in West Virginia. I mean the town was so small the fire department was one guy with an ax, a shovel, and a water pic. Well, I'm glad you're smiling. Anyhow, she was interviewed in Washington, D.C. and had never been in a town larger than Morgantown, W.Va. The university is located there. Her home, and this was told to me, had no running water other than a hand pump in the kitchen, had an outhouse, and water *was* heated and food cooked on a Ben Franklin type wood stove. In Washington, during the interview a couple of men came up to the desk to wish her well and both stated, 'We understand you're from West By God Virginia. We think you are one of the most gorgeous ladies we have even seen.' I guess she was used to the adulation so she just smiled and said, 'Thank you.'

But getting back to the interview, the Personnel Director asked where she *was* from. She answered, 'West By God Virginia.'

"West By God! Virginia, where is that?"

She answered, 'I don't rightly know, I know it's west of a my home town with, let's see, 1, 2, 3, 4—about 7 buildings But every time someone saw me or walked up to say something they always said,' By God! You're pretty!

The Director just looked at her; didn't say a word for thirty seconds or so. Then he asked, "When is your birthday?"

She said, "February 17th."

He asked, "What year?"

She answered, "Every year!"

The Director, probably overcome by her charm, stood up, closed the employment file and simply said, "Welcome aboard. You will be notified within ten days when your schooling will start. The Academy is located in Dallas, Texas. "Have you ever been to Texas?" he asked.

"No Sir," she answered. But I'll know exactly when I arrive."

"How *is* that?"

"Well, Sir, I understand that is exactly where the airplane will drop me off."

Again, he just looked at her, shook his head, and said, "We at American wish you well."

"You know what?" my friend, Jack. Stewardesses were not free to be married at that time. I dated a number of them; truly great ladies. One I dated was from American. I was still in the Air Force so I could fly and meet her just about anywhere she had an overnight. She knew 'By God!' She told me 'By God' *was* married within twelve months to a very wealthy real estate investor and was living a happy life. That will happen to Liz also, in due time, and you, my fellow friend; your happiness will come from living the life you chose—increasing in satisfaction by knowing yourself and those around you. Heck, Jack, I don't know the answers but I do remember from my philosophy studies in college but I continue to this day, I remember John Dewey said something along the lines like, 'Happiness is fundamental in morals only because happiness is not something to be sought for, but is something now attained, even in the midst of pain and trouble.' And Bertrand Russell said he believes that very few men would deliberately chose unhappiness if they see a way of being happy. Seems to me your life 'is something now attained.'

Now let's order dessert. How about a scoop of vanilla ice cream with fresh strawberries? I'm going to have black coffee. What about you?"

"I think I'll stick with the iced tea."

"OK! Do you mind if I ask you a question about monastic life?" "Of course not. Shoot!"

"How does one become a monk? But come to think of it, in lieu of answering that question for now, let me tell you about a meeting I had with Mr. Latshaw."

"Please, go ahead."

"I went up to see him in his office with an idea. It was about you. I wanted to write a column about your transition from a football hero and its concomitant adulation to the life of—well, literally, a life of solitary existence; a recluse. Of course you will have other men around you but by definition the word 'monk' comes from the <Gk, *monos.,* single. That's a hell of a change 0! change 0! if you know what I mean.

At any rate, Jack, Mr. Latshaw and I agreed that my column would be in the sports' section because of your notoriety. A lot of people would like to be kept enlightened, now and then, how your passage from one activity to the other is coming along. The name of the column will be **SOMETHING TO THINK ABOUT.** It will appear in the paper at random times. It will follow what I call 'your evolution.' Over span of time my desire *is* to keep readers interested in you. Remember, Jack, you brought a lot of excitement and pride to this community. I plan to write not only about that but other exciting days that caused happy tales and folklore to his city of *THREE RIVERS.* People love to remember pleasurable times."

And, Jack, speaking of pleasurable times, I fell sure your pleasurable times will be mental. You appear untroubled and relaxed.

May I go back to my earlier question on how one becomes a monk? Tell me about your perception and sensitiveness. I think that's a good word to help you tell me about your new purpose in life."

"Mr. Grube," Jack said, "I think, from the little I have learned, that monastic life is a vocation or calling from God. At some point in my life, and I recall lately while skiing at Deer Valley, a man feels an attraction to this kind of life. Well, my attraction, if that's what it's called, needs to be tested to see if it came from God or from some other source, to see whether it is only a passing fancy or whether it is a genuine resolve to serve God in this way of life. As I said earlier, I think this is the right thing to do but I haven't the slightest idea until I try. Trying is a test; an examination! If it's anything like my display of spectacular agility on the ski slopes at Deer Valley, I am in deep trouble. I was showing off making a jump off a steep slope. I missed calculating everything, and a disbursement of skis, gloves, sun glasses, cap, ski poles, trail maps from an open pocket, and I, covered at least a 50 yard radius from where I hit cross ways on my right shoulder. If I get like results from my test at monastic life, I won't make altar boy.

From the information I received from the **Abbey** in Utah, I will be placed under the direction of a novice master, who will instruct me in the requirements of the life, will help me discern my real motivation in coming to the monastery, and test my resolve.

I think I spend the first six months as, what is known to me, as a postulant. It's observation time! I observe and test the community and the community observes me. If I persevere for six months the **Abbey** takes it from there. What that entails I don't know. I'll get you more information after I arrive. You can count on one thing; when I'm free to communicate, I'll give you the straight skinny for your column.

I hope that partially answers your question, Mr. Grube"

"It does, and I appreciate it. I may have mentioned I have a fighter pilot friend in living Ogden. It's not far from Huntsville. I called him and he is going to send me information such as history, a review of a monk's day, more details on the Retreat House, plus he is going arrange a personal meeting for me with a Father Eugene, or another Trappist priest whomever will be in charge. I think he is known as the Guest-master. Mr. Latshaw has given his "OK" for me to travel to the **Abbey** of the *HOLY TRINITY* sometime in the future depending on how my column *is* being received regarding a Mr. Jack Flynn."

"Just spell my name right and you'll be OK!"

Jack and I finished our strawberries and ice cream. I told the waiter to please bring the check. Jack and I rose from the table, and solemnly wished each other well as we shook hands. Jack thanked me and said, with deep earnestness, "Thank you, Mr. Grube. I pray I may contribute to the happy tales of *THREE RIVERS.*"

"That depends on how I spell your name!"

"Please give my fond regards to your family."

Talk to you later!

Charles Grube
Sports' Editor

CREATION/INSPIRATION
A WAREHOUSE OF FACTS WITH
POET AND LIAR IN JOINT OWNERSHIP

-Ambrose Bierce

I received a call from Jack's older brother Jim, who told me the family had a quiet but very loving dinner party at home for Jack the evening before he left for Utah. All of the family was there including relatives plus close friends. Liz was also there. Jack asked Jim to call me and to say thanks again for the luncheon at Chartiers and that he would call when he arrived and had settled in. Also, Jim told me Jack had given him a two or three page "brochure" outlining details of the **Retreat House** at the **Abbey of Our Lady of the Holy Trinity.** It was sent to him by "The Guestmaster", a Father Eugene. Jim said, "I'll get one of the city's couriers to drop it off first thing in the morning."

Brother Jim is some kind of a "big wheel" working for the Chairman of three county commissioners handling all transportation needs for the city of Pittsburgh.

I thanked Jim. He is one of four children of the "Irish eyes are smiling" Flynn family; two girls and two boys. I met Jim through Jack after a football game last season. He was talking to his big brother while waiting for the team bus to take them back home. Everyone was jubilant! The team won by about 20 points and Jack had had a remarkable evening; scored two touchdowns on runs of 52 and 81 yards. Anyhow, Jim interrupted his discussion with Jack and said he appreciated my recognition of Jack through the paper.

All of the Flynn's have a lot of class. A note on Jim; he was a heck of a football player himself. He earned three letters in football as a 6 foot, 195 pound left linebacker for Crafton High. I remember a game I attended when Jim made a defensive tackle I will never forget.

Jim was lined up behind his left tackle—I would guess about four or five feet. It was raining very hard; a real downpour! The quarterback called his signals and at "HUP" took the ball from his center, and faked a handoff to his fullback charging through the left side of the line behind his guard and tackle. Jim was not fooled. Because of a wet ball the quarterback lost about ¾ of a second before he underhanded the ball to his left halfback headed around left end. Jim took advantage of the ruined tempo as the pulling left tackle, slowed by the soaked grass and slop, was a half step behind his halfback. Jim charged angling through the line and took a mighty lunge, and blocked the tackle with his upper body as he grabbed the runner by the ankles and pulled him to his chest. Both men, with curled bodies, knees to their breasts, slid about 15 yards across the muck and mud onto the sidelines knocking down two doused cheerleaders, a saturated photographer, and one very shocked referee who arose, very slowly, covered with wet, sticky earth. Jim helped the referee up and said something I would guess to be, "Are you OK?" The ref wiped some mud from his face, put his hand on Jim's massive shoulder and seemed to be saying he was all right as he was shaking his head up and down.

Honestly, when Jim and his opponent were sliding they looked like "Frick & Frack" the **two** comic, but exceptionally talented ice skaters from the *FOLLIES*, who looked like "**one—**" bent, knees to their chest, sliding on the pristine ice in circles around the ring.

The envelope Jim sent me was on my desk the following morning. The information on the Abbey was not only enlightening but it also got me a little excited about my future plans to visit.

THE RETREAT HOUSE

The hurried pace of life today prompts many men to seek a place of peace and quiet in which to reflect on their relationship with God; to pray and be renewed spiritually. The Retreat House at Holy Trinity has room for twelve and is open for adult men, whether Catholic or not. Retreats generally are private, allowing the individual retreatant to arrange his own time for prayer, reading, exercising or resting. Priests of the community are available for counseling and for the sacrament of reconciliation. Women who wish to make retreats may use the family guesthouse at times when it is not in use by relatives of the monks.

Retreats are usually limited to three days for persons within the state of Utah. A person coming from outside the State may have a lengthier period, which is arranged by the Guest-master. The abbey church is always open to retreatants for prayer and meditation, including the times of the monks' prayer and the celebration of the Eucharist. There is no set fee for making a retreat. A free will offering according to one's needs is requested, so that the retreat house can continue its operation.

Each guest has a private room, but there is a common washroom and shower room. A clothes washer and dryer are available for use by the retreat ants.

The retreatants' library has an ample selection of religious books. Other books and pamphlets can be purchased at the monastery's book store.

The time for rising is at the discretion of the retreatant himself. If he wishes to attend any of the monks' early hour of prayer or the Mass at 6:30 a.m., he is welcome to do so. He is expected to be present for meals in the common dining room. If he foresees that he will be absent for a meal, he should notify the Guest-master beforehand. Meal times are posted!

Well, let me think! What did I learn? Jack will be met by Fr. Eugene and with the proper arrangements he can stay as long as he desires, but has to remind himself that his Prep School probably starts in the Fall. It sounds like a good plan to me. He will have the solitude to think of his future and Jack, as the will rest of his fans and friends, will seek God's help through a prayer or two—or three—that he makes the right choice.

Talk to you later!

A BRIEF HISTORY

Monks or ascetics existed in the Catholic Church from at least the third century!

I will continue to pass on to all the information forwarded to me about the Abbey of the Holy Trinity; the organizer—Roland DeBeers—my fighter pilot friend.

**By: Charles Grube
Sports' Editor**

I will continue to write my columns about garnered information as long as we (the sport fans and I) feel it best to keep Jack Flynn on our minds. It is also in my plans to take you back in history when so many of Pittsburgh's most cherished athletes and teams made headline news. I think it will be enjoyable for all of us to reminisce.

Now, let's talk a little Monk history!

Upper Egypt housed large monasteries of community-type monks called cenobites. Meanwhile, in Lower Egypt, near the Nile Delta, lived hermits or solitaries, who built cells in the desert, where they lived in loosely structured colonies or by themselves. About the same time, in Syria, there arose a monasticism of the solitary type. Hilarion initiated monasticism in Palestine by becoming a hermit around 308 A.D. Colonies of monks sprang up around him. In Asia Minor Basil (329-379) founded monasteries and wrote rules—like "say your prayers and brush your teeth." Just kidding!!

(I will continue, but I want the readers to know I looked up Hilarion and Basil in the *THE COLUMBIA ENCYCLOPEDIA* and found nothing. Anytime I run across a name that I can contribute a little personal history, I will include it in my written soliloquy.)

Western visitors and ascetics, attracted by the fame of the Egyptian monks, visited them and wrote their histories, like Palladius' Lausiac History, and the anonymous collections of the sayings of desert fathers, called the Apophthegmata. Jerome (+419A.D.) and Rufinus (+410 A.D.) translated some of these works from Greek into Latin for the benefit of the Romans and other Europeans.

It's sorta fun to look up words I haven't the slightest idea how to pronounce. Maybe Mr. Latshaw and the paper will publish a crossword puzzle when we're finished with our history lesson. I couldn't find a word on Palladius, that is, as associated with his time and nationality. The same holds true for Jerome and Rufinus. There was a St. Jerome. His Roman name was Sophronius Eusebius Heironymus. How would a mother arrange to have her young daughter introduce *him* to her father. I would think—Carefully!

John Cassian (+c433A.D.) visited the monks in Egypt and later recorded their teachings in his famous Institutes and Conferences, which were written in southern France and had a considerable influence on western monasticism.

(Eureka! An Eastern Christian monk and theologian who brought Eastern spirituality to the West.)

In Italy, Benedict, (c480-550A.D.) founded the famous monastery of Monte Cassino and wrote his Rules for Monks, a set of prescriptions for monastic living, which we still follow in principle. Even before Benedict, and during the centuries that followed, monks established monasteries throughout Western Europe. They established schools and promoted studies and learning during the so-called Dark Ages.

Known as Benedict of Nursia, he went to Subiaco, a town in central Italy where he and his disciples lived for 33 years before moving to Monte Cassino. In an old pagan holy place, he started the first truly Benedictine monastery.

Monte Cassino was, throughout the centuries, one of the great centers of Christian learning and piety; its influence on European civilization is immeasurable.

We all learned of Monte Casino from the Italian Campaign of WW II. A concentrated aerial bombardment (1944) flattened the buildings and most of the art treasures destroyed. It was rebuilt after the war.

Monasteries have periods of fervor and of decline. In periods of decline there often appear saintly and fervent leaders who effect reforms. Once such reform took place in eastern France in 1098 A.D. Robert, abbot of the monastery of Molesme, north of Lyons, took with him twenty monks and founded a monastery at Citeaux, which became the center of the Cistercian Order. The monks of this order came to be known as the "white monks," in contradistinction to the traditional monks, who wore black and who became known as Benedictines.

The encyclopedia states: The Cistercian Order was founded by *Saint* Robert, allegedly reacting against departures from the Rule of St. Benedict.

Let's see; reminds me of someone else named Martin Luther, German leader of the Protestant Reformation. Luther was no dummy; he had a Masters in Law and Doctorate in Theology. He entered a monastery of the Augustinian friars devoutly attentive to the rigid discipline of the order. He began an intensive study of Scripture, and was ordained a priest. The church's abuse of indulgences started it all and his break from Rome became inevitable.

Martin Luther's life makes for great study; but any study, or investigation, or examination of potentially conflicting ideas offers at the same time a mental parachute. It's a causation—an inducement—to open ones' mind.

In the early 17ᵗʰ century a further reform was called for in the Cistercian monastery of La Trappe in northern France, which had fallen into decay. Armand-Jean de Rance (1626-1700 A.D.) became the abbot and reformed the community. It is from this monastery and its foundations that we get the popular term "Trappist."

(de Rance was of a noble family, was well educated, and lived at court as a worldly priest. In 1664 he retired to the Cistercian Abbey at La Trappe, establishing, as a regular abbot, a discipline stricter than the primitive Benedictine rule. In a few years La Trappe was famous, and its reform spread; out of the movement came the Trappists.)

In 1790 all monasteries and religious houses in France were suppressed, and their property confiscated by the Revolutionary Government. The monks and other religious were either guillotined, escaped into exile, or abandoned their religious status. The novice master of La Trappe, Augustin de Lestrange, escaped from France with twenty-one monks of his monastery and set up his community in a vacant Carthusian monastery in Switzerland.

When Napoleon's armies threatened to invade Switzerland, de Lestrange, together with his monks and nuns, journeyed all the way to Russia. After a year of two, not finding any welcome there, they gradually made their way back to France. Many candidates came to fill their ranks, and eventually they established monasteries in France, England, Ireland, Canada, and the United States. The first two houses in the U.S.A. were Gethsemani in Kentucky and New Melleray in Iowa. It was from Gethsemani that the monastery of the Holy Trinity was founded at Huntsville, Utah, in 1947.

(So, with our history lesson completed, it appears Jack will inherit a well-documented legacy)

THE TRAPPIST-CISTERCIAN ORDER

The order belongs to a worldwide Order of monks and nuns. In 2005 there were 101 monasteries of monks and 70 of nuns on all continents. Of these, 12 of monks and 5 of nuns are in the United States.

The highest authority in the Order is the General Chapter of each branch. Every three years the abbots and abbesses meet under the chairmanship of the Abbot General to make decisions concerning the welfare of the Order. At present time the two chapters, male and female, meet jointly in what is known as the Mixed General Meeting. Between these meetings the Abbot General and his Council, who reside in Rome, are in charge of the Order's affairs. The present Abbot General is Dom Bernardo Olivera of Azul, Argentina.

Cistercian houses are joined together by filiation. Although independent, a monastery of monks is under the supervision of the abbot of the founding monastery, who ordinarily makes a visitation of the daughter house every two years. Thus the Abbey of the Holy Trinity is a filiation of the Abbey of Gethsemani, from which it was founded. A monastery of nuns is related to a monastery of monks in somewhat the same way. The Abbey of the Holy Trinity has the paternity of the nuns' monastery of Santa Rita at Sonoita, Arizona.

The Trappist Mission in the Church

The relationship of the monks of this monastery to the Church in Utah is well expressed in the Constitutions of the Order:

"The monastery is an expression of the mystery of the Church, where nothing is preferred to the praise of the Father's glory. Every effort is made to ensure that the common life in its entirety conforms to the Gospel, which is the supreme law. In this way the community will not be lacking in any spiritual gift. The monks strive to remain in harmony with all the people of God and share their active desire for the unity of all Christians. By fidelity to their monastic way of life, which has its own hidden mode of apostolic fruitfulness, monks perform a service for God's people and the whole human race. Each community of the Order and all monks are dedicated to the Blessed Virgin Mary, Mother and Symbol of the Church in the order of Faith, love and perfect union with Christ."

The Apostolate

The apostolate of the community at Holy Trinity Abbey is that of all Trappist monasteries. It is best expressed by these words of the Order's Constitutions:

"Fidelity to the monastic way of life is closely related to zeal for the Kingdom of God and for the salvation of the whole human race. Monks bear this apostolic concern in their hearts. It is the contemplative life itself that is their way of participating in the mission of Christ and his Church and of being part of the local church. This is why they cannot be called upon to render assistance in the various pastoral ministries or in any external activity, no matter how urgent the needs of the active apostolate."

For this reason one does not normally find Trappists engaged in teaching or ministry outside the monastery. Our role in the Church, the Mystical Body of Christ, is to live the gospel in our particular way for the sake of our brothers and sisters throughout the world. We do this in part by praying for them and by being witnesses to the supremacy of God, a supremacy that all people will hopefully come to recognize in their lives.

(The next piece of information forwarded to me by Mr. DeBeers had to do with the question, "How docs one become a Monk?" Jack discussed a little bit of this with me during our lunch at the country club; I think I will hold off further discussions until I travel to the **Abbey** and ask questions myself. I hope it doesn't sound too easy. But no worry; I flunked religion in the first grade!!)

Talk to you later!

HONUS WAGNER

By: Charles Grube
Sports' Editor

For those sports' fans who may have missed my earlier column to weeks or so ago, I'll bring you up to date.

I met with Chairman and President David Latshaw around that time and we decided I would follow our consensus ALL AMERICAN Jack Flynn's new vocation as a monk in my Sport's Column. I mean, of course, *as* long as possible because I don't think I could get in the front door; and Jack probably can't sneak out the back! We will do so for as long as possible because our sports' fans knew Jack and his accomplishments through the *PITTSBURGH POST TELEGRAPH's* Sport(s) Section.

Pittsburgh, as you know, has many heroes in a variety of sports. Starting with my column today I will, at times, bring you these men of fame and notoriety. So sit back, read, and through your dreams let's bring back these intrepid stars.

In my opinion, the greatest all-around player who ever lived was Honus Wagner. [Sam Crawford]

Wagner's teammate Tommy Leah thought so, too:

> *While Honus was the best* third *baseman in* the *league, he was also the best first baseman, the best second baseman, the best* shortstop *and the best outfielder. That was in fielding. And since he led the league in batting eight times between 1900 and 1911,* you *know* that *he was the best hitter, too. As well as* the *best base runner!!*

A Pennsylvania coal miner whose ambition had once been to become a barber, Wagner was one of nine children of Bavarian immigrants. It was his older brother, Al, who first caught a baseball scout's eye, but when the visitor saw the big, eighteen-year-old Bonus scaling stones across the broad river behind his house, he signed him up.

Wagner began his career playing minor league ball in Ohio and Michigan and became a star in the Iron and Oil League. In 1897 he joined the Louisville Colonels, and three years later moved to the Pittsburgh Pirates, with whom he played for eighteen years, hitting .300 or more fourteen seasons in a row, stealing 722 bases, setting National League records for at-bats and number of games played that stood for four decades.

Wagner was an imposing man. He 5-foot-11, 200-pound frame, it was said, 'featured a massive chest that might have come from a barrel-maker's shop and shoulders broad enough to serve dinner on." But he was not prepossessing: "No one ever saw anything graceful or picturesque about Wagner on the diamond," said the New York *American.* "His movements have been likened to the gambols of a caracoling elephant. He *is* so ungainly and so bowlegged that when he runs, his limbs seem to be moving in a circle after the fashion of a propeller."

His legs were indeed badly bowed, but he had huge hands and arms so long that opposing players swore he could tie his shoes without bending over. Nothing seemed to get past him, and he threw so hard to first that pebbles, scooped up as he fielded grounders, were said to arrive along with the ball.

There is no question about it! Honus Wagner *is* synonymous with the coal mining country, the city of Pittsburgh, the State of Pennsylvania, and the sovereign game of baseball.

We all have a reason to be proud!

Talk to you later.

THE SUPERIOR

Charles Grube
Sports' Editor

Information for the sports' fans and loyal readers of the *PITTSBURGH POST TELEGRAPH!*

The abbot of a Cistercian monastery is elected by the monks whom he will lead and serve!

The monks of the **Abbey of Our Lady of the Holy Trinity,** with Fr. Damien Thompson, of Gethsemani Abbey in Kentucky presiding, chose their fifth abbot. He *is* Fr. Casimir Bernas, 71 at that time. Born in Chicago, he was living in Portland, Oregon when he entered the abbey at Huntsville in 1949. Before becoming a monk, he attended high school at Columbia Prep in Portland and the first year of college at Notre Dame in Indiana. For six years prior to his election, he served as the monastery's business manager. He brings to the office of abbot numerous skills both practical and academic. He earned a doctorate in sacred Scripture from the Pontifical Biblical Institute in Rome, the first Trappist-Cistercian to do so. Also, he *was* ordained a priest about in Rome about that time.

Abbot Casimir replaced Fr. Alan Hohl who served as the appointed superior a few years earlier. At the time of Abbot Casimir's election, **Holy Trinity Abbey** was the home of twenty-two monks and one postulant.

In the administration of the temporalities of the monastery, the abbot is assisted by the advice of his council, by committees, and for important decisions, by the entire body of monks with perpetual vows, known as the monastic chapter.

I'll continue on and tell you, next page, about a monk's day. One thing I think we will all agree on—it's a long day!

A MONK'S DAY

No, I didn't write it! Just researched it! Thought the fans would like to know!

Charles Grube
Sports' Editor

3:15 AM	Rising
3:30 ~	Vigils
6:00 ~	Lauds
6:20 ~	Eucharist
7:45 ~	Terce
8:00 ~	Work
12:15 PM	Sext
12:30 ~	Dinner
1:00	Rest
2:15 ~	None
2:30 ~	Work
5:30 ~	Vespers
6:00 ~	Supper
7:30 ~	Compline
8:00 ~	Retire

"Hours" are when the monks gather in the church to sing and pray together. The Psalms and Canticles of the Bible form the backbone of these prayer periods. There is always a reading from Holy Scripture, longer or shorter for the different hours. Taken together, these prayer periods form the Liturgy of the Hours.

Liturgy of the Hours

Vigils is the night office. Some monks, notably the Carthusians, rise at midnight to chant this hour and then return to sleep. Most monks who follow the Rule of St. Benedict, as we do, rise later at night (or early in the morning) and do not retire after this prayer. The word itself, Vigils, means "watching," and reminds us of the warning of Jesus that we must watch and be prepared at all times for his coming (e.g., at the moment of our death and at the final judgment).

Lauds means "praise" and is the morning prayer. It is one of the two cardinal prayer periods, the other being the evening prayer, Vespers. Formerly, Lauds was prayed at daybreak. Here we pray Scripture, longer or shorter for it at 6 a.m. year-round.

Terce or Tierce comes from the Latin word "third [hour]." In ancient times, people divided the day into 12 hours and started counting at sunrise, the third hour, therefore, coincided more or less with 9 a.m. Here we pray it at 7:45 a.m.

Sext comes from the Latin word sexta, meaning "sixth [hour]," which, in ancient times was our 12 noon. It was approximately the hour when Jesus was crucified.

None comes from the Latin word nona, meaning "ninth [hour]." That coincides approximately with our 3 p.m. It is Jesus died on the cross. We pray None at 2:15 p.m. Vespers comes from the Latin vesper, meaning "evening." As we saw above, it is the second of the two major prayer periods. It is intended to be prayed by daylight, says St. Benedict in his rule for monks.

Compline comes from the Latin completorium, meaning the ending of the day or night prayer. Originally it seems to have been prayed in the large common dormitory of the monks just before they retired, but for centuries it has been prayed in the church. Originally it was invariable during the whole year, so that it could easily be memorized and prayed in the dark. We pray it at 7:30 p.m

The Work Day

"When they live by the labor of their hands, as our fathers and the apostles did, then they are really monks," St. Benedict writes in his Rule for Monks.

At the **ABBEY of Our Lady of the Holy Trinity** we put this injunction into practice by earning our own living through farming and other industries and crafts. The members of the community have to be fed, clothed, and have their health needs met. Guests too must be housed and fed. Monks, therefore, are assigned to cleaning and cooking for the community and for the visitors. As far as possible we try to do our own maintenance and repair work in the monastery and the quest quarters.

On our 1800-acre farm approximately 700 acres are cultivated. We raise beef cattle as part of the farming operation. To grow crops of alfalfa and barley we need to irrigate the fields, because the climate in Utah is comparatively dry. The hay we do not need for our cattle is sold, and so the sale of the cattle, hay and grain is used for the support of the monks and other charitable purposes.

Talk to you later!

BIRDS SING, PEOPLE SING
MONKS ARE PEOPLE
SO WHY???

Charles Grube
Sports' Editor

I awakened early and went through my usual routine; you know, hit the "chamber of commerce" (bathroom), put on the coffee, and start my exercises—stomach crunches, bicycle for thirty minutes, push ups, etc. I'm single; I do not live with anyone, the distinct disadvantage being that I have no one to talk to over hot coffee, cold cereal, and a warm croissant with jelly. My true love, Gloria, lives with a girlfriend on the other side of Pittsburgh from where I work. But we do grasp the time to enjoy each other's company. In fact we were together for dinner last night plus we took in the Pittsburgh Symphony's performance of Beethoven's monumental 9th Symphony with its choral finale based on Schiller's *Ode to Joy;* a remarkable, breathtaking composition. Gloria is the secretary to the President of Pittsburgh Gauge and Supply, a very large and successful industrial supply house. She brings me all my masking tape for nothing and we wrap ourselves together and laugh and giggle and—oops! Enough of that!!

I was thinking this particular morning, while taking a shower, about last night and Beethoven, particularly the third movement of his 9th. It *is* so majestic and exalting. I just stood there; with the soothing hot water offering my neck and shoulder a peaceful calm and expulsion of all tension. There's something different about Beethoven. I mean, here's a guy who is universally recognized as one of the greatest composers of the Western European music tradition for both *his* unsurpassed piano virtuosity and extraordinary work of music. Yet, he composed the beautifully blended notes for instrument and voice while completely deaf. Yes! Stoned cold deaf! He died in 1827; he was deaf in 1817 when he started the 9th and did not finish it until 1823. Six years of composing, while deaf, one of the greatest symphonies known to man.

It just so happened that I was reading a new book entitled *IDEAS*, A **HISTORY FROM FIRE TO FREUD.** I seem to get smarter in the shower but I am remembering Beethoven because I just read about his pure genius a day or so ago in *IDEAS,* authored by Peter Watson. He was educated at the Universities of Durham, London and Rome. Smart man! He's written about six other books.

I learned from Watson that the great "generation of romantic composers" were all born within ten years of one another—Berlioz, Schumann, Liszt, Mendelssohn, Verdi and Wagner. Before all of these, however, there was Beethoven. All music leads up to Beethoven, and all music leads away from him. Beethoven, Schubert and Weber comprised a smaller grouping, of what we might call pre-romantic composers, who between them changed the face of musical thought, and musical performance.

The great difference between Beethoven (1770-1827) and Mozart, who was only fourteen years older, was that Beethoven thought of himself as an artist. There is no mention of that word in Mozart's letters—he considered himself a skilled craftsman who, as Haydn and Bach had done before him, supplied a commodity. But Beethoven saw himself as part of a special breed, a creator, and that put him on par with royalty and other elevated souls. "What is in my heart," he said, "must come out."

Goethe was just one who responded to the force of his personality, and writing, He said, "Never have I met an artist of such spiritual concentration and intensity, such vitality and greatheartedness. I can well understand how hard he must find it to adapt to the world and its ways."

In a lifetime of creating much beautiful music, two compositions stand out, two works which changed the course of music for all time. These were the *Eroica* symphony, which had its premiere in 1805, and the Ninth symphony, first performed in 1824. Harold Schonberg wonders what went through the mind of the audience on the momentous occasion when the *Eroica* was first performed. 'It was faced with a monster of a symphony, a symphony longer than any previously written and much more heavily scored; a symphony with complex harmonies, a symphony of titanic force; a symphony of fierce dissonances; a symphony with a funeral march that is paralyzing in its intensity.' This was a new musical language and for many the *Eroica* and its pathos were never surpassed. It has been said it must have been an experience similar to hearing the news of the splitting of the atom.

And I just ran out of hot water!

I finished dressing, grabbed a handful of notes, my hand-held tape recorder, and jumped in my Dodge coupe for the repeat after me, "pain in the ass" commute to the *PPT* building on the Blvd. of the Allies. I drive through Roslyn Farms and say to myself, "Don't forget to stop before crossing the bridge to enter the parkway, best keep in the center lane, go through the Ft. Pitt tunnel and zip up the boulevard to the office."

Ah, yes! Nice and easy!

Wrong! First, if one does not come to a *complete* stop before crossing the "exit" or "entrance" roadways from the parkway the shrill of a cheap siren first scares the heck out of you, and second, you're really angry because you got caught—again. This particular cop is so specific, and singular, and distinct about **STOP SIGNS** that you roll down the window, hand him your license, and get ready to sign your name after listening to the same canned, worn out, vapid speech about safety and stop signs. This guy's so intense when Roslyn Farms elected a new police chief his first job *was* to arrest the *old* police chief.

And second, traffic on the parkway; a totally intolerable, creeping, stop and go, parking lot. When I drive in Pittsburgh traffic I see more strange actions than a wrestle mania cameraman! Women take curlers out of their hair, fluff it like a mop, and break out the comb! Women tilt down the rear view mirrors to use it to apply make up to eyebrows, eyes, cheeks, lips, and always finish rubbing their index finger over their teeth that is, after they finish their coffee! All this while passing me on the left with speed of departure of at least ten miles per hour until they have to slam on their brakes! Other women turn to the right talking with their front seat companion at least 60% of the time. These women get about twenty miles to a fender. I see men shaving with an electric shaver; it's the shaver that's "steady on" while his head *is* moving around like a remedy for a sore neck. They comb their hair, drink coffee, reach for do-nuts, and some brain-surgeons balance the paper on the steering wheel so they can look down every fifteen seconds or so to read it.

As for me, I drive with my left hand on the wheel and use my right for my hand held recorder. My verbal notes this particular day was again in particular wonderment about the third movement of Beethoven's 9th which I found so majestic. I asked myself, "Do MONKS ever consider putting words to that magnificence?" I would think they would be allowed to listen to classical music as a form of prayer. They pray alone and together. Maybe they could discover a latent Gershwin or Berlin, or someone of talent like contemporary opera stars. I'll have to do some research on that subject. But right now, much to my chagrin, I'm creeping but I am thinking; it took Beethoven six years to compose his *chef d'oeuvre.* But we all know anything deemed worthwhile takes what?

TIME!

After the Wright Brothers, it took over 40 years to break the sound barrier opening a whole *new* world of supersonic aerodynamics. It took Charles Darwin 23 years before putting forth his artistic effort in the *Origin of Species.* Boy! Did that open a whole new world of discussion! Michelangelo, universally famous for sculpture (DAVID), painting (SISTINE CHAPEL), and architecture, was hired to redesign St. Peter's Church in Rome. It too him 15 years to complete only the dome and four columns! Albert Einstein, recognized as one of the greatest physicists of all time, took ten years of examining the lessons of history plus hard work to give the world **e=mc2.** That gave us a heck of a bang! The *PITTSBURGH POST TELEGRAPH* is over 50 years old; 50 years of learning from the lessons of history plus hard work to give all of us a hell of a bang for a buck!

My mind talks to me about this earnest evolution; it addresses it as *An Exchange of Value.*

Talk to you later!

IS THE LORD JESUS INVITING JACK FLYNN TO "CISTERCIAN LIFE"?

Come and observe at our next vocational live-in Retreat!!

Charles Grube
Sports' Editor

Guess what, Fans! I received a "Certified Mail" letter from Jack Flynn; it arrived eight days ago. It *was* a straight, to the point, extended stay letter from the Retreat House. I say "extended stay" because the family or I do not know how long Jack plans on staying before he matriculates to a prep school. In addition to the letter he enclosed a note saying his parents and 'Liz" McGovern were also receiving the same communication. We now have knowledge of the important questions that I feel we were all asking ourselves and each other.

I have spoken to Jack's family and discussed the missive with "Liz" over coffee in a downtown Pittsburgh deli. Our conversation *was* poignant and short lived; she had a photo-shoot and I had a deadline. I will say "Liz" seemed pleased that she heard from Jack; nothing on the personal level was talked over.

The following is Jack's non-edited letter; I think it rather brilliant!

Jesus asked two of his disciples, "Can you drink the cup that I am going to drink?" Will you respond as confidently as they did, saying, "We can"? Or even "I think I'd like to try it."

If so, consider what you will find at **Holy Trinity Abbey,** Huntsville, Utah. They are a community of twenty-one Catholic monks, who have responded to Christ's challenge and have pioneered a vital monastic organization in this fertile valley hidden in the mountains of northeastern Utah, land of the Latter Day Saints (Mormons).

The challenges facing pioneers, especially religious pioneers, are formidable. These are part of the cup that Jesus continues to hold out to us to drink. Renunciation, the narrow gate, living for others instead of for oneself, humility, and obedience, these are the contents of His cup.

Jesus himself found it hard to accept and prayed, "My Father, if it is possible, let this cup pass from me; yet, not as I will, but as you will".

Experience shows that this cup, once generously accepted, becomes a "cup of salvation", a cup of gladness, freedom, and inner peace. It is a pledge of fraternity and companionship, a call to communion with our brothers who partake of the same cup, a call to love. "[Practice] friendliness," says the Cistercian Doctor of the Church, Saint Bernard of Clairvaux, "so that you strive to be loved and to love, to show yourself gentle and friendly, to support the weaknesses of others not only patiently but gladly".

Cistercian monastic community is a school of love. Education in this school goes on for a lifetime, and our chief teacher is the divine Spirit of love himself. "The Holy Spirit that the Father will send in my name will teach you everything". The biographer of Saint Bernard, William of Saint-Thierry, says, "Although love has been implanted in the human soul by the Author of nature, in our present condition it must be taught".

Monks, because of their frail human condition, are sometimes slow learners and fail in loving others. The virtue of mutual forgiveness goes hand in hand with that of fraternal charity, as all those in the monastery strive to walk the path along which Jesus leads us.

Cistercian monastic life is a life of following Jesus in ever greater conformity to Him. Our love for Jesus in Himself and in His members is modeled after the perfect union between Jesus and Mary, His Blessed Mother. As our Constitutions put it: "Only if the brothers prefer nothing whatever to Christ will they be happy to persevere in a life that is ordinary, obscure, and laborious". Over the years, the result of living by these ideals is a relatively complete transformation of self, the birth of a new self, another Christ, so that "I live, no longer I, but Christ lives in me".

For newcomers, like me, the transition from life in today's fast-paced and stressful American society to the slowed-down, quiet way of life at **Holy Trinity Abbey** can be disorienting. Some call it liberating. Although we are not completely cut off from society, we deliberately withdraw from many features of city life, even good ones, for the sake of our religious practices. Monks do not pretend to live in the Middle Ages, free of modern technology and totally self-sufficient, but monks do filter and restrict their contacts with contemporary society.

After an initial discernment retreat, candidates to **Holy Trinity Abbey** are introduced gradually to the practices of monastic, life during the observer ship (one month) and the postulancy (six months). The difficulty of separation from family and familiar surroundings is made easier because of the welcome given to the newcomer by the senior monks, some of whom helped found the monastery. The example of perseverance and the accumulated wisdom of these seniors inspire the newcomers to overcome obstacles that inevitably come up during the early years of monastic life. "Do not be daunted immediately by fear," says Saint Benedict, "and run away from the road that leads to salvation. It is bound to be narrow at the outset".

After postulancy comes a two-year novitiate, during which the novice, clothed in white robe, scapular, and cloak, attends formation classes and deepens his understanding of the Cistercian monastic tradition. He participates to a certain extent in the work program, helping to keep the buildings clean or the snow shoveled, (no more skiing for me) helping on the farm, the lawns, or at one of our small industries. He joins the rest of the monastic community for the chanting of the Divine Office (in English) seven times during the day and night. At the end of his novitiate, if the vote of the seniors is favorable, he may advance to temporary profession (at least three years) and then to solemn profession (perpetual).

The monastic calling at **Holy trinity Abbey** is open to practicing Catholics between the ages of 21 and 45, (I am not there yet) who are single, free of financial obligations and family duties, in good mental and physical health,—with written recommendations from designated acquaintances. The vocation director will assist the candidate in moving through the initial phases of vocational discernment

---

The Cistercian Order

(Texts from the Cistercian Constitutions)

The holy abbots Robert of Molesme, Alberic and Stephen Harding gave the Benedictine tradition a particular form when in 1098 they built the New Monastery of Citeaux, and founded the Cistercian Order. About 1125, Saint Stephen established the nuns' monastery of "Tart", as Citeaux's own daughter house, entrusted to the pastoral care of the abbot of this monastery. Under the influence of Saint Bernard of Clairvaux and others the ideal of this reform spread and monasteries of monks and nuns following the Cistercian way of life multiplied even beyond Western Europe. In 1892 the three congregations of the Strict Observance combined to form a single order, now called the Cistercian Order of the Strict Observance.

This Order is a monastic institute wholly ordered to contemplation. The monks and nuns dedicate themselves to the worship of God in a hidden life within the monastery under the Rule of St. Benedict. They lead a monastic way of life in solitude and silence, in assiduous prayer and joyful penitence as defined in these Constitutions, thus rendering to the divine majesty a service that is at once humble and noble.

There are now 12 monasteries of monks and 5 of nuns in the United States Cistercian Order.

Monks:

- St Joseph's Abbey, Spencer, Massachusetts
- Genesee Abbey, Piffard, New York
- Holy Cross Abbey, Berryville, Virginia
- Our Lady of Mepkin Abbey, Moncks Corner, South Carolina
- Holy Spirit Abbey, Conyers, Georgia
- Gethsemani Abbey, Trappist, Kentucky
- New Melleray Abbey, Dubuque, Iowa
- Assumption Abbey, Ava, Missouri
- St. Benedict's Monastery, Snowmass, Colorado
- Holy Trinity Abbey, Huntsville, Utah
- Abbey of New Clairvaux, Vine, California
- Our Lady of Guadalupe Abbey, Lafayette, Oregon

Nuns:

- Mount Saint Mary's Abbey, Wrentham, Massachusetts
- Redwoods Monastery, Whitethorn, California
- Our Lady of the Mississippi Abbey, Dubuque, Iowa
- Santa Rita Abbey, Sonoita,(sp) Arizona
- Our Lady of the Angels Monastery, Crozet, Virginia

Jack said at the end that was all the info he had and he was very happy, relaxed, and pleased to be talking conversing with God.

I know we all wish Jack well; maybe will have a chance to say "hello" to him if his prep school is near or on the way to Pittsburgh.

Talk to you later!

KNOW HOW TO HAVE A BEAUTIFUL DAY?
TAKE A GORGEOUS LADY TO LUNCH!!

Charles Grube
Sports' Editor

I had just returned to my desk from a meeting with one of my journalists when the phone rang. I was lounging in my chair so I had to s-t-r-e-t-c-h to pick it up and said, "Hello! Grube speaking!" It took me 1/25 of a second to sit up straight while my countenance transmuted from a frown to a BIG smile as the voice on the other end said, "Hello to you, Mr. Grube. This is Elizabeth McGovern."

"Helllooo Elizabeth," I said. How is "Sparky" McGovern doing these days and what have you been up to? None of us have seen you since Jack left—but before you answer say, "Yes, I'll be glad to have lunch with you."

"Yes, Mr. Grube," Liz said, with a slight titter in her tone, "I was thinking lunch. I would be pleased in enjoying your company. Will you call me and let know where and when?"

"Of course I will. I already know where—THE CARLTON—best place in town. What is the better time for you? Early or later—say about 1:30PM?"

"Mmmmm, let's see! I'm off on Thursday afternoons so 1:30 sounds great. Is that a good day for you?"

"That's OK with me. I'm looking at my calendar so the 14th is next Thursday. Just tell me you know where THE CARLTON is and I'll see you there at 1:30 on Thursday the 14th. Anything in particular you want to talk about now?"

"Ooooh! Not necessarily. You know I have been working as a Power's model since my sophomore year. I am increasingly busy since graduation and I'm going to start school in about three weeks. But I'll talk to you more about that—and Jack—when we meet. It will be nice to see you again. And I know where THE CARLTON is. Do you have my home number in case something comes up?"

"No, Liz, I don't. I am glad you mentioned it."

"It *is* Walnut 6724. My Mom or one of my sisters can take a message. Say "hello" to Gloria for me. See you Thursday! Good-bye."

I slouched back in my chair while sliding a cupped hand up and down the lower part of my face. "Gee!" I said to myself, "Elizabeth McGovern. Gotta' be one of the most beautiful young ladies in all of Western Pennsylvania. No, change that; in *all* of Pennsylvania! And to add to that, she is exceptional bright! And very well mannered! And a glass-hour figure; 24 hour. To think Jack gave her up for a life dedicated to God! "Sparkey" loves Jack; Jack loves God! That could mix up any ones' emotions in a very short period of time.

When I got home around seven I changed; shorts, running shoes, athletic socks, sweat shirt and my favorite PITTSBURGH PIRATE baseball cap and headed for the running track around the LITTLE LEAGUE baseball field(s). Ah! To be young again! I couldn't get the thought of "—Loves Jack,—loves God" out of my mind. I had not the slightest reason why, but I kept running and the next thing that hit my mind was a thick New York steak off the grill, charbroiled rare, with mushrooms and a baked potato loaded with sour cream, chives, and bacon bits. I ran a little faster. I accompanied the steak and all "my stuff" down my anxious throat with a savory CHATEAUNEUF-DU-PAPE, Chateau Beaucastel, France—saved for me by a good friend who *is* a wine broker. Gosh! It's great tasting! Seemed to take its time and trickle into my stomach just to allow a few more seconds of enjoyment. But I think I had too many "trickles." Made me think of dreamy things with Gloria! Better call her; tell her about my lunch date with "Liz."

After dinner I retired to my library/den taking what was left of my friend DU-PAPE with me. I was Thinking! Thinking! Thinking! Can a theologian, or a philosopher, or a Bishop from the Mormon Church, or a Catholic priest, or a Baptist minister define what love is and what it *is not?* Can any of us? Whatever the uncertainty we cannot avoid facing questions about its relationship to desire. Is the word "love" just a synonym for the word "desire"? My THESAURUS *says* so—along with infatuation, flame, passion, and attraction. Is Jack infatuated with God? Is desire only one of the components of love? Is the kind of desire that enters into love different from all the desires that are not transformed by love? Different answers to such questions result in different conceptions of love and different classifications of the kinds of love.

These are questions the *GREAT TREASURY OF WESTERN THOUGHT* professed to me during my limited research in my library when I *was* thinking of Jack and "Liz." At this initial stage of *my* grasp of love, I do not think man can find, or agree on, an answer.

First, let's look at *The AMERICAN HERITAGE dic.tion.ar.y.* The dictionary defines love as, deep affection and warm feeling for another. The emotion of sex and romance; strong desire for another person! A beloved person! A strong fondness or enthusiasm!

Second, I am going to deviate a bit, so bear with me. On my first air-to-ground combat mission in Korea I let my flight leader down, my squadron down, and myself down. Why? Because I was so scared I couldn't think straight or fly my fighter in the correct mission profile which was, of course, to protect my flight leader and deliver my bombs in an effective manner. It was April 1953. I made a fool of myself!

A great and caring man by the name of Sherman Coffin, Capt., USAF, an extremely experienced combat pilot, took me under his wing and took the time to fly with me and talk about the erratic and capricious happenings that can take place during a combat mission. I can't tell you how much knowledge I gained on how to stay alive; but the first thing he said was, "Lt. Grube I can talk about your training, missions, and aircraft, and the enemy but the most important avenue to success is to learn to know and love yourself. It's the philosophy of life; and it's a never ending search."

Since early college days I have always been an assiduous reader of the lives **and experiences** of philosophers. They have all "been there; done that!" Early on I latched onto Socrates, "Man of Athens, Man of Greece, Man of the World." He has always been there for me—flew as my wingman. I mean, why not? If James Stewart can have HARVEY, I think I can have Socrates! People have personal trainers, or mentors do they not? So what could be wrong with Socrates being my mental trainer? Not a single thing! And believe me, it seems to be working so far—through my life of a college student fighter pilot, combat, test flying and now, a professional learning under the leadership of the Latshaws. Even today my life of love *is* being surrounded by Gloria!

In reading I learned the knowledge of Socrates comes indirectly from certain dialogues of his disciples Plato, a pupil and friend of Socrates, and Xenophon, one of the well-to-do young disciples of Socrates. I also remember reading somewhere along the line that Socrates *was* married to a lady by the name of Xanthippe. She was known as a shrew or woman of bad temper. Also she was supposed to be ugly; so ugly she could stop Switzerland! Oh well! Maybe that's why he stayed away from home so much.

I became interested in learning more about Socrates because his contributions to philosophy were a new method of approaching knowledge; a conception of the soul as the seat of both normal waking consciousness and of moral character, and a sense of the universe as purposively mind-oriented. I liked the words "mind-oriented."

I started serious study about him around the time in Socrates' life when he abandoned any interest in physics and immersed himself in *ethical* and *logical* inquires. I'm glad; I wasn't too keen on physics either. I flunked religion and arithmetic in the first grade so Socrates' decision paralleled my thoughts on a curriculum I wanted to follow in school. Socrates (then about 47) was regarded as a sophist. The sophists were itinerant professors teaching, for a fee, the skill of arête (excellence, in the sense of how to make the best of your self and continue on with life.) Socrates was the Athenian sophist in as much as his life was dedicated to the same intellectual inquiry into education—the science of effecting *arête.*

Socrates took no fees and gave no formal instruction, but he would start and dominate an argument wherever the young and intelligent would listen, and people asked his advice on matters of practical conduct and educational problems. I was only about 2400 years behind them!

It was the matter of practical conduct that interested me; maybe I could learn to take more of a common sense approach to things, or certainly learn to have more of an awareness of things as they really are. I wanted to learn to step forward and face reality regardless of the consequences. It seemed to me it would contribute to one's reduction of emotional agitation. If I could learn through Socrates what the lessons of his experience and the lessons of history have to offer, my outlook and approach to life, and living through combat, would be more practical.

Socrates also brought me awareness, through Plato, to think about ethics, logic, and self-examination; a 'know thy self' scenario. Socrates said to know thy self first before thinking one could consider the discipline of possessing, or displaying, perceptions of great accuracy and sensitivity. Common sense activity, combined with moral duty and obligation, Socrates admonished, *is* another thinking process of enormous importance.

Gee!!! I though, if Socrates could only fly my wing!!!

"It is only logical that a man in control of himself is in control of his actions," Socrates said. Well, I wasn't in control of my first mission, buy

I'm learning. Socrates continued, "The self-discipline of moral reason frees a man from the slavery of distracting appetites so that he can do what he wishes—that is, pursue true happiness."

Socrates also advocated the Delphic motto 'know thy self' and evidenced that introspection by showing how man achieves his real personality—the efficient realization of his being *(arête.)* For Socrates, knowledge was not acceptance of secondhand opinion that could be handed over for a sum of money like a phonograph record or encyclopedia, but a personal achievement gained through continual self-criticism and being able to accept the experience and criticism of others—exactly like my relationship with Captain Coffin. Philosophy involves not learning the answers but searching for them—a search more hopeful if jointly undertaken by two friends, one perhaps more experienced than the other but in love with the goal of truth and reality and both willing to subject honestly to the critical test of reason.

"God," I said to myself. "Socrates made that statement over 2400 years ago and Captain Coffin and I are experiencing a practical example of it today."

Empathetically, Socrates pulled me aside and said, "Charlie, the problem with you is you don't understand the difference between 'knowledge of and knowledge about.'" Socrates then said, "Tell me what you know about Paris, France."

I said, "Well, I know the Seine River flows through it. Paris *is* the capitol and largest city. The Charles de Gaulle airport is the main airdrome, the ARC DE TRIOMPHE, the SORBONNE, and the *Follies Brassiere,* Whoopie!! are there, as *is* the Cathedral of Notre Dame."

"OK! Whoopee! it's not brassiere it's *Follies Bergeres.*"

"Well, Socs, not much difference. One holds them in, and in the other, the chorus gals let them all hang out."

"Sometimes I think you're a real nut case! You know that! At any rate, how do you travel from Notre Dame to the Follies?'

"Socrates, I have never been to Paris, so I haven't the slightest idea."

"Right! Why? Because you know of the city of Paris but you don't know anything *about* Paris. Today, on your first mission you knew of the enemy, your jet aircraft, where you were going, and what you were supposed to do. However, you didn't know anything *about* aerial combat and the tactics of the enemy, your jet's performance under combat conditions, *your* performance under combat situations, what was expected of you as a wingman, etc., etc., because you didn't have the slightest idea!'

"You're right, Socrates! I almost lost my life and the life of others but the Navy and Air Force got wise and started "TOP GUN" and "RED FLAG.""

"Charlie," Socrates said, "let me give you some good advice based on my personal knowledge derived from participation. As you grow in experience and age, whether it in combat, test flying, business, finance, male and female relationships inciting "strong desire for another," whatever, you will learn that there *is* an enormous difference between knowledge of and knowledge about. Please keep that in mind!"

I got up from my desk and went to the kitchen and brewed a pot of coffee. When it was ready I went back to my chair, sat down, turned out the light and thought—about Socrates—and what I learned from him that near death day. This is neither the time, nor the place, to discuss my combat but after my debriefing I jumped into "the fold" with experienced pilots like Capt. Coffin, intelligent officers, armament, mission profiles, maintenance, and weather personnel plus attending every pre and post combat briefing and debriefing as possible. I listened and learned and became a damn good combat pilot and experienced flight leader.

Getting back to the initial stage of my grasp of love, Jack and Elizabeth know of love but they are too young to know anything about it. Jack knows of his religion but he doesn't know anything about it and doesn't know one thing about what he and the Abbey are getting into. Please don't get **me** wrong. I am not against any of their choices. There always has to be a first step. It's just that as a result of my first mission and my continued awareness of something not learned before, plus becoming bookish about Socrates, I am always a little bit on the cautious side. Fighter pilots are not wary *by* nature, but smart planning and "learning about" does add to longevity.

What drives me to this theory or supposition? I can't satisfy myself about, in this case, the definition of desire! My *ROGET'S* THESAURUS has about 150 synonyms!

I can understand, without attending a class on philosophy that "Liz" desires Jack because of their relationship but does Jack "desire" Christ? How can he? He doesn't even know the Guy! Therefore I think desire is evolutionary; something to emerge, or grow, depending on the one-on-one **relationship** between the two parties. Jack and Elizabeth communicated, held hands, held each other close, kissed, and may have made love. OOPS! I mean had sexual relations. Jack doesn't have a relationship with God. Relationship *is* defined as a *logical* or *natural* association between two or more things or personnel. I can't find a logical or natural relationship between

Jack and Christ. But what is important here is, in stating "'Liz' loves Jack and Jack loves Christ, is that Jack has nothing to hang on to. Yes, he has his belief system or faith in his religion but now we get into defining religion and faith—based on what—someone else's definition?

In reviewing the research publications I acquired and now have in front of me, that is, the ones I didn't spill my coffee on, literally hundreds and hundreds of sayings, and adages, and proverbs, and bywords, and statements, and talks, and voices enunciated, or announced, or broadcast, or divulged, or disclosed, or promulgated, or proclaimed, or informed, or declared, by maybe a hundred or so different philosophers, I am finding I am over my head! I thought I could impress Fr. Anton Niepp my philosophy professor in college, but I think I could get more reaction out of him by offering the good padre two strokes a side!

I did, however, find a couple of adages that I think are related to God and Jack's desire to be a monk. It makes me feel better, mentally, that this took place.

Thomas Aquinas, (1225-1274) in *Summa Theologica,* II-II, 81, 7, said, "We pay God honor and reverence, not for His sake (because He *is* of Himself full of glory to which no creature can add anything), but for our own sake, because the very fact that we revere and honor God, our mind is subject to Him."

We all take our own paths in life, with, we pray, help from Him and our loved ones.

And Ralph Waldo Emerson, (1803-1882) in *Worship,* said, "We are born believing. A man bears beliefs as a tree bears apples."

A couple of other notes! Why *was* Socrates my mentor? Daniel Boorstin, in his brilliant book *THE SEEKERS* said, "Socrates brought the search for meaning down from heaven to earth."

I, Charlie Grube, would have been a fool not to take advantage of that.

Also, I told Socrates that if he could bring the search for meaning down, I could start my own search for a beautiful lady for him.

Socrates said, "Charlie, just because you're rich and young and single doesn't mean you can go out just like that and pick up an elegant partner for me. What do you know about women?"

"Well, Socrates," I said. "I was out with ravishing blonde when I *was* younger and my lovely lady friend ended up saying I could make love to her as long as she heard birds tweet accompanied with bells and whistles."

"So?"

"So, I made love to her on a pinball machine!"

"Charlie! Charlie! Charlie!" Socrates said. "There is no hope for you. Did your mother have any children that lived?"

We both had a great laugh at that!

"Liz" made an OTA—On Time Arrival if I may speak in pilot parlance. THE CARLTON was still crowded but good service and great food will do it every time.

I said, "Welcome Miss McGovern" as I stood up to assist "Liz" in her chair. When we were both seated, we fluttered our napkins to a position on our lap, looked at each other, and smiled. Elizabeth, with a scintillating smile that matched the warmth of her two-piece pinstriped, impeccably tailored suit, was the first to speak. As she started our waiter approached and offered menus, and inquired about our desire to having a drink before ordering. We both opted for ice tea. He said he would be happy to oblige.

"I haven't seen you since graduation, Mr. Grube," Liz said. "In fact, I have seen very few of my friends because of my frequent afternoon modeling and attending undergraduate class at Chatam College. I am looking at a Liberal Arts education with a major in media, or medium, that, I understand refers to agencies of mass communications. It seems I'm running at the mouth, Mr. Grube, but I am just trying to put things together in my life. The loss of Jack still hurts."

"I can understand, 'Liz.' He surprised us all; I distinctly remember the startled look on your face. But time will take care of the hurt and you'll see that everything happens for the best. And," I said as I, per habit, looked around for our waiter, "I don't know about you but I'm hungry. What are you thinking?"

"I'm looking at a soup and salad. I see the soup du jour is cream of broccoli with a little mild cheddar. That sounds yummy! And under salads I see 'Chopped salad with mushrooms, tomatoes, and a touch of turkey, ham, and onion, blue cheese crumbled with vinaigrette.' To die for!"

As "Liz' carefully placed the menu back on the table, our waiter appeared with our ice tea and order book in hand and said, "Would the lovely lady, and gentleman care for an appetizer or what do you have in mind for lunch?"

I told the waiter what Elizabeth had in mind and said, "Make it two."

"OK!" I said to 'Liz,' "tell me all about—well, what you want to talk about. Let's start with your work. Are you pleased with the POWERS AGENCY? Are they treating you just as another pretty face or are you something special? Are you on your own time, so to speak, or do they support you with a schedule?"

"First, Mr. Grube, they treat all their models as assets, or maybe I should say capital, in a very sophisticated, professional manner. They seem to have a very good hold on what each of us, male or female, have to offer. Let's face it, if you'll pardon the expression, pretty faces and figures sell merchandise; they have the platform to create what their clients' desire and we models help fulfill their aspirations. I realize some of the girls are a bit haughty or egotistic; it seems to come with the territory. POWERS, it appears to me, manages to keep everyone under control. But you know as well as I the models, men and women, bring in a lot of dollars.

As far as I'm concern—oops! Here comes our broccoli soup."

Our waiter, Cervante, served us what I would call a gourmet's delight. The soup was creamy, like a bisque, sharpened with the right amount of cheddar. It was absolutely delicious! Elizabeth commented that it was the best she had ever tasted. She thought it was enhanced by, as she said, 'The creamy feature.'

She continued her conversation. "As I *was* saying, the Agency uses me for mostly facial commercials. They are shot in a studio. My other income comes from a variety of clothes depending on the up and coming seasons. They try to schedule the sessions at a time that suits my schooling but not to worry as most of my classes are in the evening. I usually do not go out of town for shooting because I'm a little young. Does that help you understand?"

"Yes, of course. I'm glad things are working out for you. It looks like Cervante *is* ready with our salads so let's just enjoy and finish our chatter after we finish."

We did just that. A little conversation between a bite or two—the spring weather, the PIRATES and STEELERS, the new law ordering the switch from coal to gas. "It's really cleaning up the town," I said. "I remember when you could tell the number of times it snowed in winter by the layers of snow, then soot, then snow, then more soot. One would have to carry a clean shirt to work in the event of going out to dinner. The one at breakfast would be a mess."

We ordered sorbet, a tasty lemon/coconut, and coffee. I asked `Liz' what she expected out of school.

"Well, right now I am looking for my AA and then maybe a Bachelor's in some discipline in communications; advertising, radio, TV. What I think I would really like would be a news anchor or a weather reporter, that is, if I wouldn't have to qualify with a degree in meteorology. Right now I'm up in the air about a definitive goal; I have to try to get Jack out of my mind. I really loved the guy. At least I didn't lose him to a redhead."

"You are a mature, bright young lady, 'Liz.' By the way, you know I am writing about Jack's progress in my Sports' Column. I think my reporting may ease the pain a bit. To be honest with you I am writing an editorial about love in my column and although I did quite a research, I don't understand love in terms of Jack and his decision to become a monk. I totally respect Jack but giving up a Gem like you plus a scholarship to a finest university of his choice is a bit 'much'. So, we are in this conundrum together. And, by the way Elizabeth, my article will be about my meeting with you. Is that OK?"

"Sure, Mr. Grube. Make me famous, she said with a smile. And, by the way, I have decided to take golf lessons and eventually getting some outdoor exercise by maybe walking a couple of par 3 courses with a light bag over my shoulder. I'll carry four or five clubs and a putter. I met a man at our advertising agency and he said to use his name at Chartiers (country club) and the pro would give me a good deal on cost. Maybe I'll win a tournament some day."

"Liz," I said, "you're already a winner."

We finished our coffee with a sip. I paid the check, and as I stood up I held the napkin for 'Liz' to see and said, "Look how neat I am; not a drop or morsel." As I was folding it I said, "I use to be so sloppy I had to tell people I spent $1200 on my nose, but now my mouth didn't work."

Elizabeth Mc Govern and I had a hearty laugh. Not a bad way to end an afternoon!

Talk to you later!

HOLLYWOOD HAS CELEBRITIES!
DO ABBEYS??

Charles Grube
Sports' Editor

I was watching some kind of special on TV not too long ago about Hollywood and the men who went to war in WWII. Jimmy Stewart *was* a bomber pilot and Clark Gable was in gunnery school. And I *think* it showed a picture of Wayne Morris who *was* an F-6F "Hellcat" pilot in an air battle that came to be known as the "Mariana Turkey Shoot." In fact, if memory serves me correctly, the F-6F had just replaced the F-4F "Wildcat" and the "Hellcat's" remarkable advancements over the Japanese "Zero" is the reason the aerial combat was called a turkey shoot.

I wonder if the fighter pilots said, "Gobble, Gobble, Gobble," before they pulled the trigger. I mean, Sgt. York did in WWI and won the Medal of Honor.

Anyhow, WWII had its share of celebrities—Hollywood leading men, fighter aces, Medal of Honor Winners, and even the "Hellcat" was celebrated for its advancement in the state of the art. So I was wondering—do any abbeys, or monks, or Trappists have celebrities?

I did a little research and I ran into a lot of luck. I had read Thomas Merton's *SEVEN STORY MOUNTAIN* in college and all I recall is the big words he used because I spent more time with my dictionary than I did reading the book. I recollect also that he was a monk and he died at a relatively early death. So when I went to the library and my lovely assistant from my last visit not only pulled the book from the shelf for me but also gave a summary of what a Mr. John Russell entitled *Thomas Merton: Celebrity Monk. I* don't know who Mr. Russell is but if he reads my column

I want him to know I give him credit for the information outlined in the Summary.

Thomas Merton (1915-1968) spent 27 years of his life as a Trappist Monk. When he entered the Abbey of Gethsemane in Kentucky in 1941 only days before the Japanese attack on Pearl Harbor, he looked forward to a life of obscurity, silence and contemplation; interrupted only by the daily chanting of the prayers of the church. All that changed in 1948 when he published his autobiography under the title of The *Seven Storey Mountain*. It became one of the publishing sensations of the Twentieth Century. In the years leading up to his accidental death in Bangkok in December 1968, (more on this later) Thomas Merton became increasingly famous not only as a contemplative monk, but paradoxically also as a seminal figure in Christian thinking. What kind of Christian thinking? Thinking about what we all think about and contemplate; about the complex problems of war and peace in a modern industrial society, and as a leader in the search for shared values between the Western and Asian religious traditions.

As Charlie Grube I want to be "straight on" about two things: 1.) Mr. Latshaw, as CEO and Chairman, does not object to me offering my opinions, and 2.) When I give opinions about specific tidings, I speak for myself and not the paper. That is why the *PITTSBURGH POST TELEGRAPH* is such a dynamic, compelling paper. Mr. Latshaw tells all of the reporters: Say anything you *wish* to complement your article; just be sure the foundation is accurate and honest.

Mr. Latshaw, Fr. Anton, and I have all been in war. We were subjected to the **failure** to solve the problems of war and peace. And in all due respect to Thomas Merton, **specific** values and the understanding of cultures surrounding religious traditions should be defined and agreed upon before they can be shared.

Let's move on with what Mr. Russell is sharing with *us*.

The Trappist order, which Merton joined in 1941, was an austere, reformed offshoot of the Cistercians, formed in the 17th century at the French abbey of La Trappe. Before the modernizing reforms of the Second Vatican Council (more on this later) Trappist Monks sought the contemplative life by sleeping, eating, and working in common, and by observing perpetual silence and rigorous fasts.

The primary, essential and immediate end to which all observances are subordinate, is union with God in prayer. For the Cistercian is a contemplative. With contemplation however, and as a means thereto, the monk combines penance. He lives in common with his brethren, sleeping in a common dormitory on a straw couch, retiring at 7pm in the winter, and 8pm in the summer; rising at 2am in the morning, and never eating fish or meat except when seriously ill. The monk never speaks; save to superiors or by special permission, and there is no recreation.

My mind is racing as I review what Mr. Russell is telling us; there seems to be a dichotomy here! When Jack Flynn becomes a **Trappist Monk** living the Cistercian way of life, is it expected of him to observe perpetual silence? If that is the case, how do Monks chant? Why *is* Monk Merton allowed to speak out?

Stick with me—and Mr. Russell on this!

Thomas Merton was born in the French Pyrenees on 31st January 1915 to peripatetic bohemian artists. His mother, Ruth, the daughter of prosperous Long Island Quakers, had met Owen Merton, a New Zealand artist from Christchurch, while they were both studying art in Paris. Owen refused to enlist during the First World War, and in early 1916, the family went to the United States, as France was increasingly difficult for a foreign male not in uniform. Both of the young Tom Merton's parents were dead before he was 9, by which time he had lived in the United States, Bermuda, France again, and then England.

School in England, under the supervision of a guardian, was followed by a short and reputedly wild time at Cambridge University. Eventually however, Merton tired of the rigid conventions of English life, and in 1935 he left for New York to enroll at Columbia University.

Studying in *New* York put Merton at the center of the world of high scholarship, passionate political beliefs, and intense self-consciousness. In 1938 his reading of Aldous Huxley, William Blake, Gerard Manley Hopkins, and above all of the Bible, led him to become a Catholic.

In 1939, Merton began work on a doctorate in English Literature. He was however, increasingly convinced that he should dedicate his life to God. After an application to join the Franciscan fathers was rejected, Merton heard from a friend about the Trappist Abbey of Gethsemane, established in 1848 by exiled French Monks deep in the Kentucky countryside. A stay over Easter in 1941 at Gethsemane, convinced Merton that God wanted him to live there as a Trappist, and he entered the abbey on 10 December of that year, three days after the attack on Pearl Harbor. (7 December, 1941. Who can forget it? by author)

For the time being, Thomas Merton *was* happy to follow the rigid and surprise free patterns of monastic life. However, the Abbot of Gethsemane encouraged him to write about the Cistercian way of life, for the benefit of an uninformed and possibly hostile public.

In 1948, the year before his ordination to the priesthood, and at the ripe old age of 32, Merton published his autobiography under the title of *The Seven Storey Mountain,* later released in Britain and Australia as *Elected Silence.* In its pages, Merton outlines the events of his life that led him to the Trappist world.

The Seven Storey Mountain was an overnight sensation. It sold over 600,000 copies within the first year of its publication, and in time it was translated into all the major languages of the world. It remains one of the great publishing events of the 20th century.

In later years, Merton often felt trapped and embarrassed by *The Seven Storey Mountain* and its youthful certainties and zeal. In 1963 he wrote the preface to the Japanese edition and he made his peace with the book and its legacy.

> *Perhaps if I were to attempt to write this book today, it would be written differently, who knows? But it was written when I was still quite young, and that is the way it remains. The story no longer belongs to me, and I have no right to tell it in a different way or to imagine that it should have been seen through wiser eyes.*
>
> *In its present form, which will remain its only form, it belongs to many people. The author no longer has an exclusive claim to its story. Certainly, I have never for a moment thought of changing the definitive decisions taken in the course of my life, to be a Christian, to be a monk and to be a priest. If anything, the decision to renounce and depart from modern secular society, a decision repeated and reaffirmed many times, has become finally irrevocable. Yet the attitude and the assumptions behind this decision have perhaps changed in many ways.*
>
> *Thomas Merton*

However, up to the time of the Second Vatican Council, Merton kept these feelings of self-doubt well away from his admiring and curious public. I asked Lawrence Cunningham, a Merton biographer and Professor of Theology at the University of Notre Dame in Indiana if Merton in these years *was* the perfect monk, reveling in the Trappist Life.

Lawrence Cunningham: Well I think that that was certainly the public picture that was given. He wrote his early books from the cloister, and even in the monastery itself, it was not known by most of the monks how much of a celebrity he was. So I think, yes, the fair thing to say would be that up until around 1960 the general perception was that Merton spoke from the cloister and from the point of view of a rather traditional Trappist monastic life.

John Russell: Monica Furlong *is* another biographer of Thomas Merton.

Monica Furlong: He went into the monastery I think hoping that he was going to change utterly from the sort of person he had been, but I think he understood quite soon after he entered the monastery, that somehow just trying hard wasn't all that helpful, but he tried and he tried and he tried, and I think he found quite early on that he simply didn't fit in, that the things that the others took for granted, he wasn't able to take for granted, I have to say I don't find him a very sympathetic character in those early years, I think he was acting a part really.

John Russell: Why *is* that, Monica?

Monica Furlong: Well I think he felt ashamed of his earlier life. He'd fathered an illegitimate child, he'd led a sort of a wildish life, I don't think people would think it all that wild these days, but it seemed a wild life to him. And I think he felt a great shame about all that.

I also think that he suffered a sort of a psychological injury, that he only half understood; his mother had died when he was only 6, and then he spent the rest of his childhood spending some time with his grandparents. He also spent some time with his auntie and uncle, and some time away at school. I think he had a sort of homeless feeling, and I can see that if you feel homeless, the attraction of a monastery, where everybody stays all the time, and has avowed to stay there, perhaps gives you a feeling of being secure. And I think that he hoped that by entering Gethsemane he would feel secure, and I don't think that ever quite happened to him.

John Russell: Even during the '40s and '50s, Merton's fame must have rankled with his superiors and many other of the monks. On the one hand he brought fame and attention to their hitherto hidden way of life, but on the other hand, his erudition and fame must have made others feel a bit uneasy with him.

John Howard Griffin, journalist and author of the award-winning *Black Like Me* and Merton's close friend and designated official biographer, described the circumstances of Merton's death.

When he got to Bangkok, he gave a talk on the morning of the 10th, the anniversary of his entry into the monastery. He *was* very tired, the heat was oppressive and he hadn't had a nap the day before so he went to his cabin and took a shower. He was never a very practical man about things. He put on a pair of either shorts or short pajamas, and barefoot and still damp, walked across the terrazzo floor. They had these very tall fans, and he reached for the fan to turn it on to the palette where he was going to take his nap on the floor.

It was DC current and it went into him. He was staying in a cabin with three other people, but it wasn't until about an hour later that they went, and the door was locked from the inside. It was a double kind of door, and there was a little curtain in the upper part and they saw him lying on the floor on his back with this big fan crosswise across his body. The blades had stopped rotating but the current was still alive and it *was* still burning. He was very deeply burnt, in that angle across the body.

There was a Benedictine nun superior from Korea who was, before she became a religious, an Austrian physician and a specialist in internal medicine, and a very, very fine one. He was already dead, but she gave him an immediate examination, and she determined that he died from the effects of electric shock.

Vaticanum Secundum
Vatican Two

The Second Vatican Council and its promise for the future of the Catholic Church is dedicated to the spirit of Pope John XXIII who dared open the doors and windows of the church he loved to the contemporary world. By this courageous act he allowed sunlight and rain to feed the foliage and roots of the increasingly petrified tree of the Fortress Church.

For those who read my column about Hollywood having celebrities and morphing into Thomas Merton, I would appreciate any letters you might send and let me know what you think. Please discuss your thoughts about Jack Flynn's entry into, what appears to be, a very strict and lonesome life, Thomas Merton the "celebrity", and the Second Vatican Council. Since the column is written for you, maybe we could stir up some noteworthy discussions.

In the meanwhile, I have written a few sports' articles that I trust you will find interesting. They will be in my column soon,

Talk to you later!

QUERY!!!

A REQUEST FOR DATA
TO PUT A QUESTION TO (SOMEONE)

By: Charlie Grube
Sports' Editor

I feel sure most of you will remember the article I wrote a few weeks ago about Thomas Merton the **Trappist Monk** who became somewhat of a celebrity after writing *THE SEVEN STOREY MOUNTAIN.*

In my mind I always thought monks were "way out there in mind and body;" always far from centers of human population, not readily noticed or seen, and obtaining the aura of being nameless; no one to talk to about yourself or learning about the others you sleep and pray (a lot) with. If you recollect, my article *BIRDS SING PEOPLE SING* addresses the issue of a monk's silence, yet many monasteries are incarnate with monks' chants. And the monks are uttering words or sounds in musical tones; as Russell says, "It would be hard for anyone, even with a rudimentary religious or musical culture not to be moved by a great monastic choir singing Gregorian Chant, the ancient liturgical music of the Roman Catholic church." So they are talking! To music! They are not mumbling or uttering indistinctly!

I also mentioned in my column The **Second Vatican Council.** I am hoping a few of you might comment on this no matter your church or beliefs. I know the **Council** is relatively young compared to the full flavor and richness of many aged religious practices, but your observations will be welcomed.

I'm a bit confused; that is why I asked you to write and give me your comments. You have done just that and I have listed your thoughts below. I will bring all of what you said to the attention of the **Abbots of the Holy**

Trinity Monastery when I visit Huntsville, Utah and get as many answers to your queries as possible. Mine too!!

Your letters are as follows:

Mr. Grube: I don't like the idea of men, and women, (there are woman monks) disappearing into obscurity, remaining silent, and spending their whole life contemplating God and his saints. What do they gain from that? Although I am a devout Catholic and I think it's a little stupid. Are they any closer to God than I, or my wife? The sacrament of marriage gave us freedom from concupiscence and the blessed opportunity to procreate and educate our children. Can you get any closer to God and enjoy what life has to offer than that? All those men and women rising at two to three in the morning to "praise" God! For what? For their own self! How about rising at two or three in the morning to care for a sick or dying child? Are we not, then, taking care of "gifts from God? I think the men and women in Abbeys, Monasteries, and Nunneries haven't done anything except maybe run away from the problems of life rather than facing them. At least men and women like the Brothers of Mary and the Sisters of Charity devote their lives to teach young men and women. Also, they always make an effort to bring discipline, self-respect, and truth to complement their education. And they're tough! I have the bruises to prove it!

Mr. Walter Schmidt,
Carnegie, PA

Mr. Grube: So, according to Monica Furlong, Thomas Merton, "didn't quite fit in," with the monastery life. I understand he also fathered an illegitimate child—not in the monastery, of course. But didn't the "powers to be" ask him about the support and welfare of the child?

Also, I know a young priest who "didn't quite fit in" so he gave up the priesthood, became a lawyer, and married a blonde. The church excommunicated him? Why such a foolish act and what did it gain the church? I personally know eleven parishioners that left with him.

Mrs. Gertrude O'Matheny,
McKees Rocks, PA

Mr. Grube: You spoke of the Second Vatican Council. I was in Carnegie's library a short time ago and found that JOHN XXIII, on his deathbed said, in reference to **VATICANUM SECUNDUM,** "It is not that the gospel has changed; it is that we have begun to understand it better. Those who have lived as long as I have . . . were enabled to compare different cultures and traditions, and know that the moment has come to discern the signs of the times, to seize the opportunity to look far ahead."

My first question is who is the "we" I have underlined above? I understand an invitation was extended to Protestant and Orthodox Eastern churches. The meetings were attended by representatives from many of those churches; did they help the Catholic church begin to understand the gospel better?

Question two! Were the Protestant churches significant in pushing for more lay personnel in the church?

Mr. Jim Harris,
Sheridan, PA

Mr. Grube: I have been reading your Sports' Column for a number of years and have thoroughly enjoyed every word. My father and Jack Flynn's father have been Rotary Club friends for years and I understand you are going to follow, through your column, Flynn's "exciting but often hazardous undertaking" into the life of a monk.

I was in Erie about ten days ago and just about the time I was to head for home the radio said there was "about a three hour delay" on Route 19 at the Erie/Crawford county line. The delay was due to an accident and chemical spill. I decided, therefore, to go to a library near my hotel and just for the "heck" of it I wanted to see how many monasteries and/or abbeys there were in the U.S.

Mr. Grube: I was shocked! Under the title of **Trappist Monasteries, Abbeys, and Nunneries: North America** the listing gave 22. Under **Benedictines** Men's Communities and Women's Communities the listing offered 46 men's and 30 for the women's. Plus there were pages and pages of monasteries and abbeys all over the world.

Mr. Grube: I *was* thinking if I could organize (I'm not thinking unionizing) about 1000 of those very religious personnel to say a one minute prayer for me once a day, that would add up to 365,000 minutes or over 6000 hours of prayer for me a year! Somebody "up there' is bound to hear and man, I'd be ready to walk **through** the Golden Gate. No one would even have to open it for me!! Everything would be OK except I'd have to be careful not to say, "Holy Cow, I'm in HOG HEAVEN!"

One has to go through life laughing at his self and with others, Mr. Grube. Please keep up the good work.

Mr. Thomas Witt,
Crafton Heights, PA

Mr. Grube: What ever happened to Jack Flynn's girl Elizabeth "Sparky" McGovern? I understand she was a beautiful young lady!

Mr. Bill Allin,
North Side, Pittsburgh, PA

OH! I'm single!

Mr. Grube: As I understand from what you have said, plus what I am trying to do to relieve my confused mind, *is* find out what the heck is going on. I understand the **Second Vatican Council** was formed to enable those who cared to *compare* different cultures and traditions. It didn't say anything about forging; no combining or altering. When think of the Council I think of words like "ambition", or "drive", or "stimulus". The Council wanted to open the door that would link heaven and earth and welcome the *endless variety of flocks of believers* to build nests, as my research stated, in the *vast network of branches—a* genuine **Tree of Life.**

Mr. Grube, am I right in saying that those men and women who are deemed "religious" because of a principle or system of beliefs held together with ardor and faith can be just as much a Baptist, as a Methodist, as an Episcopalian, as a Catholic?

Let me offer you an example. A Catholic boy is dating a Baptist; both involved with the tenets of their faith. His girlfriend said to him, "*We* have a dynamic, compelling, eager beaver (pardon my expression) but very effective minister who preaches believing in ones' self through, I guess, a combination of philosophy and faith. Will you attend a service with me soon and see what you think?"

Her true love says, "Yes, I'd like that." As time goes on he is drawn more and more to her and her church, not so much for his feeling toward his girlfriend as the enjoyment of the energetic speaking of the Baptist preacher. He feels he is truly learning about inward, and outward, love for himself and others. His Catholic priests offer, week after week, the same sermonizing, vapid, dull discourses with total lack of spiritedness and originality. He has soon abandoned his faith for the good feeling the Baptist minister *is* giving him.

What does the Catholic Church think about that? Is he committing a mortal sin? Would he be excommunicated? I have given this scenario much thought. The Second Vatican Council was formed to enable those "who cared to compare

Mr. Darren Bond,
Philadelphia

I purchased your paper from a newsstand that carries other cities' papers.

Mr. Grube: First, I am not a religious person but since I retired eight years ago I have just about lived in libraries studying, gosh knows how many, religions. I do this because I find the examination very interesting. The more I study and the more I listen to preachers on the radio I keep going back to the same question—do each of these religions offer a distinct, but different path to God or, as it seems to me, are the ministers just offering a crutch to dispirited souls?

Mr. Howard Ames
Mt. Washington, PA

Mr. Grube: In quoting John Russell from the analysis of Merton's book, he said, "All monasteries were to observe exactly the same rules and customs, the abbots of all the houses were to meet in an annual general Chapter, and each house was to be visited yearly to ensure the observation of uniform discipline."

Mr. Russell continues, "Before the modernizing reforms of the Second Vatican Council, Trappist monks sought the contemplative life by sleeping, eating, and working in common, and by observing perpetual silence and rigorous fasts. He lives in common with his brethren, sleeping in a common dormitory on a straw couch, retiring at 7 in the winter, and 8 in the summer; rising at 2 in the morning and never eating fish or meat except when seriously ill. The monk never speaks, save to superiors or by special permission, and there is no recreation."

My question, Mr. Grube is, "What did the Second Vatican council have to do with Trappist monks and what were their modernizing reforms?"

Ms. Janet Gaynor,
Media (outside of Philadelphia), PA

Mr. Charles Grube: Thank you for keeping your "followers" up to date on Jack Flynn and his new (tentative) vocation. I am anxiously looking forward to see how he does; my family and I say prayers before dinner to wish him well. I read Merton's *The Seven Storey Mountain* while in college; a good lesson to learn vocabulary. Mr. Russell's (I think he is the man who reviewed it) said some of the monk's were jealous and Thomas Merton had a hard time from the #1 in charge. If the monks are so busy praying and keeping their mouths' shut, where is there time for biased or prejudiced thought?

Charles J. Atkins,
Thornburg, PA

Mr. C. Grube: Editor in Charge/Sports,
Pittsburgh Press Telegraph

Sir: I am a Professor of Religion at a small Methodist Church in Eastern Ohio not far from the Pennsylvania border. I get a chance to read your paper about a week late. A member of our church has it mailed to him. My question is simple yet the answer, if there *is* one, could be discussed as long as time and religion exists. It seems to me that people, particularly my parishioners, are anxiously looking for something different from current world. We end WWI, only to start again in WWII, only to start again with Korea. And let's not forget the IRON CURTAIN! All of this seems to be creating a perception or feeling that the modern world, as we had thought we understood it, has somehow gotten out of control. All our different religions are praying for others and ourselves but to no apparent avail; we don't seem to be able to build a foundation of faith to allow us all to live in peace with our self and our God. Would you please ask the Monks about this; what do they think?
By the way; I am a STEELER fan!

James J. Hullstrunk, PhD,
Smallsville, OH

Charles Grube: Would you please give us your thoughts on the possibility of a mental collision between the Jack Flynn culture built around the dynamics of an ALL AMERICAN high school football player and the authoritarian, institutionalized, safe kind of life style of a monk. Not the Thomas Merton kind of monk!

Baron John Neff,
Dormant, PA

Well, friends and sports' fans of our great Pittsburgh paper, you have just read a synopsis of the many thoughts and questions that have hit my desk over the past few weeks. I appreciate the diversity and contrast; I found the variance creative and intriguing and—I thank you!

I will keep you informed on when I expect to hit the Utah trail. But remember, Jack is only at the Retreat House and is expected to return home soon but this is not his QUERY. It is between us—sports' fans all!

Talk to you later!

MORE PERFECTION

By: Charlie Grube
Sports' Editor

I do not know if all of our *PPT's* fans read my column not too long ago where I said I would be writing about some of Pittsburgh's heroic athlete's in addition to following the path of Jack Flynn. My first one was about Honus Wagner; I appreciate all of your thoughtful phone calls and letters.

In this particular column I address "perfection" or in this case "super excellence." This story seemed to "fit right in" since we have been talking so much about striving for perfection through prayer, church, Abbeys, etc. This man wasn't any of that; just a very proud Pirate who filled us all with a swagger of superiority and self-esteem.

His name was Harvey Haddix, known as "The Kitten," and he had been a solid but unremarkable pitcher for seven years when his Pirates faced the Milwaukee Braves on May 26th.

Then he did something extraordinary. One after another, for nine innings, he retired Milwaukee batters: twenty-seven in a row. But Pittsburgh had also failed to score, and so he went on, through the tenth, the eleventh, and the twelfth: thirty-six straight outs.

No man had *ever* pitched so perfectly so long before.

Then, his own team betrayed him. The third baseman, fielding an easy grounder, made a bad throw, letting a man on base. The runner moved to second on a sacrifice. Hank Aaron walked. And Joe Adcock hit the ball over the fence.

Harvey Haddix's no-hitter, his twelve perfect innings, ended in defeat. But for one afternoon at least, he had seemed to be the best pitcher in baseball history.

Talk to you later!

LONG-TERM RESIDENCY

A GOOD MOVE FOR JACK
AFTER RETREAT HOUSE??

By: Charlie Grube
Sports' Editor

I did a little research about Holy Trinity—I tried an encyclopedia at the downtown Pittsburgh library but I wasn't doing too well until I got lucky; pure luck. I was having a quiet lunch, sandwich and "coke", at the big ISALYS' store on Penn Avenue when I ran into Fr. Josephson from St. Philips. He was with a visiting priest from. St. Vincent College and St. Vincent Seminary in Latrobe. We all know the word "Latrobe", as well as we know the word golf. Why?? Because that is where Arnold Palmer is from! And guess the visiting priest's name! Arnold! Father Arnold Brownell! And. yes, he plays golf.

I won't bother you with details but Fr. Brownell is on a sabbatical, granted every 7th year from Rome, to travel and research the potential growth of the number of priests and monks in the USA and what could be done to enhance those numbers. At the present time he is visiting parishes within a few hundred mile radius encompassing Western Pa, Eastern Ohio, Northern West Virginia, etc. He is encamped at the St. Vincent Seminary when he isn't traveling.

Anyhow, my steadfast fans, Father Brownell sent me all the knowledge I need about Abbeys and Monasteries. The following is a synthesis of what I learned; I want all of us to know as much as possible, or practical, about Jack's future.

Holy Trinity Abbey now offers a program that permits someone to live in the monastery for a prolonged but limited period of time without intending to become a monk. Maybe it's meant to give men like Jack a chance to think more about his objective reasoning.

Our long-term residency program is offered to practicing Catholic men who are twenty-one years of age or over and who meet the specified criteria. After the first month, if all is favorable, a long term resident may stay up to two more months; after that, he may renew his residency for another three months, at the discretion of the abbey.

Long-term residents are permitted and expected to live, pray, eat, and do assigned work (at least four hours per day) along with the monks. Since the spiritual growth of the residents is of fundamental importance, they will attend classes in monastic formation during the school year, except classes on the vows. They are under the guidance of the novice director and his assistant. Throughout their residency, they are expected to know and follow the day schedule and the guidelines of the monastery in all matters.

The monastery will supply the long-term residents with all daily necessities except health-care benefits; residents are expected to show written proof of health insurance covering the length of their stay. Long-term residents also sign a legal document promising not to seek financial compensation for the work they do as residents.

Requirements

An applicant for long-term residency does the following:

Makes a week long retreat in the monastery retreat house, during which he has interviews with the admissions board, answers a general questionnaire, and writes a brief autobiographical statement. He then leaves the monastery while his application is under consideration.

1. If accepted for an initial one-month residence, he furnishes the following documents before returning:

    ❖ Original (not photocopy) certificate of Baptism and Confirmation
    ❖ Record of dental check-up
       Record of physical exam

       Photocopy of health insurance policy covering his expected length of residence

❖ List of three people from whom the abbey can request letters of recommendation

After all the paperwork has been accepted by the abbey, the applicant returns to begin his trial month of residency. During this time, and later, the residency can be terminated for sufficient reason either by the resident or by the abbey.

Purpose

The primary purpose of the Long-term Residency program at Holy Trinity Abbey is to share the benefits of our monastic lifestyle with those who are unable, for various reasons, to join our monastery as prospective lifetime members. The program is for men who are sufficiently free of obligations to be able to devote some months to deepening their spirituality in an environment of silence, solitude, and natural beauty, in the company of monks who have been seeking God for most of their lifetime. Please note that this program is not intended for those who may need a therapy program or recovery program. Likewise it is not a sabbatical for those wishing to pursue their academic or artistic goals. Instead, it is for those who wish to experience the Cistercian charisma of love for God and neighbor in a traditional setting that has been called "ordinary, obscure, and laborious".

Well, we learn something new everyday!

Talk to you later!

EXCUSE ME, PLEASE
IS THERE A MR. BERLIN OR GERSHWIN HERE?
HOW ABOUT CARUSO! OR PAVAROTTI!

By: Charles Grube
Sports' Editor

I mentioned, in one of my columns, while still in wonderment regarding Beethoven's 9th, if MONKS ever put music to the deeply concerned talks (prayers) with God. MONKS, by definition and by nature, spend time in solitude and I frankly wonder if their collective prayers would make beautiful music. Or, better said, would their collective voices in prayer make glorious music?

Well, I figured the better way to find out was to visit the library. Holy Molly! Did I learn a lot!

The first thing I learned was to call Gloria and let her know where I was. No, we do not press each other as to our where about but after three nights she was a little concerned. I answered the phone about 11:50 pm on the fourth night!

"Good evening, Grube."

"What do you mean evening? It's almost morning; I worry about you."

"Oh gosh! I appreciate that Honey; my fault. I should have called but I was going to fill you in on what I was up to over the weekend. Are we still heading for Conneaut Lake?"

"I should hope so. I bought a new bikini to drive you wild plus a couple of beautiful sundresses for our evenings at dinner. I'm not sure you're still the kind of guy that drives a motorcycle into an officers' club pool just, as you told the Air Police, 'I wanted to clean it up before going to town.'"

"Aw! Cum'on Gloria, that was after a three-martini lunch. And beside—"

"A *double* martini three times over is what you are trying to avoid saying."

"That was a long time ago; my fighter pilot days! Now, one ice cold vodka, straight up does the trick—sorta' gets me all exceeded. I mean excited!"

"Do not worry your pretty body, my love. My bikini will exceed your excitement on this trip. Pick me up after work; I'll drive in with my roommate. We could grab a bite at the new P&LE station and leave after the traffic calms down. And, Jolly Cholly, please don't let four days go by without calling. Have a nice evening—what's left of it!"

With that, she blew me a kiss and hung up.

I don't know what it was—singularly or collectively—the bikini, the martinis, the scotches and soda, the wine, black Russians, the sexy dress, the warm water, the dark night, whatever! I even forgot what we ordered. We both got completely undressed and swam naked for at least half an hour. We had an exceedingly exciting time. And we didn't have to get up because it was a "mess around" morning. That's when you stay in bed and "mess around!"

On the way to the lake I filled Gloria in on the details of my search. Here goes:

Blue Cloud Abbey: A Catholic Benedictine Abbey located in Northeast South Dakota. Individual monks express their talents in music, **plus** carpentry, tailoring, cooking, etc.

Church **Music** Association of America: A young **MUSIC** student had often heard the **Monks** of Solesmes and their recordings of Gregorian (relating to Pope Gregory XIII) Chant—a monodic (sung by one voice) and rhythmically free liturgical chant of the Roman Catholic Church. Of Solesmes comprises sixteen **abbeys** and four priories (the superior ranking next to the abbot of a monastery) of **monks**, and six **abbeys** of nuns.

Sixteen **abbeys**, four priories, six **abbeys** of nuns! Sounds as if they could give Fred Waring and his *Pennsylvanians* a run for the money!

"Honey! Did you know he also invented the Waring Blender??"

"Yes, Dear. That's what it says in print on the box it came in! It was given to me by my Mom and Dad when I went out on my own."

"You scared me there for a second. I thought you were going to say 'given to me as a wedding present'."

"Now, Charlie! You tyke! Why would I say something like that! I'm too young to be interested in marriage."

"Yes, Darlin' I understand. One of the married guys at the office told me about a week ago he saw a tombstone at a memorial service that said, "He had been married for thirty years and was prepared to die."

Gloria looked at Charlie with disdain and said, "You're about as funny as a cry for help!"

"As you say, No 1! May I continue?" Charlie said as he took the proper turn heading off the highway toward their favorite lake.

"Throughout the Middle Ages, monasteries and **abbeys** nurtured music!

—Over two hours of Gregorian Chant, Chorall and Instrumental music from the **monks**—the **monks** of Prinknash and the nuns of Stanbrook **ABBEYS.** Prinknash is located in Gloucestershire, England, UK, and Stanbrook is an **abbey** of Benedictine nuns in Callow End, Worcester, England, UK. Callow End was a community founded by the granddaughter of Sir Thomas More in Flanders in the 1600's. I can't forget auld Sir Thomas. I was doing great in History until a Brother of Mary put a big red "X" thru my Moore. Told me to learn how to spell! In red blood! Well, he was so tough it looked like blood.

Sir Thomas is the guy who lost the battle (and his head) with Henry VIII for impugning the pope's authority and made Henry the head of the English church.

—the Benedictines for ten years, at Worth and Downside **Abbeys** . . . . when we hear **monks** sing—Worth is located in South East England in 500 acres, Sussex countryside. Downside is near Bath, Somersetshire, England.

And that's what I learned so far."

Gloria said, "That was a lot of work. It must have taken you hours."

"That's true, Honey, but I had a lot of help from the librarian's assistant. Her name was Gracie; from Dormont. I told her my friends and I used to loaf at the Dormont pool but it was a long time ago.

The information I gathered was amazing to me. Hell, Gloria, they all sing, both men and nuns, from all over—Spain, France, England! Information I must find out, is, are their words to the music other than their everyday prayers. I told you I was going to visit the **abbey** Jack is very seriously considering; I think the priests and lay monks will share some information with me. Of course, I won't know 'till I ask!!

Now, what are you favoring for dinner tonight; fish, steak, chicken, pasta? The chicken breast stuffed with a special cheese with basil over angel hair is—well, it's just damn good!

Talk to you later!

WE WILL HAVE AN ANSWER

To our collective column
QUERY!!!

By: Charles Grube
Sports' Editor

Remember about a month or so ago I wrote a column entitled QUERY and asked any interested parties to drop me a line about their thoughts on Jack Flynn, or any man, becoming a MONK. I received some very interesting, poignant, engrossing letters. I also told all those who perused and pored over my column that *I* had a friend in Salt Lake City who knew the Trappist priest at the *ABBEY OF OUR LADY OF THE HOLY TRINITY* located in Huntsville, Utah, about 50 miles north and east of the Salt Lake airport. The abbey is where Jack Flynn will be matriculating into his new profession.

My friend (we were both in the same fighter squadron in Korea) hand carried a letter along with our QUERY column, to Father Tom Gillespie, asking if I could meet with him and discuss this rather provocative missive. Father Tom told my friend that he would study our query and let him know when he could meet with me at a time suitable for the two of us.

Well, friends of *THE PITTSBURGH POST TELEGRAPH,* I met with my boss, CEO and President Dave Latshaw, and he gave me permission to go to Utah with his blessing and $3.50 cents spending money. Gee! thought; how long would it take by hitch hiking?

Of course I'm kidding. Mr. Latshaw has always been exceptionally fair when it came to out of town expenses—air fares, hotels, car rentals, meals, and entertainment was never a question. "Just think of it *as* OUR money," he used to say. I'll leave it up to you." Mr. Latshaw trusted his employees because he knew thy trusted themselves. As Emerson said in *Self-Reliance,* 'Trust thyself: every heart vibrates to that iron string."

So, friends of Jack Flynn, Fr. Gillespie and I found a suitable time. Summarized below is a synthesis of my trip:

Ten days ago, I took a 7:00AM TWA flight to Chicago. Changed planes and caught a United Airlines DC-4 to Denver and then a Western Air Lines CONVAIR Liner to Salt Lake. No, I didn't try the water to see if there was enough salt to keep me afloat! I rented my car, drove to a downtown hotel, had a quick bite and went to bed. Remember, I arose at 5:00AM to get to the airport on time and with the time difference, I didn't hit my pillow until 1:00AM Pittsburgh time.

I might add, also, I made a fool of myself; something I seem to have the propensity to do when I am in an airplane—be it a single seat fighter or a crowded 4 engine airliner.

About an hour into the flight from Chicago a lovely stewardess singled me out asked if I knew how to play "Gin"? I said, "I've been known to play a game or two. Why do you ask?"

The stewardess, her name *was* Delores, said, "I have a lovely lady sitting about 4 rows in front of you and if you wish to play I can set you two up in the lounge."

"That would be outstanding! Just tell the delightful lady to taxi on back here and to bring her money."

I won't bore you will all the details, but the sparkling woman from "four rows up" and I played about 2 hours and laughed, and drank wine, had a sandwich or two and cried "gin" more times than I can count. I did win! About 40 cents!

After we got off the plane and headed for our selected gates, or baggage claim, we exchanged the usual "nice meeting you, have a nice trip," and such, I said, "By the way, my name is Jack Simpson. What *is* yours?"

The lady stopped, smiled, and said, "Ella Fitzgerald!"

I was stunned! Staggered! And felt about 2 inches high! After I caught my breath I said, "Holy Willey mouse! What a fool I am! I had no idea."

Ms. Fitzgerald smiled and graciously said, "I know. If you did, thought maybe you wouldn't have tried so hard to beat me"

"Ms. Fitzgerald," I said. "I always play to win. I'm going to frame that quarter, nickel and dime. But did I leave you enough for coffee?"

We laughed, hugged a goodbye, and went our lighthearted ways.

The good padre and I had an eleven o'clock appointment so I jumped in the car about 9:15AM with a satisfied stomach full of 2 eggs over easy, a slice of delicious ham, a glass of orange juice, toast and two cups of hot coffee. Planned flight time, oops! High-way time, 1 hour plus "a little bit."

My rental, a new Ford sedan, gracefully took me to 15 North, for 15 miles, then US-89 toward I-84E for ten miles, hit 1-84, then right, OLD HIGHWAY RD followed by a left on TRAPPERS LOOP RD and then right on UT-39 and follow the signs to Holy Trinity. And "Thar she blows;" right in front of me; a number of old, decrepit, infirm, WWII, one-story buildings positioned, well—sort of everywhere! At least they were all painted white; the achromatic color of maximum brightness—maybe something like we hope our souls will be when we pray, or obtain with difficulty, the tortuous road to heaven.

I met Father Tom in the business offices housed in a wing of the chapel; he looked at each other in the eye as we tested the firmness of our handshake. He was about 6 foot, 200 pounds, good looking with bright eyes accompanied with a sunny smile. By the time we walked the short distance to his office and sat down, I was already very comfortable.

Father *was* from, believe it on not, from West 'By God' Virginia and when I told him I used to sell bottle gas stoves to farmers near Terra Alta and Morgantown, we were buddies. I also told a 'short hand' version of our beautiful American Airlines stewardess. He said he always liked the beauty of women; face, heart, and soul.

I found myself in the company of a very intelligent, articulate man.

Over the course of our conversation I gave him the outline of my chapters in *SOMETHING TO THINK ABOUT.* I told Father Tom I had yet to finalize the cover but I gave him some of my thoughts. I did mention though, that Jack's true love in high school was a beautiful lady and was being tested daily in rough world of business; that is, being "hit on" by any number of ego oriented, vexing, jerks! I also outlined the mental struggle of the main character, and that the ending was still in question.

I then asked, "Father, what do you think about the chapter my friend brought him entitled, **QUERY?**"

Father Gillespie said, "I read it a time or two and found it very interesting. I think your sports' fans took the column seriously and asked incisive, intelligent questions. Also, the comments, particularly by a Mr. McGervey, I think that was his name, were profoundly moving; in fact, very touching. So overall, **QUERY** was a challenge I latched on to right away.

So here is what I propose. I am going to answer your **QUERY,** in writing, which I would like to see as an absorbing chapter in *SOMETHING TO THINK ABOUT.* Your, or is it Mr. Flynn's fans, offer their views in writing so I would appreciate the same courtesy. **QUERY** was great! It was honest! I would like to tell all what we monks feel about our vocation. Frankly we are surrounded by love and life's satisfaction and our happiness is possibly a direct path to God. Your happiness in the secular world may take a more discursive path. But, with the help of faith and prayer and overcoming of obstacles may put you on a more solid and rewarding trajectory. Who knows! We like our way and when you get to heaven you'll look back and say, "My way wasn't so bad either."

"Gee, Father, well said. OK! We have a deal. You tell all and I'll tell my learned readers my column, on a particular day, belongs to you. I am sure they will appreciate what you have to say. Thank you for your time. I'll make sure our mutual friend knows of your conversable attitude."

We arose, shook hands and gave each other an affable exchange of, "Take care of your self."

On the way back to the car I stopped by the Holy Trinity depository and purchased a couple of containers of Monk bottled honey. When the elderly Monk gave me the bill, I reached into my pocket and asked, "Sir, where are you from?"

"Kentucky," he said.

I said, "Oh! Not long before the Kentucky Derby. I think I may go this year."

The Monk looked at me with a smile, winked, and said, "Throw down a couple hundred on #5 horse for me."

I said, "You got it, Sir! Throw up a couple hundred prayers in the air. Maybe a few will land on #5 for ME!"

He smiled, shook my hand and said, "Pease be with you my Kentucky friend."

Life is great, isn't it! One thing T didn't say was, "Keep the change."

Talk to you later!

THE WISDOM OF CASEY STENGEL

By: Charlie Grube
Sports' Editor

As Sports' Editor for the *PITTSBURGH POST TELEGRAPH* I have the responsibility to keep all of our readers as happy, or contented, as possible. Most of you know my new "SOMETHING TO THINK ABOUT" column was initiated because of Pittsburgh's consensus All American Jack Flynn who gave up potential scholarships to become a Monk. I have been writing about his transition from high school to the Monastery but I also wanted to give our fans some historical, or contemporary sports' stories to provide "something to talk about" over a beer and hard boiled eggs at your favorite hang out!

I was thinking of all of you as I wrote this column between Denver and Chicago in one of United Air Lines new Douglas Aircraft DC6Bs. We flew higher and faster; it *was* a comfortable flight.

Here's Casey at his best:

I broke in with four hits and the writers promptly declared they had seen the new Ty Cobb. It took me only a few days to correct that impression.

All right, everybody line up alphabetically according to your height.

I made up my mind, but I made it up both ways.

On hearing that a rival manager was trying to win *the* pennant *with just three pitchers:*

Well, well, well, I heard it couldn't be done, but it don't always work.

Being with a woman never hurt no professional baseball player. It's staying up all night looking for a woman that does him in.

On players who did not drink:

It only helps them if they can play.

Good pitching will always stop good hitting, and vice versa.

The secret of managing is to keep the guys who hate you away from the guys who are undecided.

On winning the last years World Series:

I could'na done it without my players.

On being asked how the Mets were doing:

Well, we've got this Johnny Lewis in the outfield. They hit a ball to him yesterday, and he turned left, then he turned right, then he went straight back and caught the ball. He made three good plays in one. And Greg Goossen, he's only twenty and with a good chance in ten years of being thirty.

On being asked about his future in the great game of baseball:

How the hell should I know? Most of the people my age are dead. You could look it up.

To his excuse prone Mets:

You make your own luck. Some people have bad luck all their lives.

Talk to you later!

I'M LEARNING!! I'M LEARNING!!
THAT'S WHAT LIZ TOLD ME!
ONLY SHE DIDN'T TELL ME FROM WHOM!!

By: Charles Grube
Sports' Editor

Liz and I chatted on the phone for about 15 minutes the other day. She is very good at keeping in touch with me; calls about every three weeks or so. The first thing he asks is, "Have you heard anything from Jack?"

Sometimes I say "Yes", and review what he thinks about her and Lizs' classes at Chatam College and always lets me know that he is truly happy and looking forward to his entrance into Holy Trinity Abbey. I *always* choose my words carefully as not to possibly hurt Liz; I think she is still carrying a heavy load in her heart for him. But we all know that! Liz does not mind everyone keeping in touch with both Jack and her, although vicariously, through my sports' column.

But, come to think of it, to me Liz seemed a little more "at ease" with herself. She seemed to be carrying a lighter burden; no burdensome edge from the usual ruggedness or crumple in her voice. There was an accompaniment of smoothness; her words were now flowing with more precision with what was on her mind and in her heart. Remember Liz was an "A" student; mature and very proficient in verbalizing her thinking and study.

If you recall some time ago, Liz suggested over lunch that she was thinking about taking a few golf lessons to break away once in awhile from her school and modeling. Looks like Liz is making a move in that direction. She casually mentioned it to her boss, Ms. Barbara Chase, at Powers, and didn't think anymore about it. One afternoon she had a note from Ms. Chase stating a friend of hers arranged for Liz to talk about lessons to Jim Flynn, the pro at Chartiers County Club. I am sure a number of you know him, or of him, since he is Jack's younger brother. I understand Jim has gained a fine reputation over the last year or so. Heck, he was a fine athlete just like his big brother. Maybe I should talk to him also. The trouble with my golf is that I'm too close to the ball after I hit it.

Anyhow, Liz has taken a few lessons and told me she was a basket case but is now, finally, putting a few to some sort of practical success. She said, with a little sparkle in her voice, "Mr. Gruby, speaking of being a model, I am building a model backswing, you know, `right distance from the ball, height for solid contact, chin up, aligning my shoulders, etc., etc. I think my building is falling apart, though. I met a man on the range last week and I stupidly asked what he thought of my swing?"

"It seems OK to me," he said, "but frankly, Miss, I'd rather play golf!"

"He really hurt my feelings for a second or so; we both looked at each other and laughed. But five minutes later or so, he wandered over and asked, "Would you mind if I made a few suggestions?"

"Well, Mr. Grube, "He seemed very nice! Big smile! And he did help me; seemed to know a lot about golf. Thanks to this guy, I don't even know his name, I felt my swing was a little more fluid. However, I know I'll need to be practicing an awful lot before I dare approach a golf course.

Anyhow, Tell Gloria and all I send my regards and love." "I'll do that, Liz. Same to you and keep in touch," I said.

Talk to you later!

THE SAGACITY OF YOGI BERRA

By: Charles Grube
Sports' Editor

One can learn a lot about Yogi Berra; just read his book. Yogi is dumb—like a fox! I realize, as do many others, his syntax, or rhetoric, or figure(s) of speech seems about as screwed up as a drunk driver heading down a one-way street— the wrong way. At least Yogi's imagery doesn't hurt anyone; unless you laugh 'till it hurts. His famous, "It ain't over 'til it's over," actually makes sense. It's true! It ain't!

My *ROGET'S THESAURUS* defines *sagacious* as sage, wise, shrewd (wisdom). Yogi's book *is* full of wisdom!

Baseball is 90 percent mental. The other half is physical.

You can observe a lot by watching.

In baseball, you don't know nothing.

A nickel ain't worth a dime anymore.

It's déjà vu all over again.

If you come to a fork in the road, take it.

Think! How the hell are you gonna think and hit at the same time?

Hey Yogi, what time is it? You mean now?

On being asked his cap size at the beginning of spring training:

I don't know! I'm not in shape.

On why the Yankees lost the 1960 series to Pittsburgh:

We made too many wrong mistakes.

On Rickey Henderson:

He can run anytime he wants. I'm giving him the red light.

On Ted Williams:

He is a big clog in their machine.

I usually take a two-hour nap, from one o'clock to four.

On the tight *National League pennant race:*

It ain't over 'til it's over.

If the people don't want to come out to the park, nobody's going to stop them.

On being told by the *wife of New York Mayor John V. Lindsay* that *he looked cool despite the heat:*

You don't look so hot, either.

Why buy good luggage? You only use it when you travel.

On Yogi Berra Appreciation *Day in St. Louis in 1947:*

I want to thank you for making this day necessary.

I really didn't say everything I said.

Talk to you later! (It ain't over till it's over!)

QUERY

Fr. Tom Gillespie's Answer(s)!!

Forward by: Charlie Grube
Sports' Editor

I know all of you sports' fans plus many other loyal, studious browsers of the PITTSBURGH POST TELEGRAPH are aware of my trip to Salt Lake City to meet with a truly great man, Fr. Tom Gillespie. Remember, we discussed your thoughts, in writing, under the column QUERY, about choosing the life of a monk.

Father Gillespie had no problem with your vigorous, staunch comments and questions. The reason for this particular column is Fr. Gillespie's wish to answer your inquiry, in writing, with the PPT serving as a platform. I thought that very reasonable since my original column, your questions, and his answers put us in the same ring. And since I had the privilege of reading it first, I know we are not speaking of a boxing ring.

One other thing! Mr. David Latshaw, the President and Chairman of the Board of the paper is aware, first hand, of every move I made and of every word spoken. He has demonstrated once again, his broad and ravenous mind for learning something new and sharing with others thereby giving one the choice to agree or disagree. He believes it to be their privilege.

So, it is an honor for me to introduce you to Father Thomas Gillespie.

Abbey of Our Lady of the Holy Trinity
Huntsville, Utah

The Value of Monasticism

When individuals go into monasteries, they take on much the same identity as the average family: they live by themselves peacefully, sustaining themselves by making small contributions to the local economy and the social well-being of the surrounding peoples. In that exterior sense, monks don't do anything, but how many of us do? Monks live the Christian, human life as everyone does, but on a more intense level.

The problem in not appreciating the value of monasticism is that we live in a utilitarian society, where individual worth is largely measured by exterior accomplishment. The result of this mentality is chilling: those incapable of making functional contributions are considered valueless and therefore disposable. That's why human beings who are very young and very old are in fact eliminated, by abortion and euthanasia. The problem is not monks or monasticism, but in the lack of appreciation and poor evaluation of monasticism. We are not called by the Lord to be human doings, but human beings. Our value is in our identity before God, not our physically-related accomplishments.

What value is there in monasticism? Monks practice great love. Love *is* the greatest good there is. God is love. To practice love, we simply choose to unite good to the object of our love: ourselves or others. Love is good will.

The cardinal principle of life is that it is only through challenges that people grow. We see this in our formal education system, as we grow in knowledge and skills through the challenges of classroom work, study, and exams.

Love, or good will, grows in strength through the challenges of relationships. Some think that people become monks in order to escape from life, but what do people want to escape from? The difficulty is relationships, and *we* have three relationships in life: with God, with other people, and the most burdensome, demanding relationship of all: with ourselves.

Outside the monastery there are legitimate escapes from problematic relationships. Simply drop them and go somewhere else. In a monastery, however, there is little or no escape. The monk must put forth great effort to make many relationships work and grow through them.

In other words, monks face great challenges to their good will, and persevering love in the face of great challenges is a great love. Add the fact that the primary dwelling place of God is in people. We alone have an eternal destiny and we are the most highly developed beings on our planet. Since God dwells in us, whatever we say, do, or willfully think toward anyone, good or bad, we say, do, and think toward our Creator, in each other. The great love we practice toward others, then, is primarily practiced toward God, and we are relating to a God who is not going to be outdone in generosity. He rewards us with the proverbial hundredfold beyond our efforts, and not only us, but our loved ones, and all the peoples of the world.

After all, we are three-fold in our humanity: physical beings, mental-psychological beings, and moral-spiritual beings. Monks relate to everyone primarily at the moral-spiritual level, the deepest level of our being. At that level we are all brothers and sisters, sons and daughters of the one Heavenly Father. This means that when a person becomes a monk, he goes, not into isolation, but into solitude, and he becomes more intimately related in love to his brothers and sisters in the world, by drawing closer to God, who is Father to all. Monasticism *is* a universal vocation.

Monks are men and women of prayer. We know that relationships depend on communications. Good relationships mean regular, congenial communications, or else the relationship weakens and dies. It works the same way with God, and our communication process with Him is prayer. The closer we come to God, the more we bring all of humanity closer to God, just because we are human, and we are praying in the name of all humankind, another aspect of our universal monastic vocation.

Who knows, but that in God's providence, a monk's life of self-sacrificial love and prayer may be intimately connected with the success of your personal life, so that, if the monk left the monastery, or didn't enter at all, the supporting sacrifices would not be there, and your life would fall apart.

With all this love and prayer going on, why is there still so much war, division, and conflict in the world? Between the Lord's offering of happiness and peace, and our acceptance, there is the awful barrier of human free will. We have other agendas that we like to pursue, other gods that we would rather worship: money, fame, power. People worship the gods that rule them: their anger, their lust, their ideas, and their ambitions.

With our free will, in other words, too many are saying that they don't want God's gifts of life and peace. This is not a question of the value of monks or religion, but free rejection by too many people. Look at the statistics. An important example is that all the countries of Western Civilization are dying because of artificial contraception. People want pleasure, but without the responsibility of children. The result is that whole countries fall far below replacement level. If contraception fails, abortion is used as a backup. Both are country-killers. History is also filled with people who want to gain more power by conquest, and consequently destroy peace.

What has happened throughout history is that people commit the cardinal sin of humankind. They forget God. When you realize that all good comes from God, then in forgetting God, they reject good, and they are left with evil. By contrast, monks spend their lives remembering God.

In the face of moral and social problems, there is monasticism. The great love or good will that monks practice is the antidote for all the hatred and disorder in the world. Love, or good will, is the only factor that can offset hatred or bad will. As monks grow in love, they become ever more effective solutions toward the peace and happiness of the world's people. Their prayer-petition becomes more powerful. The love-lives of monks also serve to make up for the evil choices that people make. This is a valuable redemptive aspect of the monastic vocation. Monks offer their lives in sacrifice, the highest form of love, for all humankind. Parents perform this kind of love for their children, and monks practice love for the benefit of everyone.

The value in the monastic life of seeking God through prayer and good will, can also be measured by what everyone experiences.

We spend much of our time on earth seeking various legitimate pleasures and satisfactions. The Creator of all these gifts must be at least as good and desirable in Himself, as the gifts He creates, because he can only give what He has and is. God's wonderful creation is founded on His unlimited ability to create.

Multiply any pleasures and satisfactions by infinity, and you get some idea of the opportunity everyone has in his life for eternal happiness. This is the opportunity that monks live and give witness.

In failing to seek the Creator of all we have and are, so many are missing out on what monks enjoy: the greatest and rewarding and important adventure in life.

Our prayers win support for the active efforts of people who work to care for others and bring them to faith. Prayer predisposes people to receive the good works of active people, and so they both depend on monks' hidden lives of prayer and love.

Thomas Merton became famous as a monk. His wife and child were killed in the London blitz, so that he had no obligations when he entered monastic life.

When a priest leaves the active ministry, it depends on how he left. If he left with a Church dispensation, it was probably for the best, since as a priest he *was* frustrated and unhappy. He could serve God and the Church much better as a married man.

The Vatican II Council recognized the contributions non-Catholic religions can make to spirituality. The bottom line in a person's relationship with God *is* not his formal religion. It is love, because God *is* love. God is not Catholic or Protestant. He is good will.

At the same time, greater truth about God will lead to greater love. The late Frank Sheen wrote, in "Theology and Sanity," "If a person loves God knowing something about Him, he should love God more from knowing more about Him, because each new thing learned about God is a new reason for loving Him." This, the true religion of God, the religion that possesses the fullness of truth, offers the greatest opportunity to grow in love of God.

Individuals do leave the Catholic Church because of poor preaching in their parish church and they are attracted to another religion on account of a minister's personality or ability to preach. That's not necessarily sinful in each case, but it does show a lack of appreciation for Church doctrine. The problem is almost always, inadequate catechesis. Individuals who leave the Church don't know or appreciate what they are giving up.

Each religion offers its own path to God, which *is* to say, a path to personal holiness. It's like paths on different sides of a mountain. They are all in different locations, but they all lead upward to the same summit.

For Trappist Monks, Vatican II gave us the freedom to change our emphasis from spending our time and energy going from one difficult penitential exercise to another. Now we appreciate the value of close community life as a source of challenges for growth in love, understanding, and compassion. Human relationships are penitential and disciplinary enough.

Monastic, religious life *is* much like a marriage, where the primary focus *is* on efforts to make relationships work, and this is challenging work. It costs great effort at times to practice love in the context of stability.

Monastic life is primarily an interior life of mind and heart, because there's so much aloneness with God. The powerful challenges of relationships force a monk to turn to prayer, in order to maintain love of neighbor and interior peace.

When a person gets married, he chooses a spouse on the basis of mutuality: religious beliefs, social, economic, educational backgrounds, and compatibility in interests, character, and personality. When a person becomes a monk, these luxuries are not afforded him. He commits himself to a community, with often great differences in all these areas. The personal challenges are great, and the corresponding call to character-growth or holiness is great. The monk's value as a person of love and prayer becomes great.

The primary challenge in the interior life of a monk is his thoughts. Various kinds of thoughts come into play in response to the challenges of daily monastic life: the demanding schedule, different kinds of people, personal psychological and physical challenges.

Success is measured the same as in marriage: how you handle conflict, whether in your relationship with God, with others, or with yourself.

There's no mental collision between say, an All-American football player or any vocation, including monks. All lifestyles and activities are governed by laws and rules. All have penalties for violations of the rules, even to the point of being removed from the premises or the monastery. Interior peace and peace between individuals in community must be maintained, and that requires a high degree of personal discipline through training in all cases.

AN ADDENDUM

My thanks to Charles Grube and, as I understand, Mr. David Latshaw for the opportunity to discuss these important issues with you fine ladies and gentlemen.

Fraternally yours in the Risen Christ,
(signature)
Fr. TOM Gillespie

What can I say; beautifully written; straight to you folks, fans, friends of Flynn, and fair-minded. To those of you who disagree or take umbrage, it is of course, your prerogative.

It wasn't satisfied just to read Fr. Gillespie's writing; I studied it several times. He said one thing I recognized that fit the goodness of his reasoning. I found it profoundly moving.

"Monks offer their lives in sacrifice, the highest form of love, for all mankind. Parents perform this kind of love for their children, and monks practice love for the benefit of everyone."

Talk to you in my next column!!

MORE ON CASEY STENGEL

By: Charles Grube
Sports' Editor

In this past summer, the Senate Subcommittee on Anti-Trust and Monopoly held hearings on a bill that would have formally recognized baseball's exemption and extended it to cover all professional sports.

Casey Stengel was the leadoff witness, and while he shed little light on the antitrust question, his testimony provided perhaps the most celebrated example of extended Stengelese of his long career.

Senator Estes Kefauver of Tennessee was the chairman

KEFAUVER: Mr. Stengel, you are the manager of the New York Yankees. Will you give us very briefly your background and views about this legislation?

STENGEL: Well, I started in professional baseball in 1910. Have been in professional ball, I would say, for forty-eight years. I have been employed by numerous ball clubs in the majors and in the minor leagues. I started in the minor leagues with Kansas City. I played as low as Class D ball, which was at Shelbyville, Kentucky, and also Class C ball and Class A Ball and I have often advanced in baseball as a ballplayer. I had many years that I was not so successful as a ballplayer as it is a game of skill. And then I was no doubt discharged by baseball, in which I had to go back to the minor leagues as a manager. I became a major league manager in several cities and was discharged. We call it discharged because there is no question that I had to leave_

[Laughter]

KEFAUVER: Mr. Stengel, I am not sure that I made my question clear.

[Laughter]

STENGEL: Well, that's all right. I'm not sure I'm going to answer yours perfectly either.

[Laughter]

KEFAUVER: I am asking you, Sir, why it is that baseball wants this bill passed.

STENGEL: I would say I would not know, but I would say the reason they want it passed is to keep baseball going as the highest paid ball sport that has gone into baseball, and from the baseball angle—I am not going to speak of any other sport. I am not in here to argue about these other sports. I am in the baseball business. It has been run cleaner than any business that was ever put out in the one hundred years at the present time . . .
Kefauver eventually called a halt to Stengel's testimony and thanked him for his time. Mickey Mantle was next up.

KEFAUVER: Mr. Mantle, do you have any observations with reference to the applicability of the antitrust laws to baseball?

MANTLE: My views are just about the same as Casey's.

The committee room erupted in laughter. Stengel had managed to testify for forty-five minutes without ever taking a position on the pending legislation. The Senate bill died before it reached the floor. But Stengel had also hinted between the lines that all was not well with the players, and their complaints were worth looking into.

Talk to you later!

WHAT DID LIZ LEARN??

ABOUT GOLF
And The Man—With The Smile?

"I'm a little confused," Liz told her friend from childhood and high school, Joanne Flyers. "In thinking of my friend Jack who is to me something sweet and mellow. For when Jack was with me almost all the time, it was with the feeling I *was* going to lose him, and now that I have lost him, I keep feeling that I have him with me still."

Liz and Joanne were heading down Carson Street on the way to town for a rare Saturday photo shoot for Powers. Joanne, like Liz, is on top of the ultimate latter when it comes to beauty; dark hair, beautiful smile, red "come hither" lips, light skin, and the face of an Angel. She was under a part time contract with Powers because Joanne had gone to school to learn the profession of "Dental Assistant" and was working full time for a dentist in Crafton. Her captivating smile always kept her busy with the modeling agency on free days.

"I don't think you are confused, Liz," Joanne said. "I think sometimes we contemplate with our heart; other times with our mind. I don't know where the soul fits in," she continued with a smile as Liz was concentrating on the proper lane to take them over the Point Bridge. "I guess the soul just takes a glance at what one throws his or her way and places it in a position to keep it as white as possible."

Liz looked at her for a long second and said, as she picked up on the traffic, "My heart says I love Jack, but you're right about the mind. I keep thinking of this very nice guy I met on the driving range at Chartiers and my continual desire to go back. Talk about confused! I don't know whether his charm is drawing me or the fact that he's a damn good golfer. I am learning as much from him as I am from Mr. Flynn. At least he comments on my golf swing for free."

"Liz, I'm going to be honest with you. I loved a great man once. Lost him! He chose to go to Navy flight training and it's only the lucky ones that a pilot wearing gold wings would come flying home to. It hurt, but in due time I moved on and today I am very pleased with my love life. Enjoy the circumstances you're under. Learn more golf my friend; challenge him to a putting contest. Beat him on one hole and laugh and enjoy the feeling. Invite him to have a hamburger. Tell him it's for free for taking the time to help you. Just make sure you go in separate cars. And remember! Nothing is for free!"

Liz pulled into the parking garage and drove carefully to the slots saved for Powers' models and employees. When she and Joanne exited the car and started toward the elevator, Joanne said, 'You know our experience has taught us we'll be busy all day so let's meet at *JONA'S CAFE* at five. Last one there buys the drinks."

It wasn't a day of "wine and roses"; both ladies worked long and the day enervating. Liz and Joanne both reached the café about the same time so they treated each other to a fine glass of champagne followed by a dinner of filbert-crusted (hazel-nuts) wild salmon with angel hair pasta and fresh steamed spinach. No dessert! But a cup of hot coffee and a small snifter of brandy followed. They were all smiles and neither had a care in the world!

What *is* said here about Liz and Joanne not "having a care in the world" *is* true—to a point. Everyone has problems; mostly at their own fault. Philosophy tells us, in a voice not necessarily smooth, "You put yourself in that position; be man enough to get yourself out!" Marcus Aurelius suggests to us in *MEDITATIONS,* when we are troubled about anything, we should remember all things happen according to the universal nature. Aurelius suggests, "Man's wrongful act is nothing to thee. Minding one's own business *is* a nugget and treasure to the mind. Everything which happens, always happened so, and will happen again, and continues to happen everywhere. Everything *is* opinion; every man lives in the present time only, and loses only this."

As they were drinking their brandy, Liz looked at Joanne; she had a quizzical look on her face.

"What's the matter?" Joanne asked.

"Do you mind if I ask you a very important question?"

"OF course not," Joanne said *as* she slowly placed her cup of coffee in the saucer. "Liz, you are my friend;" she said, "You can't possibly do anything wrong. Shoot!" She moved her chair just a bit little closer to Liz to make her feel more comfortable during her query.

Liz asked while looking at Joanne in the eye, "Are you a virgin? Maybe I should be minding my own business, but—." Liz dropped her eyes toward the tablecloth.

"Liz, look at me! You asked me an honest question and I'll answer. You know I have been dating that very nice fellow from Dormont; met him at the Dormont pool last year. We started chatting and I found out he played football for two years and he asked me if I had been a cheerleader at Crafton. When I said 'yes', well, that started it. We talked football, my discipline in working for a dentist, his going to the Wharton School of the University of Pennsylvania majoring in business, my friends, his friends; we talked for an hour or so. We have been going together ever since, and that's been about—let's see—19 months. A beautiful man; built like Joe Palooka and just *as* nice, you know, from the comic strip. And yes, Liz, we have had sex. It was a little "fumble jumble" to start with but he has been very, very warm and tender. Then one evening something delicately lovely happened; we both had a strong—what I sensed was a tremendous gasping, grabbing sensation that threw sparkles and flashes of something through my whole body. It was a bizarre romantic experience that's tough to describe or even talk about—that is to others. Very frankly Liz, I'm glad you asked me," Joanne said with a light simper. "I have wanted to talk to someone about it and now, come to think of it, you are the perfect friend. I guess that answers, in a round about way, your question."

"Gee! Joanne, it does and I feel happiness for you. I also feel relieved that I also have someone to confess to. I had the same situation only a lot worse. I lost my virginity when I visited my grandparents with the rest of the family last Christmas. I haven't told a soul. I went to a Christmas dance with a group of friends and on the way home this guy by the name of Jeff just about raped me in the back seat of a limo he rented. I fought him off for awhile but then decided, what the hell, no use fighting him. Don't laugh, but I didn't want him to tear my beautiful new party dress. I just calmly took it off and folded it over the front seat. I *was* shaking; guess it *was* a combination of being scared and a little chilly at the same time. It was awful and damn it! It hurt. My mother has never mentioned a thing about sex and I'm lucky this jerk was smart enough to use a condom. And also, my mother has never sat down with me to discuss anything about a normal menstrual cycle. I had to find that out by visiting the school nurse.

Oh! Yes, waiter. Please a refill for our coffees. Anything else, Joanne?"

"No thanks! A hot cup will be fine."

"Anyhow enough about me! One more question! What do you do about keeping from being pregnant?

"I went to a gynecologist," Joanne said. "He gave me all the details about the menstrual cycle; average length which is about 28 days, progesterone level. If your level is low you would have a tough time in getting pregnant. But you should really make an appointment with a doctor of your choice or I'll set you up with mine if you wish."

"That's very nice of you, Joanne. I really should talk to my Mother but let you know. God! I'm glad we had this conversation. I'm really happy I asked and I'm extra happy for you! But just one more thing! I'm getting awfully tired of being hit on all the time; in stores, buying shoes, in restaurants, at school, even on a streetcar not too long ago. I think I am going to buy a fake diamond and pretend I'm married."

"That doesn't surprise me," Joanne said. "Your beautiful, great figure, being hustled goes with the territory. Go ahead, buy a cheap ring and when the next guy hits, show him the ring and say, 'Thank you, but I'm taken.'"

When Liz got up the next morning to a beautiful day of sunshine and blue skies, she took her time over coffee and thought about the good time she had with Joanne but a shiver went through her body when she remembered what Joanne said. "Remember! Nothing's for free!"

Chartiers Country Club is located a short time west of Pittsburgh. It is a private club, with over 600 members including 150 permanent golf members and over 275 members in other membership categories.

The facilities include a newly renovated pool and pool house, a large Tudor style clubhouse with four dining areas and large ballroom. The ballroom is well known to Crafton High as a formal dance is held every Christmas night and many graduates always look forward to celebrating the Christmas spirit with their long time friends. The eighteen-hole course was originally designed by Willie Park in 1924 and modified at a later date by Arthur Hills. The course, a par 70 layout measures 6,232 yards from the blue tees with lesser distances from the white and red tees.

Liz, thinking Sunday *was* as good of a time to practice as any, arrived at the club in early afternoon. She immediately went to the Tudor Chop House and looked over the menus. A bacon, lettuce and tomato on white toast seemed to fit right nicely and along with it an ice cold "coke" to quell a sudden watering of her mouth. "I knew I should have ordered an egg and a bite of toast," Liz said to herself. "Sometimes I do the dumbest things."

While enjoying her sandwich and drink, Liz gave some serious thought to what Mr. Flynn had taught her during her last few lessons. She asked the waiter if she could please borrow a pencil and a piece of paper she could steal. The waiter smiled and said, as he was handing Liz the pencil and paper, "Don't get caught."

Liz sat there and started to concentrate. She started to make some notes. Iron play! What are my points to remember? Mr. Flynn said it is easy to practice in front of a mirror so there were no excuses for adopting a poor position. When I do that at home I always stop to fix my hair. My grip should feel like an extension of my arm. Before I grip the club I'm supposed to push my hands a couple of inches ahead of the ball. Darn! I'll be thinking so much I won't be able to relax and take a descent swing. I think that man was right when I heard him on the tee say golf is *flog* spelled backward. Oh well! I'll get up and try. I paid the bill and left the waiter a tip—and his pencil.

Just as Liz was getting up from the table and reaching for her purse, a voice from over her right shoulder said, "Well! Hello! What a surprise meeting you here!"

Startled, Liz stood straight up and whirled around. In a few seconds her countenance changed from flabbergast to a faint smile. Oh! Hello! Gee, I wish I knew your name but I certainly remember where we met."

"My name, Liz, *is* Arnold Brownell, but my friends call me Arnie, and you can wipe the surprise off your pretty face. I asked the assistant pro after you left last week—or was it ten days ago, what your name was. I was not being a wise guy or excessively forward. I just wanted to know your name in the event we met on the range. If we do meet, and if you don't mind, I would be glad to help you anytime as long as it did not interfere with Mr. Flynn's plans for you."

"That's very cordial of you Mr. Crownell and I—"

"No, Liz, it's Brownell but please feel relaxed enough to call me Arnie. I think I unnerved you a little by calling you Liz and I apologize."

"Yes," ah! ah! Arnie, that you did but I'm back to normal—almost; and as I started to say I think it would be just fine for you to help me as long as *you* talk to Mr. Flynn."

"OK! It's a deal! Talk to Mr. Flynn and get his blessing under the circumstances you mentioned." Brownell looked at his watch and said,

"I have an afternoon appointment. I'll look forward to the next time we meet. In the meanwhile, take care and don't forget—keep you eye on he ball."

"I will!" Liz said with a smile. "Have a nice afternoon; and thanks!"

Liz felt a little flutter of lightheartedness; "Is Arnie a likelihood; a prospect for that hamburger Joanne was talking about?" she asked herself as *she* was getting into her cart to drive to the range and practice putting green. "He is good looking," she continued, "and a damn good golfer; probably make a good partner too!"

Liz continued to talk to her self. "If you had your fake ring on, would you remove it? I guess so; heck, he wouldn't want to mess with a married woman, I think! If we did happen to go for a snack or something, I could take my ring off as I removed my golf glove from my left hand.

STOP IT! And stop drooling for God's sake!"

Liz slowed down almost to a stop and damned herself for thinking the impracticability of it all. She started to pass the green but slammed on the brake, jumped out of the cart and grabbed her putter. "I can't think of anything sexual while trying to hit a 5 iron so I'll try my putting. At least I can keep my legs closer together."

Mr. Flynn had told Liz few things were more frustrating than hitting the green in regulation only to take three or four putts. Yet among amateurs it is an all too common scenario, turning a good round into a disastrous one. Then there is the complication of reading the line and judging the speed. "So, Liz," he said to me, "if there *is* one shot worthy of focusing on, it's surely this."

Liz dropped six balls a few feet from the hole and started; reading the putt, soft hands on the putter, walked my eyes up the line, concentrate on speed; and above all keep my head still. I missed the hole on the first two, sank three out of the last tour, and was pissed after the last one—it stopped on the edge; lost my concentration on speed.

And so I continued; three feet, five, seven and then ten; at the ten foot distance I sank two. Gettin' there! I then made up a game. Arnie against me! I bet him a hamburger if I sank a putt from anywhere outside of ten feet in one putt *vs* his two, he bought. We would play nine holes. I *was* to put first; he followed. I wanted that juicy 'burger. I was on the seventh hole; I stroked and followed the ball. Closer! Closer! Go in! Damn it! Go in!—Plunk! I let out a grandiose WHOOPE! A couple of other men on the green thought I was nuts! I looked at them and said, "I just beat my imperceptible partner." They laughed; I smiled on the way back to the cart.

I then spent about 40 minutes on my swing with an eight, nine, and wedge. Out of a one to ten scale I gave myself about four and a half. It only made me more determined. And I'm gonna' beat that Arnie in a putting match.

My rules!

Of course!

I went home, took a nice warm bath, had dinner with Mom and Dad, read some shorts from *READERS DIGEST* and went to bed. I wasn't ready to bring up the subject of **sex.**

EVER HEARD THE EXPRESSION "LAST BUT NOT LEAST"?

By: Charles Grube
Sports' Editor

If you haven't you can tell everyone you heard it from me!

This will not be my *last* column but it will be at *least* for awhile. Mr. Latshaw, as you may have read in my previous column two weeks ago, called me to a meeting in his office and told me he would like it if I went to Pitt and achieve my MBA. He said I could pick my courses, with help from a mentor, and attend lectures day or night or a combination thereof. I can also write my columns when I get the opportunity; Mr. Latshaw and I expect it will take 18 months to two years.

I want you to know it was all of you fans that made my column. Your calls, and letters, and queries, and sustained interests gave me the motives and incentive to "tell it like it is" and face truth and reality. And just THINK! Mr. Latshaw did not interfere once! Never said a word! He let our communication flow from one another just as the two rivers converge at Pittsburgh to flow into one. Oh sure! We get our share of floods but we are learning how to control the water through experience. And all of us gained wisdom in our exchange of value through what? Understanding of what is true, right, or lasting! We can throw in a little common sense and good judgment too!

I wish to leave you with a little info; Jack Flynn has started school at **Notre Dame Preparatory School and Marist Academy—Private Catholic College Preparatory.** The school is located in Michigan, Pontiac to be exact. At the request of the Archbishop of Detroit, the Marist Fathers and Brothers of the Boston Province founded Notre Dame Preparatory to provide an excellent college preparatory program with a strong Catholic identity. I know I speak for all the fans in wishing Jack well. Certainly, between the Retreat House and Notre Dame, he will be mentally prepared to enter the life as a Trappist monk.

AND, I had a very enjoyable luncheon at the Woolworth's tearoom with "Liz" McGovern just this past week. She called me at work and *was* excited about a couple of things and wanted to share them with me. We prattled over delicious "finger food" sandwiches and iced tea. We also snuck in a scoop of delicious Bryers fresh strawberry ice cream.

"Liz" was happy; I would say as a result of an arrested development in her love life. She told me she met a very nice gentleman at the driving range at Chartiers Country Club. It turns out he is a low handicap golfer and offered to assist with her swing if it was OK with Liz's instructor. Jim Flynn gave his OK so when they met on the range by happenstance her friend's help *was* immeasurable.

She told me a great story; they were at the Club. Liz told Arnie (that is his name) that she would bet him a hamburger that she could beat him in a putting match if he would play by her rules.

He said, "Your rules! What's in it for me?"

"Well," Liz said, "If you win you get a free hamburger, or BLT, or toasted cheese—anything you want as long as the decimal point is in front of the price."

"Geezz, Liz! You're a real snapshot of the "Queen of Dodge City!"

"Oh Arnie, quit complaining," Liz said. Here's what we do. We will putt for 18 holes on the putting green over there. One ball each! If I get hole in one, game over; I win the hamburger. Since your handicap is a 7 or 8, and mine *is* a 30, you will have to get 12 holes in one in the 18 to win. That's my offer!"

"Liz," Arnie said with an astounding 5 alarm fire look on his face, "you're beautiful, have a nice figure, sparkling smile, and I know if your doctor told you to go out and play 36 holes a day you would probably buy a harmonica, but you are dumb like a fox and yes, you win. We don't even have to play. You're looking for a free. hamburger, aren't you?"

"Well, I guess so,' Liz said with a demure, blushing smile. You have been so nice to me I just wanted to have a bite to eat with you some early afternoon and learn more about you."

So, Fans, she drove, he drove, and they met at a sandwich shop in Carnegie and Liz told me she liked what she learned—he is single and is a vice president for regional sales of a drug distribution corporation. I guess they will be dating on and off as his travel allows.

Funny thing about the name Arnold today! At work we were talking about the American Revolution and Benedict Arnold's name came up. I am working on an Arnold Palmer piece for the paper. I met a priest by the name of Arnold staying at St. Phillips for a few weeks, and now Liz's new friend is Arnold. Too bad they aren't Jacks. I'd be ready for a quick hand in poker.

Liz also had an additional astonishment! She is a finalist in the BRECK Girl shampoo contest. She will let us know how it turns out. Sounds like I'll be keeping in touch through osmosis.

Talk to you later!

I GET A CALL FROM THE BOSS

I was right in the middle of an imaginative article about a man inventive in spirit and prolific in delivery—that is in delivery of a baseball from the pitcher's mound to home plate. I am talking about Satchel Paige. His age evades us but his wisdom is of today, yesterday, last month, last year, and last century. Of all the sportsmen I have had the pleasure of meeting during my relatively short life, "Satch" is the one I would choose to sit down to dinner with and just listen to him speak only in aphorisms—brief but profoundly moving, touching observations of life.

But I guess I'll have to continue my article AFTER seeing Mr. Latshaw. So please excuse me!

When I arrived at Mr. Latshaw's office he, as he always does, greeted me with a heartfelt smile and forceful hand shake. "Please sit down, Charlie. Make yourself at home," he said as he slid effortlessly into an over stuffed brown leather armchair. An elegant end table fit firmly next to each arm rest was covered with a lace tablecloth and on it sat a roast beef and cheese sandwich with rye, a wedge of iceberg lettuce covered with blue cheese dressing, and two bottles of ice cold "Coca Cola." My mouth was forming a puddle as I said, "Gosh, Mr. Latshaw, is your next vocation going to be one as a chef.'

`No," said Mr. Latshaw with a smile. "I have more employees on vacation than I would care to admit so I just sent out for 'take out'. I hope you enjoy my choices."

"Sir," I said. "I just happen to love roast beef, Roquefort, and `Coke.'"

While we were enjoying out palatable lunch we disposed of the current talk such as family, friends, the Pirates and Jack Flynn. I filled him in on what I had been covering in my column about "Liz" and Jack. It was made easier by Mr. Latshaw telling me he reads my column assiduously.

"Charlie," he then said as he took a drink of coke. "I am going to send you the University of Pittsburgh Katz School for your MBA. I'll send down the Mervis Hall address, phone number, who to talk to, and any other pertinent information you need. I would like you to load up on business and management courses such as Cost Analysis for Strategic Thinking, Finance, Business Ethics, Decision Making and Risk Analysis, Marketing, Management Simulation Game, etc. We have already spoken about your choice of day and night classes so meet a good business manager at the school and you two figure what is best for you—and the *PPT*. We have also discussed the time it would take and you have an `OK' from me to write a column now and then but you must begin to think of your replacement. I am going to let that up to you. When we think you are ready I am going to promote you to a position of Managing Editor. Engleburg will be of help and Bottonley will be retiring and you will take his place. All expenses such as tuition, travel, meals, car, and maybe even a dinner for two—if Gloria *is* the number two."

"I want to say you earned this little meeting today. I know you will do well. All of you fighter pilots seem to grab a hold and hit the bang burner or what ever it is."

"It's afterburner, Sir, usually adding half again the thrust."

"Well, Charlie, thrust your self out of here as I have a management meeting," Mr. Latshaw said as he got up from his chair to wish me well as he shook my hand.

I said, "Sir, I am honored and I will not let you down."

He beamed at me and said, "You mean about school or that number two for dinner?"

Talk to you later!

SATCHEL PAGE ELUDES US, YET HIS WISDOM IS WITHOUT TIME ATTACHED

By: **Charles Grube**
Sports' Editor

"Age *is* a question of mind over matter. If you don't mind, it doesn't matter." That is according to baseball immortal Leroy "Satchel" Paige, born 100 years ago on July 7, 1906. Paige (legend has it) won 2100 games, 60 in one season, and 55 without giving up a hit. And that was before he was allowed in the majors as a 42 year old "rookie."

"How old would you be if you didn't know how old you are?" Paige once remarked. Of course, old Satch *was* known to have fudged the facts a smidge when it comes to longevity. He enjoyed shaving off a year or two to his biography, depending upon his mood and how much publicity it might attract. Satchel's actual birthday *is* one of the great mysteries of the sport.

He told Cleveland Indians owner Bill Veeck it was September 18. Wilber Hines, a childhood friend, claimed it was September 12, 1905. It was after Satch died, Cool Papa Bell reported that "Satchel *is* two years older than I am, and I'm 101." Bell was 77 at the time!

But Satch's mother, Lula, said that he was born in 1904, and she wrote the birth dates of her thirteen children down in the family Bible. The only problem was her father was reading it under a chinaberry tree one day when the wind blew it out of her hands. The family goat ate it!(this *is* getting more interesting than my column; I should have named it the *mystery of bible eating horned bearded mammal*).

Anyhow, Satch's birth date was lost forever. But the goat, according to Satch, lived to be exactly 27. (must have been his digestive tract assimilating new born again religion).

July 7 seems to be Paige's most likely birth date. Teammate Ted "Double Duty" Radcliffe (who died last August) insisted Satch was born on July 7, 1900, two years to the date before he was.

In Satch's autobiography, "Maybe Pitch Forever" he wrote, "I got to Cleveland on July 7, 1948. That was my 42nd birthday." And in 1954 the Mobile, Ala., Health Department located a birth certificate for a "Leroy Paige" dated July July 7, 1906. They've been carrying on so long about my age, nobody will believe what I say," Satch said.

We'll never know for sure when Satchel Paige was born. But when he threw his first pitch for the Cleveland Indians in 1948 (one year after Jackie Robinson broke the color barrier), Satch was an old man by baseball standards. Yet he still went 6-1 to help the Indians win the American League pennant. Paige became the first black player to pitch in the World Series and the first Negro League player inducted into the Baseball Hall of Fame (his plaque says he was 42 in 1948) Satch went on to pitch four more seasons.

Then, after being out of the big leagues for a dozen years, the Kansas City Athletics brought him back for one final appearance in the last days of September (I don't know the year—maybe early sixties).

Sept 25, 1965. Satch was pushing 60, but he pitched three shutout innings that day. It had been nearly 40 years from his first professional game until his last.

"Don't look back," Satch said, "Something might be catching up with you." Regardless of age, Satchel Paige was wise beyond his years. "We don't stop playing because we get old," Satch use to say. "We get old because we stop playing."

I say July 7 is as good a date as any to celebrate. Happy 100th, Satch! Even if it's not your birthday!

Quotable Satch.

- Ain't no man can avoid being born average, but there ain't no man got to be common.
- Don't pray when it rains if you don't pray when the sun shines.

- Money and women! They're two of the strongest things in the world. The things you do for a woman you wouldn't for anything else. Same with money!
- You win a few, you lose a few. Some get rained out. But you got to dress for all of them.
- I ain't ever had a job, I just always played baseball.
- Mother always told me, if you tell a lie, always rehearse it. If it don't sound good to you, it won't sound good to no one else.

As you may notice, I did not sign off with "Talk to you later." The reason is simple and straight to the point. Mr. Latshaw called about ten days ago and asked me to meet with him. I know some of you knew of the meeting because I was in the throws of beginning my column on Satchel Paige. Mr. Latshaw wants me to acquire my MBA at Pitt starting when feasible. I can continue writing my column but on a more limited scale. So, my friends, I am combining 'Satoh" with my new research on Roberto Clemente in order to clear my desk and prepare for school.

CLEMENTE LARGE IN LIFE

THE LATIN SUPERSTAR TRANSCENDED RACIAL DIVIDES WITH HIS FEATS ON AND OFF THE FIELD

With all the attention paid to many sluggers, I can't help but think of an equally talented, less celebrated—and far more transcendent player who's never gotten his due: Roberto Clemente, the first Latin American ballplayer elected to baseball's Hall of Fame.

It you followed baseball, you already know about Clemente. He wore No. 21 and played for our own Pittsburgh Pirates, leaving indelible images of hard slides, slashing line drives and laser-like throws from right field that gunned down even the swiftest runners trying to advance a base.

In his 17-year career, Clemente won four battling titles, played on two World Series winners, was an 11-time All-Star and won 12 Gold Glove Awards. He accumulated a lifetime batting average of .317, collected 3,000 hits and was voted most valuable player in the National League and the World Series.

He died in a plane crash on New Year's Eve, attempting to deliver food and other relief supplies that he had collected for earthquake-ravaged

Nicaragua. The private plane he chartered—loaded beyond capacity and, unbeknownst to him, riddled with all sorts of mechanical problems—plunged into the Caribbean Sea shortly after taking off from the San Juan airport in his native Puerto Rico.

Soon after his death, the Baseball Writers Association of America voted to enshrine Clemente in the Hall of Fame rather than follow the customary five-year waiting period after a player's retirement. He was the second player so honored in the history of the game. The other: the Yankees' Lou Gehrig.

David Maraniss got it right in his biography, *Clemente: The Passion and Grace of Baseball's Last Hero,* when he argued that Clemente's legacy went far beyond Cooperstown and the baseball field. Often regarded as the Jackie Robinson of the Spanish-speaking world, Clemente was 19 when he signed with the Brooklyn Dodgers—the same team Robinson played for when he broke the color barrier in 1947.

A smattering of Latin ballplayers had played in the major leagues as far back as 1902, but Clemente would become the first superstar. The Dodgers tried to hide their prize prospect in the minor leagues, but the Pirates discovered him and drafted him onto their major league roster.

At 5 feet, 11 inches, 185 pounds, Clemente was no behemoth; he succeeded because he was a passionate competitor. Beyond that, he was a compassionate humanitarian who died in service to others before he could see his dream of building a sports complex for youth become a reality.

If induction to the Hall of Fame were based solely on character, Roberto Clemente's bronze plaque would deserve its own wing.

I *will* be talking to you later!

EVEN AS A SPORTS' EDITOR I THINK I HAVE THE RIGHT TO BE DISENCHANTED!

By: Charles Grube
Sports' Editor

First, I would like all of you fans to know I did not clear this script with Mr. Latshaw before writing it. Lately, I have not been too fond of the play surrounding the competitive atmosphere among a cross section of professional sports' teams. I did, however, send Mr. Latshaw a copy and asked him to please let me know if he had any objections.

Not a word!

So here it is! A tough, ruffianly, straight examination of my observation of the "fields of dreams"! I don't like what I see; and I take privilege in saying I don't think you sports fans do either.

I have learned in my tide, though limited experience in relation to time, nothing really happens that hasn't happened many times before; only in different dimensions! My friend Marcus Aurelius, (Rome AD 121) told me so in his masterpiece MEDITATIONS. In its place, my understanding has taken on a dimension of skew-ness or distortion in the realm of accepting *and* comprehending; no matter what happens I don't get the feeling of any strong emotion. Subliminally, I'm telling myself, "Hey, I've been there, done that!"

Mark Twain, born 1700 years after Marcus Aurelius says, "The character of the human race never changes, it is permanent." Circumstances change from time to time for better or worse, but the human race never does.

Let me give you an example or two! My circumstances regarding professional sports have changed. I used to thoroughly enjoy football, baseball, basketball, and hockey as great games for fans to enjoy the tough competition between professionals who worked their way to the top. But sad for me to say, their games have now become, to me, a gigantean bore. Of course you have noticed my column is not a report on "play by play."

In football, I tire of the arrogant "look what I just did" displays of players in the end zone and three time losers from drugs back on the field after a slap on the hands and a microscopic relief of dollars from their wallet. In addition, I read where one football player, after catching a ball in the end zone, in a display egregious egoism and pomposity, runs and stepped on the rival's logo. An insult to any normal man's intelligence! Of course intelligence is defined as: mental acuteness, or the act of understanding, or the skilled use of reason, or the ability to apply knowledge. This moron didn't have the mental acuteness or intelligence of a wet brick. I say "wet" because I want to stay as far away as possible from my "dry" sense of humor.

Baseball has become a turbulent display of bean balls, chair and bottle throwing, fans running on the field, and fisticuffs; so much so TV is now showing the many team upheavals as part of a review on the championship playoff series. Managers tell players to "dust 'em off or get even." Just wait until an irate pitcher throws a 90mph fastball and hits a player on the head so hard it kills him. It's going to happen; count on it! Or worse yet, these medleys, or a jumbled assortment of players running onto the field ready to show how tough they are in a party of thirty or more! Is that why they are wearing a uniform with the proud name of **PITTSBURGH** on it? Ridiculous!

If hockey keeps up the deceitful, low life guile of deliberate injuries to opposing players it will soon be like watching the Christians vs. the Lions because the consciously unsocial, morally offensive fans will demand more!

A star-loaded basketball team shamefully lost a championship series because of envy extending far from the surface of the court. And the fans, probably the most behaved, until recently, and loyal of any, were the losers. They lost watching a star player because the poor little, 7-footer, thought only of his ungrateful self. And just in the past few days, the newspapers, TV sports shows, plus radio and TV commentators, are "shocked" at the melee between players and fans at the Detroit Pistons-Indians Packers The country is aghast and dismayed with the brawl with its naked display of fear and loathing. Pro athletes, and the fans that watch them, don't like each other anymore.

"I have been on the sidelines at 49ers games for 20 years and I have witnessed the change," says critic Harry Edwards, a San Francisco 49ers consultant. "The resentment is deeply rooted and hard-wired and it has to do with money, race, and class."

Read on! Hal Holbrook, impersonating Mark Twain on Broadway says, "We're having a greedy love affair with money."

And while I am at it, I might add a thought on boxing. A previous heavyweight champion went from excellence to excelling . . . in disdainful, haughty, supercilious un-sociability. I mean, he could do anything he pleases because, "I am rich!"

Think back to "Red" Grange, Lou Gehrig, John Wooden, and Joe Lewis! The absolute greatest; and gentlemen all! And they will *always* be remembered for having "Class." The others! Their names in my paper and your mind are ephemeral; short lived; and thankfully so!

I feel a sense of impropriety; the acts described totally lack conformity to what is socially acceptable in man's conduct and speech. My former strong emotions about professional sports are now being replaced with reality! I am intuitively aware of their "me first" attitude!

Hal Holbrook, who as a young actor in the early fifties began developing a one-man show portraying Mark Twain onstage, calls the "me first" attitude "Get Rich" because we're having a greedy love affair with money. "I mean," says Holbrook, "we're forgetting everything. We're just so in love with money, and everything in our society feeds into it, beginning with the television and the advertising and the commercialization of the human being. We have become a product. What a horrible conclusion to come to for a human being."

I recognize, in action, the professionals' excessive and arrogant self-confidence. The terrible injustice is that he doesn't recognize it. Someday, a wind will come along and blow him, his dollars, and his inflated ego away. And he will be too stupid to know the reason why.

I know the PITTSBURGH POST TELEGRAPH fans' understand I speak of only a few, with their pretentiousness grab of the headlines. Their egocentricity pushes them high above all others. Their life at the top is short lived and their fall will be—catastrophic.

Talk to you later!!

ARNOLD PALMER: A BIOGRAPH
A Little About Our "Home-Town" Boy!

By: Charles Grube
Sports' Editor

Arnold Palmer is many things to many people; a world famous golf immortal and sportsman, highly successful business executive, prominent advertising spokesman, skilled aviator, talented golf course designer and consultant. He *is* also a devoted husband, father and grandfather and a man with *a* down-to-earth common touch that has made him one of the most popular and accessible public figures in history.

His popularity and success have grown with the tremendous golf boom in this latter half of the century to heights few ever anticipated. Certainly each contributed to the other, a fact given recognition when he was named "Athlete of the Decade" for the 1960s in a national Associated Press poll. Before, during, and after that great decade, this famous golfer amassed 92 championships in professional competition of national or international stature by the-end of 1993. Sixty-one of the victories came on the U.S. PGA Tour, starting with the 1955 Canadian Open.

Beside the magnificent performance record, his magnetic personality and unfailing sense of kindness and thoughtfulness to everybody with whom he comes in contact have endeared him to millions throughout the world and led to the informal formation of the largest non-uniformed "military" organization in existence—Arnie's Army. Seven of his victories came in what the golfing world considers the four major professional championships. He won the Masters Tournament four times, in 1958, 1960, 1962 and 1964; the U.S. Open in spectacular fashion in 1960 at Cherry Hills Country Club in Denver and the British Open in 1961 and 1962. He came from

144

seven strokes off the pace in the final round in that U.S. Open win and has finished second in four other opens since then. Among the majors, only the PGA Championship has eluded him. He has finished second in the PGA three times.

Arnie's springboard to professional fame and fortune was his victory in the U.S. Amateur Championship in 1954. He turned professional a few months later. His hottest period was a four-year stretch from 1960 to 1963 when he landed 29 of his titles and collected almost $400,000. He was the leading money-winner in three of those years and twice represented the U.S. in the prestigious Ryder Cup Match, serving in 1963 as the victorious captain.

Palmer *was* born on September 10, 1929, in Latrobe, a small industrial town in Western Pennsylvania just about 50 miles east of Pittsburgh. He still spends the warm months of the year there, but makes his winter home in the Orlando area. He has numerous active and honorary memberships in clubs throughout the world, including famed St. Andrews in Scotland and prominent Oakmont in our town of Pittsburgh.

The golfing great has been the recipient of countless honors, the symbolic plaques, trophies and citations scattered throughout his personal, club and business worlds. He has received virtually every national award in golf and after his great 1960 season both the Hickok Athlete of the Year and Sports Illustrated's Sportsman of the Year trophies. He *is* a charter member of the World Golf Hall of Fame and a member of the American Golf Hall of Fame at Foxburg, PA, and the PGA Hall of Fame in Florida. He is chairman of the USGA Members Program and served as Honorary National Chairman of the March of Dimes Birth Defects Foundation for 20 years. He played a major role in the fundraising drive that led to the creation of the Arnold Palmer Hospital for Children and Women in Orlando. A long-time member of the Board of Directors of Latrobe Area Hospital, he established a major annual fundraising golf event for that institution a few years ago.

The saga of Arnold Palmer began when he *was* four years old, swinging his first set of golf clubs, cut down by his father, Milfred J. (Deacon) Palmer, who worked at Latrobe Country Club from 1921 until his death in 1976, much of that time as both golf professional and course superintendent. Before long, Arnie was playing well enough to beat the older caddies at the club. He began caddying himself when he was 11 and worked at virtually every job at the club in the ensuing years.

The strongly-built young man concentrated on golf in high school and soon was dominating the game in Western part of our state of Pennsylvania.

He won his first of five West Penn Amateur Championships when he was 17, competed successfully in national junior events and went to Wake Forest University (then College), where he became No. 1 man on the golf team and one of the leading collegiate players of that time. Deeply affected by the death in an auto accident of his close friend and classmate, Bud Worsham, younger brother of 1947 U.S. Open Champion Lew Worsham, Arnold withdrew from college during his senior year and began a three-year hitch in the Coast Guard. His interest in golf rekindled while he *was* stationed in Cleveland. He was working there as a salesman and playing amateur golf after his discharge from the service and brief return to Wake Forest when he won the U.S. Amateur in 1954 following his second straight victory in the Ohio Amateur earlier that summer.

It was during this period that he met Winifred Walzer at a tournament in Eastern Pennsylvania. They were married shortly after he turned professional in the fall of 1954 and Winnie traveled with him when he joined the pro tour in early 1955. The Palmers have two daughters—Peggy Palmer Wears, of Durham, NC, and Amy Palmer Saunders, of Windermere, FL Arnold's brother, Jerry, who succeeded their father as course superintendent at Latrobe CC, and his two sisters, Lois Jean and Sandra live in the Latrobe area. Jerry is now general manager of Latrobe CC and all Palmer properties there.

ACADEMIC HONORS

Honorary Doctor of Laws, Wake Forest University, Winston-Salem, NC
Honorary Doctor of Humanities, Thiel College, Greenville, PA

Honorary Doctor of Laws, National College of Education, Evanston, IL
Honorary Doctor of Humane Letters, Florida Southern College, Lakeland, FL

AWARDS: GOLF

Charter member, World Golf Hall of Fame, Pinehurst, NC American Golf Hall of Fame, Foxburg, PA

PGA Hall of Fame, Palm Beach Gardens, FL

All-American Collegiate Golf Hall of Fame, Man of Year Ohio Golf Hall of Fame

Phoenix Open Hall of Fame

Plus 16 others including Golfer of Century, New York Athletic Club

AWARDS: GENERAL

Associated Press Athlete of Decade—1960-69 Hickok Athlete of Year—1960

Sports Illustrated Sportsman of Year

Wake Forest Hall of Fame

Arthur J. Rooney Award, Catholic Youth Assn., Pittsburgh PA Lowman Humanitarian Award, Los Angeles, CA

Plus 20 others, including National Sports Award, Washington, D.C.

I am just beginning to make the mental transition from my Sports' Column to school. Soon you will be reading a column by a knowledgeable, experienced writer that Mr. Latshaw and I agreed on hiring with a starting date in about six weeks. I feel sure you fans know of him but as a matter of professional etiquette we will not name the individual at this time. I will let you know because he and I are planning on writing a very interesting column together. I can tell you one thing! He calls me "Jolly Cholly

   In reference to this column, I thought it a good idea to research the life and accomplishments of Arnold Palmer because I am sure it makes us all feel good about our own lives—like Casey Stengel and Yogi Berra!!
   I sincerely believe man should continually strive to go through life feeling happy about himself, and, no matter the destiny, others. Also, I have learned, sometimes in difficult arenas, to laugh at myself—and *with* others!
   Talk to you later!

THE FUTURE IS NOW!!

By: Charles Grube
Sports' Editor

Ever hear the song, "My Echo, My Shadow, and Me?" I just sat down with my pencil, my paper pad, and me!

I do this every now and then; keeps me sharp as I write a column to myself. Don't get me wrong. I continually see people of interest even while going to school but I like to catch up on what's been going on. It permits me to exchange information; but I keep the results to myself.

TIME is everywhere; everyone knows that. I frown as I scratch my head because I'm thinking—it evades me; hides out from me like a participant in "Kick the Can." We all knew that game as kids. Actually TIME gets away from all of us; yet is catches up to all because we collectively utter the same words, "Where the heck did all the time go?"

That scenario happened to me the other day! I have a good friend whose older daughter had a baby the day before his younger daughter got married. She was so determined to be at the wedding that she wrapped the baby in plenty of warm clothes and told the pediatric nurse, "I'm going!" And then, there she was—standing at the altar with her sister, baby and all. It was absolutely a thing of grandeur and, I might say, dignified distinction.

I often see my friend Bill and one particular evening we were talking about his four married daughters and that I should have married one of them to get to his money. I said, "Gee! I still remember Mary Kay and the baby. She must be in 5th or 6th grade by now." "Chuck," Bill said laughing, "the baby you saw in her arms enters her senior year in high school in September."

I could not believe it!

TIME is so bound up in our universe and ourselves that it resists our efforts to isolate and define it. TIME haunts our experience like some invisible spirit of things, some irretrievable truth. And when we try to manage our own time, setting new goals, cleaning and rearranging the little houses of our days, TIME gently mocks us—not so much because we lack wit or will as because TIME operates on a deeper psychological level that conscious effort can normally reach. It seems to me TIME operates most dramatically on our dearest values and concerns. It is operating against me now as I am trying in this darn traffic to meet Liz at noon at the entrance to her school; The School of Continuing Education at CHATAM COLLEGE. "I know its not far north of Schenley Park," Charlie said to himself. "I remember I have seen it before but there's that word TIME again; acts on your brain like it does your beautiful five year old *PLAID* golf pants. It fades!"

I continued on; eye on the traffic; eye on my watch. "There! There it is" Turn right on Woodland Road," I mumbled to myself. "Down a half a block and she should—there she is! Right in front!" I pulled right to the curb, came to a stop, I leaned over, rolled down the window and said, "Hey, pretty lady. Wanna' mess around?"

"Mr. Grube," she said with a short outcry as I leaned farther to open the door. "What an enormous pleasure seeing you again," she continued as she slid into the front seat, closed the door and artfully, in one swish of her left hand, smoothed her skirt to meld it with the front seat upholstery and cover her knees. She was wearing a pale yellow dress with a narrow skirt and bolero style jacket. "How's school? How's Gloria?" she asked. "And I guess no one has heard from Jack as he ensconced in **Holy Trinity**. I don't think Monks are even allowed to talk to themselves." She looked at me and flashed her brilliant smile as she asked. "Where are you stealing me off to today?"

I looked into my "added accessory" side view mirror and gunned my chariot into traffic. "I'm pilfering you to a small Italian restaurant hidden in an alley behind the GULF BUILDING; you have to know somebody to get in. I discovered it about three years ago—named **ABELLA ITALIAN KITCHEN**. Abella means 'beautiful' just like you. Are you hungry?"

"Of course I am! Starving! I always seem to get hungry whenever I'm offered a free meal," Liz said as a spark of light streaked from her smile. I'll probably even have a glass of wine. I'm delighted that you gave me a call. Besides, I am in need of a friend like you, Mr. Grube."

"OH!" I said as I pulled up to VALET PARKING. "It must be important."

"It is," Liz said as she got out with the assistance and courtesy of the valet; "probably working his way through college," I said to myself.

We were greeted by the owner, Louie D'Ambrosio, as Italian as spaghetti and meat balls. The first time I met him he had just seated Mr. Latshaw and me at a fine table. When Mr. Latshaw introduced me, Louie said, "Gee, Mr. Grube, look'it that double-breasted suit you're wearing. You're cleaner than dah board of health!"

I'll tell you, Dave Latshaw and I broke up laughing. Louie and I have been close ever since. He can kid around but when you are with someone, as I was with Liz, he is extremely circumspect; even after being introduced.

We were seated at a small table against a wall—my favorite. Our waiter, I call him Amigo, said "hello" as he smiled as Liz and asked, "Same drink, Mr. Grube?"

"Not today, my friend. I think Miss McGovern and I will have a glass of *ZENATO* Pinot Grigio. And how's the house Minestrone?"

"Just as good as ever," Mr. Grube! Will you and the lovely lady care for a cup?"

I told Amigo "No thanks" for now Miss McGovern and I are going to visit for fifteen minutes or so and he may present the menus at that time.

So Liz and I talked—and talked—through our wine and minestrone, and Classic Caesar with grilled chicken breast for Liz and with succulent prawns for me.

Everything was going along great for Liz. She is majoring in COMMUNICATION and likes it; communication skills, public speaking, diction, business courses, organization, responsibilities, some minor math, grammar, English, vocabulary—the whole works. And she is enjoying it.

The Breck Shampoo and the Breck Girl hair and shampoos ads of 1956 offered three shampoos for three different hair conditions. The pretty portrait of a young lady in the ad is Liz. She was so delighted; so was everyone else. She kept her charm and amiability throughout the whole campaign. But, then, Liz was never affected by any accolades or special acknowledgements sent her way.

"Did I tell you my friend Joanne got married? She had an elegant but small wedding in Bellvue. She married a guy she met about four years ago at the Dormont pool. His name is Tim—Timothy Robert Sterling. Heck of a nice man; graduate of the Wharton School of Business from the

University of Pennsylvania. He was one of the winners in the Business Plan competition—Yes, Mr. Grube?"

"Oh, I didn't want to interrupt, Liz, but wasn't Joann a cheerleader about the same time you were. If so, I think I met her one evening after a game. Jack introduced us when you went to say good bye to your parents or somethin'. Also, I am sure Tim is of the Sterling family; real estate, banks, big investments in Wall Street."

"Yes, you're right. You did meet her! Anyhow, her 'Joe Paloka' as Joanne kids him, was one of the Grand prize winners and rang the NASDAQ stock market closing bell. One of her bridesmaids at the wedding brought a bell and rang it when Joanne said, 'I do'. It was really funny. He landed a great job working at Westinghouse. But no worry, the family has tons of money so Joanne deserves much happiness."

Amigo came over to remove the salad dishes and offered coffee and dessert. I didn't hesitate a second. I told Amigo to bring us two coffees and two forks for an order of *Torte de Le Nova*, a delicious lemon tart—with a small scoop of vanilla ice cream. Liz looked at me and just shook her head. I said, "It's only a half and we both work out so no worry. Besides, you deserve something sweet—goes with your disposition. Now tell me why you need a friend like me!"

"Maybe I could have a little more coffee first," Liz asked.

"Sure" I said as I signaled to Amigo by holding a clandestine cup between my forefinger and thumb while raising it to my mouth. He caught on immediately and was on his way.

"Well, Mr. Grube," Liz said as she watched Amigo pour her coffee and moved to fill my cup at the same time. "You remember me telling you about the man—the golfer—I met at Chartiers while practicing my golf swing. He has asked Mr. Flynn, my pro, if it was OK if he helped me after my lessons and of course Mr. Flynn said it would be fine with him. So as the time moved on, Arnie, that's his name, has been a tremendous help. Also he is—what do they call a golfer who is par most of the time?"

"A scratch golfer," I said to Liz.

"Yes, that's it. He is damn good, pardon me, and has been a tremendous help. I'm actually swinging the clubs pretty good; not scoring worth a darn but I'm learning and I'm happy just to get out on the range or playing nine holes with a couple of girls I met. With the play I'm learning the rules too! I hope I'm not boring you!"

"Of course not, Liz! I am pleased; you seem more relaxed and happy."

"Well, darn it I am. Arnie travels, for a drug distribution company or something like that, and when he's in town, and most of the time when we meet by happenstance at the club, I feel invigorated. We've even been out to lunch a couple of times at the club or one time I made him a loser on a trumped up putting match so he had to take me out for a hamburger. We each drove our own car.

I like my hamburger thick, medium rare with lots of ketchup, onions, dill pickle, plenty of mayonnaise on the tomato and iceberg lettuce gently placed a toasted bun. I spend half the time wiping my face off; go through three or more napkins. But gee! It sure tastes good! We talked about golf mostly. Arnie wants me to put a little bit of more power in my strike—maintain my height from start to finish best achieved by holding my chin off the chest at address and keeping it off until after impact. He said, 'Liz, a useful thought to promote the necessary wide swing arc for distance is to start the club head back low and slow. It also helps to promote good tempo.' He was demonstrating as much as he could at the table but stopped and continued, 'Try to think you're swinging at about 85 per cent.'

We each had a second "Pepsi" and kept on with our—what's it called—confabulation, or something like that, until we checked our watches and decided it was time to go."

"You were right, Liz, I mean about the word confabulation. It is another word for conversation. But is that the reason you were anxious to talk to me—about your wide swing arc for more distance?"

"Oh, no! Of course not! When Arnie and I walked to my car we continued to chitchat until I suggested, innocently, there was no need for him to continue standing and to sit down on the passenger side—I had the top down—and be comfortable. Well, Mr. Grube, he did and every time we laughed we got closer until we were looking at each other in the eye. And then, just like that, he put his arm around my neck and gave me a long, tender, warm, and very sensual kiss that sent waves of sensuality through my whole body. And the harder he pressed the more indulgence I felt and I put my hand on the back of his neck so he would press all the harder. We ended sucking on each others' tongue and—and I was so full of titillation and tingle I wanted him to devour my whole body. But we both realized, at the same instant, that we were in public and stopped immediately. We looked at each other and slowly came together for a touch of the lips and then Arnie whispered, 'I better go' and opened the door and walked to his car. He did wave as he drove out of the lot and signaled he would see me at the club."

I told Liz I was glad she told me and I felt honored that she would confide in me. "There is no doubt," I said, "that if you two were alone in an isolated area you would have had a front seat that at the time it was manufactured it did not know it would partake in a frenetic love making hustle-bustle that wore you both out to the bone. Heck, Liz, I'm happy for you. A woman of your beauty and panache needs someone to hold and if the right man comes along, and I think maybe he has, why not go for it! Just be careful and don't get hurt. And I also think we better get going."

I dropped Liz off at school and headed for the office; I was thinking about what a shame it was that Liz didn't have anyone at home she trusted and could share her stories with.

I wanted to tell Liz I found my eventual replacement in "Doc" Giffin; he was a couple of years behind us in high school. "Doc" had been the Editor of the school paper and has been working at the PITTSBURGH PRESS for about six years starting out writing columns about the Pittsburgh Renaissance, the development of "The Golden Triangle" and clearing of the air from soot and smog to clear blue skies. He then found his niche in writing about Pittsburgh's college athletes signing pro contracts in football, baseball, and basketball. I talked to Mr. Latshaw about hiring him to take over my column so he called the Editor of the "PRESS" as a matter of professional courtesy and asked if we could speak to Mr. Griffin. The Editor, Mr. Charles Mahoney, appreciated the call and said it was OK with him. So Mr. Latshaw and I started with lunch and we made the deal with "Doc" about six weeks later.

I shared my thoughts with "Doc" on writing a column about Golf's Legends (I thought we could write three columns posted about every other week) which would give the *PPT* fans a chance to meet "Doc" through his verbal professionalism. I'll write an introduction about our new star when we write the column.

Well, enough of the "talking to myself." I have to crack the books. Talk to you later!

LIZ HAS MUCH TO THINK ABOUT!

By: Charles Grube
Sports' Editor

"Almost too much to figure out," Liz said to herself as she headed out town. She had thought of this trip for the past several months but wanted to "get her head on straight" first, as she used to say when talking to herself. She had today, Friday, clear of any commitments and had spoken to her Mom about taking a trip to see a girl friend, Dahlia Walsh. Her mother knew Dahlia, a bright classmate who was on the debating team with Liz. She was also the president of the Chemistry Club, a soprano with a beautiful voice in the Glee Club, and had hit the Honor Roll with nothing but "A's" since she walked into her first class as a high school freshman. She wasn't what you would call beautiful but she was attractive with an unblemished face, and a knockout smile. The guys used to call her "Robin Red Breast"—red hair, polished cheeks and a heck of a body.

Dahlia's parents lived near Toms River in New Jersey and she very much liked to visit them when she was on vacation or had a few days off from her college of choice—the Benedictine Academy founded by the Benedictine Sisters of Elizabeth, New Jersey.

There was something about the presence of mind in Dahlia; composure, self-possession, aplomb. Liz first noticed it during their chemistry club meetings; everyone talking about some formula or the right way to balance an equation and it always seemed that it was through Dahlia's calmness that coalesced every ones' thinking into forming one collective answer. Jack and Liz double dated several times with Dahlia and her date—a powerfully voiced tenor from the Glee Club. He was complaining one night about his performance at a recital and Dahlia told him in short order to stop being so petulant and to thank God for giving you such a voice that "you will have years to develop." He looked at her for a short time and said, "You're right! And, Jack and Liz, I apologize."

Dahlia's stoicism came from her profound Catholic faith; her equanimity allowed her to step forward in any situation with the thought that God had His hand on her shoulder.

Liz was talking to herself as she took a right on E. Crafton Ave. and a left on to PA-60 where after a right onto W Carson onto US-22/US-30E toward MONROEVILLE to the PENNSYLVANIA TURNPIKE. During the next 171 miles she could talk to herself loud and clear. "I need someone's hand on my shoulder," she said. "I would be kidding myself if I said I didn't thoroughly enjoy my deep throat kissing with Arnie. It drove my sexual desire to an elevation I have never felt and damn it, why did it have to end so suddenly. Why did Arnie push away so suddenly? We sat there looking at each other as my nymphomania drained from my body while my brain screamed 'Impurity! Unclean! Shame!' I was so full of desire under my breath I shouted back as Arnie and I softly touched lips, 'go to hell!, damn brain! leave me alone!'"

Tears were sliding, slowly, down her cheeks as Liz merged onto I76/Pa. Turnpike via Portions toll. "My one chance to enjoy a warm kiss and 'just like that' it was gone. My only other experience was a debauchery with that asshole in the back of a limo. And on top of that everyone in my family would be shocked and would ask with scandalous quest, 'Did you talk to a priest! Did you go to confession! Nothing about 'Where you hurt! Did you see a doctor! How about protection!'"

Face it Liz, you are on your own. Prepare for a huge mental battle between a fulfilling sexual relationship and the uncleanness of mortal sin.

Liz stopped on the turnpike for gas and a bite to eat. In the ladies room she looked into the mirror with red saddened eyes and asked, as Schopenhauer once did, "Why, with so many mirrors in the world, does one not know what they look like?" Liz answered her own question as she rubbed her lips together to even the shade of her lipstick, "Because not one takes the time to even try to know and love oneself; a never ending goal. How can I love anyone else if I don't know how to love myself and return love with a delicate artistry," she asked herself. "And I can't even start loving myself with a broken heart and desolate dreams. Why, Lord, did you take Jack away from me.?"

She hurried to the car so no one would see her tears again.

Her unfailing Mustang took Liz onto HARRISBURG PIKE, then it was ALLENTOWN, HILLSIDE, Maple, Williamson, N. BROAD ST. and

Liz was there: 362 miles, seven and one-half hours later; BENEDICTINE ACADEMY, 840 N. BROAD ST, Elizabeth, NJ.

Liz made a right turn into the entrance and immediately saw a sign ADMINISTRATION BUILDING. She followed the arrows and parked in front. Inside she asked the receptionist for Ms. Walsh.

"And your name?" asked the petite blonde with a smile.

"I am Liz McGovern from Pittsburgh and Ms. Walsh is expecting me," Liz answered returning the smile.

"Oh yes! Ms. McGovern. I am awfully sorry. Yes, off course! Ms. Walsh called about 15 minutes ago and told me to expect you. I'm sorry! I'll call her right away."

"That's perfectly all right. I'll just sit in that comfortable chair right over there," Liz said as she turned to the left and started to walk away.

"A big, comfortable expansive reception area," Liz said to herself." Bright rays of sunshine crept stealthily along the white marble floor in cadence with bringing sparkle to the windows and adding brilliance to the dark tan curtains. Liz sat peacefully in her chair; eyes closed; a cloud of uncertainty lingered overhead but she mentally took her two hands and shoved it away!

Dahlia's excited outcry, "There you are, Liz. How happy I am to see you," snapped Liz back to reality as she arose to greet her loving friend. They both hugged for a long five seconds or so as they whispered enthusiastic greetings in each others ear. "I'm so glad you're here," Dahlia said as she held Liz at arms length and then brought her close with another embrace. "My roommate is out of town and you can stay with me and all we have to do is visit and talk and catch up and laugh and throw in a few tears. I have a reservation at a local pub tonight and dinner on me tomorrow at a very nice French restaurant east of town at seven! So I'll show you where to park and let's gather your stuff out of the car head for my room in the dorm. I think you'll like it!

So—Liz and Dahlia visited and laughed and cried and drank beer and ate good food for thirty six hours or so and enjoyed each others' company as only two great friends can. There was one somber discussion on Sunday morning over coffee and delicious "bear claws". Liz told Dahlia about her inflamed kisses with Arnie and as Liz said, "My sexual desire turned me inside out and I wanted him to caress my whole body with his tongue and lips and mouth. Gee! Dahlia, I was going crazy. Look at the ring I wear—just to hold off guys from hitting on me but I get so lustful at times; drives me goofey."

Dahlia started to say something but Liz said, "Just a second; OK! Sorry! I want to hear what you have to say but first the thing that drives me—I don't know—mentally unbalanced—is FEAR! Fear of mortal sin! Fear of dying with sin on my soul! Fear of going to hell! But all I really want is to love someone who loves me and if it leads to sex that's OK as far as I am concerned because sexual intercourse is a physical and heartfelt union between two consenting mature people. With those parameters, why the hell is it a sin? Now it's your turn," she said to Dahlia as she went back to sipping her cup of coffee.

"Well, my beautiful friend I can only tell you what I have learned and what I believe. You know me! I'm religious because I am comfortable with my beliefs. Doesn't say I'm narrow minded or 'square.' I have been 'French Kissed' a number of times; even had a man, or two, bare my breasts—kissed them and licked my nipples but when they wanted to go farther I stopped them by saying, quite emphatically, 'NO.' I was worked up but my Christian strength helped me. That is not to say I'm right and others that go all the way are wrong. I did not have a strong sexual feeling for these men. It was great to have a few beers with them and relax in their company. It sounds like you have something different. I have two classes where we have serious discussions about sin and who is guilty of committing—say—a mortal sin and who gets off with only a venial. I once had a Jesuit priest tell me it's only in the eye of the beholder. He said, in a prepared speech that, "Things considered by the Magisterium of the Roman Catholic Church to be a grave matter can usually be considered violations of the Ten Commandments, whether directly such as perjury, adultery, lust, murder; or indirectly in the cases of heresy, or despair, which contravene the first commandment, or the use of contraceptives, which contravens the sixth commandment. All of these, however, are subject both to the conditions on what meets the tone or situation for a mortal sin and to mitigating circumstances of the individual situation."

"So, Liz, if you fall in love with Arnie, who is to say you are even committing a sin! God gave you the innate sexual desire. Why would he send you to hell for enjoying it through love. Wish I had an answer!"

Liz had tears in her eyes. She had great ardor for her friend; her talk made her feel a little more comfortable about what the future may hold. She knows, but doesn't know when, that Arnie and she will go all the way and she told herself she would not rationalize or fear sin any longer. It made her loins feel warm and moist.

Liz wanted to stay and visit her friend a little longer but Dahlia has an early morning class and she decided to leave about 1:00pm which would get her home no later than eight. Liz had Monday morning free so if the trip tired her she could sleep in and then have lunch with her Mom.

It was an uneventful trip; her Mom was interested in Dahlia and her school and was pleased her daughter had a pleasant visit with her good friend. The whole family had a cheery, amiable Bar Be Cue with Dad in his chef's hat and apron doing all the cooking.

"Honey, what's on the schedule tomorrow"? Liz's Mother asked during dinner.

"Let's see! I have two classes in the early afternoon and a powers' shot or two at five pm and then I plan on having dinner with Joanne. You remember! She got married to her "Joe Paloka" several months ago. She is still doing some modeling though. She's absolutely beautiful; face of an angel!"

IS JOANNE UNHAPPY?
ALREADY!!

By: Charles Grube
Sports' Editor

Liz told Joanne she would meet her at a small French restaurant on the Blvd. of the Allies called PARNASSUS, named after a mountain in central Greece N of the Gulf of Cornith. That's right! A French café with a Greek name! Everyone finds it captivating but it's quite simple. The owner is French but his wife is Greek and he was so much in love with her (they met in Athens) he promised if she would marry him he said he would create the French menu but she could give the restaurant a name of her choice. So his new wife thought the restaurant would be of high choice so she named it after an 8000 ft. mountain near her hometown. Well, it turned into a mountain of enchantment as the food is a gourmet's delight, the service is second to none, the selection of wines unequalled, and most patrons can't wait to tell their friends they ate French food in a Greek restaurant. I was introduced to PARNASSUS by the vice president of marketing and sales from Breck Shampoo.

Joanne arrived at 7:30 right on time. When I slid off my bar stool to greet her with a hug I knew at once that I had my arms around a disenchanted angel. I have no idea why, nor did I act any manner other than an ecstatic lady greeting her dear friend. I took her hand and led her to our reserved table.

Earlier, when I was given our table I asked the waiter to open a bottle of Nuevo Beaujolais and let it breath. Our waiter's name was Franz Joseph. I said to him when he first greeted me, "Franz Joseph! Why Franz Joseph was an Emperor of Austria! Any relation?"

He said, "No madam, but it makes me feel good that you asked!

After we were comfortably seated Franz Joseph took the wine bottle in his hand and palm and showed us the label. 1957 Beaujolais Village, Domaine Manoir du Carra. He added, the village was located South of Burgundy and North of Rhone Valley. We both smiled and said, "Looks great" and he poured me a taste and when I told Franz it was delicious he poured Joanne and me a glass.

Seconds thereafter he presented us both with a menu—with a beautiful painting of Mt. PARNASSUS on the cover. We both commented on its beauty and he said, "We lose lots of menus because of that illustration and, I hope, also the good food."

Joanne said, "It's a tremendous advertising piece; the name, the mountain and the exceptional food. I think I'll steal one. I'm getting excited. I haven't stolen anything since the third grade when I lifted a boy's pair of gloves when it started to snow."

"Don't worry, Miss Joanne. I'll steal it for you. You can visit me in jail but in the meantime, ladies, I would like to address our specials for the evening.

"Yes, please, go ahead!"

"We have two; BOEUF en BROCHETTE. Marinated and grilled tenderloin cubes with a rich tomato sauce, and DAURAUOE PROVENCALE, sautéed red snapper with tomatoes and peppers! I'll return at your notice to take your order; Oh, one more thing. Our French onion soup is always the early evening specialty! More wine Miss Joanne?

"Yes, Franz, please. Thank you!"

After Franz literally brought their mouths to a waterfall of impeded juices, Joanne asked Liz, "How did he know my name?"

"Easy! When I ordered the wine I told the maitre d' my name and mentioned I would be with my friend Joanne who had the face of an angel."

"Yeah! Angel of Mercy is a better description!"

"Joanne I wasn't going to say anything but I felt—or had a feeling when we first met tonight you were extremely taut, you know, tense, withdrawn. I perceived a bogus smile as if, as if—oh, what can I say—I know! As if you were hiding a deleterious contusion to the inside of your mouth or worse a broken tooth or something. What's wrong?"

"What's wrong? I think everything is wrong and I'm going crazy because maybe it's me that's mistaken or acting improperly."

"Look, Honey," Liz said. "Let's start at the beginning. What do you consider wrong? How long have you had this feeling? And, oh! just a second! Franz is here to take our order."

"And what have you ladies decided," Franz asked with a smile as he lifter his notepad.

"Hmmm! He's left handed," I said to myself.

"Miss Joanne you'll be first. Does the onion soup sound luscious to you?"

"Right you are, Franz. My favorite! I think I'll skip the salad though, and fully enjoy the grilled tenderloin cubes. Sounds wonderful!"

"And you Miss Liz? Are you going to join Miss Joanne in the soup tasting contest," he asked with a smile.

"Yes, Lefty, I am," Liz said with a grin. But my entrée will be the sautéed red snapper; tomatoes and peppers are my favorite.

"So you caught that left hand," Franz said with a smirk. "Very observant! And I have observed you will need another wine? Am I right and may I serve the ladies?"

"Thanks, Franz. And yes, please do."

When Franz left the table Joanne said, "Liz you are right. I feel like hell. I was so happy with my time and life with 'Joe Palooka', as you say, the day we met until we were married. Even after we were married we were enraptured with our lives; full of great sex and the thought of being together, but then things started to change; it was the Oakmont Country Club, the Pittsburgh Athletic Club, the Duquesne Club, golf, meetings, out of town trips, late, cold dinners, and 'too tired' to make love too many times. I am positive he has not met someone else and I am aware of the pressures of his important position at Westinghouse but God sake, it leaves little time for me. And on top of that—"

Franz appeared and said to the ladies, "Ah! the soup of the day to two lovely women. You will find it delicious—and hot! So sip and enjoy!"

Liz and Joanne lifted their glasses of wine and touched them with a "Cheers" and then Joanne said, "Do you know what fighter pilots say when they toast one another?"

"No, I haven't the slightest idea," Liz said.

"Cheers ASS!" Joanne said just loud enough to bring smiles to a couple of men sitting at the next table.

"Where the heck did you hear that?"

"Oh! At a fighter pilot reunion one afternoon at the athletic club. I was dining with some friends of the family. One of them tried to pick me up. I was flattered but I showed him my ring."

While enjoying their soup Liz said something about Joanne being interrupted in her chain of thought when Franz showed up. "You started to say something about 'on top of that—'"

"Oh! Yes, the parties we are invited to are vapid, inane, flavorless BS sessions. Everybody telling stories of how they did this and that for charity and all the wheels they know and met. A gathering of rich blowhard old ladies seeking to get their names in the paper! That gives them reason so they can tell everyone at the next vapid, inane party. It drives me crazy. I have to be 'with your loving mate' as some lady with the face of a recently plowed cabbage patch told me. I know it's rude, Liz, but I can't help it; I am so unhappy." Tears watered Joanne's beautiful eyes. "I'm just so full of melancholy," she said as she wiped her eyes and dabbed the tears from her cheeks.

Liz stared at Joanne frozen; didn't say a word. Her mental facilities bolted; her intellectuality latched but in a struggle to say something. Nothing came! Yes, Liz was self-composed; she kept her poise; but she was totally lost for words. Her elegant, angelic Powers' model friend was at a low point in her young ornate, luxurious life and Liz's mind was at stage zero.

Thank God! Franz appeared seemingly out of nowhere to remove the soup dishes and said, "Are you two ladies ready for your early evening delight?" He answered his own question as he placed our two selections in front of us. The presentations were beautiful! Absolutely mouth watering! He also added more wine to our glasses.

Franz appearance allowed Liz to put her thoughts together. "Joanne," she said, "I am in a daze; what you have told me is ah—well, a bombshell. I remember at the wedding celebration you showered us all with your happiness so what you have said is puzzling and to be honest, baffling. You have evidently given the whole passage some thought but even as your good friend I have zero experience in this kind of thing. I was heartbroken when Jack left me but at least all cards were on the table and time has allowed me to recover some. All I can think of to say is give things some time and don't do anything rash."

"Funny you should say that, Liz. I do have sort of a wise and trustworthy teacher; met her at the Duquesne Club. She reminds me of Maggie Brown. You know, *The Unsinkable Molly Brown,* an American socialite and philanthropist who became famous as one of the survivors of the sinking of the **Titanic**. Believe it or not she started talking to me in the woman's lounge and actually asked me, "Why is a beautiful young lady like you carry such a heavy heart? Can you believe that? How did she know?"

"She knew because she probably has daughters that have had their heart broken and maybe a marriage that broke hers too. You are lucky. Spend time with her and listen! I know one thing she probably told you. Get involved in some charity that is low key; no newspaper stories or pictures. Get your husband Tim involved only if it's money and tell him how you spent it and what good it's doing. Screw those other ladies and their ostentatious gabble."

"Liz you are right; she did tell me to get involved in something on my own. She also said go skiing in the winter and join a slow pitch softball league in the spring. Quit feeling sorry for yourself and live your own life. Be kind and true to your husband, He's a wonderful man; known him for years. You married into one of the wealthiest families in the East. And anytime he wants to make love to you wear his ass out! Honest, that's exactly what she said. 'Wear his ass out!'"

"I am going to try that out one day myself! Well, let's finish dinner and get your ass on the way home," Liz said with a smile; the first she had since they sat down to dinner. Liz also told Joanne that Molly Brown and her husband separated in 1909, but stayed connected and cared for each other. JJ, her husband, was cheating on her but that didn't stop her from carrying on. "Did you know she headed the **Titanic** Survivors' Committee, she asked Joanne." Without waiting for an answer she said, "It was a group of wealthy survivors which raised funds to help those less fortunate among surviving passengers and crew."

Liz nodded to Franz to please bring hot coffee and two surprises for Miss Joanne and me. "The surprise dessert is on me with my love and good fortune to you," my great friend. "And don't worry. Tim is true! In fact, think TITTY; that's easy! We each have two. Tim Is True To You! Things will work out OK."

The dessert was CREMEUX a'l'ANANAS, a pineapple cream with rum. It was the sweet of sweets. Everyone went home with a sweet smile too!

ARNIE AND LIZ
ANOTHER CONTEST!!
TO THE VICTOR, ANOTHER HAMBURGER??

By: Charles Grube
Sports' Editor

Liz had called Jim Flynn and scheduled two lessons for an early Saturday afternoon and Sunday morning "about eleven." She inquired as to whether or not Arnie had been around and she received a "Roger," on that and he asked about her and he would inquire about an 8AM starting time with his normal foursome. Liz said, Thanks, Mr. Flynn," and hung up.

A busy week was in store for Liz; two days and a night in school, a POWERS session—new makeup and jewelry which will last as least four hours on Wednesday and then, on Friday, an encompassing all day round trip by company plane to Harrisburg, Pennsylvania for a sitting for the newly employed Ralph William Williams as the Breck artist. Liz had learned that when Edward J. Breck, the son of Dr. John Breck, Sr, the founder of Breck Shampoo, assumed management of the company he hired commercial artist Charles Gates Sheldon to draw women for their advertisements. Sheldon's early portraits for Breck were done in pastels, with a soft focus and haloes of light and color surrounding them. He created romantic images of feminine beauty. He preferred to draw "real women" as opposed to professional models.

In 1957 Williams succeeded Sheldon as the Breck artist. Unlike Sheldon, he often used professional women. Breck ads ran regularly in Woman's magazines and Breck girls were identified through the company's sponsorship of America's Junior Miss contests.

Today Liz was to have her portrait painted by Williams and attend a Junior Miss contest. Her portrait turned out to be strikingly beautiful and her short unprepared speech to the teenagers and their mothers was received by a warm enthusiastic applause.

The plane became airborne just at the time Liz fell into a deep exhaustive sleep. She had had a superb time and everyone surrounded her with pleasantness. But when you think about it, Liz was the kind of lady that consistently attracted attention through her beauty and well developed figure but she always acted with extreme prudence, heedful of potential circumstances if she acted with snobbishness or with an unduly high opinion of herself. She seemed to exactly know her place in all occasions; she was respected and loved by all who met her.

The manager of flight operations met the plane. Arrangements were made to have the co-pilot drive Liz home in her car, and a cab would take him back to his hotel near the airport.

Liz awakened at nine, was in the kitchen on time to have juice, scrambled eggs and conversation about her trip while she sipped coffee with her mother. And after a quick kiss on the cheek and a "Love you Mom", she was out the door on the way to Chartiers.

Jim Flynn was ready 11:45; Liz noted that Mr. Flynn never asked her any questions other than about her health, her family and her school. He never asked anything about her modeling for POWERS or winning the Breck's contest. Jack Flynn was his brother; enough said!

Jim grabbed her bags and put them in their proper position in the back of the cart. He headed toward the practice green but stopped about 35 or 40 yards away. After he stopped he turned and looked at Liz and said, "You may never hope to be a female Arnold Palmer or a winner like Babe Didrikson Zaharias, or Betsy Rawls, or Patty Berg because you are not planning on being a professional golfer. But I watch you in practice and your visage tells me you have that determination to win even if it's against Arnie in a putting contest. Yes, I heard all about it! But any advice I can give that might knock a precious shot or two off your score is worth listening to. From swing technique and the long game, to putting, chipping and getting out of trouble, these are the tips that work for the best players in the world and, with a bit of practice, will work for you two. Are you with me?"

"Yes, Mr. Flynn, I am. So you heard about the contest, huh?" As Jim was shaking his head Liz said, "Well he's too good. I needed to knock him down a bit and besides, the hamburger tasted a lot better when he had to pay."

"Someday Miss McGovern, I'll play you for a half a ham sandwich.'

"With lettuce and tomatoes and pickle and mustard and mayonnaise on rye?" Liz asked.

"Sounds cheaper for me if I just bought you a vegetable garden," Jim said as he stepped out of the cart. "Come on, follow me. For an hour or so, we're going to work on "the short pitch" and the "pitch and run.""

And so they did! Jim talked through the short pitch swing, demonstrated it a few times and turned the iron over to Liz. "Most amateurs get into a complete mess, technique-wise," he said, "when they're faced with a shot that is neither a chip nor a full pitch. It's somewhere in between the two, and frankly, that's pretty hard to deal with for a lot of golfers. The secret lies not in any complicated, fancy swing theories, but in simple no-nonsense fundamentals applied with authority. With a lot of practice, anyone can do that. So, let's review: 1. Good posture; remember your feet at a slightly open stance and open clubface. They're very important for this kind of shot. 2. One statement sums this up. Turn your body as you swing your hands and arms back. And don't forget, add a little wrist hinge for good measure. Remember, I demonstrated that! 3. The left arm leads the club into the hitting area, and the angles established in the wrists are maintained to ensure a crisp downward blow. 4. Keep your nerve and your rhythm. Accelerate the club head smoothly down and through impact. Let the club create loft and don't flick at the ball. 5. As in the backswing, the follow-through reflects the importance of turning the body as you swing the hands and arms through.

OK! Let's aim for the center of the green and don't make any bets.""

Liz smiled; she started her practice in earnest. Shot, after shot, after shot, with the only break being Jim's voice expressing a few mistakes to be corrected plus words of encouragement. The green, and approaches to the green were covered with balls.

After 40 minutes or so Jim said, "OK, stop and follow me. He took her wedge and they walked back to the cart where Jim reached into a container behind the seat and brought out two cokes dripping with ice water and said, "Sorry, Miss McGovern no half a ham but an ice cold refresher. You worked hard; you deserve it!"

"OH! Terrific! Thank you! The pause that refreshes! I wonder how many they bottle a day? Probably millions!"

"Well, Miss McGovern I don't know but three facts. Coca Cola is the world's most recognized trademark; recognized by 94% of the population. The company supplied the armed forces of WWII with 5 billion bottles. In 1917 they were selling 3 million per day and in 1926 it was six million. I just memorized 3, 5, and 6 only the 5 was billion. So today it could be 40 to 50 million. Who knows? The only thing I know is we have to move on with our lesson. Just throw the empty bottle in the container."

Jim and Liz took a position he thought was best suited for the "low pitch and run." He said to Liz, "In general if the green is fairly flat then the safest shot to play is the running shot. Select a club with less loft, such as a 7-or8-iron, and play the ball a little further back in your stance. I always use a pretty narrow stance as it feels more comfortable. I push my hands a little bit ahead, but keep the club head square. I also grip a little further down for added control. I always aim to pitch the ball the same distance. I hit the ball further I simple take a less lofted club.

Now I'll demonstrate and we will go through the same practice as we did on the 'short pitch.' On the **Set-up** open the stance slightly. Grip down a little for control. The ball position is a little further back, towards your back foot. **Backswing**: Swing slowly with less wrist break, no further than waist high. The swing path should be wider and flatter than normal."

Jim then demonstrated the swing several times showing Liz the proper swing. He then continued with the follow thru telling Liz to keep her left wrist firm through the impact and the follow through should mirror the backswing. He turned the club over to Liz and told her to hit twenty balls but he wanted to see a practice swing before each shot. It worked! Liz hit the last six balls without a remark from Jim.

As they headed back to the pro shop Liz saw Arnie approaching from the left of them on an intersecting cart path. Her heart stated to pump a little faster as body started to slowly stir to activity. She said, "Look, Jim, Arnie is arriving. I must thank you for arranging his foursome's starting time so we could meet after my lessons."

"My pleasure, Miss McGovern; the starter owed me a favor and I didn't want you waiting around too long. Besides, I didn't want you to challenge me to a putting game," Jim said with a grin.

When the carts were parked and Liz and Arnie gave each other a short tender kiss, Arnie asked Jim if he could buy him a drink at the club house.

"Not declined but deferred," Jim said. "Besides, if you two are going after another hamburger with pickle and a vegetable garden between the buns, you better freshen up and get out of here in a hurry before Miss McGovern gets hungry." They all had a laugh.

"Come on, lovely lady, get in your car and follow me," Arnie said. "I'll buy you that 'burger."

"Oh no! You aren't getting off that easy. Gee! It's almost 5:15 and I haven't eaten since breakfast.'

"OK! Then I'll but you a *PITTSBURGH PIRATE* hot dog too. I'm parked two cars down from yours so let's go."

"OH Boy!" Liz said with a smile. "Can I get it with plenty of ketchup and mustard and onions and relish?"

"It's OK by me but you buy the ALKA *SELTZER*. Now get in the car!"

THE IMPERIUM OR OMNIPOTENCE OF SEXUAL NYMPHOLEPSY

By: **Charles Grube**
Sports' Editor

Liz followed Arnie down the hill from Chartiers to the stop sign where the driver, when stopped, had one of three choices. Straight ahead over the Thornburg Bridge to Crafton; right to the town of Thornburg, or left toward Moon Run! Arnie made a left and had gone about two miles when he signaled with his arm that he intended to make a left into what turned out to be "Buzz" Loggerman's Night Club and Restaurant.

"Buzz" had purchased the nightclub several years earlier but also built a beautiful eight room, private motel with first class appointments meant primarily for him and guests to "sleep it off" since he was very rigid about his rule in not allowing anyone to leave his club or restaurant while under the influence. Word was that he had trained his bartenders and waitresses to judge when it was time for his patrons to stop drinking in exchange for a hot cup of coffee or if the combination of a few libations and lack of sleep was deemed to lead to a potential accident. No one would argue with "Buzz." At 6'3" and 265 pounds, no one desired to do so.

Arnie walked over to Liz's car, opened her door to help her out, closed the door behind them, took Liz's hand, gave her a peck on her cheek, and they strolled happily into the first class house of piquancy. When one walked in, the patronage was surrounded with a quality delightful to senses of the mind.

The waitress, Anne Louise greeted Arnie with a smile and led him and Liz to a table for two. Arnie assisted Liz with her seating and as he walked around the table Anne Louise removed the "RESERVED" sign and then asked Arnie what the lady and he would care to drink. Arnie politely introduced the two ladies and ordered two blended margaritas with light salt. "And Ann Louise," he said, "Do you have your famous veal chops broiled with sage, a little salt and pepper, then mix the juices with a touch of butter, flour, garlic and red wine then pour the sauce on top just before it's served?'

"Gee, Mr. Arnie, Mr. Loggerman should hire you as an assistant chef or head of public relations! You remember that from the last time."

"I remember every 'last time' when then food is excellent and the service peerless."

As he sat down he told Liz that he met "Buzz" during the earliest part of his trip to the Pittsburgh territory and always stopped in when he had the chance. "The food is matchless compared to other restaurant/night club places I have visited," Arnie said, "and I wanted you to say after dinner than it was better than your hamburger without all the stuff that you put on top. See how I think of you!"

"I think of you too but it isn't about hamburgers," Liz said with a smile. You tell me about your trip and your golf game today and then I'll tell you about my trip to Harrisburg and other flurry that kept me busy; but not enough that I didn't think of you often.

The club was not crowded at the time of evening Liz and Arnie sat down to visit and enjoy each others' company and dinner. There were a few patrons, three men and a couple of well dressed ladies, probably secretaries, who seemed to be enjoying themselves. There was another couple at a table near the dance floor.

Liz told Arnie all about her day in Harrisburg and the Williams' painting plus her short speech she gave to Junior Miss contestants. Also, she related how nice she was treated by the company's co-pilot because of her sheer exhaustion. "But today I feel great," Liz said, "I had an exceptionally beneficial golf lesson and now I'm here with you." She reached over and gave his left hand a squeeze—since the right hand was holding a fork full of a delicious house salad made of field greens, tomatoes, feta cheese, pine nuts, and lemon oregano vinaigrette dressing.

"Now tell me about your trip," Liz said as she buttered a soft roll and started eating her own salad.

"Well, Honey, nothing exciting except the white clouds and blue skies as I visited our distributors as far west as Dayton then worked my way back through Wheeling, Steubenville, and Bethany. You should be jealous because Wheeling and Steubenville houses those places of ill repute and gambling."

"You mean hookers"?

"Yes, that's what I said. Now don't get excited because I never touch *any* woman who is a stranger to me and besides, the company isn't paying me to have the police call the home office some night and tell management they found me knocked out in an alley somewhere. It's too dangerous! I think I told you I do entertain but it is always with wives; never one-on-one with a buyer."

"Why is that?" Liz asked just as Anne Louise served the dinner of veal chop, creamed spinach, and angel hair pasta with a marinara sauce. The wine steward appeared with a rich Napa Valley Merlot.

"Because, Liz, let's say I invite a buyer out for dinner and he agrees but 'wanted to start early' so he could be home with the family before the kids go to bed. Sounds great until the wife calls you in your hotel room at 11:00 o'clock and asks where her husband is. Now you have to tell a lie and say something to the effect that he met a couple of other salesmen and they invited him to an after dinner drink."

"Well!"

"Well! Miss Beautiful hair, don't you see! He used me as an excuse for and early dinner so after he could go shack up with his secretary."

"Oh! That's crazy. Men don't do that!"

"My Darling! My beautiful naïve, innocent, except in putting contests, partner in crime. It happens all the time. Please pass the wine and I'll pour for both of us."

"Well!" Liz said, "it's hard for me to believe but—but why did you call me your partner in crime?"

"Take a big sip of your wine and I'll tell you."

"OK! A big sip passed my lip and I'm hip; so speak to me."

"Liz," Arnie said in a very serious inflection. "I have not breathed three times in the past two and a half weeks without thinking of the last time we held each other with a closeness that uplifted my desire for you to the point where I wanted to tear your clothes off and smother you with my wet kisses. But I drew back because—well, because I was afraid you would think I was trying to rape you when all I wanted to do was treat you with tenderness and affection."

Liz looked at Arnie for a full minute or so. She was fighting to quell her excitement as her mind rushed to that minute in the front seat of her car when she was in the middle of serious, utterly passionate, inflamed French kisses that sprinkled her whole body with flames of sexual desire. She needed time to think! To say something mature and sensible! She said, "Honey, give me a little more wine, please."

Arnie obliged! She took a sip to wet her dry mouth and then said, "Arnie, my beautiful friend, you *were* very tender; and I shared in your tenderness. I was so "turned on" by your warm kisses that I wish you *would* have raped me. I thought you pulled back because you thought the kisses frightened me. They did not! I have never felt so warm and cozy in my life and I actually wanted more."

"I understand. I am going to tell you something. I didn't exactly know how you would react but I wanted to do it again so this time I talked to "Buzz" and all we have to do is walk out of here and go directly to room 3 in his motel. It has a king size bed and he said, 'If you are going to hold a lovely lady like Liz for a few affectionate kisses, at least go first class. Just leave when you are ready; don't worry about the bill. I'll be seeing you again.'"

"I told him, 'Thanks' but my girl is so beautiful I want to kiss her mouth and lips and breasts and—well, whatever!"

"So!" Liz said. "Why are we sitting here?"

Liz looked at him. She knew she was ready. She reached over and took his hand and said, "I am available, my love, and I'm prepared!"

About the time Liz and Arnie started to enjoy their delicious veal chop, Charlie Grube was kissing his true love, Gloria, goodbye at the airport. Gloria was on a TWA flight to Chicago to attend a conference on "Executive Secretaries" and she wanted to catch the 5:00PM non-stop to arrive early enough to have a light supper and get a good night's sleep. She told Charlie to behave and she would see him at 7:00PM on Friday night. "But be sure you call TWA and make sure my flight is on schedule."

"Yes, dear! Call me when you arrive. I'm going to grab a bite to eat on the way home at "Buzz" Loggerman's. You know it well. We have often eaten there."

"Yes! I know! Have a nice evening. I gotta' run! They're calling my flight."

Charlie turned into the parking lot with the thought of a good steak on his mind. He pulled into a parking slot near the front and stopped. Before he had a chance to put out his headlights he was, for a second or so, lost in amazement as he saw Liz walking out the front door arm in arm with a man.

He studied them both and was about to get out of the car and wave to Liz but he stopped dead! He fell into a deep meditative state; his eyes zeroed in on her companion. "Who is that guy?" he said to himself. "I've met him! I never forget a face!" His body had stiffened as he continued to follow Liz's friend. They were arm in arm around each others waist, laughing, having a good time. The guy, in one swift movement, dropped his arm from around Liz's waist and patted her on the left cheek of her ass. Liz seemed to snuggle closer but Charlie soon had only an "angle off" view of their bodies until they disappeared into the front entrance of the motel. He continued to sit straight; thinking—thinking! "Where? Where? With Gloria! At work? Did I pass him while running at the track?" He kept talking to himself!

Charlie's spell was broken as he got out of the car and closed the door. But just as he put the key in the lock to secure the car he froze. "I know that guy," he said to himself. "I met him not too long ago! He's the priest I met when I was having a short lunch in downtown Pittsburgh. Yeah, Father Josephson introduced me! It's the priest on a sabbatical from Rome. His name was Arnie—Arnie Brownell. That's it! Father Arnold Brownell! WOW! He was one of the Arnies I was talking about.

Holy Moley! Holy Good God! He banged the bottom of his hand against his forehead as he started toward the front door of the restaurant as told himself something he could not believe. Liz! Liz for God sake! Liz is shacking up with a priest!"

Time passed; a relatively short time! At the time Charlie had a sip of his first drink to relieve his tension, the lights in room 3 were dimmed. Liz and Arnie had walked out of the bathroom at two short intervals. Completely naked, they fell into each others arms and history commenced to repeat itself with deep, warm, titillation in the form of French kisses. They were followed by and hour or so of complete scrutinization of each other body with warm lips and wet tongue.

Both were in a heavenly state—on earth.

EIGHTEEN MONTHS LATER
IF I REMEMBER TIMES AND DATES
CORRECTLY

By: **Charles Grube**
Sports' Editor

The act of concentrating on a given subject, or two, is conversely, the act of temporarily forgetting everything else. This is one reason why, in most cases, highly successful people seem to be possessed of great calm and impressive reserves of energy. Capable of intense concentration on basic questions, they are not worn down by superficial difficulties, distracting side issues or the enervating friction of a divided mind. Professionally hard at work, they are psychologically on vacation; this is one case where conventional achievement is completely in accord with mental and physical health.*

I had the feeling I was splitting my learning from the historical side, *MEDITATIONS*, by Marcus Aurelius and from the practical side Latshaws, but after reading about what I said above, I knew I had to make some changes in my professional whirlwind, particularly since the day I was told I was to pursue my education.

I took the "time" to think through the past eighteen months; lost contact with a few, kept up with others. Time haunts our experience like some invisible spirit of things, some irretrievable truth. And when we try to manage our own time, like I did, setting new goals, cleaning and rearranging the little houses of our days, time *gently* mocks us—not so much because we lack wit or will as because time operates on a deeper psychological level than conscious effort can normally reach.**

Well, I think I grabbed time on some level and used it properly because I am about to receive my MBA, I know Jack Flynn has completed his college preparatory education at Notre Dame and is now with the monks at Holy Trinity Abbey. "Liz" McGovern is about ready to graduate, or maybe she has graduated from Chatam College and she has been named the winner in the *MISS BRECK* contest. I do not know how her golf game is progressing but I will find out soon enough because my wife Gloria and I have a twelve month anniversary dinner planned with "Liz" and her new found love of a year or so. Yes, I finally used my head and realized what a beautiful gem I had in Gloria and asked her to be my wife. I ended up marrying my best friend; we are extremely happy. We had a short but eloquent honeymoon that only a poet could describe.

As I said above, I am about ready to graduate with my Masters from Pitt and I have been given permission by the paper to continue my column but I must look hard until I find a replacement. I have someone in mind now but I must check with a few people to make sure his move is done in a professional manner. I also want to say that if any news of Jack Flynn in the way of vocal or written communication is given to me I still intend to pass it along to the fans. It may not be under the title of "Sports' Editor" but I don't think it will make any difference.

It will be good to get back talking to all of you once again.

Talk to you later!

A LETTER FROM JOANNE

By: **Charles Grube**
Sports' Editor

Liz was a little puzzled as she gazed at the post office stamp, and date on the envelope. It read: Novem (or something like that—it was smeared) **Champion, Pa.** "I don't know anyone from Champion", she said to herself as she headed toward the kitchen. "In fact, I have never even heard of Champion, Pa. Hope I didn't get on someone's damn mailing list. Powers or Breck wouldn't be the reason—or would it"?"

Liz slid a sharp paring knife under the smaller end of back flap of the envelope and pulled. She opened the neatly folded 8x1/2 sheet inside and saw two things at once; it was a letter from her great friend Joanne and it was written on *SEVEN SPRINGS SKI RESORT, Champion, Pennsylvania* stationery.

The letter *was as* follows:

Dearest of Friends, Liz,

I know you were probably surprised when you saw Seven Springs writing paper. Well Liz, I surprised myself after our beautiful evening together. I decided to stop being such a baby by complaining and just do something. So I took my lady friend's advice from the club. You remember me telling you about her and the **Titanic.** Well, here I am—taking ski lessons, hitting the slopes in the afternoon, and believe it or not, stopping by the local hangout with the ski instructors and having my favorite vodka martini, straight up, ice cold with an olive and an onion. But just one; honest!

Seven Springs is Pennsylvania's largest ski resort. It is located in the beautiful Laurel Mountains and just a hop, skip, and a jump away—1 hour south and east from home. It's located off of exits 9 or 10 of the Pennsylvania Turnpike. So I just jumped in my new station wagon with snow tires and here I am. Tim was actually very sweet. He said, "Go, Darling, and have a good time, I am sorry I have been so tied up in business. Also, Dad brought me in to our family business by giving me a Board seat, so please understand." Gee! Liz, we even made mad love the night before I left. But I found it too—oh! Mechanical!

This mega-resort offers me much more than skiing. It has a large base lodge hotel, shopping gallery, good restaurants, bars, indoor pool, rental rooms in the large hotel, condos, and cabins. At first I thought I could drive back and forth but I was concerned about driving the mountain roads at night so I rent a beautiful, well appointed cabin each time for two or three days depending on Tim's schedule. I don't want to try to fool you, Liz. I still feel alone but I'm not lonely. Tonight three instructors and their girl friends (ski instructors also) asked me to go to dinner with them.

I plan to tell them about my wonderful friend in Pittsburgh and *we* will all drink a toast to you. I'll yell out, "Cheers Ass!"

Guess what! Do you remember Pete Niepp—friend of Dave Latshaw? Anyhow I saw him in lift line and we recognized each other. He was a senior about to go in the Navy and we were freshman. He has been ordained a Jesuit (I think) priest and *is* a principal at a boys' school in Harrisburg. He takes two weeks off in the winter to ski and two weeks in the summer to play golf. He told me he knows Chuck Grube—met him in Korea where Chuck was a fighter pilot. In fact, they played golf at Chartiers in August, I think it was.

Well, Father Anton Niepp and I hit the slopes for a couple of runs, had a beer in the hotel bar, shook hands and bid each other a fond farewell. Nice man!

I know you have been busy; finishing school, Powers and Breck. I am so happy for you. I am about to wash my face, try to look pretty and maybe I'll yell "Cheers Ass' with my instructor friends a couple of times tonight. I love that expression! Let's keep in touch. Maybe you could drive up with me for a day or two. I love you.

Fondly,
Signed Joanne

While reading he letter from Joanne, Liz managed to grab a glass, open the refrigerator door, and reach for the bottle of cold orange juice. She sat down at the kitchen table and poured herself a glass. While taking a sip now and then she reflected on every word Joanne had to say. "I am alone but not lonely." I am going to yell out "Cheers *Ass!*" A dry martini! We made "Mad passionate love." "Maybe you could drive up with me."

"I don't know," Liz said to herself as she took savored her drink. "That doesn't sound like the Joanne I know. She seems to be communicating by banging out Morse Code rather than face the everyday with the strings and music of a violin. I know! I know! She has gotten away from the dread of a lonely home and just wanted to be around people. But there's something somber among those words of hers but don't know—I don't know!"

No, Liz didn't know but her foreboding, or premonition, *was* accurate. They would be together, but under circumstances so far removed from even the GRIM REAPER'S vista that—what is the soliloguy; "Truth *is* Stranger Than Fiction!"

A TELEPHONE CALL FROM DAHLIA

By: Charles Grube
Sports' Editor

RINGGGG! RINGGG! RIN!

"Good morning, McGovern residence! May I help you? Yes, just a moment, please.

"Telephone, Honey," her mother called. "Do you want to take it upstairs or in the living room."

Liz *was* sitting in her favorite reclining chair in the den reading some of her favorite authors from a series of short stories. "I'll take it up here, Mom," she called out! With that, Liz left the comfort of her chair, walked over to her Dad's desk, picked up the phone and said, "Hello, this is Liz McGovern. May I help you?"

"Gee! Such formality!" the voice on the other end of the line said. "Liz, Honey, this is Dahlia. Just wanted to call to thank you for your sweet card you wrote me about our visit and I am also wondering if you will be taking your normal Christmas visit to your grandparents?"

"Dahlia! What a surprise!" Liz said in an excited tone. "How are you? What a pleasure to hear your voice. And yes, we are traveling to meet our grand folks but I don't know the date as yet. Probably around the 22nd! We'll be getting together again, won't we?"

"Of course! That's the reason I called. Well, one of the reasons. Same hospitality applies. My roommates will be gone for Christmas vacation and we'll celebrate the season to be jolly. Now tell me—how have you been and how is Mr. Thrill by the Minute?"

Liz smiled at the thought of Arnie. "He's fine," Liz said as she looked around to see if anyone had entered the den. "We did it," she whispered to

Dahlia. In fact we've done it a number of times and it's more thrilling for me as we get to know more of each other, if you know what I mean. It may be because he travels so much but when he returns it's—well—it's wonderful. And Dahlia, about our discussion on sin I'm too passionate and into other sensual areas to be troubled. Let's be honest, I just didn't stop him at my breasts; I guess I am missing your moral strength."

Dahlia was quiet for a few seconds; Liz could hear her breathing but didn't say a word. Dahlia then said, "Honey, I am happy because you are. You might as well enjoy it when you can. I mean, even newly weds get worn out after a period of time. I may have said this before but you can on only count so many flowers on the ceiling—or wall, or floor, or however you do it. And one just hopes lovers have more to offer one another after the bright lights fade to dusk. Anyhow, his absence makes your heart grow fonder, both alone together, no kids, no time strain, nothing but laugh and giggle and make love. I'm jealous just talking about it."

Liz, still in a "whisper mode" said, "I'm surprised at your open mind, Dahlia. You're so intelligent and broad-minded. Seems your mind is like an open parachute; always ready to save someone from falling into a mental abyss. You are my closest friend and I love you for always being there for me. I'm looking forward to Christmas vacation. Anyhow, changing the subject, I had dinner with Joanne Bowers Sterling a couple of months ago and then received a letter from her. She was skiing at a resort named Seven Springs about an hour from Pittsburgh. I'll tell you all about our dinner when I see you and the skiing seems to be bringing joy into her life since her husband Tim also travels. What is it with these guys?"

"Oh, I think they all like to get away from things once in awhile."

"And they always come home with a joke," Liz said. Arnie told me one last time. Seems a guy walked into a male clothing store and the salesperson said, "What is your pleasure, Sir?"

He answered, "My pleasure is making love, but I came in for a tie."

They both had a hearty laugh and said they would see each other soon and hung up.

Liz walked slowly back to her chair saying to herself, "I feel sorry for Dahlia. Her parents had to go to North Dakota to take care of their ailing Mother but she died soon after and her father inherited a 200 acre farm and decided to stay and work it. I think they do well in corn and sunflowers. Dahlia doesn't get the chance to see her parents too often but she remains positive about life and seems to always have the time to assist others."

GOLF'S LEGENDS LOOK BACK
—AND AHEAD!

Doc Giffin
Sports' Editor
and C. Grube

I, Charlie Grube, can't take credit for the following editorial; Doc Giffin our new sports editor did most of the work. I told all of you in an earlier column about Doc, his evolution to success and how pleased the *PITTSBURGH POST TELEGRAPH* is in having a real pro. Although I have a new assignment, I did, however, want it as part of my **SOMETHING TO THINK ABOUT** columns because it is the antithesis of the article I wrote about my perception of how baseball, football, hockey, etc., is now being played. Read it carefully. It strikes at the heart of what I have said! Besides, you fans of the paper and golf: I think we should take a few minutes away from the Abbeys and monks and relax and smile with these great men as they conquer their profession with DIGNITY.

Charlie Grube

They are among the greatest players ever to grace the game of golf, set apart as much by their combination of sublime talent, competitive zeal and unparalleled sportsmanship as by their remarkable records.

In some cases, these members of the World Golf Hall of Fame are winding down their playing careers, moving on to different challenges. In others, they are simply switching gears, making the move from the PGA Tour to the Senior Tour, where they will find new courses and old friends.

In one very special case, it is a time to look at the game from the unique perspective of its oldest and, perhaps, wisest champion.

For Jack Nicklaus, the paradigm of all that is good and great about the game, his emotional good-byes were mutual love affairs played out over three of his favorite places: Augusta National, Pebble Beach and, of course, his beloved Old Course at St. Andrews.

It is said that a man can truly be called great if he doesn't remind you of anyone who went before or after him, and by that or any other measure, Nicklaus is a great man. For all his success, however, it is likely that history will judge Nicklaus by his generous and instinctive sportsmanship, which he inherited, in a very real sense, from Bobby Jones. As Gary Player often observed, "Jack is a great winner and an even better loser."

"The game we play is a game and nothing more," Nicklaus says. "It's a wonderful game and a game that I love, and it's a game that needs to be played in that spirit. I feel very strongly about that, whether it's The Presidents Cup, the Ryder Cup, the U.S. Open or week end club play."

He adds, "I think that the vast majority of players today have a sense of what is the right thing to do. If they don't, maybe they need to learn that. As I leave the game, hopefully if the example that I've set is followed, and if it helps one young guy change what he's doing, then I'm successful. This would be a pretty lousy game if we had guys coming out and pounding their chests after they made a putt. I wouldn't have much use for that game."

It speaks volumes for Nicklaus that when asked about his legacy, his answer has precious little to do with his playing career.

"I'm not really concerned about what my legacy is in relation to the game of golf," he says. "I'm more concerned with what my legacy is with my family, my kids, and grandkids. That's by far more important to me. If I've done it properly out here and I can hold my head up to my kids and grandkids, that's the most important thing to me."

What Legends Are Made of: Palmer's Purism to Player's Passion

It is futile to try to think of Nicklaus without thinking about Arnold Palmer, one of the game's most beloved figures and the dominant player when Nicklaus joined the PGA Tour. When Nicklaus beat Palmer in a playoff in the U.S. Open at Oakmont, it marked the beginning of a new era, but it did nothing to diminish what has been an unrivaled, 50-year affair of the heart between Palmer and golf fans around the world.

Palmer has essentially retired from competitive golf, a decision made all the more difficult because no one ever loved being out among the people more than Palmer. In a career that saw him win 62 TOUR events, including four Masters Tournaments, a U.S. Open and two British Opens (plus the 1954 U.S. Amateur), Palmer absolutely reveled in his sheer love of competition.

"When I was winning tournaments, I didn't even know what first prize was," Palmer notes. "I had to ask when it was over, because I was playing to win and playing because I love it. I hope the guys today play because they love it and not just because of the monetary values."

Palmer's innate modesty was captured in his emotional comments to the press at the U.S. Open at Oakmont, his final appearance in the national championship.

"As I've said so many times, I just loved the whole experience," he said, wiping tears from his eyes. "I haven't won all that much. I have won a few tournaments. I have won some majors, but I suppose the most important thing is the fact that [golf] has been as good as it has been to me."

And as good as he has been for the game.

Nicklaus and Palmer were joined by South Africa's Gary Player as the dominant players of their eras. Throughout his career, Player has been known for his unshakable determination, his belief in himself and his ability to overcome whatever problems have come his way. He is the true believer.

"The longer I live, the more I realize the impact of attitude on life," says Player, whose record includes victories in nine majors on the PGA Tour and nine on the "Old Mans'" Tour. "Attitude is more important than fact. It is more important than the past, than education, than money, than circumstances, than failures, than successes and what people say or do. It is more important than appearances, giftedness or skills. It will make or break a company, a church, a home. The remarkable thing is we have a choice every day regarding the attitude we will embrace for that particular day. We cannot change the past. We cannot change the fact that people will act in a certain way. We cannot change the inevitable. The only thing we can do is play the one string we have, and that is our attitude. "Golf has been so great to me," he continues. "What a difficult, humbling experience this game is. It reminds me of a puzzle without an answer, because today you have it and tomorrow you've lost it."

Talent and Hard Work, the Tenets of Success

Joining Palmer and Player as worthy rivals to Nicklaus' supremacy is a player who grew up in stark poverty in Dallas and epitomized Ben Hogan's dictum that the path to success in golf lay in hard work—and plenty of it!

"The secret is in the dirt," Hogan famously said. "You have to dig it out." And dig it out is just what Lee Trevino did. The result was a remarkable career that saw him win on TOUR 29 times, including victories in two U.S. Opens, two British Opens and two PGA Championships. He also had 29 wins on the Senior Tour that included four victories in majors.

"I don't think I was nearly as accurate as Mr. Hogan, but I thought I could hit more shots than anyone else," Trevino explains. "I learned to play golf in a completely different way and I probably spent more time at it than anyone else. When you have bad fundamentals, you have to spend three times longer than anyone else. No one ever taught me to play. I did it in the back alleys, the back of ranges, did it in fields. It was never on the golf course, but I learned to hit the ball well and work it left to right.

"Now, if you take me out of my environment and put me on a long, demanding course, I am a dead man. I am totally dead. I can't play. But if you put me on a Donald Ross-type course, I'll eat your lunch. I will eat your lunch every day. Those kinds of courses give me options. You can't put me in a position where I don't have an option—by that I mean going into the greens I can hit six different shots. That's why I had a problem with Augusta National. I couldn't hit the ball high enough into those greens and I wasn't going to change my game to go right to left and high for one tournament."

As one of the game's shrewdest and most insightful observers, Trevino has an interesting take on the comparison between Nicklaus and some of the younger players coming to center stage.

"Jack's record is out there for everyone to see," Trevino says. "It's the greatest of all time. I used to love to go head-to-head with Jack because I knew if I was going to beat him I had to play my best. He inspired me to play better. Now to me, up and coming players will need Jack's golf swing and mental capacity to map out a course, and he must have my work ethic, and that combination is real dangerous, believe me."

Another player who combined considerable talent with a Trevino-like work ethic is the greatest player of his generation: Tom Watson, Watson, who won 39 PGA Tour events, including five British Opens, two Masters and the U.S. Open, didn't come to the TOUR with overwhelming amateur credentials on a national stage, but he had something every bit as important: a dream.

"I dreamed I could be a great player and it turned out just the way I dreamed it," says Watson. "I was lucky that I got to compete against Jack, because how you measure up against the best is how you're defined. The game is very healthy today because some of the young man's influence is very similar to Jack's. There will be a man to beat and the players will raise their games to try and beat him. The game's been very lucky because it has been graced by great players who conducted themselves with decorum and played with etiquette. That's not always the top priority in other sports."

Price on the Changing Game

As Nick Price explains, these great players acknowledge the changes the game has seen in recent years, but not all of the changes have been entirely welcome.

Price, the winner of 18 PA Tour events, including two PGA Championships and the British Open, has always been respected for his shot-making skills. But he argues that today's game is far different from the game he learned to play.

"In golf, we've always tried for as much power as we could generate while still having control over the ball," Price explains. "Well now, it's very much a power game. Guys are swinging hard with these new drivers because there's a much greater margin for error. I also think they should take the 60-degree wedge out of the game. It eliminates a certain skill level. Now it's easy to just loft a shot up around the green. I might be looking at it wrong, but I'm a purist. Anyway, the average fan wants to see a power house hit a driver and a 5-iron to a 580-yard hole and that's fine. Besides, I can't complain. I'm 49 and still playing golf and you can't do that in any other sport."

If indeed golf is the sport for all ages, Johnny Miller likes what he sees when he looks at junior golfers today. Miller, who won 25 Tour events, including the U.S. Open and the British Open, is positively bullish on the kids.

"I've got four sons who play, so I've gone to collegiate events, junior events, the whole deal, and these kids are as well-behaved and as together a group of kids as we've ever had in history. I mean, you never even see an incident anymore. You don't see kids taking helicopters to clubs, and if they do, they're out of there. It didn't use to be that way. I remember when it was like [tennis players] Connors, McEnroe and Nastase time.

"One time, watching a tournament with my dad at Harding Park in San Francisco when I was about ten years old, I watched a player bury the club up to the neck. I said to my dad, 'I guess that's what you do when you miss an iron, huh, dad?' My dad said, 'No, you don't need to do that.' It was a great lesson."

The Wisdom of the Ages

In fact, golf remains a game that teaches great lessons. No one knows this better than 94-year-old Byron Nelson, whose 52 Tour victories include two wins in the Masters, the 1939 U.S. Open and two PGA Championships. In 1945, Nelson set two records that will almost certainly stand forever: He won 11 tournaments in a row and 18 in all. But even given all that, his enduring legacy transcends his victories.

"People will always argue who is the greatest player of all time, but there's no question that Byron Nelson is the game's greatest gentleman," says U.S. Open champion Ken Venturi, who polished his game under Nelson's wise tutelage.

Today, Nelson and his wife Peggy live comfortably on the ranch he bought with his winnings. He still follows the game and the years have done nothing to diminish his love for it.

"Golf is the greatest game in the world because the people connected with it are wonderful," Nelson says. "You also run into the nicest people around golf. I remember seeing a friend of mine at a club in Florida. I asked about her son, John. She said he was at the golf course. I said, 'That's wonderful, because whenever children are at a golf course, they're at a good place.'"

I wish to thank all of you fans for welcoming me to your great paper. I will do my best to follow in Mr. Grube's footsteps regarding truth in reporting and integrity in employment.

Doc Giffin

THAT CERTAIN SOMEONE
ERNEST HEMINGWAY

By: Doc Giffin
Sports' Editor

Sports Fans: I thought you might enjoy this column!

Veteran out of the wars before he was twenty: Famous at twenty-five: thirty a master—

Whittled a style for his time from a walnut stick

In a carpenter's loft in a street of that April city!

Thus Poet Archibald Macleish recalls one of the great American writers in his days of early glory, back in the 1920s, when it always seemed to be April in Paris. Last week Ernest Hemingway was a long way from Paris and a long way from April. He was 55, but he looked older. He cruised in a black and green fishing boat off the coast of Cuba, near where the Gulf Stream draws a dark line on the seascape. The grey-white hair escaping from beneath a visored cap was unkempt, and the Caribbean glare induced a sea-squint in his brown, curious eyes set behind steel-rimmed spectacles. Most of his ruddy face was retired behind a clipped, white, patriarchal beard that gave him a bristled, Neptunian look. His leg muscles could have been halves of a split 16 lb. shot, welded there by years of tramping in Michigan, skiing in Switzerland, bullfighting in Spain, walking battlefronts and hiking uncounted miles of African safari. On his lap be held a board, and he bent over it with a pencil in one hand. He was still whittling away at his walnut prose.

Five thousand miles away in Stockholm, a white-starched, tail-coated assembly of the Nobel Foundation was about to bestow literatures' most distinguished accolade on the products of his pencil. This week, "for his powerful, style-forming mastery of the art of modern narration," the Nobel Prize for Literature will be awarded to Ernest Miller Hemingway, originally of Oak Park, Ill. and later of most of the world's grand and adventurous places.

Few would deny that Ernest Hemingway deserves the trumpets of fame. As an artist he broke the bounds of American writing, enriched U.S. literature with the century's hardest-hitting prose, and showed new ways to new generations of writers. He was imitated not only by other writers but by uncounted young men who, in fact or fancy, sought to live as daringly as he. From Paris bistros to Chicago saloons, he is known as a character—not the sallow, writing type with an indoor soul, but a literary he-man. When his plane crashed on safari in Africa last winter and for nearly a day he was believed dead, even people who do not like his books felt a strange, personal sense of loss, and even people who never read novels were delighted when he walked out of the jungle carrying a bunch of bananas and a bottle of gin, and was quoted, possibly even correctly, as saying: "My luck, she is running very good,"

Battered but Unbowed. The hero of the great Hemingway legend was still not sufficiently recovered from his accident to travel to Stockholm for his latest, biggest honor. Furthermore, the first announcement of the Nobel award and the bustle of publicity that followed had thrown Hemingway off his writing pace. He took to his boat in hopes of getting back to work on his new novel about Africa. "I was going real good, better than for a long time, when this came along." He said. "When you're a writer and you've got it, you've got to keep going because when you've lost it you've lost it and God knows when you'll get it back.

Hemingway's African injuries were a ruptured kidney, bad burns, cracked skull, two compressed vertebrae and one vertebra cracked clear through. These were added to scars that cover perhaps half his body surface, including half a dozen head wounds, 237 shrapnel scars in one leg, a shot-off kneecap, wounds in both feet, both arms, both hands and groin, all acquired in the two World Wars. By last eek he was much improved, but his back *was* still bothering him. His daily quota of alcohol, though still substantial enough to keep him in good standing among the all-time public enemies of the W.C.T.U., had fallen far below the old records. Gone were the uninhibited, wine-purpled, 100-proof, side-of-the-mouth bottle-swigging days of the swashbuckling young Ernest Hemingway, the lion-hunting, trophy-bagging, bullfight-loving Lord Byron of America. "I am a little beat up," Ernest Hemingway now admits, "but I assure you it is only temporary."

The Private World. Even though held in by injury and age, Hemingway's life—on a small plantation ten miles outside Havana, called *Finca Vigia,* or Lookout Farm—*is* till the special Hemingway blend of thought and action, artistry and nonconformity. As early as 5:30 in the morning, before any but some gabby bantams, a few insomnia cats and a cantankerous bird called "The Bitchy Owl" are awake, he goes to work in the big main bedroom of his villa. He writes standing up at the mantelpiece, using pencil for narrative and description, a typewriter for dialogue "in order to keep up."

Rising up from one side of his villa is a white tower from which he can gaze meditatively at Havana and the sea, or at his own domain—the *Finca's* 13 acres, including flower and truck gardens, fruit trees, seven cows (which provide all the household's milk and butter), a large swimming pool, a temporarily defunct tennis court. In the 60-foot-long living room, heads of animals Hemingway shot in Africa stare glassy-eyed from the walls. But most imposing of all are Hemingway's books. He consumes books, newspapers and random printed matter the way a big fish gulps in plankton. One of the few top American writers alive who did not go to college, Hemingway read Darwin when he was ten, later taught himself Spanish so he could read *Don Quixote* and the bullfight journals. Hemingway has never slept well, and reading is his substitute. *Fines Vigia* holds 4,859 volumes of fiction, poetry, history, military manuals, biography, music, natural history, sports, foreign-language grammars and cookbooks.

The Perpetual Weekend. For 15 years Hemingway has lived in Cuba. "I live here because I love Cuba—this does not imply a dislike for anyplace else—and because here I can get privacy when I write." But his life in Cuba is not quiet. Guests at the *Fines* are apt to include friends from the wealthy sporting set, say Winston Guest or Alfred Gwynne Vanderbilt; pals from Hollywood such as Gary Cooper or Ava Gardner; Spanish grandees, soldiers, sailors, Cuban politicians, prizefighters, barkeeps, painters and even fellow authors. It is open house for U.S. Air Force and Navy men, old Loyalists from the Spanish civil war. And even if there are no guests, there is always the long-distance phone, which may carry the husky voice of Marlene Dietrich, calling to talk over a problem with "Papa."

For Mary Welsh Hemingway, an indefatigable former newspaper and magazine correspondent from Minnesota, it is a fortunate day when she can reckon by 7 p.m. how many are staying for dinner, by 10 how many for the night. Life at *Finca Vigia* is, as she once reported it, a "Perpetual weekend_ involving time, space, motion, noise, animals and personalities, always approaching but seldom actually attaining complete uproar."

To escape the uproar, Hemingway turns to his boat, the *Pilar,* a hardy-42-foot craft with two Chrysler engines, built to Hemingway's specifications 20 years ago. Its mate is an agile, creased Canary

Islander named Gregorio Fuentes. "It's the last free place there is, the sea," the writer declares as he sets off for a day's fishing for bonito.

Symbols & Style. In the past, hardly anyone ever suspected Hemingway novels of. symbolism. Then, in *The Old Man and the Sea,* people saw symbols—the old man stood for man's dignity, the big fish embodied nature, the sharks symbolized evil (or maybe just the critics).

"No good book has ever been written that has in it symbols arrived at beforehand and stuck in," says Hemingway. "That kind of symbol sticks out like raisins in raisin bread. Raisin bread is all right, but plain bread is better." At the wheel of the *Filar,* he opens two bottles of beer and continues: "I tried to make a real old man, a real boy, a real sea and a real fish and real sharks. But if I made them good and true enough they would mean many things. The hardest thing is to make something really true and sometimes truer than true."

Keep 'em smilin'!

AT TIMES, ONE WOULD RATHER—NOT!!

We were all standing on the porch of the cabin by the door; the entrance to a large four piece structure designed to protect the front entrance of any dwelling during the ravages of winter cold and snow. The door, perpendicular to the front door of the cabin, had a large window but it was covered with what appeared to be a thin layer of white ice. Visible were more uniforms and badges and specialty outfits than a Hollywood costume contractor carried in inventory. One man, the General Manager of *SEVEN SPRINGS SKI RESORT* said, to no one in particular, "We better wait about five minutes or so; I hear the siren in the distance." "We" being the Champion, Pa. police Captain, the sheriff of Bucks County, the assistant general manager—the man with the key—and I, waited while we stomped our feet and twirled our arms trying to keep some kind of warmth in our bodies!

The sheriff asked, "What are we all doing here? I got the call to report to Seven Springs; the General Manager here told me to follow him. The Captain has been helpful as much as possible but none of us know what the hell we're doing here.'

Since everyone seemed unaware as to why, I spoke up. "Sir", I said, "Mrs. Tim Sterling has been taking ski lessons from me every morning while visiting from Pittsburgh. We had a lesson day before yesterday, Tuesday, Sir, and had one scheduled for yesterday, and one for this morning, Thursday. And I might the added was a bit unusual because Mrs. Sterling usually leaves on Thursday mornings. She said something about her husband coming up to visit and possibly ski. I haven't seen her since Tuesday.

"What's your name, Son?'

"Well, thanks but I'm 26, Sir; My name is Blahosky, Fred. They call me the Polish Prince!"

"No kiddin! My name, hidden under my mackinaw, is "Breezy" to my friends. It's spelled Brcywczy. You and me ain't Irish that's for sure," the Sheriff said with a smile. Everyone else smiled too!

But then things got serious. "Tell me more, Prince, since you are the only one who seems to know what the hell is happening. And don't give me that 'Sir' crap."

"Yes, Sir—I mean OK! When Mrs. Sterling didn't show up after skiing, she usually had a drink with all of the ski instructors, I didn't give it much thought but just on a hunch drove by the parking area right on the side of the cabins; her station wagon was there with snow all over it.

Well, Sir, that really didn't mean too much to me then; thought maybe her husband came up early and they were out in his car.

I drove to Pittsburgh on Wednesday, when she didn't make the lesson, to sign some papers and when I got back last night I checked again. Nothing had moved or removed; that is her station wagon or the snow. I checked with the front desk; they hadn't seen Mrs. Sterling but I asked the operator if she knew anything. She said she couldn't tell me but when I told her of my worry, Mr. Mitchell, the General Manager here, said it was OK to tell me that Mr. Sterling had left a message saying he couldn't make it! That's it, Sir!

Blahosky, you should be in the goddamn Army with that "Sir" shit and I'll tell you—"

A short, piercing, jabbing sound of a siren cut "Breezy" off and turned everyone around to see a large red van with the silver printing INTERNATIONAL on the front of the engine. On the side were painted the letters *CHAMPION CITY FIRE DEPARTRMENT.* It hadn't stopped for a second when two men in black uniforms covered with white parkas jumped out of the rear. They were each carrying gas masks and a red box with *EMERGENCY* on the side. Did they know something none of the others' minds could possibly, at this time, comprehend?

They jumped up the short stairway and asked, "Who's in charge?"

"My name is Mitchell. I am the General Manager and I have access," Mr. Mitchell said.

"OK, folks! Listen up," the fireman who seemed to be in charge said. "Open the door please, Mr. Mitchell. You other Gentlemen keep away. This is either nothing or we have a suicide on our hands. By what means we don't know but experience tells us we didn't bring these masks for an exercise. Sheriff, Captain, keep these people away from the door. OK! Mitchell, let's get started but as soon as the door opens, step back and away. Got that?"

Mr. Mitchell, after opening the storm door stepped inside and unlocked the front door and opened it. Immediately we were all driven back by an invisible cloud of noxious gas. The firemen donned their masks in seconds; their flashlights already illuminated, started sweeping the room(s). We heard windows being slammed open, doors being slammed, and then—silence. We waited!

After five minutes or so, a fireman came out, removed his mask, nodded to the Captain and Sheriff and said, "You two gentlemen can come in. And you other gentlemen, we found Mrs. Sterling, is it? She was sitting in a chair, dressed in what appears to be expensive 'after ski clothes', in front of the stove, door open. She was smart enough to have turned out the pilot light or she and the cabin would have been blown to bits; there was that much gas. The sheriff will call the coroner. And Mr. Mitchell, I am sure you will notify the family." With that he walked back inside shaking his head while saying to himself, "Jesus, a beautiful woman like that! Tragic! Tragic!"

At about the same time on that fateful, momentous morning, Liz was packed and dressed waiting for a Breck chauffer to drive her to the airport. The company wished for Liz to appear for a short stay at East Carolina University, located in Greenville, NC.

There were planned activities on Friday night and a breakfast on Saturday morning at two honor societies, Golden Key and Phi Kappa Phi respectively.

East Carolina University was no longer known as "Easy-U". It *had* been known as a major party school. That was when Greenville was still a very small rural town with very little left to do than party. But Greenville and the surrounding areas have grown and there are many activities and associations to be found for those who are not party animals.

ECU offers a range of academic programs such as the **Thomas Harriot College of Arts and Sciences, College of Business, College of Education, College of Fine Arts and Communication,** and **Health and Human Performance.** Also, ECU offers the **Brody School of Medicine, Nursing,** and **School of Allied Health Sciences.**

Liz asked the pilot before takeoff, "Why East Carolina College?" She had read the literature provided by corporate and left in her seat by a window. "Oh!" the captain said, "I thought you knew! Breck has two very bright ECU graduate women in management and I think they would be pleased if you made the trip. Here, I have a copy of your agenda. A Ms. Amity Greenway will meet the plane."

"Captain, I was briefed, but not to the extent you just gave me. Thank you."

Liz's trip was letter and socially perfect. She was in her environment—encouraging, cheerful, brilliant, and, in speech, noticeable intelligence. She was always surrounded by lovely women and "Gee, I wish she was mine," men. Breck had arranged through Ms. Greenway for Liz to host a dinner for 19—professors, doctors, nurses, and PhD's from the different colleges. Her trip was later to be known as the "Triangular Triumph"; for ECU, Liz, and Breck!

At Sunday morning breakfast in Pittsburgh Liz's Mom was casually reading the paper. She turned to the third page; a headline read, **"BEAUTIFUL YOUNG SOCIALITE TAKES HER OWN LIFE."** Mrs. McGovern was aghast, struck with an amazement of horror. Liz's Dad was on the golf course. Mrs. McGovern, although in deep thought immediately got up and made two phone calls: the first was to the country club with orders to "find him" and the second was to a special number given to her by Liz to call "just in case." She dialed; waited for a male voice, and told the man on the other end, "Mr. McGovern and I will meet Liz's plane. What is the expected time of arrival?"

Liz was relaxed just being awakened from a light sleep by the stewardess. She went to the restroom on the plane, freshened up face and hair and was seated by the time the plane touched down. She was glancing out of the window as the private jet was about to park when she saw her Dad and Mom standing by his car. They waived with a faint smile. Liz waived back but was in wonderment! "Why", she said to herself. Her mind was racing; "My sister, Dahlia, grandma, pa? They're here for some important reason. Gee! What could possibly be the reason?"

Her Mom and Dad met her at the bottom of the stairs. They embraced and walked toward the car. They asked about her trip; small talk completely void of any strong warmth of feeling or fervor.

Once in the car, as it was heading out the "General Aviation" road, Liz said, "OK, Mom, Dad, let me know why you're here to pick me up. Who died, is in the hospital, or crashed? You mentioned something about dinner before I left but that's not the reason you're here."

"You are right, Liz," he Mom said. "We have some very bad news and we wanted to be with you when you found out. Joanne Sterling committed suicide while on her ski trip to Seven Springs. I'm terribly sorry, Honey."

Liz sat for a few seconds then screamed at the top of her lungs; one blood curdling scream after another. With her hands over her face she mumbled,

Stop! Stop! Stop the car! Quick!" Her Dad pulled over and Liz leaped at the door, opened it in a flash and started throwing up, one convulsion after another. She was gagging, crying, and in convulsions at the same time. Her Mom went to the trunk and pulled a picnic like table cloth and handed it to Liz and stood back and waited until Liz had a chance to get a hold of her self. Slowly, oh so slowly, the convulsions ebbed, and the screams turned into whimpers as she was wiping mascara, make up, and lipstick away her "drowning from tears" face.

"How, How? Why? When?" she asked her Mother as she got up off her knees! "Just the other day Joanne was telling me—Oh God, this can't be" as she started to cry very hard again. "This can't be," she said over and over again. "Suicide! Suicide! That means she killed herself purposely. Did Joanne do that? To her self! This can't be!"

She got back in the car dragging the tablecloth with her. Once seated her Dad started for home. Her Mother said, "We'll have some nice hot chicken noodle soup, my dear and then I think you should get some rest. One thing I failed to mention. The paper stated that the memorial service would be private and Joanne would be buried in the Sterling plot in St. Jude Cemetery in Lancaster, Pa. next to the family's great grandparents, grandparents and a great uncle.

JOANNE'S SUICIDE
LIZ'S MENTAL TORTURE

By: Charles Grube
Sports' Editor

Liz tossed and turned all night. She couldn't sleep! The more she thought about the fearful and shocking loss of Joanne the deeper her groans being accompanied by an outpouring of weeping and expletives not suited even for a hardened truck drive or hoodlum.

"I must stop thinking! I must get some sleep!" Liz would say to herself. "But why? Why Joanne? For Christ sake, Why??" She tossed and turned! The hands on her clock, sitting at the small table beside her bed, seemed mournful for Liz; they tried to slow the approach to 7:00AM so Liz's desire for just forty winks would cast anchor and allow her the relaxing sleep she so richly deserved.

The large hand swung by "12", while the smaller one inched past seven. The large hand then swerved around the "7" and hurried again toward "12" but it didn't stop. Finally, when they passed each other again, while the small one was creeping toward "8", they agreed to "one more swing" then let the bell ring at "9".

Liz awakened in a startle; she sat up and looked around taking more than a few seconds to reach out and pull her thoughts together. She flopped back on her pillow while grabbing her other one and drew it into her face and chest. Her stream of consciousness rolled into her brain sifting thoughts until she snatched one that said, "Stop the crying! It's too late for Joanne! You wonder, Why? You're a bright woman! A test of character! Leave your bed—and try to find out!"

Liz stood in front of her bathroom mirror aghast at her looks; rumpled air, red puffy eyes, makeup streaked across cheek and chin—a real mess. A shower of warm water released her pensive skin and bone, and shampoo and body soap brought Liz back to the reality of a refreshing "wake up and make up" call.

At a light breakfast she told her mother her plans; a call on the Powers model office to make sure everyone knew of the Joanne's misfortune, a meeting with her professor of *COMMUNICATION* to set the date for her final exam. Because of her travels and the fact that Liz was an "A" student called for an oral test only: "The Pros and Cons of Women News Reporters on Television." Liz didn't know it at the time, but KDKA, the Westinghouse TV and Radio station, was sending her a letter offering her a position as a newscaster for a late evening ten minute Pittsburgh news report and weather forecast. With her college education, her singular beauty and personality (management was aware of her Powers and Breck contracts), KDKA thought Liz would be the perfect woman to break the uniformity of men.

Liz's next stop was to try to answer a couple of her brain sifting thoughts; a trip to the library. She asked herself, "What are the causes and factors for the failure of a marriage?" Certainly, Joanne was disposed in that arena. And, "What does the Catholic Church say about suicide?" Also, the church has their opinions, but how about the secular, and what the philosophers from history thought?

She called home and told her Mom she may be late for dinner.

After an hour or so of researching many volumes and written documents Liz was ready to peruse and cogitate; she needed to "think out" and reason, to the best of her ability,—WHY?

Her first body of material was from the *Suicide Reference Library.*

What Does the Catholic Church Say About Suicide: by Fr. Peter Daly

My brother committed suicide two years ago after struggling with depression his entire life. A Franciscan priest reassured me that the Church currently shows compassion in cases of suicide. People who take their lives are assumed to do so due to mental illness. The Church does not presume to know their fates after death, since it cannot know their experiences during life.

E. H. Virginia

The priest who comforted you at your brother's death also gave you a correct interpretation of the official teaching of the Church.

Liz kept reading! The article continued:

The best place to look to find the official teaching of the Church on any topic is the **Catechism of the Catholic Church.** The Catechism summarizes the teaching in paragraphs 2280 through 2283 as part of the overall teaching on the fifth commandment: THOU SHALL NOT KILL.

First, the Catechism reminds us that life is a gift from God, who is master of our lives. We are stewards "not owners" of our lives. Also, we believe that life is good.

Suicide is opposed to our instinct to self-preservation. It is also contrary to a just love of self. It violates our obligation to love our neighbor, since any suicide inflicts great suffering on others, especially family members. No Catholic should ever encourage or assist suicide. We should always seek to preserve life if that is possible.

We should never have a careless disregard for our own lives either. Therefore, playing Russian roulette, reckless driving, drug and alcohol abuse are wrong. They might take our life or the life of another. They show a lack of love for life.

But the Catechism of the Catholic Church says, "Grave psychological disturbances, anguish, or grave fear of hardship, suffering, or torture can diminish the responsibility of the one committing suicide.

It continues, "We should not despair of the eternal salvation of persons who have taken their own lives. By ways known to Him alone, can God provide the opportunity for salutary (health-giving) repentance. The Church prays for persons who have taken their own lives.

Today, we offer Masses and say funerals for those who have committed suicide. We trust that God, who alone can search hearts, understands what was going on in a mind tortured by depression.

Liz got up from her library table and walked to the water cooler. She had a soothing glass of cold water and as she was drinking, looking up past the ornate ceiling toward Heaven, she said with tears welling in her eyes, "Joanne, I know you are up there my loving friend. You were always so good. I don't know of your torture but I am sure it gained you an early date with God. *You* pray for me; someday we will be together!"

Liz went back to her table and reached for another paper. The word "torture" deeply bothered her. The credential asked, in bold print, **What Are Causes and Factors for the Failure of a Marriage?**

ANSWER!

This is a very complicated question because men and women are complicated creatures. The main reasons are money problems, not getting along with in-laws, immaturity, not willing to work at marriage when everyday problems arise and not trying to COMMUNICATE one's feelings. Like any good thing in life, it takes work. It's not easy, but if you love each other you can conquer the world. Poor or rich, we all have the same problems. Some just have more property and monies to deal with in a divorce.

Marriages also fail for the following reasons: Lack of love, Lack of respect, Lack of emotional maturity, not putting the spouse needs ahead of you own, Cheating, and Lack of trust.

"WOW", Liz said to herself. "If I ever get married I better be prepared. I know Joanne was very mature but I also wonder if she knew what she was getting into? Impossible to answer! There was no problem with money. She had more than she knew what to do with. She said she was sure he wasn't cheating. Therefore, no lack of trust! They had love and respect for one another. Was there a lack of emotional maturity on both parties? I don't have an answer for that! Not putting Joanne's needs before Tim's could have been part of it. She needed him for company; looked forward to having her ski with him but he cancelled. And she was skiing only because her club member suggested it as a means to get out and meet people. When we dined together Joanne was in torture then, but I don't think anyone could tell how deep; my God! Enough to take your own life! Maybe Tim wasn't around enough to work at the marriage. With all the Sterling money maybe she was expecting a life of glamour but her tortured mind convinced her she was just another dollar in the Balance Sheet!

Liz felt lonely. It was already dark outside. She would have loved to be in Arnie's arms; that must wait until next week.

Liz pulled a heavy textbook toward her; she opened it to page 133, one out of 1771. A real treasury of western thought! She wanted to consciously inquire about what the philosophers thought of suicide. She found Job, Plato, Aristotle, Virgil, Seneca, Plutarch (who had much to say), Augustine, Dante, Shakespeare, even Kant and Schopenhauer, and Tolstoy and a few more masters of thought, experience, and ability to write poignant, affective verse.

Job said, in 7:13-16 "—then thou scarest me with dreams, and terrifiest me through visions: So that my soul chooseth strangling, and death rather than life.

Socrates, through Plato, in *Phaedo,* 61B, "Then, if we look at the matter (suicide) thus, there may be reason in saying that a man should wait, and not take his own life until God summons him.

Plutarch, *Themistocles*—he, [Themistocles] determined to put a conclusion to his life, agreeable to its previous course. He sacrificed to the gods, and invited his friends; and having entertained them and shaken hands with them, drank bull's blood producing instant death. The king being informed of the cause and manner of his death, admired him more than ever, and continued to show kindness to his friends and relations.

Aristotle, *Ethics*, 1138a4, "For (a) one class of just acts are those acts in accordance with any virtue which are prescribed by the law; e.g. the law does not expressly permit suicide, and when it does not expressly permit it forbids."

Shakespeare, *Julius Caesar,* I, iii, 91—Nor airless dungeon, no strong links of iron, Can be retentive to the strength of spirit; But life, being weary of those worldy bars, Never lacks power to dismiss itself.

Voltaire, *Letter to James Marriott* (Feb. 26, 1767) "There are said to be occasions when a wise man kills himself, but generally speaking it is not an excess of reason that makes people take their own lives."

Schopenhauer, *Suicide* "They tell us that suicide is the greatest piece of cowardice, that only a madman could be guilty of it; and other insipidities of the same kind; or else they make the nonsensical remark that suicide is *wrong*; when it is quite obvious that there is nothing in the world to which every man has a more unassailable title to his own life and person."

Nietzsche, *Beyond Good and Evil*, IV, 157 "The thought of suicide is a powerful comfort: it helps one through many a dreadful night."

Tolstoy, *On Life*, XXII—I no longer feel any attraction to life. I see that it is absurd and impossible to live for the one thing I want. That is my personal happiness. It would be possible to live for reasonable consciousness, but it is not worth while and I do not want to. Serve that source from whence I came—God? Why? If God exists, he will find people to serve him without me. And why should I do it?

One can contemplate this play of life as long as one does not find it dull, and when it is dull one can go away and kill oneself. And that is what I will do."

Liz closed the substantial volume; her mind twirling with mixed messages none of which came to a conclusion. "I guess," she said to herself, "the Catholic Church sees to have a more straightforward answer. An all loving God will make the decision in His court of law, and for reasons given, will find for the defense."

BASS HAS A LURE OF ITS OWN

By: Doc Giffin
Sports' Editor

After a trophy fish gets off the hook on a technicality, anglers swarm a small lake in hopes of reeling it back it—along with riches.

On a rainy June morning in 1932, a poor farm boy named George Perry decided to forgo plowing for the day to fish with a friend in Montgomery Lake, a muddy oxbow off the Ocmulgee River in southern Georgia.

After an hour of casting with a "wiggle-fish" lure from a handmade boat, the lanky 20-year-old farmer set his hook on fishing immortality. His lure snared something so heavy he assumed he had snagged an underwater root. But as he reeled in, he realized it was a gargantuan fish, the biggest largemouth bass Perry and his friend had ever seen.

"The first thing I thought of was how nice a chunk of meat to take home," Perry later told a reporter.

But first Perry drove to a nearby post office where the fish tipped the scale at 22 pounds, 4 ounces, breaking the previous world record by more than 2 pounds. Perry's catch earned him top prize in a *Field and Stream* fishing contest: $75 worth of outdoor gear.

In the 74 years since, the most talented anglers in the world using the latest gear have scoured the world's lakes for a bass to surpass Perry's mark. Some have sacrificed marriages and jobs in their pursuit.

But Perry's record has been intact for so long, some anglers started to wonder if it could ever be broken. Maybe, some suggested, largemouth bass don't grow that big anymore.

That kind of thinking ended March 20. Carlsbad, California casino worker Mac Weakley, 33, reeled in a largemouth bass at Dixon Lake in northern San Diego County that surpassed Perry's mark by more than 2 pounds. But Weakley had snagged the fish on the side instead of the mouth, and a fishing regulation forced him to return the giant bass to the lake.

Since then, fishermen from as far away as Florida, Texas and Mississippi have swarmed the tiny reservoir's docks and piers, jostling to be first on the water each morning while television crews and reporters stalked the shores, waiting for someone to yell: "I got it!"

So far, no one has.

Outsiders may find it difficult to understand all the excitement. But to freshwater anglers, landing the world record largemouth bass represents the conquest of one of the most sought-after records in sports, akin to Hank Aaron's career home run mark or Wilt Chamberlain's 100-point game. Whoever hooks that fish will become a fishing legend. And unlike Perry, who died not too long ago, the new record holder could probably retire on the income from tackle endorsement deals alone.

So now, the chase is on.

Largemouth bass are the fishing world's favorite quarry because these resilient fish can thrive in rivers, lakes, reservoirs and even golf course water hazards. They are the common man's fish, pursued with a vengeance across the country by more than 11 million hard-core bass fishermen. And when they are hooked, largemouth bass put up a good fight, squirming and flailing until they exhaust themselves completely.

But not every angler has the patience to pursue such a challenging quarry. In the 74-year history of the world-record pursuit, some record seekers have been caught trying to stuff scrawny bass with cement or lead weights to tip the scales. Others have bee accused of fishing at night or grabbing a dead fish and claiming it was caught live—two cardinal sins of fishing.

The official keeper of the world's fishing records—the International Game Fishing Assn.—tries to quash cheating. They require record applicants to include photos, the names of witnesses, scale certification records and the signature of the ichthyologist (a branch of zoology that deals with fish) who examined the fish.

Keep 'em smilin!

CHARLIE! GLORIA! LIZ! ARNIE!
SO CLOSE! BUT WORLDS APART!

By: **Charles Grube**
Sports' Editor

Jolly Cholly, and his not so glorious Gloria, were what one might call "hung over". But they so rightly deserved it! Last night, Mr. and Mrs. Latshaw had an elegant dinner party for them at the DUQUESNE CLUB to celebrate the new Managing Editor for the *PITTSBURGH POST TELEGRAPH*.

In his short address with his right arm held high with a sparkling glass of champagne in his hand, ready to toast, the CEO and President said, "Mr. Grube's responsibilities as the new junior executive will include directing news coverage, coaching reporters, writing editorials, paginating pages, but he also understands the value of excellent customer service and interacting with the public. Mr. Grube received acclamation from his fans and many of the *PPT's* readers for his, and his devotees' collective expressions on the subject of Jack Flynn. Also Monks, the WHY's about becoming a Monk from our public, and the personal response from Father Tom Gilispie of the Holy Trinity Abbey in Utah. As a matter of fact, Mr. Grube, with his followers in mind, flew to Salt Lake City and drove to the Abbey and personally met with Fr. Gillespie. My right arm is getting tired so 'Congratulations' Charlie and 'Welcome'."

Everyone voiced, "Here! Here!" and took a hearty swig of a savory French sparkling wine. Also, Mr. Latshaw was pleased to announce that Charlie had worked hard and received his Maters' degree from Pitt so up went the arm, as did many others, accompanied by another "Here! Here!" and one could HEAR the gurgle, gurgle! Someone yelled out, "Keep toastin', Mr. Latshaw, we love this French liquid!"

"OK!" Mr. Latshaw called back. "We'll drink to Charlie again. He was on expenses when he went to Utah. But have no fear. It's so easy to meet his expenses these days. I meet them everywhere I look!"

The dinner party loved it! Up went the champagne glasses again—and again—and again.

"Gee! What a wonderful dinner party," Gloria said as she held an ice bag on her forehead. "Please don't get promoted again for awhile and stop being educated." Charlie didn't say a word other than "I love you," as he held her as she sat up in bed trying to keep the world from going around and around.

"It's all the Duquesne Club's fault," Charlie said as he sat on the edge of the bed next to her. "But Mr. Latshaw knows his stuff. The Duquesne Club is one of the city's more prominent institutions. It's a former men's-only club but it's now where business and civic leaders gather. We are staying in one of the 30 rooms available to guests but only through Mr. Latshaw. This club was built would you believe in 1887 and continues to provide an "Old World" experience. Take your time getting back to normal, my love. We can check out as late as we wish. I'll make sure he receives a note of "thanks" from us."

One of the first things Charlie wanted to do was meet with Liz to congratulate her on graduating from college and accepting a position with KDKA CBS Channel 2 Television. He would not mention the death of Joanne unless Liz brought it up.

Channel 2 originally signed on as WDTV Channel 3 as part of the DuMont system. It was decided that Channel 3 would switch over to Channel 2 and be known as KDKA . . . . sister to the radio station. Pittsburgh's famous news anchor, Bill Burns, not only had viewers switch their sets from 3 to 2 one day at noon, but he made the big switch to Television from radio. KDKA once held the "Eyewitness News" Moniker, but now calls its news the "Hometown Advantage." The idea behind the name came as a result of the number of anchors/reporters are from the area or have lived in Pittsburgh a lengthy period of time. Channel 2 also boasts their weather with ACCU-Weather. Those two facts held the reasoning behind hiring Liz!

Charlie had Liz's home number from the last time they met. Which reminded him; he had, not for a second, forgotten the thought of seeing Liz walking to the cabins at Loggermans with a Catholic priest. He had talked to no one about it including Gloria. He had, however, made up his mind he would talk to Liz.

They agreed to meet at 402 Fort Duquesne Blvd., the TV station's address. Liz said she was pleased Charlie called and mentioned a small café nearby.

Liz and Charlie greeted each other with a warm hug. After the normal but heartfelt pleasantries they walked into *MARIE'S CAFÉ, SINCE 1937*. "Nineteen thirty seven," Charlie said. "I was 10 years old and had a paper route—in competition with my boss. But keep it a secret!" Liz smiled; she was missing her normal exuberance. He decided at that time he would not mention Joanne's suicide.

They both ordered; Liz and her famous "ketchup, pickle, lettuce, tomato, onion, mayonnaise, thick beef patty with sharp cheese burger with don't spare the fries" and ice tea with extra lemon. Charlie just gawked. When the waitress said, "And you, Sir,' Charlie didn't even look up. He started to say something but just exhaled and said, "What the hell; I'll have the same!"

Liz and Charlie always enjoyed each others' company. She loved and trusted Charlie and was pleased about his position and graduation. He felt the same about Liz and told her the invitation to lunch was to personally congratulate her on graduation and the new job. She thanked him and said, as she smiled, "If it was not for me you wouldn't be eating a famous burger. Of course neither one of us can eat another thing until Tuesday a week." Charlie laughed and said, "How about two weeks from Tuesday. How did you ever come up with this massive Dagwood martyr maker?"

Liz did not get a chance to answer. Charlie though it time to "made his move". He asked, "Liz do you, or did you, know Arnie is a Catholic priest on sabbatical from Rome? Just by chance, I saw you walking with him into Loggerman's motel. Two things! One, I was shocked but realized you probably didn't know, and two, I have not said a word to any one."

Liz sat frozen; in her seat and facial countenance. She didn't move for seconds then slowly raised her face and looked at Charlie in the eye and a whisper came out of her mouth. She said, "I didn't then but he told me the time before the last time we were together before we made love, so I know now.'

Charlie was a bit startled and quite alarmed at her answer. "You mean to say you knew from then and you still sleep with a priest with no compunction of conscious. You are not bothered at all," Charlie asked.

"Mr. Grube," Liz said in a slovenly almost dingy way, "Please don't start talking about sin and the blackness of my soul. I'm sorry if it bothers you, I really mean that. I met Arnie under normal circumstances, at least for me. And I am sure he had no intentions of sexual behavior toward me but with our loneliness combined with our closeness in our golf one thing just led to another. And after our deep throated kisses, our sexual desire was liberated for each of us and we knew, at least I did, we wanted more. His tenderness was something I needed and to be honest, I still do. I'm so damn fed up with guys always hitting on me with smart ass, juvenile remarks that I longed for someone with the mellifluence of Arnie, priest or not."

"Liz, I have nothing to say about your sin or soul. Who is to say anything of someone else's business? I read not too long ago where an Italian priest admitted publicity to be in love but still wants to be a priest. He said he had not violated the church law of celibacy. He professed his love for the woman and said he wanted to be her boyfriend while remaining chaste. What do you think of that?'

"Good luck. Our relief from our strong sexual desire certainly won't abate with the nearness of someone you love.

Men in the Easter rite of the Catholc Church who are married can become priests, and the Vatican has accepted into the priesthood some married Anglican priests who converted to Catholicism. Look, Mr. Grube, there is one God, and supposedly one church but everyone has their own ideas about what is right or wrong. Why is a priest that agrees, in all good faith, to celibacy at a young age, all of a sudden condemned because he can't overcome the concupiscence that God gave him in the first place. Please order me a cup of coffee. I'll tell you what Arnie and I discussed in detail. Heck, I love the guy no matter the position of his collar. But I am not *in love* with him. Right now I am in love with myself. I'm not going to be tortured with lonesomeness like Joanne. I know Arnie has to go back to Rome but until he does I am going to let him love me anyway he wants until then. And I am going to return the favor. I'm young. I'm nice looking, single, with no desire to marry in the foreseeable future and I am not going to use a plastic penis or dildo to relieve my concupiscence. Now if that is a mortal sin, I am not afraid to die and I'll let God decide."

A bus boy brought Charlie and Liz coffee. Charlie also ordered one piece of New York cheesecake and two forks. Before the cake arrived Liz continued. "Arnie and I had a serious conversation about some literature he had with him. I have a copy of it here in my purse. It was written (excerpted) from a Vatican Document. It said: We see the spirit of moral perversion is evident throughout the apostate element of Christianity. It has always been evident in the Roman Catholic Church, with its wicked forced "celibacy." The history of Roman Catholicism reads like something out of a Sodom and Gomorrah chronicle. Large numbers of Popes, even, were morally perverse, and countless Catholic priests were given over to homosexuality. Even Roman Catholic histories admit this, and they are usually less than forthright about the moral failure of the "mother church."

"OH! Here's our cheesecake. Thank you, Sir," for splitting it," Liz said. "Now my friend won't take a bigger piece." She smiled at Charlie. He smiled too but was shaking his head slowly from left to right as he was looking deep into Liz's eyes in disbelief.

"I am meeting a totally different Liz here today," he said to himself as he took a sip of coffee then lifted his fork to begin to enjoy the cheesecake. "I am lost for words," he continued under his breath. "But that will be OK because what can I possibly say to a woman who is totally engulfed in sexual vigor or deep rationalization, or both, in trying to find plausible, but less than faithful reasons for her conduct. Or maybe she is really trying to convince me. Well, that's OK too!"

"Hey! That cake is very good, don't you think?" Liz asked.

"Delicious," Charlie answered. "But remember what I usually say. The best part about any meal is the company. Why don't you continue with what you were reading."

"Thank you. In an essay printed in ST. ANTHONY MESSINGER, a national Franciscan magazine, a priest said that the law of celibacy was routinely flouted by many priests, some of whom have married secretly and who pass off their wives as live-in housekeepers in the rectory. Others have lovers, he adds.

"The sanctions against sexual activity for priests, the priest suggests, have led to 'rampant psychosexual problems' including an upsurge in reported cases of Catholic clergy involved in child molestation and a 'noticeable increase in the number of gay seminarians at Catholic divinity schools.'"

"Mr. Grube, we can't be that wrong. I know he's a priest and I am a single woman and Arnie is as far from being gay as the deepest star in the universe, measured in light years; and he certainly has no psychosexual problems. Did you ever see him play golf? Or poker? He's as normal as a one dollar bill in a man's wallet!"

"One or two more points and I'll—ah, yes, Sir, I will take a refill on the coffee. And please offer the same to Mr. Grube. I think the hot coffee will relieve Mr. Grube of what I believe is adding up to a headache!

Anyhow, as I was saying, in a nationally known newspaper, an ex-nun that will remain un-named, accuses celibacy of being a major cause of priests' wasted lives (a tragic number become alcoholics and quietly drink themselves to death) and explains, That mandate was issued under the assumption that celibate men and women are somehow more pleasing to God than married people. Like other man-made rules, it is totally without scriptural validity."

"One more and this will be it; this is from the GREENVILLE NEWS. 'Up to half the Roman Catholic priests in the United States do not uphold their vows of celibacy, according to the estimates from a twenty-five-year study from a FORMER Roman Catholicism priest who is now a psychotherapist. The study indicated that 20% of the priests have a clear pattern of heterosexual behavior, 10%to 13% are homosexually active, and 6% are involved sexually with minors.' "The surprise," Mr. Grube, "is while half the priests *generally support* the idea of celibacy, **only 2%** fully achieve it."

"So, Mr. Grube," Liz said as she folded her notes and put them in her coat pocket, "here I am right in the middle of a storm of thunder, lacking the knowledge of canon law and study of theology but history tells me there will be change. Theology studies for me; no! But philosophy examination; yes! I learned from history. 'Laws and institutions must go hand in hand with the progress of the human mind. As that becomes more developed, more enlightened, as new discoveries are made, new truths disclosed, and manners and opinions change with the change of circumstances, institutions must advance also, and keep pace with the times.' Thomas Jefferson wrote that in 1816. And I might add that the Catholic Church is not immune."

"Well, Mr. Grube, I must go back to my new job. If I do make it, that is, some day when I speak in front of the camera, I'll wink and that will be for you. Thank you for the invite, and for being such an excellent listener. Tell your new bride I send my love and I know this discussion will go no further than this table. Now give me a hug so I can remember you as a warm, giving man."

"You're welcome! I will tell Gloria you send your love. Our conversation this afternoon is already forgotten! And I do not want this to be our last hug."

Little did he know!

WILLIAM MCGARVEY DUDLEY
BULLET BILL AND THE BLUEFIELD BULLET

By: Doc Giffin
Sports' Editor

Since we are right in the middle of the Steelers' season on these cold Sundays I thought I would bring you a warm story about a contemporary of our Pittsburgh fans. I'm talking 1942 to 1953; just about the time our former Sports' Editor and now Associate Editor went to Korea in his jet to save us younger juveniles.

"Bullet Bill" Dudley was born on December 24, 1921 in Bluefield, Virginia. His ability as a passer to hit his target led to his nicknames. His ability to be born one day before Christmas wasn't too notable; what happened to all his birthday presents!!

Dudley was recruited to the University of Virginia after impressing scouts there with his performance at Graham High School. Although he was originally slated as a punter and placekicker, he eventually came to play the tailback position. He started every game for the Cavaliers as a junior. In his senior year, he became Virginia's first All-American and won the Maxwell Award. He was selected first overall by the Pittsburgh Steelers in the 1942 draft.

I did a little research for all you gentlemen—and ladies. The Maxwell Award, College Player of the Year, is presented in honor of *Robert W. (Tiny) Maxwell,* legendary college player, official and sports columnist.

Robert Maxwell, a native of Chicago, began playing college football at the University of Chicago in 1902 for Amos Alonzo Stagg. At 6-foot-4, 240 lbs., he also boxed and set school hammer and shot-put records.

(Stagg (1862-1965) was a renowned American collegiate coach in multiple sports, primarily football. He attended Phillips Exeter Academy, played at Yale and was an end on the first All American team, selected in 1889. His innovations in football included the huddle, lateral pass, man in motion, tackling dummy, and helmets.)

"Tiny" Maxwell, continued:

It was in 1905, while playing guard for Swarthmore College, that Maxwell made a major impact on the game of football as we know it today. At the end of a savage contest with Penn, in which he turned in his customary stellar performance, Maxwell's nose broken, his eyes swollen nearly shut, and his face closely resembled steak tartare. According to gridiron historians, a newspaper photo of his face so shocked President Theodore Roosevelt, that two days later, in a meeting with major college representatives, the President demanded that they "clean up football," or he'd ban the game outright. Three months later, rules were changed to double the yardage required for a first down from five to ten, reduce playing time from seventy minutes to sixty minutes, add restrictions against roughing, establish a neutral zone on the line of scrimmage the length of the football, and to legalize the forward pass.

After a brief, post-graduate career playing for such teams as the Massillon Tigers and Canton Bulldogs, Maxwell's career as a referee began when he was called at the last minute to fill in for an official who didn't show up. Because of his tremendous size, quickness, and knowledge of the rules, he was soon in demand for such major games as Harvard-Yale and Army-Navy.

In time, Tiny's role as an official would influence football considerably. Walter Camp said Maxwell set the standard for fairness and competence. His apartment near City Hall in Philadelphia became a gathering place for fellow officials. Out of their meetings grew the East's first formal association of football officials.

Maxwell also became one of the rare players to make the leap from field to press box. In 1914, after a journalistic apprenticeship in Chicago as a reporter for the *Record-Herald*, he began writing a sports column for Philadelphia's *Public Ledger*. Two years later, he became Sports Editor of the *Evening Public Ledger*, a position he held until his death, at thirty-seven, as a result of an auto accident.

Now, back to Dudley!

As World War II was raging in Europe, the armed forces were drafting all able-bodied young men. In 1942 Dudley was called up by the Army Air Corps, but because of a delay in training he was able to finish his season with the Steelers. Dudley ended up leading the league in rushing and won Rookie of the Year honors (before the Associated Press began giving the award). Once he joined the Army in 1944, he played for a team fielded by Randolph Field, an Army Air Corps training facility, leading them to a 12-0 intercollegiate record and a #3 ranking by the Associated Press poll, while winning the Most Valuable Player award.

Upon the close of the war in 1945, Dudley returned to the Steelers. As a testament to his ability, he managed to lead the team in scoring for the season despite only playing in four games. In the 1946 NFL season, Dudley set a record that is unlikely to ever be broken: because of his versatility as one of the "60-minute men" who played both offense and defense, Dudley led the league in four diverse statistical categories, rushing (604 yards), interceptions (10), punt returns (27 for 385 yards), and lateral passing (which is no longer recorded). As a result, Dudley was the NFL's choice for the Joe Carr trophy, which went to the league's MVP.*** The award was discontinued after this season and did not return until the AP brought it back in 1957. Dudley became the first (and as of 2005), only person to win MVP awards in college, service, and professional levels. Dudley was traded to the Detroit Lions after 1946, partly because of his contentious relationship with Steelers coach Jock Sutherland. After three years in Detroit, he was traded to the Washington Redskins. After sitting out the 1952 NFL season, he returned to the Lions in 1953, where he finished his career mostly as a placekicker and defensive player

Dudley was elected to the College Football Hall of Fame in 1956 and Pro Football Hall of Fame in 1966.

*** Joseph F. Carr (1879-1939) was an early figure in professional football. Carr was born in Columbus, Ohio. As a mechanic for the Pennsylvania Railroad in Columbus, he directed the COLUMBUS PANHANDLERS football team in 1907 until 1922. The "Panhandlers" was one of the largest draws in early professional football and were nearly unbeatable at home. Carr helped to reorganize the American Professional Football Association (APFA) in 1921, and moved the offices from Canton to Columbus. The league would be renamed the National Football League in 1922. Carr served as its president from 1921 until his death in 1939. He was elected to the Pro Football Hall of Fame in 1963.

The NFL's original Most Valuable Player award was named for Carr in 1938.

Keep 'em Smilin'

A LETTER FROM JACK FLYNN
SOON TO BE KNOWN AS FATHER JACK

By: Charles Grube
Managing Editor

Well, friends and fans of the *PITTSBURGH POST TELEGRAPH*, and Jack Flynn, this is my first column since accepting my new position and it could possibly be my last one since "Doc" Giffin has taken my place as Sport's Editor. And my complements to the good "Doctor" for doing such a fine job! I thought his article on bass fishing was unparalleled.

I received quite a long epistle from Jack Flynn. He has decided to give up his desire to become a monk and follow a well thought out plan to be ordained a priest. I spoke to Mr. and Mrs. Flynn; they received the missive also. I am writing you ladies and gentlemen because that was our deal; my responsibility to keep you informed.

I did not edit what Jack wrote. I think he wrote what came to his mind whether they be short thoughts or ones attended by long periods of melancholy. He slipped a note into the rather large envelope; it said, "Be home before Easter. Probably stay at St. Philips."

It's all here and it's all yours!

Dear Mom and Dad and Mr. Grube,

When the annual meeting in France of the world's Trappist abbots authorized a change, reveille in a Trappist monastery was never later than 2:00 A.M.,-1:30 on Sundays, and 1:00 on days of major liturgy. It wasn't a far-off bugle that did the deed, but a thirty-pound bell hung, it seemed, just outside your eardrum.

Even so, early rising seemed to be viewed by most monks more as the beginning of another day of inner adventure than as a hardship. Except when deep in a cold or flu, few ever gave evidence of having difficulty starting the day in the middle of the night. Early rising is like monastic living as a whole: it sounds a lot harder than it is.

The ambience of a 2:00 A.M. is different depending on whether you are meeting it as you get up or leaving it as you go to bed. I've done both, many times, and the difference is dramatic. From the first morning I smelled the Utah night air sliding into the monastery valley from the surrounding Wasatch Mountain. When birds in the cloister garth began their own chanting about four, still another dimension of charm was added. By the time the sun arrived on the scene, the day for both monks and birds had been in full swing for some hours.

As most of you know, the abbot insisted that I spend a second year at Notre Dame after my first visit to the monastery before he would admit me as a postulant. It was a normal requirement—"to try the spirit." Finally I passed for what I was sure was the last time through the gate that had promised me its *pax* on my first visit the summer before.

Three days of twiddling my thumbs in the guest house followed—another requirement, another final frustration to help an irresolute recruit change his mind

Was I irresolute? Did I wonder if, just maybe, my father was right after all? Did I reconsider the forfeiting of all future travel, vacation, recreation, possessions, freedom, family ties, sex? Not for a minute. I was consciously eager to find God and his bliss—and so unconsciously eager to escape my sense of personal poverty—that I had not a trace of hesitation.

Finally, on the third day, a couple of hours before vespers, I was unceremoniously ushered into the papal enclosure—so called because for centuries monasteries had been forbidden to women under pain of excommunication by the Pope—and I became a postulant and began two years of basic training, sort of a medieval boot camp. Then, if I still wanted to continue, and if the community voted to accept me, I would make temporary vows for and exchange my white scapular for a black one. After that, with now a total of five years under my belt, and again after a community vote, I would chant my final and solemn vows in front of the gathered monks and become a full-fledged Trappist.

The first thing they did was cut off all my hair. I was rid of that stuff at last! It didn't escape my notice that a closely trimmed red or blond cranium looks much better than those that once sported black hair. Black stubble left a head looking downright grungy. Shaved blonds and redheads looked steam-cleaned by comparison. I had arrived! I was going to be all right after all.

During orientation that first afternoon, the father master of novices alerted me that after the bell for rising I would have only fifteen minutes to get my clothing on, dash cold water in my face, and get into my newly assigned choir stall in church. The next morning when I made my way to where monks do this early morning cold-water trick, I forgot the part of his guidance about there not being time to brush my teeth and started to do so. The observant father master frowned and shook his head. Lesson number one! I remember being a bit disgusted.

The collection of psalms, prayers, and other texts monks recite in monotone or chant in Gregorian plainsong is called the divine office or, more simply, choir duty. The portion in the wee morning hours is the night office

It doesn't take long to learn how to function in a monastic choir. You stand, face the high altar, and respond to the plaintiff monotone cry of the *hebdomadarius,* a priest-monk who leads the liturgy for the week: *Deus, in adjutorium meum intende* "O God, come to my assistance." All respond, *Domine, ad adjuvandum me festina*—"O Lord, make haste to help me." All then turn to face the center of the choir, and add the Latin doxology:

Gloria Patri, et Filio, et Spiritui Sancto. Sicut erat in principio et nunc et simper

Et in saecula saeulorum. Amen. [Glory be to the Father, and to the Son, and to

The Son, and to the Holy Spirit! As it was in the beginning, is now and ever

Shall be, world without end! Amen!

No ritual or romance of outer circumstance, however, can compare with the weekly, monthly, year-by-year *inner* experience that comes with being in a monastery choir. The ritual eventually becomes second nature. Piece by piece most of the Psalter and other texts are memorized. As attention is thus freed, the inner occupation of a gentle and overpowering vision—wordy and reasoned only for a time—takes over. It's not a true vision at all, but an experience so real that *vision* seems its only accurate analog.

What is it you begin to "see?" Not lights or saints, one hopes. Not anything at all if you're lucky. Rather, you begin to experience the perfect harmony and proportion and benevolent nature of the universe. Ultimate meaning lying integral and uncompromised within any and every event! Life—*the* Life—within every person and thing! If the word *peace* weren't so run to death and misapplied to what often amounts to not much more than the satisfaction of getting one's own way, it would be accurate to identify this experience as the coming of peace.

During my first months in the abbey I kept busy learning rituals, the Trappist sign language, and a sizable book of daily usages. Knowing the ancient monastic signs was immediately critical, because while keeping silent was considered essential, some form of communication was equally necessary in order to follow instructions at work. Even communicating signs was forbidden in many places and at certain times, but speaking was forbidden always except when asked a question in class, when in the confessional, and when, with permission asked each time and customarily while kneeling, speaking to the abbot. Everyone took silence seriously, sometimes too much so. Years before my time, a major building burned to the ground one night at the Trappist Abbey of Gethsemani in Kentucky because the one brother who awoke and saw the beginning flames out a dormitory window would neither speak nor make signs to alert anyone during the so-called Great Silence of the Night (signs strictly forbidden).

But from my first day in the abbey, something absorbed me far more than rhapsodizing about an ancient lifestyle. I was unaware of it myself, and apparently there was no one around astute or unvested enough to recognize it for me. I thought I was busy learning sign language and usages, but what I was mostly busy at was learning to turn my self-management over to others. I had come to the abbey to find myself, and I immediately set to work to make sure I never would. We recognized the self-submersion, of course, because it would have been impossible not to, but at least those of us who stuck it out didn't know how to assess it. We missed a basic and horrendously fallacious principle that is still at work in much of Christianity and that was only present in higher relief in monasticism. A major part of organized Christianity, like the monastic life, openly justifies the subversion of the personal and social values of this world for the sake of the next.

Rome has traditionally called Trappist, Trappistines, and other cloistered monks and nuns its favorite children. Why wouldn't it? They're the most diligent of anyone in the church in giving up every trace of self-expression and self-determination. Rome's gauge of excellence is the care individuals show for minutely prescribed church directives and, by consequence, for having no self-determination in anything of consequence. Who in the Roman curia would not love monks and nuns of the Trappist variety, men and women who had given over every semblance of self-direction to the church?

Being a Trappist novice was like having a doting mother who cares not a whit whether her son grows into maturity, but only that he respond to every whim of mama, be no trouble whatsoever to control, be the model conformist in school, and them magically graduate in a manner that will make mama proud of her totally capable young man. The only thing that matters is this brand of institutional formation is, as one rakish translator of church doctrine put it, "pie in the sky when you die by and by."

The year I entered the monastery was a holy year in Roman Catholicism. It will be difficult for anyone who didn't live then to appreciate how different from today were the attitudes in that era toward churches, especially among Catholics. Catholicism was counting it burgeoning membership with glowing gratification. It was the day of the nationally broadcast Monsignor Fulton J. Sheen who spoke across sectarian lines and regularly made cases for despising the progress of this world for the sake of the next. It was the era of Pope Pius XII, who routinely held audiences for world-class scientists, historians, and scholars, many of who listened to him as to an oracle when he expounded on virtually all topics. It was an era of increasingly widespread education, when Catholicism was reaping the benefits of a backlash against the anti-intellectualism of so many Protestant denominations—*and* when the intellectual riches of the Catholic tradition blinded many from noticing some less-evident accompanying corollaries.

During the years I was in the abbey, priests and monks were obliged to swear and sign a solemn oath against the "errors of Modernism." And they did it with vigor—I did it with vigor. I signed it twice: before solemn vows in 1955 and again before ordination as a priest in 1958. By 1958, however, I did it with the beginnings of a grimace.

The monastery held this reactionary, simplistic, self-submerging view and multiplied it into every detail of life. All answers were provided. Quoting Jesus in a manner as ridiculous as it was arbitrary, the abbot regularly reminded his monks that anyone who obeyed the abbot was obeying God, and anyone who did not, was not. Every single action was assured of being right it was prescribed or permitted by Holy Mother Church, which, tugging confidently on her won bootstraps, proclaimed in a loud voice that it was God's voice we were hearing. As did the abbot she had set over us. This overseeing by the church and our divine-right abbot was total.

A minuscule monastic practice of that era illustrates this self-reduction well and deserves careful preservation as the outrageous prank of uproarious angels that it is, a prank played on overly pious men, a monument to the inane extremes reachable by organized religion.

During my years in the abbey it was the custom for monks to file singly past the abbot and bow profoundly to him when leaving the abbey church after the last bit of choir duty of the day. The bow was a sign of our belief in him as God's representative.

For the first few years that I was in the abbey, there was a detail in that ceremony that probably went unnoticed by visitors. While bowing to the abbot, we would, if natured demanded, raise the sleeve of our cowl to our lips to request his permission to visit the toilets before going to our individual cells for the night. He would grant divine endorsement for this blessed event by nodding his head. I have never, before or since, urinated with such a conscious sense of heavenly support! Today, when nature calls, I simply go somewhere and peacefully pee, never even considering the possibility of asking permission from anybody—so far have I fallen into the errors of Modernism.

Somebody telling me when to urinate was not exactly what I needed in my life then. But since I thought it was a question of spiritual growth to embrace everything put before me, I eagerly conformed and obeyed and waited with anticipation for my superiors to spell out ever-greater detail as to how God wanted me to hold my face while I thought the thoughts they told me. He wanted me to think. That description, unfortunately, is fact and not fiction. And it was the practice of a whole monastery of men, not just of one admittedly neurotic fledgling. If Trappists in those days carried dependence to extremes and turned the church's expectation into caricature, and we certain did, it was from conscious hunger for holiness as much as from unconscious neurotic self-diffidence. I recognized the diffidence only in myself then, but in retrospect I notice there were no senior monks around free enough of the same drives to pull junior monks back from such silliness. Monks far more mature than I were asking permission to urinate right alongside us newcomers.

Indignant Catholic churchmen will hotly deny the picture I've just painted. Unfortunately for their position, there are countless inactive priests, ex-monks, ex-nuns, ex-lay people—"recovering Catholics," as many call themselves—who have abandoned the church, and sometimes all religion, simply because what I'm recounting here was so oppressively true.

Novices in Trappist life typically experience a severe crisis soon after entering. Shorn of hair; wearing stiff, canvas like underclothing and scratchy woolen outer garments both day and night; shorted of sleep on stone-hard straw mattresses; locked in a silence never punctuated by recreation, sports, or conversation; spending five to eight hours each day in choir; forbidden under pain of eternal hell to even think about masturbation; fed on a diet of bread and boiled vegetables with no meat, fish, or eggs, seldom butter, and only sometimes milk or cheese; the majority of new monks in my day quickly decided to run their vocational plans through one of those multi vacuum tube IBM computers one more time.

Shortly before I decided to leave the monastery, I researched the personnel records it had become my duty to maintain. Roughly five percent of those men who applied to the abbey were eventually admitted, and, curiously, five percent of those admitted were still there five years later to make their solemn vows.

My appreciation of cloistered life changed substantially during my time in it. For the first few years or so, I loved it for its great dignity, its in-depth and protracted training, its open-ended potential for idealism, and, unknowingly, for the effective escape it offered to my lingering fear and guilt. Starting out in the neurotically pure delight of having my life run for me by others, and continuing for a time in the infantile joy and superficial semblance of peace that such submission provided the insecure, I slowly evolved until eventually I found myself running afoul of much of the edifice in which I had until then found my security. During my last years in the abbey, I felt a growing and increasingly defined criticism for what many of my fellow monks and I had come to see as the confused priorities of local and Rome-based managers.

During my first year there, I was a novice, dressed completely in white, except for the denim habits we wore when working outdoors. My college education was interrupted for daily classes in spirituality, meditation, and the history of monasticism, particularly of the Trappist order, officially named the Order of Cistercians of the Strict Observance, or, more simply, Trappists. After two years as a novice, the community voted to accept me as a member of the community, and I made my temporary vows and became a "simple professed." This meant that I was given the hooded black scapular that has been characteristic of Cistercians since their founding in 1098. At the end of that three-year period, the community voted again to accept me, permanently this time, and I chanted my solemn vows during the solemn Mass in the abbey church, vows *usque ad mortem*—"until death." I was now known as one of the "solemnly professed" monks. These five vows meant that I agreed that, for the glory of God and the salvation of souls, including my own, I would for the rest of my life on this earth be perfectly chaste, would own nothing whatsoever, would obey the abbot and church authorities in all good things, would never leave the abbey for any reason whatsoever except the need for hospitalization, and would never quit striving for perfection. When I sat down amid the senior monks on the evening of August 15, 1955, in my great white cowl, the outer garment that covered the black scapular and white tunic beneath it, I was a full-fledged Trappist at last, and fully determined to remain one until death.

The daily routine of choir duty, meditation, study, and work continued virtually without change from day to day over the years. Christmases and Easter came and went. Trappists in my era had neither television nor radios. As an example, a Korean War came and almost went before the abbot, who alone was permitted to read the daily *Salt Lake Tribune*, told all about it. A president was shot, and for some reason the abbot told us the same day. A Pope died, and the abbot kept us posted on each detail of the election of a new one. Eventually the abbot even posted color photos from *Life* magazine showing the old Pope's burial and the new Pope's coronation. Postulants became novices, novices became junior monks, and junior monks became senior monks. More and more monks completed the long studies for the priesthood and were ordained.

Such a life would have been lethally boring but for the inner dimension, which was our whole reason for being there and what we were busy doing beyond appearances. The monastery was a place where one learned to contact God, where one ordered his whole life to do precisely—and only—that.

The surface of the pond was without ripple, but new currents were beginning to move beneath the seeming tranquility. Some of us were uncovering forgotten selves and sensed a heretofore unknown restlessness. The abbots of the Trappist order, with a few remarkable exceptions, reacted by marching smartly backward. One conservative side began digging in as the progressive began to dig out.

One day I asked Father Thomas, a professor of moral theology, why the church's rejection of birth control was held to be adequately justified by a simple appeal to natural law, when the same "law" is ignored in identical applications elsewhere. He furrowed his brow, and, pressured by a now curious class, reluctantly asked me to explain my question. Catholicism has always taught that to dam the flow of semen by condoms or other forms of birth control, or to "spill" it in masturbation, is eternally damnable and will send the perpetrator to hell. "Such acts deny the seed its natural, God-intended purpose" went the institutional wisdom." Why then, I asked the professor, does the church not equally condemn our grinding of wheat to make bread and our crushing of grapes to make wine? Wheat kernels and grape seeds are, just as clearly as human seeds, intended by nature to reproduce their own kind. Sacrificing the former for food flies in the face of natural law every bit as much as do condoms and spermicides. Could it actually be God's will that horses eat oats and thus deny those innocent seeds their natural reproductive goal—or is that practice, too, but a result of "original sin"?

The professor was aghast and, significantly, had no answer.

Shortly afterward the abbot called me into his office and spoke to me about their common concern for my faith. I reassured him I was full of faith, but while faith for me might at times exceed the reach of reason, I refused to let it ever contradict reason. I went on to wonder, in his presence, if most or all church doctrines and practices did not require reevaluation now that the human race was becoming more broadly educated and less uncritically credulous. The abbot heard, I think, not a word I was saying, such organizational filters did he have over his ears. He was a brilliant man, and, but for those filters, would have been out front with the rest of us rethinking the nonsense we have inherited from the church's past.

When I finished formal studies for the priesthood, two years after being ordained (a common practice in monasteries where studies stretch substantially beyond the usual seminary curricula), I was restless and well-trained monk. And I had only begun formulating questions, questions that I was addressing most of all to myself.

Studies had been demanding, but I still had ample time for substantial amounts of additional research in the abbey library. Even after my classes were completed, I continued to read voraciously, and the insights began to come once I started daring to do my own thinking.

A statement in a book by the French philosopher Jacques Maritain startled me one evening in a way I shall remember forever. I was sitting in the chapter room, the place where monks gather before going into the church for the final bit of choir duty at the end of each day. This is evening chapter, during which the abbot briefly addresses the community and then one of the monks reads from a spiritual or philosophical work for about fifteen minutes, a leftover from the centuries when only priests and students for ordination could read.

I remember staring wide-eyed at the reader after he had read a sentence from Maritain that instantly became for me a major breakthrough.

I can no longer name Maritain's specific book, much less quote verbatim his actual sentence, but he wrote something to the effect that none of us will ever move beyond the mechanical, institutional, legalistic formulations of "faith" and get to its actual content unless and until we gain a contemplative experience of existence. In less metaphysical terms, he was saying that we must take care lest we forever prattle on in kosher formulae and never go after a far deeper grasp of the meaning and experience of existing.

That chapter room event was my first indication that the thrust of my urgency to get well, to grow, would demand that one day I break out of every monastic mold of conformity. Maritain hooked something in me I didn't yet understand, and for most of my years in the monastery would have been frightened by had I understood it. But life is a process, and process is why we're here. Process takes time, and that's what time is for. First I gained fleeting insights, then fuller and fuller understanding, and eventually the time arrived when I was invited to act on that understanding. And finally I found I had the courage to act.

In the end, it was not studies or intellectualizing, or even the hours of chanted prayer in choir, but meditation itself that gave me such a new and undeniable experience of my existence that I dared to launch out on my own. From classes, reading, and consultation with my spiritual master I gained new conceptual tools with which to better understand, Reality, yes. And these were priceless. But it was the actual *experiencing* of that Reality in meditation, as I have explained, that caused my tires to touch the road and carry me out of fear-based conformity to freedom.

The course of studies on the road to the priesthood at the abbey required that we inch our way through every page of the thirteenth—century *Summa theological* of Aquinas and through much of his *Summa contra gentiles*. We plowed-groaned-through a soporific, four-volume, fine-print-Late expose of the theology of morality (as a certain Italian organization man, Professor

Fanfani, understood morality, that is). Course by course we marched through the seven traditional facets of scholastic philosophy, and were always studying one aspect or another of the Bible. A few ancillary subjects like church history, cannon law, and "sacred eloquence" (how to give a homily were added.) But to have said all that is only to have reproduced a page from a college catalog. It's to have said nothing about the real nature of monastic studies. Listing courses doesn't mention the impact that meditative silence and choir duty seven times a day has on those studies.

When we start to meditate with regularity, something happens inside that absorbs, reshapes, and infuses everything we think and feel and do. Until then we may have thought our inner life was made up of thoughts and feelings only, with an intuition thrown in here and there. Meditation opens a higher and deeper, more expanded and more centered dimension—a dimension that begins to shape our lives long before we're conscious of it.

When mediation becomes a significant part of each day, everything else in our days appears in its beyond-the-physical—"metaphysical"—and, properly understood, "spiritual" context. This isn't a conscious process, and we may not become aware of it for a long time. But it happens inevitably.

In a life lived in silence, the impact of philosophy, theology, and sacred writings quickly transcends all the specific data being learned. Study indirectly assists mediation, but meditation substantially transforms study. Study is suddenly more than a matter of learning facts; it becomes an integral part of an inner adventure.

Studying to become an ordained priest in a monastery is one thing in church managers' minds, but it's something else for the men they send through it. Monastic studies can precipitate more than what these churchmen had in mind—something, in fact, quite opposed to what they had in mind. The freedom that resulted for many of us after our protracted training didn't come merely because we had dedicated professors and a fine library. It resulted because of the meditative context with which monastic life supplemented the studies. Accumulation of facts doesn't set one free; what one does with, how one experiences, those facts is what sets one's heart dancing in freedom.

It was in meditation that I caught my first glimpse of the transcendental experience of Existence that Maritain had written about. And it was that experience, when more complete, that freed me once and for all from dogmatism, fear, dependence, and the obsessive gyrations of anxious self-perpetuation in institutionalized religion.

It is impossible to say when this took place other than to say it was the process of many years. Slowly—*very* slowly, for fear plays a powerful role when we start to reassess familiar faith—I began to see that my experience in meditation neither supported nor matched what the church told me about its big separate God. During my last year at the abbey, especially, I consciously met a Source within me that was far more like what I had read about Emerson, Holmes, and the Hindus that what Catholicism had taught me.

The church had set out to teach me to pray, and even when it used the word *meditation*, it actually only meant inner prayer, mental prayer. In fact, willy-nilly, I moved beyond mental prayer and into the experience of meditation. I eventually saw that Datur, Kiefer, and Topel were correct and the monastery wrong about the ideal way to approach and respond to religious, transcendental fact—to God. Meditation is not a dissecting and deepening absorption of doctrine as Catholic practice, if not theory, presents it. Meditation is the experience of that Ultimate Reality, the *conscious* experience of it.

I could almost hear those learned men heaving a sigh of relief when I began spending more and more time in private meditation, increasingly undistracted by the tabernacle on high altar, totally turned inward to find there the Source and Self of all things.

Years later I found a Buddhist metaphor that aptly describes my state during my last year in the abbey. I was like a rock in a stream, smiling as it lets anything and everything float over and around it.

One of the retreatants who came to the abbey for a week of spiritual R and R, was a General's chief of chaplains, back briefly from his outfit in Korea.

Free to talk to him as the monastery's retreat master for guests, I spent hours with him walking in the hills, he with his problems, I with mine. During this interchange with someone back from the intensity of a past war, I began for the first time to see real-world implications to the insights I had gained. By the end of the week, I suspected—also for the first time—what I had to do.

It took a special hour of meditation a couple of weeks later for me finally to find the courage to tell myself, and only then the abbot, that I had decided to leave the monastery.

That memorable meditation was a scary invitation that could have been couched in words straight out of the Bible: Friend, come up higher.

I was a well-educated, increasing self-confident, a relatively young priest with an uncanny eye for ecclesiastical bullshit—and the testicular fortitude to call it what it is—when Brother Nicholas drove me to the Salt Lake City airport on a bright but cold day in February. I was off on an adventure I couldn't have fantasized six months before. Off to the City of Three Rivers and then back to another City by the Bay for another graduate program in theology at the Jesuit University of San Francisco.

As we pulled away and past the sign that was still promising its *pax* to all who entered, I remember being surprised at how easy it was for me to leave. I felt not a trace of guilt, fear, hesitation. *Au contraire!* I was feeling vital, whole, in charge as never before. The singing in my heart made me think of those heady months when I entered years before.

Many others had left ahead of me, and still more were to leave later. I was glad I wasn't leaving in bitterness as some had. The reasons some gave for going ranged from ridiculous and resentful to idealistic and informed. Peter left after reading that fish is good brain food and when the abbot proved unwilling to give the order to start serving fish. Augustine left simply because the celibate life was too lonely for him. Cyprian left because he resented even the two hours of daily manual labor that interrupted his scholarly pursuits. One young man left in a great huff within three weeks of his arrival when he found out he had been misinformed about monasteries being places where homosexual activity was part of the observance. A few withdrew to join other monastic orders where, they judged, their talents or spiritual tastes would be more effectively engaged. Two particularly admirable and memorable young left to become hermits. Several stormed out in outspoken anger and seemed unable to pinpoint any specific complaint, although to most of us it seemed fairly evident that diet and early rising were the probably unrealized reasons. At least one withdrew simply because the abbot's personality rubbed him the wrong way.

Anyhow, family, my high school friends, Mr. Charlie Grube *et alii* (oops! Excuse the Latin), my wish is to see all of you soon. In the interlude, I wish you all peace in the heart accompanied with lots of love.

Signed,

Father Jack

We are now all aware of Jack Flynn's new life. When I see him I'm going to take him down to the football field where he became an icon and our hero. I remember in Korea when I was assigned my own fighter, F-86F #52-4401. I named it *CHOLLY CON CARNE*, my favorite dish of spicy peppers, meat, and plenty of beans. I figured if I couldn't shoot a MiG down, I could kill him with home made gas or bad breath. I asked our Chaplin to please visit the flight line and bless my airplane. Father Bill Worrell was his name. He did just that and I never had an abort, or close call in 61 rough air-to-ground missions. I know I was scared 61 times but that is a different story.

Maybe I can get Fr. Jack to bless our high school athletic field with the thought that no athlete, visitor or home team, would ever get hurt or injured to the point of permanent disability.

Talk to you later!

CHRISTMAS TIME BRINGS AN END TO MELANCHOLY! NEW YEARS DELIVERS AUSPICIOUS EXPECTATION!

Liz was happy; the New Year was about to be born and she was with Arnie. They were alone in the small but beautiful Mountain View Hotel in Greensburg only about four miles from St. Vincent College and Seminary in Latrobe, Pa. Liz had driven from Pittsburgh during the morning and met Arnie at the hotel. She told her mother she was staying at the hotel where she registered in her name and would be going to a New Year's party at one of the fraternity houses off campus. Not one person, friends, family, or otherwise (with the exception of Mr. Grube) knew of their liaison. Arnie was housed at the seminary when not traveling for less than two days or so and was not restricted, or questioned about where he went or what he did. The "management" of the seminary knew only that he was on a sabbatical from Rome and would be returning about the middle of March.

The afternoon Liz arrived she fell into Arnie's arms and launched into a series of warm, sensual kisses followed by nth degree saturnalian sexual intercourse enjoying every second without compunction, or contrition, or regret, or guilt. They knew no barriers; nor blockades, mental or physical. Liz felt she was at last becoming a wholehearted, salubrious woman learning to give and take in the determination to satisfy her man. Humpty Dumpty Arnie put her back together again after losing Jack and Joanne whose memories seemed to float farther and farther away with every glimmering climax.

During dinner that evening she recounted her trip to her grandparents' home near Scranton and her visit with Dahlia in Elizabeth, N.J.

She related to Arnie about Dahlia being in school under the Benedictine Sisters of Elizabeth but does not travel as her parents were now farming corn and sunflowers in North Dakota. They are pleased to be able to meet all her costs with extra for "having a few nights out with the girls." But Arnie, Liz said, "Dahlia was a little more subdued than the last time we visited. I'm not sure that she is not very seriously entertaining the thought of joining the Benedictine Sisters. One evening in the library at school," Liz said as she broke away from holding Arnie and rolled on her back while grabbing a big while pillow and pulled it to her chest, "I looked up general information on nuns. I was surprised to learn that Roman Catholic Church law uses nun to refer only to women with solemn vows and those whose vows are not solemn. Interesting!"

"That's true, dear. The nuns are devoted to a purely contemplative life or to a life of charity, including teaching and nursing. Why don't you roll back over here and teach me something," Arnie said with a big smile.

"Me! Teach you! Are you kidding? If it weren't for you I'd still be a pent up sissy pan—." She didn't finish she drew more comfortably close and started a torrent of caressing his lips.

Liz woke up; it was dark. She was flat on her back with a warm comforter over her. "Arnie," she said!

"Yes, my love. I'm right here next to you. You were in a deep sleep! You snore! Kept me awake!"

"Aw, you're crazy," Liz said. "You just say that to put me on."

"Who, me!" Arnie said.

"No! The guy next door! What time is it?"

"Time for us to freshen up and find a nice place serving turkey," Arnie said as he pivoted on his rear end and with his two legs and feet together started pushing Liz out of bed.

"Stop that! Stop!" Liz yelled. "You big bully," she said as she was pushed to the floor in an aggregate of sheets, pillows and blankets. She was laughing as she said, "OK! Tough boy! I owe you one!" Liz had never been as happy in her life as she was then!

They found a "gourmet's delight" restaurant and enjoyed a dinner of a fine white wine and a turkey dinner with all the trimmings. Over coffee and pumpkin pie Arnie said, "Liz, you knew I had to return to Rome sometime; the sometime will be by St. Patrick's Day. I had a letter waiting for me when I returned from my Cleveland, Geneva, Lake Erie, Warren trip. I feel we love one another but our separate lives and our calling requiring specialized knowledge keep us from being *in* love. I never knew, never knew I would meet someone like you. I really was a devoted priest but forgot all that the day I saw that lousy golf swing of yours." Liz smiled. "We are both mature enough to have realized it couldn't last but for this past—what is it, ten, twelve months I carried only you in my heart. Thought of nothing else! But now I must face the aftermath. When I confess I won't be facing the wrath of God. He understands these things happen. But when I confess I must be sure I can take the loss of you. It will take a long time."

"I know, my beautiful loving man. Not many women have a chance to say that. I can, and I mean it. I told Mr. Grube I couldn't allow myself to be *in* love. Heck, Arnie, we both knew we were on shallow ground but we pushed away the quicksand and enjoyed a fabulous time. We gave our hearts and souls to one another with all of the passion that could possibly come from us. Now we have to "pay the piper," so to speak. It won't be easy; I'll cry at times and miss you terribly. But I don't want to talk about it anymore. We separate in the morning but we still have tonight."

A clear cold day surrounded by the rays of the sun faced Liz as one of the rays awakened Liz from an intense sleep. She wiped her eyes with her fists and blinked them into clarity. She looked! Once! Twice! Arnie was gone. Silence encircled her. She knew it had to end. Looking back she said to herself, "I am more of a woman; but less of a lady!"

FR. FLYNN; THE FAMILY'S EASTER BUNNY

WILL THE RADIANT SUN TAKE RESIDENCE IN LIZ'S SOUL??

There was no doubt in her heart; Liz missed Arnie. Yes, the sex was something she missed but the real problem was her lonely heart. She could play golf but first Chartiers Country club ground keepers would have to sweep off six inches of snow. "But", she said to herself, "March roars in like a lion and sneaks out like a lamb." Since I'm on the late hours shift at KDKA, I'll work out in the mornings, hit a few golf balls, clean up at the women's spa and go to work from the country club. "One of these days, I'll give myself a present and start taking my golf lessons again from Mr. Flynn."

Liz had met, and dated, a couple of pleasant and amiable men at the TV station but each seemed to have too much baggage; one was living with his overbearing mother, the other, more mature, very successful entrepreneur, was going through a nasty divorce. He was up front about it and wasn't looking to sleep with her but the conversation always ended up about *his* problems. The talk of money and their unhappiness brought back too much of Joanne. Her dear friend seemed to have taken up a slot in her heart and wouldn't go away. Which was OK with Liz; at least she had someone to talk to although the cerebral conversation always brought up the same mysteriousness; WHY!

The station, KDKA, had given her what was considered a fair and potentially lucrative contract. Her experience with Powers and Breck plus her intrinsic beauty will, in time, ease the way to a newscaster's position. In the interlude, she was prepared for hard work. Liz realized TV and radio announcers perform many responsibilities both on and off the air.

They generally announce all of the important information relating to the public, including news, time, weather, and commercials. Often they will even do the necessary writing and research for a certain on-air prompt or discussion. Others perform interviews or commentary for certain public events. Successful announcers are usually quite popular with their listeners and occasionally make public appearances to promote special events.

Announcers on the radio are often referred to as disc jockeys (DJs) that may specialize in a particular area of music. They typically do not make their own choices when selecting music, as this is left up to management teams who prepare talk, music, and commercial schedules. These DJs perform common tasks of on-air interviewing, taking listener requests, managing on-air contests, and commenting on news, traffic, and weather.

Liz was pleased she had chosen the right vocation for study at school.

One evening at the studio while Liz learning how to manage on-air contests, one of the most popular disc jockeys, a big guy originally from New Orleans by the name of "Gordie" Jenkins approached Liz and said, "Honey, I gotta' grand idea, and I was wunderin' if you all would help me gather some data?"

Liz looked up at Gordie (he was always a gentleman) and said, "Mr. Jenkins, you know me well enough by now that I would be happy to assist you. Besides, I have learned you are a low handicap golfer so I must be nice to you to get a few lessons."

"Child, Gordie said," You all's so full of that female pulchritude that I'd spend 'nuff time with you to put you on the tour. Why, you'd be the female Arnold Palmer. Instead of "Arnie's Army," we'd have "Liz's Ladies." Have a good time too! They both laughed.

"Well, Liz," Gordie continued, "I've been a thinkin'! This week is the 20th anniversary of the downtown flood. My Dad had just been transferred to the capitol of Harrisburg as an assistant Public Works Director, but he was soon up to his you know what in Pittsburgh's horrific problems. I'll never forget how hard he worked and now that he is gone I thought I would pay tribute to him and many other of those fine heroes with a series of two-way talks with our fans. Would you help me gather a few details? Gonna' cost yaw'l a trip or two to the library!"

"Gordie, I will be happy too and I'm honored that you asked. I'm sorta' new around here. Everyone has been happy to help me get acquainted with the business end and your request will only make it better. Where and when do I start?"

Liz spent long hours for several days between the library, the very hospitable librarian, KDKA, and Gordie. She gathered, in detail, (so Gordie could edit out anything deems not necessary) the following information:

Rapidly diminishing water supply!

The specter of thirst and pestilence joining the twin horror of fire and flood!

At least 135 persons were believed dead in 11 states and the District of Columbia!

Estimate damage downtown—$35,000,000—would be multiplied when the havoc is counted.

Deaths by drowning, fire, and explosions were numerous!

A happy note! Twins were born in Mercy Hospital; a child was born to a woman isolated by the flood. Two Coast Guard boats saved them!

St. Francis periled!

Few street lights! The Golden Triangle stricken where Pittsburgh's towering office and mercantile buildings ravaged by flood. Banks, stores, hotels struggling out of mud and water!

Household Life! Bathing suspended. No radios blaring. Candles furnished light. Cups, bottles, jugs, filled with water. Pantries stocked with canned food. Electric refrigeration useless! Housewives postpone washing, ironing, sweeping, cleaning. Dishes frequently unwashed! Some heating systems useless! Milk deliveries good. Gasoline for the family auto scarce! Walking discovered by many!

These were the highlights of the dreadful low life of the mud and contaminated water existence for residents of Western Pennsylvania, Ohio and West Virginia. Liz had done a noteworthy job and Mr. Jenkins rewarded her by letting her handle many of the in-coming calls. "She was comfortable and comparable to others who had been in that position in the past," Gordie told his management. It was duly noted!

Twenty four hours after the good Brother dropped off Jack at the airport, he was perusing the rental ski and boots department of one many sports' shops in Park City. He had wired his Dad from a Western Union office in Salt Lake asking for a "loan" after he decided to cancel his flight and ski for two or three days in remembrance to the time before he entered the Abbey. He was anxious to start on the "bunny slope" and advance to the time when he could parallel down the slopes, standing straight up, arms out wide with dangling ski poles yelling to himself, "I'm Free! I'm Free"!

Fr. Jack was happy; with himself, his priesthood and with what the Catholic Church offered to him as a young priest. His Dad sent him plenty of money. He could go to dinner, have a delicious meal to his choosing, plus a dry, straight up, vodka, ice cold, with an olive and an onion—martini!

His friend Augustine left Holy Trinity because celibacy bothered him. Jack had been tested; the future of a celibate life did not bother him. He often prayed for the help needed to overcome *any* temptations; for now he was very comfortable with himself.

Two and a half days in the sun, on the slopes, gave Jack a red face with the outline of his protective goggles. He was one of the gang that retreated to the bars and grills after the last run. A recently ordained priest, obvious to no one, "Bull Sh—ing" with the guys and gals, enjoying his independence that no one could imagine after years of restraint and restrictions! Jack felt like he just gottin' out of jail. All things were turning out well.

More accurately, Jack realized all things were well all along. More days were passing in gentleness and humor, and dawns were consistently getting brighter.

Jack arrived at Pittsburgh's County airport to a happy and ardent family. Many years had passed, but soon he felt very comfortable. He thought of Homer, 800 years before Christ, and one his masterpieces, *Odyssey*, "Where shall a man find sweetness to surpass his own home and his parents! In far off lands he shall not, though he finds a house of gold."

Coming home meant more to Jack than returning to a bit of familiar geography. Home is a context that includes values, emotions, thoughts, and special persons. He would be lying if he said to himself that he hadn't thought of Liz. Coming home to one's Self in developed spirituality means something similar: a returning to renewed familiarity with oneness, to conscious union with love for everything and everyone.

It's been a long journey for Jack, but there in no bemoaning in that statement. It's simply a fact that it was a long difficult journey to today from the evening of his high school graduation speech anxious for an OK from everyone's, anyone's approval. But now, at last, the journey has brought Jack home to his Self where, all along, fulfillment and complete blessedness lay in waiting as a priest.

Jack took the long way around to learn that spiritual masters were not talking in metaphor, but meant literally what they were saying when they told us that the kingdom of God lies within us. The place of our source of fulfillment and bliss is only found within. Jack learned that Heaven is not a place, but a condition. Jack's mind slipped back to his football days where conditioning was "God." The moniker for Heaven will again will give him a boost, like his high school linemen did, and allow him a broken-field run for a rapturous ninety five yard kick-off return.

The rectory at St. Philips had been enlarged a bit while he was gone and he was enjoying the freedom of a private guest room and bath. The meals were deliciously prepared by a young woman from Germany who married a GI now in his third year of college. The GI bill and the salary from the parish tendered great help.

One night during a dinner of a top sirloin steak smothered with mushrooms the priest in charge of the parish, sixty five year old Fr. Thomas Becket, named by his great grandmother after Saint Thomas Becket, (1118-1170) archbishop of Canterbury, asked Fr. Jack if he would give a sermon of his choice at a Sunday mass.

"Of course," Jack said. "Any Mass you say."

Padre Tom, as everyone called him, lived a saintly life accompanied with a sense of humor.

If St. Thomas Becket had one he didn't get a chance to use it. He was murdered in the Cathedral itself and was canonized in 1173. Canterbury became an immediate shrine; immortalized in Chaucer's *CANTERBURY TALES*.

Anyhow, Fr. Tom would always have a joke to tell at dinner.

One night he said, "A minister made a home visit to one of his congregation, a deaf lady. She was apologetic at having missed the sermon. He said, "That's all right. You didn't miss anything."

"That's what I heard."

Padre Tom always loved to laugh at his own jokes! A saint! At 72! We all hoped he would live to be a hundred.

One evening he said he had a joke and it really fitted him. He said, "The sermon had been going on endlessly. Finally the rector's voice cracked and said, 'What more can I say?'"

One parishioner yelled, "How about 'Amen'!"

Everyone loved that one!

Fr. Becket picked the 9:00AM mass on Palm Sunday. Jack said to himself. "Hmmm! A week before Easter! Many of the parishioners will be fulfilling their yearly obligation of the Latin rite requiring that its **practitioners** confess at least once a year. So I think I'll speak on the Seal of Confession!"

Jack spoke! With few notes! He stood straight up, shoulders back, but in a relaxed sort of comfortable way, high in the pulpit (he said to himself that if this thing was any higher he would need oxygen) and began; first by telling them that their "once a year" was up and "come see me in the confessional" and you'll walk out with a great sense of relief with a smile on your face. And then he added, "And don't worry! I can't say a word to anyone!"

He thought he caught a few expressions of amusement.

"For Catholic priests, the confidentiality of all statements made by penitents during the course of confession is absolute. The strict confidentiality is known as the Seal of the Confessional. According to the Code of Canon Law, 'The sacramental seal is inviolable; therefore it is absolutely forbidden for a confessor to betray in any way a penitent in words or in any manner and for any reason.' Priests may not reveal what they have learned during confession to anyone, even under the threat of their own death or that of others."

He stopped and looked over all the parishioners and said with a smile, "Don't worry about me and that death threat, folks. I have heard confessions that have already scared me to death!" That brought many snickers and smiles. "What the heck," he said to himself. "The Catholic church needs to stop taking itself too seriously. This is one of the reasons I gave up trying to be a monk."

Jack continued, "This non-revelation is unique to the Seal of the Confessional. Many other forms of confidentiality, including in most states attorney-client privilege, allow ethical breaches of the confidence to save the life of another. For a priest to break that confidentiality would lead to what is known as a *latae sententiae* automatic excommunication reserved to the Holy See. In a criminal matter, a priest may encourage the penitent to surrender to authorities. However, this is the extent of the leverage he wields; he may not directly or indirectly disclose the matter to civil authorities himself."

Jack then told the parishioners that he wanted to keep the sermon short but it didn't "short change" the importance of a confession being extremely strict about what is said staying between the priest and confessor. He also reached for his notes and announced, "Confessions will be heard from 1:00PM until 8:00PM on Saturday and an hour before each mass on Easter Sunday."

"Go in Peace and God bless all of you!"

One parishioner was heard to say, "Gee! Here we have, as I understand it, a real high school hero preaching to us and he was a humble as can be. I often wonder what goes on behind the gates of a monastery. I'm sure the monks don't beat 'em into mortification!!"

"You're right, Mama," said a man with an authoritative demeanor. Physically, Jack was not touched. But mentally, the strict, controlling severity of the practice of trying to beat faith into a man that, through his ingrained love of God, wanted to be there in the first place. It was just too demoralizing for Father Jack. It weakened his spirit; his soul. What kind of a religion would be proud of that?"

Jack thought he would start hearing confessions starting about 3PM. The three priests in three confessionals could "handle the load," if you will excuse the expression. Most, until later in the day, would be the kids from third to sixth or seventh grade anyhow. Jack took a flask of cold water and some cookies from the pantry in the rectory.

The first confession was a young boy. "Bless me Father for I have sunned. It's been three weeks since my last confession."

"Yes," Jack said. "It's nice that you go to confession child but it's not sun, but sin. Do you understand that?"

"Yes," Father. I think so! Doesn't sun burn you and doesn't the sun send you to hell so you'll be burnt?"

"Oh yes! Ah! You are right young man. Please, go ahead."

"I hit my sister because she told my Mommy that I gah gahed and pee peed in the woods!"

"You hit your sister? That's not being a good boy. Wha—Wha—What did you hit her with? Did she cry?"

"No, Father. She just him me back; with her tennis racket; and I cried!

"Now wait a minute! You were a bad boy for poop'n in the woods in the first place. And your sister was only trying to help you and you had no right to hit her. What did you hit her with?"

"My jump rope"!

"Now that's not right. You should be ashamed! A jump rope is for jumping not hitting girls. Now ask God to forgive you and say three Hail Mary's and say your act of contrition and God bless you. And be a good boy! Do you hear?"

A meek voice answered, "Yes Father."

Again, another young boy! "Bless me Father for I have sinned etc, etc. I have been a bad boy."

"A bad boy"! Jack said. "Now why were you a bad boy?"

"My Mommy made me stand in the corner—with my face to the wall."

"You must have been a bad boy. What happened?"

"I farted"!

Silence! A complete quietude inside the confessional as Fr. Jack muffled his laugh until he finally asked, "Did you get any on you?"

"No," came the somewhat saturnine answer. "Just gas"!!

Jack couldn't keep his guffaw back but covered his mouth with a bogus laugh while telling the boy not to worry, his mother still loved him, say an Our Father and Hail Mary and, as he blessed him he said, "Don't worry about the Act of Contrition. You're a good boy!"

"Ah! The ingenuousness of kids," Jack thought.

The hours kept moving toward the evening in dull monotonous murmuring sounds as the exclamations of "Bess me Father, missing Sunday mass, fingering of girl friends, cheating on spouses, birth control practices, female and male masturbations. Fr. Jack told one teenager who masturbated so often his penance was to "get an eight hour job swinging a heavy sledge hammer so at night he would be too tired to play with himself."

And, just as life sometimes seems so lacking in luster, it has a way to manage or treat "things" with little spark of brilliance. A young boy confessed that he was told by his Mother he talked too much and had put him to bed without dinner and took away half his allowance.

"Why was that?" Jack asked.

"My Mother had some friends at the house playing cards and one of them asked me if I missed my Daddy since he went to the Army?"

I said that I did. And then she asked me if I "enjoyed sleeping with Mommy?" I said, "Yes, I do and I sleep with her every night except Saturday night because that's when my uncle comes over and sleeps with her."

Mommy jumped up and yelled, "TOMEEEFY! GO TO YOUR ROOM!" She seemed very mad so I just turned around and ran upstairs. I stopped at the top and listened. It was very quiet and soon the ladies left."

"Well, Tommy, you did the right thing by obeying your Mommy. So just say a Hail Mary and be a good boy and then you can pray to Jesus and ask if he can get you your money back!"

There was a little commotion outside of the confessional; minor, short lived. Jack wondered?? But his thoughts were immediately directed to his right where someone was struggling to enter the confessional and kneel down. Someone said, in a lady's voice loud enough for him to hear, "Damn it!"

It was now quiet! Noiseless! The party had evidently "settled in" and was waiting for the priest to slide back what Jack called "the window of opportunity."

Mission accomplished! It was always a little dark inside; just an outline of the priest and confessor. A specter whispering to an apparition under Middle Ages circumstances; but the sins to be confessed were modern; prophylactics, birth control pills, lesbian women, homosexual men, cheating on the sacrament of marriage, adultery, and even going to communion with known mortal sins on someone's soul. The person didn't want to be embarrassed and hit with a fusillade of questions from the Nuns in Monday morning's Religion class. That's what is known as "taking a chance on Dove." Peace be with you until next Saturday's confessions!

"Be peaceful," Fr. Jack said to the frustrated woman on the other side of the screen. Please go ahead."

"Bless me Father for I have sinned. It's been at least 36 weeks or more since my last confession. I have been lying to myself because I have been committing adultery; many times. And I was rationalizing by saying it was "OK" because it was so enjoyable. My partner is now gone and in his absence I realize now how wrong and shameful I have been."

Jack was taken aback but not startled. The Abbey had prepared him for shock and circumstance. He asked, "Was this with a married man with family, or unhappily married, divorced or what?"

"This was not the situation, Father. I met this man by chance at the golf course. He offered to help me with my game and we had lunch, then dinner, then sex. This was over a period of about eight to ten weeks. My abominable, awful offence against God is I found out he was a priest on a sabbatical and the intercourse was so pleasurable I didn't want to stop. He's gone now; back to Rome with both of our lives ruined (she was crying) but hoping that time and the church will put us back on the right paths to honest conduct and happiness."

"Young lady," Jack said. "It appears to me you have been thinking about this confession for a period of time the amount of which I can't fathom, and you've come up with a pretty good speech. My wonder is, are you sincere? I think I detect bona fide reality and I know you are crying so there must be truth, but do you have anything else to say?"

"Yes, Father! I am so sincere and overpowered with guilt that I could only confess to you Father. Jack, it's Elizabeth McGovern!"

Silence! A bombshell! Narcosis! Jack could not believe what he just heard! He fell back in his chair, arms raised and elbows bent allowing his hands and fingers to press against the sides of his stupefied head. Liz!—LIZ!—Liz, my high school sweetheart; love of my life! I knew something might happen; certainly not in the confessional. I *knew* you must have known! I know you must have known; I wrote to the family and copied Mr. Grube. But I couldn't pick up the phone and say, "Let's go to dinner. Not that there is anything wrong with that but everything in life is timing and I couldn't put it together. And now, by Gosh Almighty I meet you, voice only, in a confessional. It's mind boggling! An overwhelming sea of fright and amazement! Forget the

Act of Contrition. I'll say it for you! I know you're sorry! 'Oh my God, Liz is heartily sorry for having offended you. And she detests all her sins—Oh! you know the rest God; we'll both forgive her!'"

"Go in peace, my love! I will see you before I leave."

"I hope so," said Liz. "Remember the club downtown we went to after graduation. It was *Club Exquisite*, where the under aged went. The club for the ones old enough to drink was Café la Liberte. Well, Father Jack, I made reservation for two for tonight: I mean, priests have to eat and there are no restrictions on your dinner date. I know it's best if you drive yourself so I'll meet you there at 9PM."

Jack was still stunned! His mind was still scampering to solidify these—these expressions of "Bless me Father, sex, offense against God, intercourse, adultery, abominable, sabbatical, Act of Contrition, discussing dinner reservations; in a confessional? It's crazy! Absolutely crazy! Lord, in this particular confession you have to forgive *me*!"

All of these importuned, insane goings on as Jack conveyed to Liz through his mental fog, "I'll be there! At 9PM!"

YES, MY STUDIOUS FRIENDS, WE ALL HAVE—*SOMETHING TO THINK ABOUT*

Before he left the church Jack stopped at the statue of the Blessed Virgin and said a prayer in the form of asking for support. "Virgin Mary," he said, "I know just because I now wear a clerical collar does not automatically free me from temptation; *any* kind of temptation! I will be with a beautiful woman this evening and we expect to have a good time. Please give me the extra courage and fortitude to remain steadfast in my vows. And please talk to St. Jude; I know I did him a favor once and tell him if he doesn't help me to remain true blue I'll have to come up there and bite his dog. Amen"

Jack undressed starting with the removal of his ankle-length cassock, undergarments, shoes, socks and jumped into the shower stall under what felt like a cascade of warm water on his back, his shoulders, and back of his neck. The teeming water gave him an heir of luxury. The soap was a bar of green with the suds giving up the smell of fresh mint; the thought of a green apple martini weaved through his mind.

He shaved then slapped his face with the fragrance of an exotic lotion his sisters had given him on his return home. He dressed wearing the clerical dress code.

The church is insistent that her ordained ministers wear the ecclesiastical garb. The reason is simple. The ecclesiastical dress is an external sign, a symbol that is replete with meaning. The clergy who wears it is sending a message to the community of believers as well as to the people in general. The message of the Gospels that the clergy is commissioned to transmit is expressed with words and communicated effectively with external signs, easily understandable to the world of today that is so sensitive to the language of images.

To quote the words of Pope John Paul II, to wit: "Ecclesiastical dress, therefore, is a sign which makes it easier for others to approach the ministry that the priests represent. In the present society, in which the sense of the sacred has become so diminished, people have even more need of those calls to God, which cannot be disregarded without a certain impoverishment of our priestly service."

Jack arrived just before nine and was greeted by the "valet parking" attendant and shortly thereafter by the *maitre d`*. He greeted Jack with a pleasant smile, a firm handshake, and said, "A pleasure meeting you Father Flynn. Miss McGovern is waiting for you at her selected table. She wanted to be here when you arrived. Ah huh! I see the wine steward is aware of your presence and is already pouring a glass of your favorite, Korbel Dry Champagne in celebration. Miss McGovern told me she was hosting your dinner tonight doing honor to your new vocation as a priest. I am happy for you, Father."

Jack thanked the gentleman and then stopped. For the first time in many years Liz and Jack's eyes were locked in a laser clasp. Jack staggered; her beauty was that of a Madonna—unmitigated pleasure to the senses! Talk about the argument of "Intelligent Design" vs "Darwinism"! *Some bright somebody* in the college(s) of Design, Art, Beauty, Architecture, and Brick Sh—Houses, coalesced their designs and deserves an "A+ for "introducing" Liz McGovern to our fellowship. Jack stepped forward and they reached for each other and hugged in a warmhearted, congenial embrace. Her firm breasts against his chest made his heart skip beat—or two!

"You look so great," Liz whispered as she brushed away a tear. "To think we have been apart for so many, many months but after this afternoon in church, and now having you so near makes me exalted and proud. She kissed him lightly on the cheek as they eased away from each other. Jack, forever the gentleman, helped Liz to her seat.

"I have ordered your favorite meal," Liz said as they toasted with the champagne. "Steak with mushrooms piled high, fresh spinach, baked potato, and salad with blue cheese dressing and a dry red wine; but first, your dry martini!"

"You know, Liz, you are beautiful inside and out. This will be one of my happiest nights in a long, long time. You said 'after this afternoon' and I said 'beautiful inside.' Here comes my martini. I will raise my drink to you and say, the afternoon is past, something to be gained, but then forgotten.

You were always elegant; every morning, every afternoon, and every night, every day, month and year.'"

Liz started to say something but Jack said, "No Liz! Let me finish! The words of the Absolution in the Latin Rite gave you, through me, the **right** to absolve you from your sins. God the Father, through the death and resurrection of His Son sent the Holy Spirit among us for the forgiveness of sins. I'm giving you a heck of a speech but it's true. God sent the Holy Ghost to forgive you, Elizabeth McGovern. So let's forget the past and laugh and giggle and enjoy our time together."

Liz looked at him and sat silently for a time, until she had to look for her handkerchief and wipe away another tear. She said, "You're right. I do feel relieved and I will not bring it up again,"

So, for the next hour and a half the former ALL American and Powers model had a pleasurable evening. At one time Liz did ask Jack about his thoughts on celibacy and chastity. "Please forgive me," Liz said, "there are rumors about some priests in Pittsburgh and their relationship with young boys."

"Well, pretty Lady, it's a very fair and incisive question. I honestly think the Catholic Church has a problem. I read not too long ago, I forget where, said that homosexuals who are thinking about the priesthood would save themselves a lot of grief by dropping the idea. But if the Vatican's treatment of these men is morally wrong—and the author seems to think that it is—then his conclusion seems to endorse an injustice.

The author I mentioned above uses the terms "celibacy" and "chastity" interchangeably. When I studied canon law, celibacy was defined as the "state of not being married" (the Latin caelibatus means ("unmarried"). Although morally reprehensible, sexual sins did not contravene the celibacy canons, but attempted marriage did. The Catechism of the Church, while it does not define celibacy, seems to understand celibacy in this traditional sense. Meanwhile, Liz, chastity is a virtue everyone is called to embrace. According to the Encyclopedia of Catholicism, chastity is 'the virtue that pursues the integration of the true meaning of human sexuality and intimacy, whether one is married or not.' The author, by the way, is a Catholic theologian and I think he could have used these terms with more precision."

"May I have a little," Jack asked as he pointed to the wine bottle.

"Thank you!"

"Anyhow, I, and nearly everyone else would agree that seminaries need to do more to foster chaste (pure), celibate (unmarried) priests capable of mature, nonexclusive relationships. I do not pass judgment on the morality of homosexuality, but seek to examine the stigmatizing practices that make it more difficult for gay seminarians to develop chaste, celibate, intimate relationships. The data suggest that this stigmatization causes some candidates 'a lot of grief.' Despite the extensive formation that American Catholic priests have received, they are nonetheless statistically more likely to become depressed, HIV positive, to suffer from alcoholism, mental breakdowns, and heart attacks, and to die younger than other college graduates. These facts are never mentioned in the Catechism or in cannon law, but they strengthen my sense that there is a need for prudence when it comes to implementing the policies and practices that relate to the training of priests. I do not have a problem now, but that is not to say it would never happen. To be honest, I am scared; it's not so much the sexuality bit but the seemingly narrow-mindedness of the church. Why can't priests marry? What could possibly be wrong with a woman priest? And, heaven help us, a married woman priest?"

Jack told Liz that he honestly hoped what he said brought more light to the both of them. "And now," he said, "let's talk about you."

Liz sat back, relaxed, and told Jack all about her college, modeling for Powers, the Breck shampoo contest and the win, and her hiring by KDKA. She said to Jack, "Frankly they chose me because of my experience speaking at beauty pageants and honestly because of my looks. You know me, Jack, I never gave my looks that much of a thought but the station needed a lady that attracted attention when she starts to broadcast the news and/or weather reports."

"Makes sense to me, Liz. The word will spread; not about the weather or what latest country was facing an insurrection, but 'you gotts' see that beautiful blonde doin' the talkin'.'"

"You may be right," Liz said as her facial expression indicated pleasure. I must say, though, I have been blessed."

"We have both been blessed; and I must confess I have a 7:am early Mass to say. I am going to get up, lean over and give you a peck on the cheek that is topped full of love and good wishes. Then, I am going to turn around and walk out and pray to God that you, and me to, live a life of our chosen happiness."

As Jack walked toward the entrance, he didn't look back. He didn't want Liz to see him reaching in his back pocket to pull out his handkerchief. He used it to wipe away a tear.

FR. JACK FLYNN

ACCEPTING HIS NEW FREEDOM
AND A CHANCE TO THINK!

Ralph Waldo Emerson said, "TO THINK" is the toughest of tasks any man can undertake.

Jack smiled as he settled into the front seat of his new Chevrolet two door sedan the family gave him for a "welcome home" gift but now he is ready to travel 2600 miles and use it as a "going away" present. He was happy inside; in being free from the overwhelming mirthless drudgery in the life of a monk. But as Fr. Gillespie reminded all, it was a beautiful rewarding life to a few but Jack felt he was certainly not one of the chosen. It would be a long trip to Jesuit University of San Francisco, "Baghdad by the Bay" as the city was so eloquently named by a newspaper reporter. "But", as Jack said to himself, "I have a detailed map, motels along the way, money to travel, and a light hearted soul surrounded by cord of heartfelt love for Liz. And I am going to learn more about theology as I study religious faith, practice, and experience. I'll be able to study God and of God's relation to the world. 'God's relation to the world'! What a mess of a relationship I learned about in the confessional a week or so ago. Beautiful, lovely Liz even now warmer in my heart! Who in the whole world who have ever thought that I, through the love and grace of God, would be chosen to bless her as she said the "Act Of Contrition" and say, 'Go in peace and God bless you.'"

I could not be a parish priest he thought. Confessions never really change; same old masturbations, fornications or "fingering" among single young adults, birth control practices through the midst of the loving married, and all based on the inability of man, in a less than sterile society, to overcome an ardent sexual desire. *Concupiscence! LUST!* Innate in a man! He didn't study for it or win it in a poker game! If playing with yourself, or "fingering' a young lady, or two married lovers seeking freedom from concupiscence does absolutely no physical or mental harm, why is it a mortal sin? Condemned to hell?? Come on!!

In Pittsburgh Jack started out going NORTHEAST on GRANT ST. toward 6th toward I-579N/PA-380 E, pickup I-279 N, merge I-76 toward YOUNGSTOWN, OHIO then merge onto I-89 toward CLEVELAND, crossing into INDIANA. "That's about 400 miles," he said to himself, "enough for the day!"

To kill time during the elongated trip Jack took the time to make some notes so he could THINK about how lucky he was in learning to appreciate the printed word; and how Socrates became his mentor.

One day in the college library Jack found a treasure trove of the philosophers and Great Authors of Ancient Greece and Rome, plus the Middle Ages through the 18th century. He was talking about Homer, roughly 800 B.C. to Descartes and Milton, Locke and Newton about 1600 A.D. to 1700 A.D. Then Jack had Voltaire and Rousseau, Adam Smith and Jefferson into 1800 and a little beyond. This discovery, plus luck, pushed Jack into the study of Socrates, Plato, and Aristotle. In his "checks and balances" life, his luck appeared to offset the loss of the lovely blonde that broke his heart while at the same time he could slowly reproach the sadness because of his determination to stick with his initial plans of at least reviewing, with scrutiny, a monk's life. It was at this time he happened to pull from the college library shelf, Marcus Aurelius' *MEDITATIONS*. His friend Marcus guided him to patience in trying to understand the illogical turns of life, the study of philosophy, and the search for wisdom. A never-ending search, Jack might add!

Somewhere along his broken-line ups and downs of college life, he needed a flight leader, particularly when he entered the Abbey of the Holy Trinity. Jack zeroed in on Socrates; man of Athens, Man of Greece, Man of the World. He thought, and it made sense to him, "If Jimmy Stewart could have "HARVEY" he figured he could have Socrates."

WHY PHILOSOPHY

Jack, in his dreams, spoke of meeting Socrates, one of the great philosophers from Greece. Jack wanted him to "fly his wing" because, in his limited studying of the lives of philosophers, he needed someone to lead him in the right direction; the direction which would offer him the chance to better understand his self and his fellow man. Jack wanted Socrates to be his coach about life. He wanted Socrates, and his friends, to talk to Jack and tell everyone their story about what he, Socrates, could do, through philosophy, in helping man "think through" the capriciousness of life.

It is really that simple! He knew he had a lot to learn; Jack picked Socrates and **philosophy** to be his intellectual coach.

Socrates agreed to "fly his wing" and tell Jack's story.

Jack believes the chance to roam a bookstore, or library, with the thought in mind to carefully consider what book would contribute to, or further enhance his study of philosophy, is an unadulterated gift. Maybe he didn't wish to study, per se, but he would buy a book just to see what additional information philosophy had to offer.

Jack and I spoke many times about his numerous trips to the Pittsburgh library, or Notre Dame Library. This is what I found out about how Jack cogitates:

He thinks, in addition to the lessons of history, philosophy offers a pure endowment of man's experiences that are voluntarily transferred by one person to another—without compensation. The study of philosophy extends to man the chance to learn to love and pursue wisdom.

With this study, many men and ladies would probably find themselves tyros when it came to pure intellectual investigation. Heck, Jack did! However, he totally prepared himself for a great deal of reading and mentally groomed himself to think through what would be gifted to him in book form.

For the many years in college and in the abbey Jack, once out of bed, when he had the chance to be alone, would sit or kneel down in a quiet, dark atmosphere of study and reflect and ponder over what eminent philosophers, such as Aristotle, Plato, and Socrates, were trying to say to him. He knew it would take a long time to sift through the never-ending exploration in regards to a general understanding of values; and a continual search for some degree of excellence. He told me one morning what he was learning **about** philosophy was like the last drop of water from a canteen held to the lips of a thirst craved downed fighter pilot in a one-man raft. As he squeezed the canteen with his shaking, bony, sun burned fingers, he kept saying, "There has to be more! There just has to be more!"

It was the same thing with Jack in *his* particular approach to philosophy. The longer the time of the search, there grew within him an evolved appreciation; and he just couldn't let go. Just as the downed pilot couldn't let go of his canteen! In philosophy it becomes a love of the pursuit of wisdom. "Love of Wisdom!" Beautiful words but be careful—nothing comes easy. It may be better stated that philosophy is the 'search for' moral self-discipline and ethical strength. Tough order! And in order to prepare to do that, one must read, study, think, love one self, and develop personal self-esteem.

Believe me, Jack does not preach. It's just that philosophy, to him, means generating an awareness of how great life and living among his fellow man can be.

What Jack was saying earlier about being an amateur means only his lack of education in the many disciplines of Philosophy. Part of his recent studies included a book entitled THE OXFORD COMPANION TO PHILOSOPHY. It's very thick and heavy; Heck sake, I could use it for my bench-pressing exercises. According to the author, Tom Honderich, Professor of the Philosophy of Mind and Logic at University College London, Philosophical inquiry includes, among many disciplines, EPISTEMOLOGY, the study or a theory of the nature and grounds of knowledge. It also includes METAPHYSICS the branch that examines the nature of reality and the relationship between mind and matter. LOGIC is concerned with the laws of valid reasoning. ETHICS deals with the problems of correct conduct, and AESTHETICS attempts to determine the nature of beauty and the criteria of artistic judgment. Well, if you know fighter pilots like Jack's friend Chuck Grube all the guys in the 8th Fighter Bomber Wing passed AESTHETICS with an A+. And! With all the Las Vegas chorus girls he and other pilots met while going through gunnery, it didn't take them long to determine the nature of beauty and the criteria of artistic judgments. They determined a minimum of a 9 ½; pretty face, scintillating smile, great bust (at least, and he meant at *least* a 36,) plus hips, rear end, and legs to complement the first three.

There goes the moral self-discipline bit Jack was trying to sell me!

With all kidding aside, philosophy attracted Jack by the challenge to pursue wisdom and the search for a general understanding of values and **reality.** He wanted to take on a mental sphere of activity that would allow him to encompass the overall value by which one lives and to try to entertain the calmness, equanimity, and detachment revered as that befitting a philosopher.

You probably noticed above I put a bold face on the word reality. Jack and I had a long time deliberation about **REALITY.** We agreed that reality is, quite simply, the quality of being factual, an actuality. In my own little philosophical thought processes I say to myself, "If man grasps the *quality* of reality, he grasps and understands the *quality* of truth. He understands the *quality* of relationships by telling the truth Socraties. Jack says that too many men in high executive positions can't face reality or the truth Socraties." Jack said to me, "That is exactly why, and believe me, I know, many of these men do not understand, nor have they taken the time to understand, the quality of relationships through facing the truth. And I am talking relationships from the executive suite to the janitor on the manufacturing floor.

Jack had a grim look on his face. He said to me, "I'm going to tell you a story; it's truthful, poignant, and virulent. And it's not going to be easy. I learned of this when I ran into a fighter pilot/test pilot friend of mine while skiing when I was in Utah for a short time. He dated my sister's girlfriend so I had known him for years; fellow by the name of Eugene. He was flying for Lockheed out of a base called Palmdale and an Air Force base named Edwards.

He told me Lockheed was losing a lot of airplanes and professional pilots on the development of a new supersonic fighter. Twenty two crashes and nine dead pilots! He said he was a statistic in those numbers having survived a crash landing and an ejection from a crippled jet when the tail was torn off by an errant tip tank during what was called "a lateral—longitudinal" stability test. He said he ejected upwards, upside down at 25,000' at over 500 miles per hour.

Anyhow, the top General at what was called the Air Research and Development Command in Baltimore wanted someone from Lockheed to personally meet with him and tell him what the hell was wrong. Lockheed management and Tony LeVier, Lockheed's illustrious experimental test pilot (who hired Eugene) decided he should be the one to go to since he had more test time and experience at high altitudes and speeds than anyone in the company.

Jack told me Eugene objected! He told Tony that management, or the designers, or the Program Manager, or the Vice President of Manufacturing, or Chief of Quality Control should go. 'Hell,' he said to Mr. LeVier,' I'm just an employee who happens to attract a lot of attention not because I'm anything special except that I'm a survivor.'"

"Eugene," Tony replied, "I want you to go."

He said, "Yes Sir! I'll go but my intention will be to tell the truth as I see it. I realize the General is a powerful man but that doesn't scare me a bit. I remember something from Bacon; 'Truth will not make us rich, but it will make us free.'"

"Well, my good philosopher friend, Eugene flew back east and met with the General; a disaster! A total disaster! He started to tell him about how he believed aerodynamics had advanced the state of the art but systems engineering and engine development was lagging behind and the jet was turning into a killer. 'And, Sir,' he continued, 'no one at Lockheed, or General Electric (engine) seems to be taking charge; no one is managing.'"

The General fluffed him off and said, "That jet is just like any other jet."

Eugene said, "But Sir, it isn't just like any other jet. And the officer from the Systems Project Office (Wright Field, Dayton, Ohio) isn't even jet qualified. We don't have anyone qualified to talk to. And, in all due respect Sir, the jet's accident rate speaks for itself and"—he cut me off, stood up and told me bristly, 'Mr. Coniff, this meeting is over.'

Eugene sat there devastated, wasted, almost ravaged of character; his manner of thinking short-circuited. He couldn't stand up at first but then he said to myself, 'Eugene, get off your ass! Stand up! What were you reading just last week? You read that science, such as the new jet, gives us knowledge, but only philosophy gives us wisdom. You have the *understanding* of what is true.'

So Eugene stood straight up, internally defiant but outwardly calm, and looked the General right in the eye, and said, "Sir, I'll go but before I leave I want to say that new jet will kill one of your great test pilots one of these days and you will remember everything I said."

The failed meeting was flashed back to Lockheed in a nanosecond. Management had a piranha on its hands. But Tony LeVier stood up for him.

"So my friend Socrates, time moves on; the General at the Air Research and Development Command had control of all testing—aircraft—engines—systems, and the Flight Test Center for test pilots at Edwards. The Grim Reaper got confused about Eugene telling the General about "one of his pilots" so he killed one from all three; a great USAF test pilot and fighter ace, a General Electric engine test pilot, and one from Lockheed. All personal friends of Eugene! The General and Eugene attended the funeral of the pilot from Edwards; he was Eugene's instructor when he was in gunnery school before going to Korea and a great friend. The General didn't have the guts to look at him and not one—NOT ONE—executive from Lockheed said a word. I learned the hard way! None of these men could face reality or the truth!"

"I might was well continue. Eugene told me months later Lockheed's chief of production flight test was killed on take-off (engine fire) and the

Group Commander from the USAF's first active squadron of the new jet was killed on the same day of introduction—engine failure on final approach while landing.

The USAF stopped production."

I told Jack, "Truth offers man what? It offers man freedom from deceit or falseness. If something is going on in a man's life that is factual, and only he in his own conscience can determine such, then he can't possibly tell a lie, or fix the books, or falsely report testing data. Man can be deceitful, but then he is only lying to himself. Fools are those who try to impose their own selfish desires on reality."

"You're so right, Socrates," Jack said to me. "What else?"

"Well, let's see! It takes courage to face reality and tell the truth. The world owes much to its men and women of courage. I do not mean physical courage, in which a man is at least equaled by the bulldog. What I mean is the courage that displays itself in silent effort and endeavor—dares to endure all and suffer all for truth and duty. It is courage that is more truly heroic than the achievements of physical valor, which are rewarded by honors and titles, or by laurels steeped in blood."

Jack is learning from his studies of philosophy, that it is **moral** courage that characterizes the highest order of manhood and womanhood. It takes courage to seek and to speak the truth; courage to be just; courage to be honest; courage to resist temptation; and courage to do one's duty. Jack tells of Eugene having a hell of time with "one's duty" on his first combat mission and, later, telling the story of facing hundreds of men glaring at him with fierce, piercing eyes just after he wrecked a jet airplane in pilot training; it was over a very beautiful lady. Eugene said he danced, and laughed, and giggled into the wee small hours while drinking too many bourbon "snow cones". Eugene says she was gorgeous! And he came pretty close to getting kicked out of jet pilot training! What saved him? Telling the truth!

Yes, Jack and I had quite a discussion on reality and truth.

I suggested that if men and women do not possess this virtue, they have no security whatever for the preservation of any tests of moral courage.

Truth and reality are *the* important parts of the evolution of the mind that continually pursues the search for a general understanding of values. And it is the measure of those qualities that determine a man's worth.

My friends and I, friends like Plato, Aristotle, Augustine, even Mark Twain and Emerson, speak to Jack about moral courage, truth and reality all the time. "OK, Socrates," Jack said, "Here comes a chicken or the egg question. Which comes first, truth or ethics? In other words, if I speak the truth am I ethical, or am I ethical because I speak the truth? And, while you are looking at me with your quizzical stare, answer this also; can you *teach* truth? Can you *teach* ethics?"

I looked at Jack for at least thirty seconds; stroking my beard as was my usual countenance while thinking. "OK!" I said. "I'll answer your question, but I'll diverge a bit! You know me by now that my discourse moves in two directions—outward to objective definitions, and inward, to discover the inner person, the soul. I believe the soul to be the source of all truth. No, the search for truth among man cannot be conducted at a series of weekly lectures, for it is the quest of a lifetime. I ask myself a lot of questions that I am hardly ever able to answer. Nevertheless, my query has to continue—for a lifetime. You are aware of my dictum, 'The unexamined life is not worth living.' I cannot possibly give or teach my disciples the truth. Each of us must find it out for ourselves. The history of philosophy is enveloped with statements of brilliant men trying to define truth but you'll find no one wanting to specifically teach it. I am talking about Aristotle, Plato, Aquinas, Gibson, Boswell and Emerson. Even Emerson said that truth is such a flyaway, such a sly-boots, so un-transportable a commodity that it is as difficult to catch as light.

Who can teach that?"

I continued! "Let's see," I said to Jack. "John Locke, in addition to gaining fame with his essay *CONCERNING HUMAN UNDERSTANDING* wrote *A LETTER CONCERNING TOLERATION* in which he said, 'The truth certainly would do well enough to shift for its self. It seldom has received and, I fear, never will receive much assistance from the power of great men, to whom it is but rarely known and more rarely welcome. It is not taught by laws, nor has it any need of force to procure its entrance into the minds of men.'

"So, no," my friend; "I think truth is too fleeting to teach. Have I answered your question?"

"Of course it does. Thank you." Jack told me. "Now the next question: Can ethics be taught? I had a friend of mine working for an aerospace company and one of the mid-management executives got caught in a payoff scandal. The president of the company is now making all executives attend a class on learning ethics. I think he is going down the wrong road. I don't think you can teach ethics or, as it is said, 'More formally known as moral philosophy'!"

"I agree with that," I told Jack. "I don't think ethics as it stands alone can be taught. But let's ask this question. What is ethics?"

"Well, Socrates, as you have made me aware," Jack said, **"Ethics is the discipline dealing with what is good or bad and with moral duty and obligation."**

"You're right!" I told Jack. I remembered the night sometime ago; we were having dinner-—Oh! some place—Jack couldn't remember either. Jack said the church was shoving the TEN COMMANDMENTS down his throat and he was extremely angry because the Nun said, 'God gave them to us, so follow them.' He was young then. I asked Jack, "What did the TEN COMMANDMENTS tell you?"

"Told me not to miss church on Sunday, not to steal, not to kill, don't take another man's wife, honor my mother and dad, not to—"

"So you knew what was good or bad. Can you *teach* good or bad?"

"No, Sir, I don't think so." Jack said. I can *learn* by knowledge about. I know by common sense; I learn what happens to others when they kill or steal. I know you can make people aware of duty and obligation. But, morality among men! It is up to the individual! I don't think you can teach 'good'! And in all practicality I don't think it '*bad*' to miss church on Sunday."

I told Jack he answered his own question.

EPISTOMOLGY, METAPHYSICS, ETHICS and LOGIC makes for extremely interesting study, but individually, these particular disciplines do not interest Jack. In studying philosophy, with practical learning experiences from my friends and me, he seems to be more interested in learning about self-knowledge and self-love. Also, an offer of the general recommendations for the conduct of life! He thinks that would entail honor, friendship, fear, characteristics and conditions of human nature and knowledge, morality, truth, courage, values and happiness.

According to Jack's *OXFORD COMPANION*, Honderich says, "Philosophy, the search for wisdom, brings together, first of all, the work of the great philosophers. As that term is commonly used, there are perhaps twenty of them. By anyone's reckoning, this pantheon of philosophers includes Plato, Aristotle, Aquinas, Hobbes, Spinoza, Leibniz, Locke, Berkeley, Hume, Kant, Hegel, and Nietzsche."

But Jack asks? "Where the hell are my pals Marcus Aurelius, and Socrates?" He was ready to jump all over Honderich but then he remembered what he added and it made *me* feel good. Honderich said, "Socrates, teacher of Plato, is one of the most significant yet enigmatic figures in the history of philosophy; significant because his relation to Plato was crucial to the development of the latter, and thus indirectly in the development of much later philosophy.

Socrates was enigmatic because he wrote nothing himself, and therefore presents the challenge of restructuring him from the evidence of others."

Jack discussed how he learned **of** me in when he quoted Daniel Boorstin in his brilliant book *THE SEEKERS* who said, "Socrates brought the search for the meaning of philosophy down from heaven to earth," Jack also said, "I would have been a fool not to take advantage of that".

No, I didn't write anything down but people have learned about me through Xenophon, and in three of Plato's works. The *APOLOGY* is an idealized version of his defense at my trial. Crito, gives reasons for my refusal to take the opportunity to escape. And *PHAEDO*, a moving re-creation of my final hours, containing first a Platonic treatise on the philosophy of life, death, and immortality and then a description of the ideal philosophic death.

In one of his thirteen books on philosophy, *THE EXAMINED LIFE*, Borden Parker Browne, Professor of Philosophy at Boston University, Jack learned, "Plato and Xenophon affirm that I, Socrates, turned away from the natural science that engaged me in my youth. It is said I brought philosophy down from my contemplation of the heavens, caused it to enter into the cities and houses of men, and made it concern itself with human beings.

Jack also acquired additional knowledge from *THE EXAMINED LIFE*. It has 35 excerpts from the philosophers who shaped Western thought. Augustine, Machiavelli, Locke, Rosseau, and Dewey, among others, discuss thought, culture, beauty, capacity of man, wisdom, and need for open-mindedness. "I mean," Jack says "how more fortunate can man get to be able to use these great minds to learn to be better persons. You pick up a book and start thinking about what you can do to know yourself better, learn to be more open-minded and enjoy a better world that you will, subliminally be contributing to."

Jack has also read *CRITO*, *PHAEDO*, and the *APOLOGY*. In addition, he read the best selling novel entitled, *THE TRIAL of SOCTATES!* Here's a guy, me, well respected, who was, in practice, a loyal citizen, served with distinction on the battlefield (Peloponnesian War,) and adhering strictly to his ideals of legality and justice. Once under the democracy I was alone in opposing an unconstitutional proposal. And once under the tyrannical regime that briefly ousted the democracy at the end of the war, I refused an order to participate in the arrest, and subsequent death, of an innocent man.

None-the-less, my association with notorious anti-democrats, led to my accusation on vague charges of impiety and corruption of the young, and to my condemnation to death.

I think I am teaching Jack what kind of man he should be; a man of character, truth, moral strength, honesty, dignity, and integrity. And I taught him about the influence of reading books! "It builds character while learning," I told him.

I told Jack, "Man is usually known by the books he reads, as well as the company he keeps. There is a companionship of books as well as of men; and one should live in the best company, whether it be of the book or of men."

"Companionship of books, as well as men," I continued in talking to Jack. "Keep the two in mind; temper those words. Although genius always commands admiration, character most secures respect. The former is the product of brainpower, the latter of heart-power: and in the long run it is the heart that rules in life. Men of genius stand to society in the relation of its intellect, as men of character of its conscience; and while the former are admired, the latter are followed."

"You know! Socrates is right!" I said to myself. "How else do you learn about a man's character and his genius or brainpower other than by history; and that leads to books," I told Socrates one Sunday a longtime ago when we were discussing a national magazine's best seller list. "A good book can be among the best of friends. The way you talk, Socrates, it is the same today as it was way back in your time—almost 500 years before Christ. So it will probably never change. I find a book the most patient and cheerful of companions. It does not turn its back upon me in times of adversity or distress. It always receives me with the same kindness; it is always ready to speak to me; fill me full of information. And I control the conversation! It's not like being married. I guess, my good friend, you heard the one about the judge who said, 'I understand that you and your wife had some words.'"

The defendant said, "I had some but I didn't get a chance to use them."

Ah marriage! The cooing stops with the honeymoon; the billing goes on forever!

Socrates also told me, "Men often discover their affinity to each other by the mutual love they have for a book—just as fighter pilots bond by the mutual admiration they have for each other."

"Jack," Socrates said to me, "The book is a truer and higher bond of union. Men can think, feel, and sympathize with each other through their favorite author."

I also suggested to Jack that books possess an essence of immortality. They are by far the most lasting products of human effort. Temples crumble into ruin! Pictures and statues decay! But books survive! Time is of no account with great thoughts, which are as fresh today as when they first passed through their authors' minds, ages ago. What was then said and thought, still speaks to us as vividly as ever from the printed page. The only effect of time has to sift and winnow out the bad products; for nothing in literature can lone survive but what is really good.

The great and good do not die, even in this world. Embalmed in books, their spirits walk broad. The book is a living voice. It is an intellect to which one still pays attention. Hence we will ever remain under the influence of the great men of old. "You're under their influence Jack," I said. "You are under the effect and authority of Plato, Aristotle, Epictetus, Aurelius, Gibbon, Darwin, Tolstoy, etc. You mention their names in your studies. They become your silent partners in war, religion, business, friendships and love.

The imperial intellects of the world are as much alive now as they were ages ago," I continued. "Just think" Jack. "Homer still lives; and though his personal history is hidden in the mists of antiquity, his poems are as fresh today as if they had been newly written. Plato still teaches his transcendent philosophy; Horace, Virgil, and Dante still sing as when they lived; Shakespeare is not dead: his body was buried in 1616 but his mind is a much alive in England now and his thoughts as far-reaching, as in the time of the Tudors."

I remember when one of Jack's mentors told him of insufficient evidence to support his premise regarding the following:

> You fail to define "good" or "bad".
> What is moral?
> On what basis do we judge "good" or "bad"?
> Where does "common sense" come from?
> How does one obtain 'common sense'? What is it?
> You mention the TEN COMMANDMENTS! Why were
> they handed down?

Good questions if one wanted to enter into philosophical discussions that would not, in Jack's opinion, give an answer. It's like discussing politics or religion. No one wins! Jack doesn't agree, or disagree with his mentor; he considers him a very bright man and there is respect for him. But Jack's **WHY PHILOSOPHY** is not a printed and bound work about the tenets of philosophy. It reviews, sometime in great detail, his experiences as a student, an inspired monk candidate, a priest, grabbing the lessons of history, and capturing a learning process about philosophy, free enterprise, study, and the rewards of thought.

Jack did the examination! He opened his mind, like a parachute, to exposure! He participated in, or partook of personally, as much information as possible to learn to be a better man. And he appreciated, in depth, what he learned from a great number of philosophers including the American born, Ralph Waldo Emerson, (1803-1882), who said, "In every man there is something I may learn of him, and in that, I am his pupil."

Jack knows what "good" or "bad" is. His life is based on the fact that he knows the difference. It is due to being exposed plus "been there", "done that". It is his responsibility to know and act accordingly.

Jack knows "common sense" is the unreflective opinions of ordinary men like himself. He knows it is *sound* and *prudent*, but often unsophisticated judgment. That is all he has to know! He knows from the experiences of doing, in a particular discipline, whether a man or woman is making "common sense". If *he* thinks good, that's good. If not, he has the ability to determine "if there is something he may learn of him," If there is something he *may* learn, he'll stick around. If not, he'll leave.

Moral, in Jack's earlier thinking relates to him, the principles of right or wrong in behavior. *He* makes those judgments and accepts the responsibility of his ability to make sensible decisions in these matters.

The TEN COMMANDMENTS, according to the Bible, is the summary of divine law given by God to Moses on Mt. Sinai. They have a paramount place in the ethical system in Judaism, Christianity, and Islam.

Most Christians know, or can recite, what the COMMANDMENTS teach. If one believes, good for him. If not, it's his business. Jack has always acted according to his beliefs. He doesn't kill, or steal, or commit adultery, and he loved his great, warm, loving father and mother. The TEN COMMANDMENTS didn't tell him to do what is mentioned above. They COMMAND by fear. Jack is not and will not be surrounded by fear. He is surrounded by love—of his self, and because of these circumstances he has learned to love others.

WHY PHILOSOPHY? Jack thinks my friends and I know the answer. That is why he hangs around with us.

It can't get any better than that!

"Well," Jack said to himself, "That thinking about my vicarious life with Socrates made the time go by fast. Let's see, I've done a couple of hundred miles. Time for a late lunch, gas, and I'll stop just before crossing into Indiana. Starting tomorrow I have about 2100 miles more; four days depending on weather and San Francisco traffic. I know the university is down town but I'll worry about that later.

I'm looking forward to learning, lector when asked, leading a happy Christian life, and loving every minute of it—along with my dry, vodka, straight up, ice—Aw! You know the rest!

I kept looking around for a gas station. I was a little worried, but just as I looked up from my gas gauge, I saw a large sign ahead on my right with the letters GULF. I pulled in and told the attendant to "Filler 'er up" and while he was doing so, I asked if there was a combination restaurant and motel "not too far" from the highway.

He said, "About a half mile up, Sir, you will see a sign HOWARD JOHNSONS. The restaurant has good food and the motel right beside the restaurant is warm and clean. Just as soon as I finish checking your oil, I'll send you on your way."

I paid the gentleman and not more than 15 minutes later I was in a comfortable booth ready to order my dinner of "New York steak charred rare, baked potato, salad with blue cheese dressing and a side order of peas." I love to put peas in my baked potato. They had a bar so you know what I ordered for a drink.

During my meal, I asked the waitress where I could buy an evening paper. She told me I could probably buy one at the motel, but a diner just finished and left behind a copy of the *CHICAGO TRIBUNE* and she would be happy to give it to me.

"What luck!" I said to myself. I finished my meal and then spread out next to a hot cup of coffee and folded out the paper before me. I skipped over a couple of articles. One that caught my attention was a story about, "She Wore a Yellow Ribbon." I remember hearing it from a couple of guys from WWII. A gal wore a yellow ribbon—around her neck she wore a yellow ribbon, she wore it in the springtime and in the month of May etc. Many are now tying a yellow ribbon around trees dedicating it to the hostages in Iran. Boy! That's a mess.

A lot of articles about the hostages in Iran! Another, a Robert Westbrook wrote, "I want a girl, just like the girl, that married Harry James." I think that is Betty Grable!

Another story about a former CIA official who sometimes publicly identified US agents! Why the heck would he do something like that?

Anyhow I continued; I was looking for the SPORTS section when something caught my eye under CLASSIFIED. *The Chicago School of Professional Psychology* was looking for a professor with at least a Masters to lecture students in their quest for a "Master of Arts Degree in I/O Psychology in Organizational Effectiveness." A minor in Philosophy would be of imposing assistance. (The I/O mean industrial/ organizational)

I was awestruck! A sudden respect combined with fear. My mind unexpectedly went in two directions. I could see myself in my position at my school in San Francisco—getting up early everyday, saying Mass, wearing the same black suit, doing the same thing, seeing the same Brothers of Mary, wording my prayers, eating at the same time every meal. And, honest, at the same time, I saw myself on the Chicago School campus, greeting the students with a smile as we continually try to keep pace with the ever growing applications of our discipline in real world contexts. I was smiling at the coeds, waving to other professors—women and men. I felt light hearted; I was back with the ball team; back with Elizabeth. After all my years of silence, and total lack of being able to be myself! After years of a tyrannical, draconian, repressive atmosphere of sultry living under a bully autocrat, I could now get up, leave the booth and take a piss without permission.

The restaurant! The waitress! The Chicago Tribune! Was it horse crap luck or something of a set up for a nightmare?

I asked the waitress for my bill and, "Could I keep the paper?"

I checked in at the hotel, took a long, hot shower, hit the sack, and immediately fell into a deep sleep.

A lazy morning walk to the restaurant put me back in a booth with last night's paper. I looked at the ad. I looked at the address. The college was located at 30 North LaSalle, Suite 2400. There was also a phone number. My mind would now require careful handling. I ordered a cheese omelet, fresh orange juice, whole-wheat toast, and coffee. As I finished my last sip, my mind was thinking "way out there", but I had made it up. I went to the motel and placed two calls. The first to San Francisco; the second to Chicago! I made an appointment! My plans were I would be a week late to my new assignment, but I would not leave Chicago until it was determined whether I was, or was not, able to be approved and offered the position as a professor in the discipline of Master or Arts.

A YEAR HAS PASSED

Well, I was accepted as a professor in the **Chicago School of Professional Psychology**; it's going extremely well. And I must say the handling of the paper to me that night at HOWARD JOHNSONS changed my life. I have explained earlier why I was distraught and disconsolate at the abbey and becoming a priest did lift my frame of mind. The white collar gave me a warmer perspective and I was proud; I can't find the church out of line in any way. It was my line that was taut and rigid, but relaxed a bit as a man of the cloth. I believe my destiny was changed by the ad in the Chicago Tribune.

The Catholic Church didn't like it; I was excommunicated. Excommunication, in the sense of a formal proceeding, is not a penalty, but rather a formal proclamation of a preexisting condition a more, or less, prominent member of the Catholic Church. When such a person commits acts that in themselves separate him from the communion of the faithful—it is necessary for the Church to clarify the situation by means of a formal announcement, which informs the laity that this is not a person to follow, has separated from the church and is not longer to receive sacraments.

Excommunicated persons are barred from participating in a ministerial capacity. So, that's me! I'm out! I still go to church on Sunday and I am happy with my life. On my Fridays and Mondays off, I sometimes fly to Pittsburgh to visit the family: and I met a beautiful, Irish red headed stewardess on a flight who lives in Chicago. We have started dating.

I did not see Liz on any of my trips. I was told she was spending a lot of time, on her time off, with her friend Dahlia.

FINIS

Each of us occupies two temporal modalities of being: one which exists in the present and on which stretches through time to our lives' limits, while the former constantly demands our attention, it is upon the latter that every precept of behavior and hope of happiness is based. Our broader selves are our better selves, and our present attitude toward them is optimally one of attentiveness and humility. Conspicuously admirable people seem to inhabit these broader selves and strike us as living in mansions of time; the rest of us, who give up projects in a day's despair, renounce friendships in anger, and follow fads and read magazines as oracles, are pent up in temporal hovels. Characteristically anxious or distracted, we inhabit tiny fractions of our full being; and like small patrols, isolated from the main army and ambushed, we respond weakly and are overcome by the shocks of experience.

Self-confidence, on the other hand, often consists merely of the ability to connect our fragmentary present with our wholeness—in due time. The past *AND* future gives it meaning and importance.*

Liz McGovern, after spending time, hard work hours, and study for an eventual chance to brightly shine as a weather person or nightly local newscaster, wasn't really happy with her life. Did she have too much—too soon?

One Saturday morning, Liz, after spending extended hours on Friday evening and night talking to her parents, got up early and said goodbye to her family and friends. She was going to see Dahlia in Elizabeth, N.J. After the long 71/2 hour, 365m mile drive, Liz *was* glad to meet Dahlia at the front door. "Oh! Liz, I am glad you made it," said Dahlia. "We are all very happy for you."

After the luggage was in, Dahlia closed the door and smiled at Liz. There was a sign on the front of the door:

BENEDICTINE SISTERS of ELIZABETH

St. WALBURGA MONASTERY

Jack sat in the back of the beautiful chapel. He *was* alone for over an hour contemplating his last few provocative years; the more he studied about his religion and his church the more disengaged he became. The time had arrived. He smiled; his future was, at last, bound to have meaning and accomplishments:

DO YOU JOHN B. FLYNN TAKE JOAN PAULINE SULLIVAN TO BE YOUR LAWFUL WEDDED WIFE—
"I DO"

DO YOU JOAN PAULINE SULLIVAN TAKE JOHN B. FLYNN *TO BE YOUR LAWFUL WEDDED HUSBAND—*
"I DO"

I NOW PRONOUNCE YOU HUSBAND AND WIFE, YOU MAY KISS THE BRIDE!

IN THE FACE OF A TRUE FRIEND
A MAN SEES
AS IF IT WERE A SECOND SELF.
SO THAT
WHERE HIS FRIEND IS,
HE IS!!

CICERO
FRIENDSHIP, VI

LOVE IS A MANY SPLENDORED THING!

OR, IN TIME,

IS IT A MANY SPLINTERED THING?

Jack Simpson

APPENDIX

The names Jack Flynn, Dave Latshaw, Charles Grube, Anton Niepp, RolandDeBeer are authentic. They are the names of friends I grew up with, or in the case of Roland DeBeers, an executive in the procurement department of a client of mine for over 20 years.

Elizabeth "Sparkey" McGovern is pure fiction.

The background information, or I might say, the evolution of Charles Grube's growth into the position of Sports' Editor for the fictional *Pittsburgh Post Telegraph* is, in fact, the background of one of our friends from high school. The paper was the *Pittsburgh Press*; he became, over time, Sports' Editor. I thank him for sharing this important intelligence. I did not use "Doc's" full name because I failed to ask permission.

My meeting with Father David at the Retreat House, Holy Trinity Abbey, arranged by Roland DeBeers, is authentic. Also, the narrative about the meeting with Ella Fitzgerald is true only I met her on a flight from New York to Los Angeles when I was a test pilot in the USAF. I was carrying my helmet while waiting to be picked up by the North American courier. Ms. Fitzgerald began the conversation by asking if I were a football player. The meeting is detailed in *SOCRATES 'n SUITS*, BOOK I, of the trilogy. And, yes, the stewardess' name was Delores; I was dating her at the time.

In regards to the QUERY columns, particularly the one where Fr. Tom Gillespie addressed, in writing, his answers to those who "queried" about the life of a monk. I did meet with a priest from the Abbey whose name will not be revealed; his are the answers to the QUERY. The mentions Vatican Council II. Vatican Council II was from September, 1962 until December, 1965. This fictional novel (with the exception of my trip to the Abbey of the Holy Trinity and Fr. Secret's treatise) takes place in the '50's but I did not want to destroy the tranquility brilliantly introduced by Fr. Our secret priest.

The statement regarding trusting thyself from Emerson's *Self-Reliance* was taken from *GREAT TREASURY OF WESTERN THOUGHT*, 1.4.46.

All of the information regarding location, the life of a monk, the Holy Trinity Abbey, Huntsville, Utah, the Retreat House, The Cistercia Order, etc., was taken from the INTERNET.

The SPORTS' EDITORIALS under the different "Contents" written by Charlie Grube are, in fact, taken from the sports section from *THE LOS ANGELES TIMES, THE PITTSBURGH POST GAZETTE, USA TODAY*, and *BASEBALL/AN ILLUSTRATED HISTORY*, Geoffrey C. Ward and Ken Burns, Alfred A Knopf, New York, 1994. As an example, the story on the age of Satchel Paige is from *USA TODAY*, July 6, 2006, by Dan Gutman, the author of Satch & Me. All of the articles were written after the early 50's when the story was written

Information on the lives of the Monks and priests are, in part, are taken from George Fowler, *dance of a fallen monk*, Addison-Wesley

Publishing Company, New York, 1995.

SOMETHING TO THINK ABOUT

The ALL-USA Football First team information was obtained from *USA TODAY.*

RETREAT HOUSE

The facts regarding Murray Gell-Man are detailed in the chapter.

LEGACY AND CULTURE

A compendium of philosophers' allegations listed below resulted in a common thread of my learning about legacy and culture and applying my thoughts of such to the Latshaws and their newspaper.

Everyday Zen by Charlotte Joko Beck

The Conquest of Happiness by Bertrand Russell

Character by Smiles

Forbes Scrapbook of Thoughts

Ethics and Rhetoric by Aristotle

City of God, Augustine

Meditations, Marcus Auerlius

BASEBALL, An Illustrated History,

Hippocrates and the other Greek philosophers from a short summary, *GREAT TREASURY of WESTERN THOUGHT*

JACH FLYNN; IRISH EYES

The discussion on happiness was complimented by Bertrand Russell and John Dewey, *THE GREAT TREASURY of WESTERN THOUGHT,* p3

In reference to the verbal exchange Charlie Grube and Jack Flynn had considering Jack's answer to the question, "How does one become a Monk?" the information came from the Internet but surreptitiously from my friend, Roland DeBeers. He is brought into the story here because later, he actually set me up with a meeting with the Guest-master of the Retreat House, Abbey of the Holy Trinity.

In reference to the SOMETHING TO THINK ABOUT columns throughout the book, dealing with steroids, and John Daly, (if in fact I use them) and bass fishing, they presented a synthesis of articles from *THE LOS NGELES TIMES*' Orange County Edition, regular edition, and from *USA TODAY* (John Daly) article. I did not include the names of the staff writers or dates because the SOMETHING TO THINK ABOUT ARTICLES were supposed to be written 30 or more years ago. I have them on file, however. I want to avoid anyone's thought of plagiarism.

Speaking of fishing (bass fishing above) the article on Ernest Hemingway was taken from *TIME*, 1954, "The Year In Review". In fact, Hemingway was featured on the cover. The tie in to fishing! His novel, *The Old Man and Sea!*

The articles on baseball about Stengel, Berra, Haddix, and Wagner were taken from *BASEBALL/AN ILLUSTRATED HISTORY.*

The article on the biography of Arnold Palmer was taken from the Internet.

My commentary on unparalleled sportsmanship, *Golf's Legends Look Back . . . . And Ahead,* was copied from *FORBES*, June 19, 2006.

EXCUSE ME

The information pertaining to the question of music in Abbeys and the naming of a very few came from the Internet. Since SOMETHING TO THINK ABOUT is fiction from the fifties, my vicarious search had to be through libraries.

WHY PHILOSOPHY

The discussion Socrates and I had about books is an excerpt from Samuel Smiles, *CHARACTER*, A. L. Burt Company, Publishers, NYC, no date.

The discussion on why I picked certain disciplines of philosophy playing an important role in the development of character was taken in part from the *THE OXFORD COMPANION TO PHILOSOPHY*, Oxford University Press, New York and London, 1989.

The discussion with Socrates on, "Can you teach truth and ethics?" was taken, in part, from David Palmer, *LOOKING AT PHILOSOPHY*, Mayfield Publishing Company, Mountain View, Ca., 1988.

The joke about the wife "having some words," is from *MILTON BERLE'S PRIVATE JOKE BOOK*, Crown Publishers, New York, 1989.

Additional discussions with Socrates about truth and ethics came in part from *GREAT TREASURY OF WESTERN THOUGHT*, Edited by Mortimer J. Adler & Charles Van Doren, R. R. Bowker Company, New York, 1977.

When Socrates told me what he thought of history, his notions were taken from *THE COLUMBIA ENCYCLOPEDIA, 5th EDITION*, edited by Chernow and Vallas, Houghton Mifflin Company, 1975

To remain ignorant of things, etc., Cicero, *ORATOR XXXIV*, (106 BC-43BC).

The study of History, etc., Livy, *EARLY HISTORY OF ROME, I, 1, (*60BC-17AD*).

It was for the sake of others, etc., Plutarch, *TIMOLEON*, (46-120AD).

BIRDS SING, PEOPLE SING

In reference to *IDEAS*, the book was first published in Great Britain in 2005 by Weidenfeld & Nicolson. I didn't mention the date in the text because this fictional novel takes place in the early '50s.

However, given to the use of irony, the last performance of the 2005-2006 season of the Pacific Symphony, Orange County, CA, was Beethoven's 9th. It brought the house down! AND, the opening performance of the Los Angeles Philharmonic's 2006-2007 season featured the *Eroica* symphony. I attended both performances.

A BRIEF HISTORY

Although sports' writer, Charles Grube, has theoretically received his information from his friend DeBeers, a former fighter pilot living in UTAH, the history of monks in the Catholic Church was obtained from the Internet. The info was under *http://www.holy* trinityabbey. org—history, retreat house, monks' daily life, long term residency, invitation to Cistercian life, the Superior, etc.

I, Jack Simpson the author, have not at this stage of my fictional novel been to the Abbey of the Holy Trinity. I do, however, plan to visit thanks to my friend from Utah, Mr. DeBeers who has actually attended a retreat there. Mr. Grube's article, soon thereafter, following more closely the life of Mr. Flynn, will tell his readers he obtained in information from, if you will pardon the expression, "the horse's mouth."

Query

The chapter(s) associated with "A Request for Data" and Mr. DeBeers are basically non-fiction. I, the author, created the questions and I did meet with a Trappist Monk at Holy Trinity in Huntsville who wrote his answers in a brilliant letter to me; it is published as a chapter. The name Fr. Tom Gillespie is fictional to protect the Monk but Tom, a Marine fighter pilot, was my mentor in pledging a fraternity in college.

ONLY LOSERS PLAY IT SAFE

From contributing writer Tim Wendel, *USA TODAY*, February 3, 2005

HOLLYWOOD CELEBRITIES; CELEBRITY MONK

Although I write about Thomas Merton and *The Seven Story Mountain* as coming from the Pittsburgh Library, it was taken, in fact, from the Internet; *encounter*, Radio National, with John Russell, Sunday 1/07/01.

I do not know the background or experience of John Russell but the foundation for my synthesis on Merton belongs to him.

The Second Vatican Council information came from the Internet.

JACK'S LIFE IN THE SEMINARY

The information in respect to Jack and his Seminary education was derived from two sources:

1. *WHAT TO EXPECT IN SEMINARY* THEOLOGICAL EDUCATION AS SPIRITUAL

    FORMATION, Virginia Samuel Cetuk, Abingdon Press, Nashville, 1998.

2. *THE STRUGGLE FOR CELIBACY*, The Culture of Catholic Seminary

    Life, Paul Stanosz, The Crossroad Publishing Company, New York, NY 10001, 2006

I'M LEARNING!! I'M LEARNING!!

Liz tells Charles Grube that the stranger at the golf driving range told her, "He would rather being playing golf," when she asked him about her swing. The joke came from MILTON BERLE'S PRIVATE JOKE FILE, Crown Trade Paperbacks, New York, 1989.

WHAT DID LIZ LEARN?

When Liz was telling Joanne about her mixed up feeling about Jack's departing friends I used, partially, a quote from Seneca, *Letters to Lucilius, 93*, 3.4.22, p239, *GREAT TREASURY OF WESTERN THOUGHT*.

In reference to all dialogue about Golf, I took everything from, GOLF TIPS FROM THE PROS, Edited by Tim Baker, Guild & Charles Publications Inc. Company. Cincinnati, OH 45236, 2006.

The dialogue between Liz and Joanne regarding menstrual cycle, etc., was taken from the Internet.

In SOMETHING TO THINK ABOUT, An Exchange of Value, the information regarding the conductors of the middle 70's to middle 90's and their symphony orchestras is a statement of truth since I had tickets to attend the Los Angeles and Orange County symphony halls for twenty five years. I did, however, search the INTERNET for the same "exchange of value" for the 50's and found Leonard Bernstein conducting the New York Philharmonic in Handel's *MESSIAH* and Mahler's 4th Symphony. In the mid fifties we had Eugene Ormandy of the Philadelphia Orchestra, Fritz Reiner of the Chicago Symphony Orchestra, conducting his version of Bartok's *CONCERTO for ORCHESTRA*, and one of his best was his recording with the Pittsburgh Symphony Orchestra conducting Shostakovich's *SYMPHONY #6*.

On the one page, SOMETHING TO THINK ABOUT, More Perfection, I say Harvey Haddix's mind-boggling pitching for thirty six straight outs occurred on May 26th. It was on the 26th, in May of 1959. Some of the stories told in the book are not in tune with real time.

SOMETHING TO THINK ABOUT, I Get A Call From The Boss, The information on MBA Essentials (Mr. Latshaw in conversation with Mr. Grube) came from the University of Pittsburgh, Katz Center for Executive Education.

SOMETHING TO THINK ABOUT, Eighteen months later. The first star * and the second two stars ** represents testimony to TIME AND THE ART OF LIVING, Robert Grudin, Harper and Row, Publishers, San Francisco, 1982. The same holds true in the chapter beginning the second half of the book.

When Liz talks about her friend Joann getting married to a graduate of the Wharton School of Business and winning the Business Plan competition that dialogue and information was from the INTERNET.

Also, the discussion about gaining additional yardage from Liz's golf swing was taken from *GOLF TIPS FROM THE PROS*, edited by Tim Baker.

SOMETHING TO THINK ABOUT, Liz Out Of Town, The discussion about mortal sin and sexual desire etc., between Liz and Dahlia was created by the author. However, the statement by a Jesuit priest about sin was taken from the Internet, Mortal sin, Wikipedia, the free encyclopedia.

SOMETHING TO THINK ABOUT, Is Joanne Unhappy, The wine and the two French entrees was garnered from the internet. The life of "The Unsinkable Molly Brown" was also taken from the internet. All other dialogue is fiction created by the author.

SOMETHING TO THINK ABOUT, To the victor another hamburger! The information on Coca-Cola was obtained from the Internet. The golf lessons taught by Mr. Flynn to Liz McGovern were taken from *GOLF TIPS FROM THE PROS, Edited by Tim Baker,* A DAVID & CHARLES BOOK, David and Charles is an F+W Publications Inc, company, Cincinnati, OH 45236, 2006

SOMETHING TO THINK ABOUT, Golf Legends Look Back etc., the information was taken from an advertising section of *FORBES,* June 19, 2006. I could not relate the exact times and dates since the fictional novel was written for the mid 50's and 60's. I am sure the reader understands!

SOMETHING TO THINK ABOUT, Bass has a lure of its own. I gave credit to the newspaper where I obtained a copy (see page 2) The only statement adjusted was the death of George Perry. The time of "74 years passing" was not changed because it would have destroyed the integrity of the sport in reference to time.

SOMETHING TO THINK ABOUT; AT TIMES, ONE WOULD RATHER NOT. The name of the ski resort, *SEVEN SPRINGS* in Champion, Pennsylvania is real. All conversations regarding the death of Joanne is fictional although I might add it was a true event in my life; only the names and dates, if any, are fictional. The death did occur at *Seven Springs.* The information on East Carolina University came from the internet. The school was selected at random; the only criteria was location due to the "radius of action" of the jet. The names Blahosky and Brcywczy are real but not vocationally.

SOMETHING TO THINK ABOUT, Fr. JACK FLYNN ACCEPTING HIS NEW FREEDOM . . . ! The chapter is deemed as fictional with

Socrates speaking about Jack's pursuit of wisdom through Philosophy. The pursuit is non-fictional and is published in another book by the author. And the story Jack is telling Socrates about Truth and Lockheed's new fighter, actually the YF-104A, is non-fictional with the exception of fighter pilot/test pilot Eugene Coniff. Eugene Coniff is a fictional name for the author, a former experimental test pilot for Lockheed.

There is a real Eugene Conniff, however. He was a P-39, P-63 fighter pilot in the USAF and he married the lady referenced to in the chapter.

The only thing fictional about this chapter is the dialogue between Socrates and his friends, Socrates speaking of real issues, and Socrates' conversing with Jack and visa-versa. All of the authors of the mentioned books are given their due.

SOMETHING TO THINK ABOUT; JOANNE'S SUICIDE LIZ'S MENTAL TORTURE, The information Liz found at the library on the Catholic Church's view on Suicide was obtained from the Internet. The same applies to the main reasons for divorce. In reference to the thoughts of the philosophers on suicide, the information came from *THE GREAT TREASURY OF WESTERN THOUGHT, 1.9, p133-140*

SOMETHING TO THINK ABOUT; A LETTER FROM JACK FLYNN, Jack's letter to Charles Grube is a synthesis of a number of pages about the author leaving the monastery, from *DANCE OF A FALLEN MONK,* George Fowler, ADDISON-WESLEY PUBLISHING COMPANY, Mass., New York, 1995

SOMETHING TO THINK ABOUT; CHARLIE, LIZ, GLORIA, ARNIE, In Mr. Latshaw's speech about Charlie's new responsibilities, the info came from the Internet under *Classified Job Bulletin.* The information on the Duquesne Club, YAHOO TRAVEL, on the Internet. KDKA, CBS, PITTSBURGH AREA TV STATIONS; the Internet. Liz's discussion with Mr. Grube about CELIBACY came from *The Associated Press and The Vatican Bank,* on the Internet. And Liz, when talking about things changing, was taken from *THE GREAT TREASURY OF WESTERN THOUGHT,* CHANGE, p. 1487.

SOMETHING TO THINK ABOUT; William Harvey Dudley, All information, Bill Dudley, Carr, Maxwell, and Stagg came from the Internet.

SOMETHING TO THINK ABOUT; FR. FLYNN'S FAMILY EASTER BUNNY, In reference to TV and radio station's personnel duty, and the knowledge of the Pittsburgh flood came from the Internet. The discussion of Jack's "things well along" and "Heaven not a place but a condition" was taken from *HOME* chapter of *DANCE OF A FALLEN MONK*. The quote from Homer came from his *ODYSSEY*, GREAT TREASURY OF WESTERN THOUGHT, as mentioned, edited by Adler & Van Doren. The jokes told by the fictional Fr. Becket came from *MILTON BERLES'S PRIVATE JOKE FILE*, Milton Berle, CROWN TRADE PAPERBACKS, New York, 1989. The speech on the *SEAL of CONFESSION* came from the Internet, Sacrament of Penance, Catholic Church. The info on Saint Becket, his murder, his sainthood, Chaucer's *CANTERBURY TALES*, came from *THE COLUMBIA ENCYCLOPEDIA*, SIXTH EDITION, Edited by Paul Lagasse, Columbia University Press Publisher, New York, 1893, p2833.

SOMETHING TO THINK ABOUT; MY STUDIOUS FRIENDS, discussion of the Sacrament of Penance (Catholic Church) came from WIKIPEDIA, the free encyclopedia, the Internet, plus Fr. Jack's talk about celibacy, from Free On-Line Library, the Internet, plus The Dress Code of Priests, from TID BITS, the Internet.

The information regarding the Chicago Tribune's stories on the hostage situation, "yellow ribbon" and CIA came from the INTERNET!

The subject: The Chicago School of Professional Psychology and the Master of Arts Degree came from the internet. The teaching of Organizational Effectiveness combined with philosophy is fiction.

Time and the Art of Living by R. Grudan * Last sentence slightly modified

CPSIA information can be obtained
at www.ICGtesting.com
Printed in the USA
FSOW01n2244300715
9414FS